Praise for the Soul Screamers series
by *New York Times* bestselling author

RACHEL
VINCENT

"*Twilight* fans will love it."
—*Kirkus Reviews*

"The story rocks (for teens and adults, I might add)."
—*Book Bitch*

"Fans of those vampires will enjoy this new crop
of otherworldly beings."
—*Booklist*

"I'm so excited about this series."
—*The Eclectic Book Lover*

"A must for any reading wish list."
—*Tez Says*

"A book like this is one of the reasons that I add authors to my
auto-buy list. This is definitely a keeper."
—*TeensReadToo.com*

SOUL SCREAMERS

‹ VOLUME ONE ›

RACHEL VINCENT

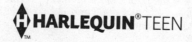

HARLEQUIN®TEEN

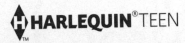

HARLEQUIN®TEEN

ISBN-13: 978-0-373-21060-2

SOUL SCREAMERS VOLUME 1

Copyright © 2011 by Harlequin Books S.A.

The publisher acknowledges the copyright holder of the individual works as follows:

MY SOUL TO LOSE
Copyright © 2009 by Rachel Vincent

MY SOUL TO TAKE
Copyright © 2009 by Rachel Vincent

MY SOUL TO SAVE
Copyright © 2010 by Rachel Vincent

Recycling programs for this product may not exist in your area.

This edition published by arrangement with Harlequin Books S.A.

For questions and comments about the quality of this book please contact us at Customer_eCare@Harlequin.ca.

® and TM are trademarks of the publisher. Trademarks indicated with ® are registered in the United States Patent and Trademark Office, the Canadian Trade Marks Office and in other countries.

www.HarlequinTEEN.com

Printed in U.S.A.

CONTENTS

MY SOUL TO LOSE

Thanks first of all to Lisa Heuer for the technical advice
and consultation. Without your contributions,
this story would have been impossible for me to write.

Thanks also to my early readers, Rinda, Chandra, Heather,
and Jen. Your opinions and advice were invaluable,
and the story is so much better for them both.

Thanks to Mary-Theresa Hussey and Natashya Wilson for so
much enthusiasm and encouragement, which keep me smiling.

And thanks finally to everyone out there reading about Kaylee
for the first time. I've poured my heart into her continuing story,
along with some delicate pieces of my own soul, and
I'm so very honored and excited that you've decided
to give her a chance. I hope you like her as much as I do.

"Thanks for the ride, Traci!" Emma slammed the back door, then opened it again to free the end of her filmy red skirt as her sister leaned out the open driver's side window.

"Be ready to go at eight, or I'm leaving you here."

Em gave a mock salute, then turned toward the mall entrance without waiting for the car to pull away from the curb. We would be nowhere near the parking lot at eight o'clock. Finding a ride home would be no problem—Emma could cock one hip and smile, and guys all over Texas would throw their car keys at her feet, if that's what she wanted.

But sometimes a ride was more fun, because she could flirt with the driver. See how much he could take before his concentration wavered and he had to force his attention back onto the road. She'd never actually caused a wreck, but Em went a little further every time, ever eager to push the limits of... Well, of anything.

I went along for the ride because it was a delicious rush of power and freedom—living vicariously through Emma was usually more exciting than living my own life for real.

"Okay, Kaylee, here's the plan." Em stepped up to the glass doors, and they whooshed open. The artificial cool inside was a mercy on my damp skin and overheated cheeks; Traci's car wasn't air-conditioned, and September in the Dallas metroplex was still hot enough to make the devil sweat.

"So long as it leads to Toby's public humiliation, I'm in."

"It will." She stopped in front of a mirror built into the wall of the main walkway and her reflection grinned at me, brown eyes sparkling. "And that's the least he deserves. You really should have let me key his car."

And I'd been totally tempted to. But I was less than a year from getting my license and couldn't shake the certainty that if we keyed someone's fresh paint job—even if that someone was my rat of an ex-boyfriend—new-driver karma would come back to bite me on the bumper.

"So, what are you going to do? Push him into the snack table? Trip him on the way into the gym? Unbutton his pants while you're dancing, then scream for help?" I wasn't too worried about homecoming-dance karma. But Toby should have been...

Emma turned from the mirror, her pale brows high in surprise. "I was just gonna stand him up, then make out with his best friend on the dance floor, but that last one has real potential. Maybe we'll do both." She grinned again, then tugged me around the first corner to the huge main corridor of the mall, where the center of the floor opened to reveal the first level below. "But first we're gonna make sure you look so good that he spends every minute of this stupid dance wishing he was there with you."

Normally I'm not much of a shopper. Thin and small chested looks just as good in jeans and skinny tees as it does in anything more complicated, and I must have been dressing to my advantage subconsciously, because finding a new date had only taken two days.

But that didn't make Toby any less of a human cockroach— less than an hour after he'd dumped me, he'd asked Emma to homecoming. She'd accepted with a plan for revenge already half-plotted.

So I'd come to the mall the weekend before the dance armed with my aunt's credit card and Emma's good taste, prepared to dump a metaphorical shaker of salt over my slime-filled leech of an ex-boyfriend.

"We should start with…" Emma stopped and gripped the brass rail, looking down at the food court on the lower level. "Yum. Wanna split a soft pretzel first?"

I knew from her tone that food wasn't what had caught her eye.

A level below us, two guys in green Eastlake High baseball caps were shoving two tables next to a third, where four girls from our school sat in front of an untouched pile of junk food. The guy on the left was a junior named Nash Hudson, whose pick of the week—Amber something-or-other—was already seated. Showing up at homecoming with Nash would have been all the revenge I could ask for against Toby. But that wasn't gonna happen. I wasn't even a blip on Nash Hudson's social radar.

Next to Amber sat my cousin, Sophie; I would have recognized the back of her head anywhere. After all, that was the part of her I saw most.

"How did Sophie get here?" Emma asked.

"One of the other dancing monkeys picked her up this morning." She'd been ignoring me consistently—mercifully—since dance-team tryouts a month earlier, when she'd become the only freshman member of the varsity dance team. "Aunt Val's picking her up in about an hour."

"I think that's Doug Fuller across from her. Come on!" Emma's eyes glittered beneath the huge skylight overhead. "I wanna drive his new car."

"Em…" But I could only run after her, dodging shoppers hauling bags and small children. I caught up with Emma on the escalator and rode down one step above her. "Hey look." I nodded toward the group at the food court, where one of the dancers had just switched sides of the table to whisper something into Doug's ear. "Meredith's gonna be pissed when she sees you."

Emma shrugged and stepped off the escalator. "She'll get over it. Or not."

But the moment my foot hit the ground, a cold, dark sense of dread gripped me, and I knew I couldn't go any closer to the food court.

Not unless I wanted to cause a scene.

I was seconds from losing control over the scream building deep inside me, and once it broke free, I wouldn't be able to make it stop unless I could get away.

Better to leave before that happened.

"Em…" I croaked. One hand went to my throat; it felt like I was being strangled from the inside.

Emma didn't hear me; she was already strutting toward the cluster of tables.

"Em…" I said again, forcing that single syllable out firmly, ahead of the pressure building in my throat, and that time she heard me.

Emma turned and took one look at my face, and her forehead wrinkled in familiar concern. She glanced longingly toward the food court, then rushed to my side. "Panic attack?" she whispered.

I could only nod, fighting the urge to close my eyes. Sometimes it was worse then, when I saw only darkness. It felt like the world was closing in on me. Like things I couldn't see were creeping toward me.

Or maybe I watch too many scary movies…

"Okay, let's go." Em linked her arm through mine, half holding me up, half dragging me away from the food court, the escalator and whatever had triggered this particular…episode.

"A bad one?" she asked, once we'd put a good two hundred feet behind us.

"It's getting better." I sat on the edge of the huge fountain in the center of the mall. The jets of water shot all the way up to the second floor at certain points during its routine, and little droplets pelted us, but there was nowhere else to sit. The benches were all full.

"Maybe you should talk to somebody about these panic attacks." Emma plopped down beside me with one leg tucked beneath her, trailing her fingers through the rippling water. "It's weird how they seem to be locked on specific places. My aunt used to get panic attacks, but walking away didn't help her. The panic went with her." Emma shrugged and grinned. "And she got really sweaty. You don't look sweaty."

"Well, at least there's a bright side." I forced a laugh in spite of the dark, almost claustrophobic fear still lurking on the edges of my mind, ready to take over at the first opportunity. It had happened before, but never anywhere so heavily populated as the mall. I shuddered, thinking how close I'd come to humiliating both me and Emma in front of hundreds of people. Including half a dozen classmates. If I freaked out in front of them, the news would be all over school by the tardy bell on Monday morning.

"Still feel like cooking up a little revenge?" Emma grinned.

"Yeah. I just need one more minute."

Em nodded and dug through her purse for a penny. She couldn't resist feeding the fountain, despite my certainty that no wish you had to pay for could possibly come true. While she stared at the coin on her palm, eyes squinted in concentration, I steeled myself and turned to face the food court, my jaws clenched tight. Just in case.

The panic was still there—indistinct but threatening, like the remains of a nightmare. But I couldn't pinpoint the source.

Usually I could put a face on the dark dread looming inside

me, but this time the crowd made that impossible. A group wearing our rival school's colors had taken the table next to Sophie and her friends, and both sides were deeply engaged in a French-fry war. Several families stood in line, some parents pushing strollers, one pushing a small wheelchair. Some kind of moms-'n'-tots group had descended upon the frozen-yogurt place, and couples of all ages shuffled their way through the cattle shoots in front of each restaurant's counter.

It could have been anybody. All I really knew was that I couldn't go back there until the source of my panic had gone. The safest thing to do was to get as far away as possible.

Em's penny plunked into the water behind me, and I stood. "Okay, let's try Sears first."

"Sears?" Emma's frown puckered both her forehead and her glossed lips. "My grandmother shops there."

As did my style-conscious aunt, but Sears was as far from the source of my panic as we could get and still be in the mall. "Let's just look, okay?" I glanced at the food court again, then back at Emma, and her frown faded as understanding sank in. She wouldn't make me say it. She was too good a friend to make me voice my worst fears, or my certainty that, at that moment, they could all be found at the food court. "They might have something…" I finished weakly.

And with any luck, by the time we'd scoured the juniors' department, whoever had triggered my panic attack would be gone.

Maybe I should have tossed a penny in the fountain too.

"Yeah. They might have something." Emma smiled, and we made our way quickly down the central corridor. The tension in my neck eased with each step, and I only realized I'd been grinding my teeth when my jaw suddenly relaxed. By the time we stepped into the cloud of perfumed air near the Sears makeup counter, the panic had completely receded into memory.

It was over. I'd narrowly escaped complete terror and utter humiliation.

A little giddy from relief, Emma and I glanced through the dresses, then spent the next hour trying on goofy, pastel-colored pants and flamboyant hats to pass the time, while I kept my mental fingers crossed that, when we left, the coast would be clear. Metaphorically speaking.

"How you feelin'?" Emma tilted the brim of a neon green hat and smoothed the long blond hair trailing beneath it. She grinned and made a face at herself in the mirror, but her eyes were serious. If I wasn't ready to go, she would hide out in the Sears granny section with me for as long as it took.

Em didn't truly understand about my panic attacks—no one did. But she'd never pushed me to explain, never tried to ditch me when things got weird, and never once looked at me like I was a freak.

"I think I'm good," I said, when I realized that no traces remained of the shadowed horror I'd glimpsed earlier. "Let's go."

The boutique Em wanted to hit first was upstairs, so we left our hats and sherbet-colored pants in the dressing room and laughed our way through Sears until we found the in-store escalator.

"I'm gonna wait until everyone's there—till the dance floor's totally packed—then I'll press up really close to him." Clutching the rubber handrail, Emma twisted to face me from the tread above, a mischievous grin lighting up her eyes. "Then when he's *really* happy to see me, I'll yank his zipper, shove him back, and start screaming. They'll probably throw him out of the dance. Hell, maybe they'll expel him from school."

"Or call the cops." I frowned as we stepped off the scrolling stairs and into the bed-and-bath department. "They wouldn't do that, would they?"

She shrugged. "Depends on who's chaperoning. If it's Coach

Tucker, Toby's screwed. She'll stomp his balls into the ground before he even has a chance to zip up."

My frown deepened as I ran my hand across the end of a display bed piled high with fancy pillows. I was all for humiliating Toby, and I was certainly up for wounding his pride. But as satisfying as the whole thing sounded, getting him arrested hardly seemed like a fitting consequence for dumping me the week before homecoming. "Maybe we should rethink that last part…"

"It was your idea." Emma pouted.

"I know, but…" I froze, and my hand flew to my neck as a familiar ache began at the base of my throat.

No. *Noooo!*

I stumbled back against the bed, suddenly swallowed whole by a morbid certainty so vicious I could hardly draw my next breath. Terror washed over me, a bitter wave of anguish. Of grief I couldn't understand, or even place. "Kaylee? Are you okay?" Emma stepped in front of me, half blocking me from the other shoppers' sight, and lowered her voice dramatically. "It's happening again?"

I could only nod. My throat felt tight. Hot. Something heavy coiled in my stomach and slithered toward my throat. My skin crawled with the movement. Any moment, that swelling screech would demand freedom and I would fight to contain it.

One of us was going to lose.

Emma's grip tightened on her purse and I recognized the helpless fear in her eyes. They probably reflected my own. "Should we go?"

I shook my head and forced out two last whispered words. "Too late…"

My throat burned. My eyes watered. My head swam with pain, with echoes of the shriek now trying to claw its way out of me. If I didn't let it, it would tear me apart.

Nononono…! It can't be. I don't see it!

But there it was—across the aisle, surrounded by rainbow-hued mountains of bath towels. A deep shadow, like a cocoon of gloom. *Who is it?* But there were too many people. I couldn't see who swam in that darkness, who wore shadows like a second skin.

I didn't want to see.

I closed my eyes, and shapeless, boundless terror closed in on me from all sides. Suffocating me. That bitter grief was too hard to fight in the dark, so I forced my eyes open again, but that did little good. The panic was too strong this time. Darkness was too close. A few steps to the left, and I could touch it. Could slide my hand into that nest of shadows.

"Kaylee?"

I shook my head because if I opened my mouth—or even un-clenched my jaws—the scream would rip its way free. I couldn't force myself to meet Emma's eyes. I couldn't tear my gaze from the shadows coalescing around…someone.

Then the crowd shifted. Parted. And I saw.

No.

At first, my mind refused to translate the images sent from my eyes. Refused to let me understand. But that blissful ignorance was much too brief.

It was a kid. The one in the wheelchair, from the food court. His thin arms lay in his lap, his feet all but swallowed by a pair of bright blue sneakers. Dull brown eyes peered from a pale, swollen face. His head was bare. Bald. Shiny.

It was too much.

The shriek exploded from my gut and ripped my mouth open on its way out. It felt like someone was pulling barbed wire from my throat, then shoving it through my ears, straight into my head.

Everyone around me froze. Then hands flew to cover un-protected ears. Bodies whirled to face me. Emma stumbled back, shocked. Scared. She'd never heard it—I'd always avoided catastrophe with her help.

"Kaylee?" Her lips moved, but I couldn't hear her. I couldn't hear anything over my own screaming.

I shook my head. I wanted to tell her to go—that she couldn't help me. But I couldn't even think anymore. I could only shriek, tears pouring down my face, my jaws open so wide they hurt. But I couldn't close them. Couldn't make it stop. Couldn't even dial back the volume.

People moved all around me now. Mothers let go of their ears to herd their kids away, foreheads furrowed with the headache we all shared. Like a spear through the brain.

Go...I thought, silently begging the bald child's mother to push him away. But she stood frozen, both horrified and somehow transfixed by my audio onslaught.

Motion to my right drew my attention. Two men in khaki uniforms ran toward me, one yelling into a two-way radio, his free hand over his other ear. I only knew he was yelling because his face was flushed with the effort.

The men pulled Emma out of the way, and she let them. They tried to talk to me, but I couldn't hear them. Couldn't make out more than a few words from their silent lips.

"...stop..."

"...hurt?"

"... help..."

Terror and grief swirled inside me like a black storm, drowning out everything else. Every thought. Every possibility. Every hope.

And still I screamed.

One of the mall cops reached for me, and I stumbled backward. I tripped on the base of the display bed and went down on my butt. My jaw snapped shut—a brief mercy. But my head still rang with the echo of my shriek, and I couldn't hear him. And an instant later, the scream burst free again.

Surprised, the cop stepped back, speaking into his walkie again. He was desperate. Terrified.

So was I.

Emma knelt next to me, hands over her ears. Her purse lay forgotten on the ground. "Kaylee!" she shouted, but made no sound I could hear. She reached for her phone.

And as she dialed, color suddenly drained from the world, like *The Wizard of Oz* in reverse. Emma went gray. The cops went gray. The shoppers went gray. And suddenly everyone stood in a swirling, twisting colorless fog.

I sat in the fog.

Still screaming, I waved my hands near the ground, trying to feel. Real fog was cold and damp, but this was…insubstantial. I couldn't feel it at all. Couldn't stir it. But I could see it. I could see things *in* it.

On my left, something twisted. Writhed. Something too thick and vertical to be serpentine. It twisted somehow *through* a shelf of towels, without ever touching the shoppers pressed against them, as far from me as they could get without leaving the department.

Apparently I was enough of a freak show to justify the pain of listening to me.

On my right, something scuttled through the mist on the ground, where it was thickest. It scurried toward me, and I leaped to my feet and dragged Emma away. The cops jumped back, startled all over again.

Emma pulled free of my grip, her eyes wide in terror. And that's when I shut down. I couldn't take anymore, but I couldn't make it stop. I couldn't stop the shrieking, or the pain, or the stares, or the fog, or the eerie movement. And worst of all, I couldn't stop the certainty that that child—that poor little boy in the wheelchair—was going to die.

Soon.

Dimly I realized I'd closed my eyes. Tried to block it all out.

I reached out blindly, desperate to get out of the fog I couldn't feel. Could no longer see. My hands brushed something soft and high. Something I no longer had the word for. I scrambled up on it, crawling over mounds of material.

I curled into a ball, clutching something plush to my chest with one hand. Running my fingers over it again and again. Clinging to the only physical reality that still existed for me.

Hurt. I hurt. My neck hurt.

My fingers were wet. Sticky.

Something grabbed my arm. Held me down.

I thrashed. I screamed. I hurt.

Sharp pain bit into my leg, then fire exploded beneath my skin. I blinked, and a familiar face came into focus over me, gray in the fog. *Aunt Val*. Emma stood behind my aunt, face streaked with mascara-stained tears. Aunt Val said something I couldn't hear. And suddenly my eyes were heavy.

New panic flooded me. I couldn't move. Couldn't make my eyes open. And still my vocal chords strained. The world was closing in on me, dark and narrow, with no sound but the harsh wail that still poured from my abused throat.

A new darkness. Pure. No more gray.

And still I screamed…

My dreams were a jumble of violent chaos. Thrashing limbs. Bruising grips. Churning shadows. And through it all was that never-ending screech, now a hoarse echo of its former strength, but no less painful.

Light shone through my closed eyelids; my world was a red blur. The air felt wrong. Too cold. It smelled wrong. Too clean.

My eyes flew open, but I had to blink several times to make them focus. My tongue was so dry it felt like sandpaper against my lips. My mouth tasted funny, and every muscle in my body ached.

I tried to push myself up, but my arms wouldn't work. *Couldn't* work. They were tied to something. My pulse raced. I kicked, but my legs were bound too.

No! Heart pounding, I pulled on my arms and legs, then jerked them left to right, but couldn't move more than a few inches in any direction. I was strapped to the bed by my wrists and ankles, and I couldn't sit up. Couldn't turn over. Couldn't prop myself up on my elbows. Couldn't even scratch my own nose.

"Help!" I cried, but my voice was only a hoarse croak. No vowels or consonants involved. Blinking again, I rolled my head to first one side, then the other, trying to get my bearings.

The room was claustrophobically small. Empty, other than me, the camera mounted in one corner, and the high, hard mattress beneath me. The walls were sterile, white cinder block. There were no windows in my line of sight, and I couldn't see the floor. But the decor and the antiseptic smell were dead giveaways.

A hospital. I was strapped to a hospital bed. All alone.

It was like one of Emma's video games, where the character wakes up in a strange room with no memory of how he got there. Except, in real life, there was no chest in the corner holding the key to my chains and survival advice written on parchment.

Hopefully there were also no video-game monsters waiting to eat me the moment I got loose, because even if someone had left me a gun, I wouldn't have known how to use it.

But my objective was clear: Get out. Go home.

Unfortunately, that was easier said than done without the use of my hands.

My pulse swooshed in my ears, a hollow echo of real fear. That overpowering need to scream was gone, but a different kind of panic had settled into its place. What if there was a fire? Or a tornado? Or more screaming? Would anyone come get me, or would they leave me here to die? I would be easy prey for those shadow things, or a natural disaster, or any random psycho who wandered past.

I had to get off the bed. Out of these stupid…bed cuffs.

"Please…" I begged the camera, frustrated by my own weak whisper. I swallowed thickly, then tried again. "Please let me out." My words were clearer that time, if no louder. "Please…"

No response. My pulse spiked, pumping adrenaline through me. What if they were all dead, and the last person on earth was strapped to a bed? Was this how civilization would end? With leather straps and padded handcuffs?

Get a grip, Kaylee.

The reality was probably much less far-fetched, but just as scary: I was trapped. Helpless, and exposed, and vulnerable. And suddenly I couldn't breathe. Couldn't make my heart stop racing. If I didn't get out soon, I was going to start screaming again—from normal terror this time, but the result would be the same. They'd shoot me up again, and the cycle would repeat ad nauseam. I'd be in this bed for the rest of my life, cowering from shadows.

So what if there were no windows and the overhead bulbs bathed the room in light? Eventually there would be shadows, and they would come for me. I was sure of that.

"Please!" I shouted, almost giddy to hear my voice coming back. "Let me—"

The door opened seconds before I would have started fighting my bindings in earnest. "Hi, Kaylee, how are you feeling?"

I strained to lift my head and put a face to the smooth, masculine voice. He was tall and thin, but looked strong. Bad skin, good hair. "Like a frog about to be dissected," I said, as he unbuckled my left arm.

I liked him already.

"Fortunately for you, I was never very good with a scalpel."

His smile was nice, and his brown eyes were kind. His name tag read: Paul Conners, Mental Health Technician.

Mental health? My stomach tried to twist itself in knots. "Where am I?"

Paul carefully unbuckled my other wrist. "You're at Lakeside Mental Health Center, attached to Arlington Memorial."

Lakeside. The psych ward. *Shit.*

"Um, no. I can't be here. Somebody made a mistake." Panic poured into my bloodstream fast enough to make my skin tingle. "I need to talk to my aunt. Or my uncle. He'll fix this." Uncle Brendon had a way of straightening things out without pissing people off—a skill I'd always envied.

Paul smiled again and helped me sit up. "After you get settled in, you're welcome to call them."

But I didn't want to settle in.

My own sock feet caught my attention from the end of the bed. "Where are my shoes?"

"They're in your room. We had to take them off to unlace them. For everyone's safety, we don't allow shoestrings, belts, drawstrings, or robe ties."

My shoestrings were dangerous? Fighting back tears, I leaned forward to free my right leg.

"Careful. You might be a little stiff and shaky at first," he said, already working on my left ankle. "You were out for quite a while."

My heart thumped painfully. "How long?"

"Oh, just over fifteen hours."

What? I sat up and felt my eyes glaze over in horror. "You left me strapped to a bed for fifteen hours? Isn't there some kind of law about that?"

"Lots of them. And we follow every single one. Need help getting down?"

"I got it," I snapped. I knew my anger was misdirected, but I couldn't help it. I'd lost fifteen hours of my life to a needle and four-point restraints. I wasn't capable of friendly at the moment. "Why was I buckled in?"

I slid carefully off the bed, then leaned against it while my head spun. The dingy vinyl tile was cold through my socks.

"You arrived on a stretcher, screaming and thrashing though under heavy sedation. Even after you lost your voice, you kept flailing around, like you were fighting something in your dreams."

The blood drained from my head so fast I got dizzy again. "I was?" No wonder I hurt all over; I'd been fighting my restraints for hours. In my sleep. If chemical comas even qualified as sleep.

Paul nodded solemnly and stepped back to give me space when I stood. "Yeah, and that started again a couple of hours ago, so they had to buckle you back up to keep you on the bed."

"I was screaming again?" My stomach had become a bottomless pit of horror, swirling slowly, threatening to swallow me like a black hole. What the hell was wrong with me?

"No, thrashing. You went still about half an hour ago. I was on my way to unbuckle you when you woke up."

"What did they give me?" I reached for the wall when a fresh wave of dizziness rolled over me.

"The usual mix. Ativan, Haldol, and Benadryl to counter the side effects of the Haldol."

No wonder I'd slept so long. I had no idea what the first two drugs were, but Benadryl alone was enough to knock me out for most of the night during allergy season. It was a miracle I'd woken up at all. "What if I'd been allergic to any of that?" I demanded, crossing my arms over the T-shirt I'd worn to the mall. So far, waking up in my own clothes was the closest thing I'd found to a bright side.

"Then we'd be having this conversation in the E.R., instead of the restraint room."

The restraint room? I was vaguely disturbed by the fact that they had a name for it.

Paul pulled open the door. "After you."

I steeled my spine and stepped into the bright hallway, unsure what to expect. People walking around in straitjackets, mumbling to themselves? Nurses in white uniforms with starched hats? But the hall was empty and quiet.

Paul stepped past me, and I followed him to the last door on the left, which he pushed open for me.

I shoved my hands into my pockets to hide how badly they were shaking, then made myself cross the threshold.

Another white room, not much bigger than the first one. The bed was a mattress set in a heavy wooden frame, too narrow and too low. Draped with a plain white blanket. Empty, open shelves were bolted to the wall in place of a dresser, and there was one long, high window. No closet.

My stringless shoes lay at the end of the bed. They were the only things I recognized in the entire room. Everything else was foreign. Cold. Scary.

"So…I've been committed?" My voice shook. I couldn't help it.

"You've been hospitalized," Paul said from the doorway.

"What's the difference?" I stood at the end of the bed, unwilling to sit. To get comfortable.

"This is temporary."

"How temporary?"

"That's up to you and your doctor." He gave me a sympathetic smile, then backed into the hall. "One of the nurses will be by in a minute to get you settled in. Hang in there, Kaylee."

I could only nod. A second later, Paul was gone. I was alone. Again.

From outside the room came the steady rattle-clank of a cart being pushed down the hall. Shoes squeaked on the floor. And somewhere nearby, someone cried in great, dramatic sobs. I stared at my feet, unwilling to touch anything for fear that it would make the whole thing sink in. Make it real.

Am I crazy?

I was still standing there like an idiot when the door opened, and a woman in pale pink scrubs came in carrying a clipboard and pen. Her name tag read: Nancy Briggs, R.N.

"Hi, Kaylee, how are you feeling?" Her smile was wide and friendly, but felt somehow…measured. As if she knew just how much to give. How to appear friendly without welcoming actual conversation.

I missed Paul already.

"Confused and homesick." I gripped the edge of the shelf with one hand, willing it to dissolve beneath my touch. To fade into the bad dream I'd surely wake up from any minute.

"Well, let's see if we can't fix at least the first part of that." The nurse's smile grew bigger, but no warmer. "There's a phone in the hall. Someone's on it right now, but when it's free, you're welcome to use it. Local numbers, legal guardians only. Tell someone at the front desk who you want to call, and we'll connect you."

Numb, I could only blink. This wasn't a hospital, it was a prison.

I patted my pocket, feeling for my phone. It was gone. Fresh panic exploded in my chest and I shoved my hand into my other pocket. Aunt Val's credit card was gone. She'd kill me if I lost it! "Where's my stuff?" I demanded, trying to stop the tears that blurred my vision. "I had a phone, and some lip gloss, and a twenty-dollar bill. And my aunt's credit card."

Nurse Nancy's smile thawed a bit then, either because of my tears or the fear they no doubt magnified. "We keep all personal items locked up until you're discharged. Everything's there except the credit card. Your aunt took it when she left last night."

"Aunt Val was here?" I used my bare hands to wipe my eyes, but they filled again instantly. If she was here, why didn't she take me home?

"She rode in the ambulance with you."

Ambulance. Discharged. Locked up. Those words played over and over in my head, a litany of fear and confusion. "What time is it?"

"Eleven-thirty. They'll bring lunch in about half an hour. You can eat in the common area, down the hall and to the left. Breakfast is at seven. Dinner's at six." She reached to her left with the hand holding her pen and pushed open a door I hadn't noticed, revealing a tall, white industrial toilet and a shower stall. "You can shower whenever you like. Just come to the nurses' station first for your hygiene kit."

"Hygiene kit?" My eyes went wide as my insides went numb. *This isn't real. It can't be.*

"We hand out soap and shampoo as needed. If you want to shave, you'll have to be monitored by a staff member." I blinked, uncomprehending, but she continued. "There's a group session about anger management at nine, one about coping with depression at eleven, and one at two this afternoon about symptoms of mental illness. That's a good one to start with."

She smiled patiently, like she expected to be thanked for passing out information, but I just stared at the empty shelf. Her entire briefing was irrelevant to me. I'd be out very soon, surely, and the only group I was interested in was the group of my own family members who could make that happen.

"The boys' rooms are in the opposite wing, on the other side of the common area. Girls are not allowed on that wing, and vice versa. Visitation is every night from seven to nine. Lights out at ten-thirty. Someone will check on you every fifteen minutes when you're out of sight of the nurses' station." She paused again, and I made myself look up to meet her detached gaze. "Do you have any more questions?"

My eyes watered again, and I didn't bother to wipe them. "Why am I here?"

"That's a question for your doctor." She glanced briefly at her clipboard. "Dr. Nelson. He makes rounds after lunch, Monday through Friday. So you'll see him tomorrow." She hesitated, and this time set the clipboard on the shelf bolted to the cinder-block wall. "How's your neck? You didn't need stitches, but they did clean out the wounds..."

Wounds? My right hand flew to my neck, and I flinched at how tender the skin there was. And how...rough. My heart thumping, I rushed into the bathroom. The small, reflective aluminum mirror over the sink showed that what little mascara I'd worn the day before was now smeared beneath both of my eyes. My skin was pale, my long hair hopelessly knotted.

I tilted my chin up and angled my body toward the overhead light. My gasp echoed in the small room. My neck was a tangle of blood-crusted scratches.

And suddenly I remembered pain at my neck. Wet, sticky fingers.

My right hand shook as I held it up to the light. Dark crust still clung to my cuticles. Blood. I'd done this to myself, trying to make the screaming stop.

No wonder they thought I was crazy.

Maybe they were right.

The nurse had said I wasn't allowed to close my door, but I closed it while I showered, and again when I got out of the bathroom, because she'd left it open after one of the fifteen-minute checkups.

Were they afraid I was going to kill myself? If so, it'd have to be a pretty creative suicide. The only things not nailed to the floor or the wall were the towel on a shelf over the toilet and the tiny bar of hand soap on the sink. In the end, my pride won out over vanity and I washed both my body and hair with hand soap, rather than go begging for basic hygiene supplies from people I'd never met.

After my shower, I found a clean set of purple scrubs folded on the bed, but I'd have to go without underwear until someone brought me some clean clothes. Nurse Nancy had said Aunt Val was supposed to bring them, but when and if my aunt showed up, she was *not* leaving without me.

Clean and dressed—if not exactly to my satisfaction—I stared at the door for a solid three minutes before working up the nerve to open it. I'd missed both dinner and breakfast, so I was starving, but less than eager to mingle. Finally, after two false starts, I shoved still-wet hair back from my face and pulled the door open.

My laceless sneakers squeaked in the empty hallway, and I walked slowly toward the clinking of silverware, acutely aware that while I did hear a couple of soft voices, there was no actual conversation. Most of the doors I passed were open, revealing room after identical room. The only differences between those and the room I'd been assigned to were the personal possessions. Clothes stacked on open shelves and pictures taped to walls.

Halfway down the hall, a girl a couple of years younger than me sat alone on a bed in a room almost as bare as mine, talking to herself. Not whispering under her breath, or reminding herself not to forget something important. Actually talking to herself, at full volume.

When I turned the corner, I found the source of the other voice, as well as what passed for the cafeteria. Five round tables were set up in a large room occupied with normal-looking people in jeans and T-shirts. Mounted on the far wall above their heads was a small television tuned to *SpongeBob*.

"The trays are on the cart."

I jumped, then whirled around to see another woman—this one in cranberry-colored scrubs—sitting in a hospital waiting-room-type chair near the doorway. Her name tag read: Judy Sullivan, Mental Health Technician. "Find the one with your name on it and take a seat."

I took a covered tray labeled Kaylee Cavanaugh from the second shelf of the cart, then glanced around for somewhere to

sit. There were no empty tables—most had two or three occupants—yet everyone ate in silence, but for the sounds of chewing
and silverware scraping plastic trays.

The edges of the room were lined in more stiff-looking
waiting-room chairs and small couches with pale green vinyl
cushions, and one girl sat alone on one of these with her tray on
her lap. She picked at the edge of a slice of meat loaf with her
fork, but seemed more interested in whatever patterns she was
creating than in actually eating.

I found a table and ate in silence, suffering through half of
the dry meat loaf and a stale roll before I looked up from my
tray—and directly into the eyes of the girl sitting alone on the
edge of the room. She watched me with a creepy sort of detached
curiosity, as if I were a bug crawling across the sidewalk in front
of her. I wondered briefly if she was the ant-stomper type. Then
I wondered why she was at Lakeside.

But I purged that thought quickly—I didn't want to know.
I didn't want to know why any of them were there. As far as I
was concerned, they were all locked up for the same reason: they
were crazy.

Oh, and you're the shining exception, right? some traitorous voice
asked from deep inside my head. *The girl who sees things that aren't
there and can't stop screaming. Who tries to rip her own throat out in
the middle of the mall. Yeah, you're sane.*

And suddenly my appetite was gone. But Meat Loaf Girl—
Lydia Trainer, according to her tray cover—was still staring at
me, limp black hair falling over half of her face, revealing only
one pale green eye. My return stare didn't faze her, nor did it
force her to acknowledge me. She just watched me, as if the moment she looked away I might jump up and dance the cha-cha.

But then someone else walked between us and caught her
attention like a ball of yarn rolled in front of a cat. Lydia's gaze
followed a tall, heavyset girl as she carried an empty tray toward
the cart.

"Mandy, where's your fork?" Judy the mental health tech asked, standing so she could see the girl's tray. The tense way she held herself made me nervous. Like she expected Mandy to lean forward and take a bite out of her.

Mandy dropped her tray on the cart with a clatter of silverware, then stuck one hand into the waistband of her jeans and pulled out a fork. If I'd had any appetite left, that would have killed it. Mandy tossed the fork onto her tray, spared a contemptuous glance at the aide, then shuffled in sock feet into another large common area across the hall.

Lydia still watched Mandy, but now her features were scrunched into a tense grimace and one hand clutched her stomach.

I glanced at her tray to count her utensils. Had she swallowed her knife, or something stupid like that, while Judy's attention was occupied with Miss Fork-in-Drawers? No, all of the silverware was there, and I could see no obvious reason for Lydia's pained look.

Creeped out now, I stood and turned in my tray—all utensils accounted for—then rushed back to my room without looking up until I'd closed the door behind me.

"Hello?"

"Aunt Val?" I wound the old-fashioned, curly phone cord around my index finger and twisted on the hard plastic chair to face the wall. That was all the privacy I'd get in the middle of the hallway.

My kingdom for a cell phone.

"Kaylee!" My aunt sounded bright and cheery, and I knew even without seeing her that her hair would be perfectly arranged and her makeup expertly applied, even though she didn't have to be anywhere on the weekend.

Unless she was coming to get me. Please let her be coming to get me…

"How are you feeling, sweetheart?" Aunt Val continued, a sliver of concern denting her otherwise impenetrable armor of good cheer.

"Fine. I feel good. Come get me. I'm ready to come home."

How could you let them bring me here? How could you leave me? She would never have left her own daughter in a place like this. No matter what Sophie had done, Aunt Val would have taken her home, made a pot of hot tea, and dealt with the issue privately.

But I couldn't say that. My mother was dead, and I'd had no one but Aunt Val and Uncle Brendon since my father moved to Ireland when I was three, so I couldn't vocalize the soul-bruising betrayal twisting through me like a vine choking me from the inside. At least, not without crying, and crying might make me look unstable, which would give them a reason to keep me there. And give Aunt Val a reason to drop off my clothes and run.

"Um…I was actually just about to head your way. Have you seen the doctor yet? Do you think I'll be able to talk to him?"

"Yeah, sure. I mean, that's what he's here for, right?"

According to Nurse Nancy, the doctor didn't do his rounds on weekends, but if I told Aunt Val that, she might wait for official visiting hours. Doctor or not, I was sure she would take me home once she saw me. Once she'd had a look at this place, and at me in it. We might not share the same blood, but she'd *raised* me. Surely she couldn't walk away twice, right?

From somewhere near the common area, a booming male voice announced that the anger management group was about to start, then specifically suggested that someone named Brent should attend.

I leaned my forehead against the cold cinder blocks and tried to block it all out, but every time I opened my eyes—every time I even took a cold, sterile-scented breath—I remembered exactly where I was. And that I couldn't leave.

"Okay. I'm bringing some things for you," my aunt said softly into my ear.

What? I wanted to cry. "No. Aunt Val, I don't need things. I need out."

She sighed, sounding almost as frustrated as I was. "I know, but that's up to your doctor, and if he gets delayed…or something, wouldn't you feel better with a fresh change of clothes?"

"I guess." But the truth was that I wasn't going to feel any better until Lakeside was a distant, unpleasant memory, instead of my current waking nightmare.

"They won't let you have anything but clothes and books. Do you want something to read?"

All I wanted to read was the exit sign on the other side of the locked door by the nurses' station. The one you had to be buzzed through.

"Um…I have a paper due next week. Could you grab *Brave New World* from my nightstand?" *See? I'm not crazy. I'm responsible and focused on schoolwork. Don't you want to take me home so I can live up to my true potential?*

Aunt Val was silent for a moment, and that uncomfortable feeling in the bottom of my stomach swelled. "Kaylee, I don't think you should worry about homework right now. We can tell the school you have the flu."

Footsteps shuffled past me, headed toward the group session. I stuck a finger in my ear, trying to block it all out. "The flu? Doesn't it take, like, a week to get over the flu?" I wouldn't miss that much school. I wouldn't miss any, if she'd take me home today!

My aunt sighed, and my gut twisted around the lump of dread anchoring me to the chair. "I'm just trying to buy you some time to rest. And it's not really a lie. You can't tell me you're feeling one hundred percent right now…"

"Because they shot me full of enough crap to put an elephant to sleep!" And I had the cotton mouth to prove it.

"And for all we know, you might actually be coming down

with a bit of the flu. I heard you sneeze the other day," she finished, and I rolled my eyes.

"They don't lock up people with the flu, Aunt Val." Not unless it's the bird flu or Stephen King's end-of-the-world flu.

"I know. Listen, I'll be there in a bit, and we can talk about this then."

"What about Uncle Brendon?"

Another pause. Sometimes there was less meaning in what Aunt Val said than in what she didn't say. "He took Sophie out to lunch to explain all this to her. This has been really hard on them both, Kaylee."

Like it's easy on me?

"But we're both coming to see you tonight."

Except I would be out by then, even if I had to get down on my knees and beg her to take me home. If I had to wake up here again, I'd lose my mind. Assuming I hadn't already.

"Promise?" I hadn't asked her to promise me anything since I was nine.

"Of course. We just want to help you, Kaylee."

Yet somehow, I didn't feel very comforted.

I waited in the common area, stubbornly resisting the jigsaw puzzles and crossword books stacked on a shelf in the corner. I wouldn't be here long enough to finish one anyway. Instead, I stared at the TV, wishing they'd at least show some *good* cartoons. But if there was a remote available, I had no idea where to find it.

A commercial came on and my attention wandered, in spite of my best efforts to ignore my fellow patients. Lydia sat across the room from me, not even pretending to watch the television. She was watching me.

I stared back at her. She didn't smile. She didn't speak. She just watched, and not with an unfocused stare, which was obviously all some of the residents were capable of. Lydia actually seemed to be observing me, like she was looking for something in particular. What, I had no idea.

"Weird, isn't it?" Mandy dropped into the chair on my left, and air whooshed from the cushion. "The way she stares."

I glanced up to find her looking across the room at Lydia. "No weirder than anything else here." And frankly, I wasn't looking to make conversation—or friends—with someone who stuffed forks down her pants.

"She's a ward of the court." Mandy bit into a half-eaten chocolate bar, then continued with her mouth full. "Never talks. You ask me, she's the strangest one here."

I had serious doubts about that.

"What're you here for?" Her gaze traveled south of my face, then back up. "Let me guess. You're either manic depressive, or anorexic."

Inside, my temper boiled, but I was proud by how calm my reply sounded. "I don't talk either."

She stared at me for a second, then burst into a harsh, barking laugh.

"Mandy, why don't you find something constructive to do?" A familiar voice said, and I glanced up to find Paul standing in the wide doorway, holding…

My suitcase!

I sprang from the couch, and he held the rolling bag out to me. "I thought that might make you smile."

In fact, I was oddly excited and relieved. If I had to be locked up, at least I could be miserable in my own clothes. But then my enthusiasm flashed out like a burned-up bulb when I realized what that suitcase meant. Aunt Val had dropped off my clothes without coming in to see me.

She'd left me again.

I took the bag and headed back to my room, where I dropped the suitcase on the floor beside the bed, unopened. Paul followed me, but stopped in the doorway. I sank onto the bed, battling tears, my suitcase forgotten in spite of the rough scrub bottoms chaffing me in all the wrong places.

"She couldn't stay," Paul said. Apparently my emotions were as transparent as the tempered glass windows. Wouldn't my therapist be pleased? "Visiting hours don't start until seven."

"Whatever." If she'd wanted to see me, she would have, even if it was just for a few minutes. My aunt's tenacity was a thing of legends.

"Hey, don't let this place get to you, okay? I've seen a lot of kids lose their souls in here, and I'd hate to see that happen to you." He ducked his head, trying to draw eye contact, but I only nodded, staring at the floor. "Your aunt and uncle will be back tonight."

Yeah, but that didn't mean they'd take me home. It didn't mean anything at all.

When Paul left, I heaved my suitcase onto the bed and unzipped it, eager to wear, see, and smell something familiar. After just a few hours at Lakeside, I was already terrified of losing myself. Of fading into the glazed eyes, slow steps, and empty stares all around me. I needed something from real life—from my world outside this room—that would help me hold on to *me*. So I was completely unprepared for the contents of my bag.

Nothing in it was mine. The clothes still had price tags dangling from waistbands and collars.

Fighting back fresh tears, I lifted the first piece from the suitcase: a pair of soft pink jogging pants with a wide, gathered waistband and a complicated arrangement of flowers embroidered over one hip. At the front were two holes where the drawstring should have been. It'd been snipped and removed so I couldn't hang myself with it. The suitcase held a matching top, along with an entire collection of clothes I'd never even seen. They were all expensive, and comfortable, and perfectly coordinated.

What is this, psycho chic? What was wrong with my own jeans and tees?

The truth was that, in her own twisted way, Aunt Val was probably trying to cheer me up with new clothes. That might have worked for Sophie, but how could she not understand that it wouldn't work for me?

Suddenly pissed beyond words, I stripped and tossed the borrowed scrubs into a pile in the corner of the room, then ripped open a five-pack of underwear and stepped into the first pair. Then I dug through my bag for anything that didn't look like something Martha Stewart would wear on house arrest. The best I found was a plainish purple jogging suit at the bottom of the pile. Only once I had it on did I realize the fabric *glittered* beneath the light over my bed.

Great. I'm psychotic and *sparkly.* And there was nothing else in the bag. No books, and no puzzles. Not even any of Sophie's useless fashion magazines. With an angry sigh, I stomped down the hall in search of reading material and a quiet corner, silently daring Paul or any of the aides to comment on my epic wardrobe disaster.

After supper, Aunt Val and Uncle Brendon walked through the door next to the nurses' station, both empty-handed; they'd had to empty their pockets and turn over Aunt Val's purse to the security guard. That way, I wouldn't be tempted to try to kill anyone with her lip gloss and travel-size pack of tissues.

Seeing them standing there was like seeing my dad every time he came home for Christmas. Part of me was so mad at them both for leaving me there that I wanted to shout until I went hoarse, or ignore them completely. Whichever would come closest to hurting them like they'd hurt me. I wanted them to feel scared, and alone, and without even basic comforts like their own clothing.

But the other part of me wanted a hug so bad I could

practically feel arms around me already. I wanted to smell the outside world on them both. Soap that didn't come in tiny, unscented, paper-wrapped packets. Food that didn't come on labeled, hard plastic trays. Shampoo that didn't have to be checked out from the nurses' station, then turned in along with my dignity.

In the end, I could only stand there staring, waiting for them to make the first move.

Uncle Brendon came first. Maybe he couldn't resist our actual blood bond; my bond to Aunt Val was by virtue of her wedding vows. Either way, Uncle Brendon hugged me like he might never see me again, and my heart raced a bit in panic at that thought. Then I pushed it aside and buried my face in his shirt, smelling his aftershave, and Aunt Val's favorite spring-scented dryer sheets.

"How you holding up, hon?" he asked, when I finally pulled back far enough to see his face, rough with evening stubble.

"If I'm not crazy yet, I will be after one more day in this place. You have to take me home. Please."

My aunt and uncle exchanged a dark glance, and my stomach seemed to settle somewhere around my knees. "What?"

"Let's sit." Aunt Val's heels clacked all the way into the common area, where she glanced around and looked like she wanted to take her suggestion back. Several other patients sat staring up at the TV, most with glazed looks of half-comprehension. Two more worked on puzzles, and one thin boy I'd hardly seen was arguing with his parents in the far corner.

"Come on." I turned toward the girls' hall, leaving them to follow. "I don't have a roommate." In my room, I sank onto my bed with my feet tucked beneath me, and Uncle Brendon sat next to me. Aunt Val perched stiffly on the edge of the only chair. "What's wrong?" I demanded, when all eyes turned toward me. "Other than the obvious."

Uncle Brendon spoke first. "Kaylee, you haven't been released. We can't take you home before the doctor has even seen you."

"Why not?" My jaws were clenched so hard they ached. My hands curled around fistfuls of the blanket. I felt freedom slipping away like water through my fingers.

"Because you tried to rip your own throat out in the middle of Sears." Aunt Val frowned, like it should have been obvious.

"That's not…" I stopped, swallowing back tears. "I didn't know what I was doing. I was just trying to make the screaming stop."

"I know, honey." She leaned forward, frowning in serious concern. "That's the problem. You could have seriously hurt yourself without meaning to. Without any idea what you were doing."

"No, I…" But I couldn't really argue with that. If I could have stopped it, I would have. But a stint in Lakeside wasn't going to make that any better.

My uncle sighed. "I know this is…unpleasant, but you need help."

"Unpleasant?" That sounded like a direct quote from Aunt Val. I gripped the footboard of the bed so hard my fingers ached. "I'm not crazy. I'm not." And maybe if I kept saying it, one of us would actually believe it.

"I know," my uncle said softly, and I glanced at him in surprise. His eyes were closed and he took several deep breaths, like he was preparing himself for something he didn't want to do. He looked ready to cry. Or to beat the crap out of something. I was voting for the latter.

Aunt Val stiffened in her chair, watching her husband carefully, as if silently willing him to do something. Or maybe not to do it.

When Uncle Brendon finally opened his eyes, his gaze was steady. Intense. "Kaylee, I know you didn't mean to hurt yourself, and I know you're not crazy."

He seemed so sure of it, I almost believed him. Relief washed over me, like that first air-conditioned breeze on a hot summer day. But it was quickly swallowed by doubt. Would he be so sure if he knew what I'd seen?

"We need you to give this a shot, okay?" His eyes pleaded with me. Desperately. "They can teach you how to deal with it here. How to calm yourself down and…hold it back. Val and I… We don't know how to help with that."

No! I blinked away unshed tears, refusing to let them fall. They were going to leave me locked up in here!

Uncle Brendon took my hand and squeezed it. "And if you have another panic attack, I want you to go to your room and concentrate on not screaming. Do whatever you have to do to resist it, okay?"

Stunned, I could only stare for a long moment. It took all of my remaining focus to breathe. They really weren't going to take me home!

"Kaylee?" my uncle asked, and I hated how concerned he looked. How fragile he obviously considered me now.

"I'll try."

My aunt and uncle knew that my panic attacks always seemed to be triggered by someone else. So far, always someone I'd never met. But they didn't know about the morbid certainty that came with the panic. Or the weird hallucinations I'd had at the mall. I was afraid that if I told them those parts, they'd agree with Dr. Nelson, and the three of them might put me back in that restraint bed and weld the buckles shut.

"Try hard." Uncle Brendon eyed me intently, his green eyes somehow shining, even in the dim overhead light. "Because if you start screaming again, they'll pump you so full of antidepressants and antipsychotics you won't even remember your own name."

Antipsychotics? They really thought I was psychotic?

"And Kaylee…"

I looked up at Aunt Val and was surprised to see visible dents in her armor of relentless optimism. She looked pale, and stressed, and the frown lines in her forehead were more pronounced than I'd ever seen them. If someone had shown her a mirror at that moment, she might easily have wound up my roommate in the loony bin.

"If you even look like you're going to hurt yourself again—" her gaze strayed to the scabbed-over scratches on my neck, and my hand immediately flew to cover them "—you'll wind up strapped to that table again." Her voice broke, and she pulled a tissue from her purse to blot tears before they smudged her mascara. "And I don't think either one of us can handle seeing you like that again."

I woke up at four in the morning and couldn't go back to sleep. After an hour and a half of staring up at the ceiling, ignoring the aide who came to check on me every fifteen minutes, I got dressed and headed down the hall in search of a magazine I'd started the day before. To my surprise, Lydia sat on a couch in the living-room half of the common area.

"You're up early." I sat next to her, uninvited. The television played in the corner, tuned to the local news, but no one watched it. As far as I knew, the other patients weren't up yet. Neither was the sun.

Lydia watched me just like she had the day before, in mild interest, no surprise and almost total detachment. Our gazes met for a long minute, neither of us blinking. It was an odd sort of a challenge, as I silently dared her to speak. She had something to say. I was sure of it.

But she stayed silent.

"You don't sleep much, do you?" Normally I wouldn't have pried—after all, I didn't want anyone else poking into my alleged mental instability—but she'd stared at me for hours the day before. Like she wanted to tell me something.

Lydia shook her head, and a strand of lank black hair fell in front of her face. She pushed it back, her lips firmly sealed.

"Why not?"

She only blinked at me, staring into my eyes as if they fascinated her. As if she saw something there no one else could see.

I started to ask what she was looking at, but stopped when a purple blur caught my attention on the other side of the room. A tall aide in eggplant-colored scrubs checking in on us, clipboard in hand. Had it been fifteen minutes already? But before she could continue with the rest of her list, Paul appeared in the doorway.

"Hey, they're sending one over from the E.R."

"Now?" The female aide glanced at her watch.

"Yeah. She's stable, and they need the space." Both staff members disappeared down the hall, and I turned to see that Lydia's face had gone even paler than normal.

Several minutes later, the main entrance buzzed, then the door swung open. The female aide hurried from the nurses' station as a man in plain green scrubs stepped into the unit, pushing a thin, tired-looking girl in a wheelchair. She wore jeans and a purple scrubs top, and her long pale hair hung over most of her face. Her arms lay limp in her lap, both bandaged from her wrists to halfway up her forearms.

"Here's her shirt." The man in green handed the aide a thick plastic bag with the Arlington Memorial logo on it. "If I were you, I'd throw it out. I don't think all the bleach in the world could get rid of that much blood."

On my right, Lydia flinched, and I looked up to see her eyes closed, her forehead furrowed in obvious pain. As the aide wheeled the new girl past the common area, Lydia went stiff beside me and clenched the arms of her chair so tightly the tendons in her hands stood out.

"You okay?" I whispered, as the wheelchair squeaked toward the girls' hall.

Lydia shook her head, but her eyes didn't open.

"What hurts?"

She shook her head again, and I realized she was younger than I'd first guessed. Fourteen, at the most. Too young to be stuck at Lakeside, no matter what was wrong with her.

"You want me to get someone?" I started to stand, but she grabbed my arm so suddenly I actually jerked in surprise. She was a lot stronger than she looked. And faster.

Lydia shook her head, meeting my gaze with green eyes brightly glazed with pain. Then she stood and walked stiffly down the hall, one hand pressed to her stomach. A minute later, her door closed softly.

The rest of the day was a blur of half-eaten meals, unfocused stares, and too many jigsaw puzzle pieces to count. After breakfast, Nurse Nancy was back on duty, standing in my doorway to ask a series of pointless, invasive questions. But by then I was annoyed with the fifteen-minute checkups, and beyond frustrated by the lack of privacy.

Nurse Nancy: "Have you had a bowel movement today?"

Me: "No comment."

Nurse Nancy: "Do you still feel like hurting yourself?"

Me: "I never did. I'm really more of a self-pamperer."

Next, a therapist named Charity Stevens escorted me into a room with a long window overlooking the nurses' station to ask me why I'd tried to claw open my own throat, and why I screamed loud enough to wake the dead.

I was virtually certain my screaming would not, in fact, wake the dead, but she seemed unamused when I said so. And unconvinced when I insisted that I hadn't been trying to hurt myself.

Stevens settled her thin frame into a chair across from me. "Kaylee, do you know why you're here?"

"Yeah. Because the doors are locked."

No smile. "Why were you screaming?"

I folded my feet beneath me in the chair, exercising my right to remain silent. There was no way to answer that question without sounding crazy.

"Kaylee...?" Stevens sat with her hands folded in her lap, waiting. I had her undivided attention, whether I wanted it or not.

"I...I thought I saw something. But it was nothing. Just normal shadows."

"You saw shadows." But her statement sounded more like a question.

"Yeah. You know, places where light doesn't shine?" *Much like a psychiatric hospital itself...*

"What was it about the shadows that made you scream?" Stevens stared into my eyes, and I stared at her crooked part line.

They shouldn't have been there. They were wrapped around a kid in a wheelchair, but didn't touch anyone else. They were moving. *Take your pick...* But too much of the truth would only earn me more time behind locked doors.

I was supposed to be learning how to handle my panic attacks, not spilling my guts about what caused them.

"They were...scary." There. Vague, but true.

"Hmmm." She crossed her legs beneath a navy pencil skirt and nodded like I'd said something right. "I see..."

But she didn't see at all. And I couldn't explain myself to save my life. Or my sanity, apparently.

After lunch, the doctor came to poke and prod me with an entire checklist of questions about my medical history. According to my aunt and uncle, he was the one who could really help me. But after my session with the therapist, I was skeptical, and the doc's opening lines did little to help that.

Dr. Nelson: "Are you currently taking any medications?"

Me: "Just whatever you guys shot me full of yesterday."

Dr. Nelson: "Do you have a family history of diabetes, cancer, or cataracts?"

Me: "I have no idea. My dad isn't available for questioning. But I can ask my uncle when he gets here tonight."

Dr. Nelson: "Do you have a medical history of obesity, asthma, seizures, cirrhosis, hepatitis, HIV, migraines, chronic pain, arthritis, or spinal problems?"

Me: "Are you serious?"

Dr. Nelson: "Do you have any family history of mental instability?"

Me: "Yes. My cousin thinks she's twenty-one. My aunt thinks she's eighteen. I'd call them both mentally unstable."

Dr. Nelson: "Do you now, or have you ever, used or abused caffeine, alcohol, nicotine, cocaine, amphetamines, or opiates?"

Me: "Oh, yeah. All of it. What else am I supposed to do in study hall? In fact, I better get my stash back from your rent-a-cop when I check out of here."

Finally, he looked up from the file in his lap and met my gaze. "You know, you're not helping yourself. The fastest way for you to get out of here is to cooperate. To help me help you."

I sighed, staring at the reflection shining on his sizable bald spot. "I know. But you're supposed to help me stop having panic attacks, right? But none of that stuff—" I glanced at the file I was secretly desperate to read "—has anything to do with why I'm here."

The doctor frowned, pressing thin lips even thinner. "Unfortunately, there are always preliminaries. Sometimes recreational drug use can cause symptoms like yours, and I need to rule that out before we continue. So could you please answer the question?"

"Fine." If he could really help me, I was ready to get cured, then get out. Short and sweet. "I drink Coke, just like every other teenager on the planet." I hesitated, wondering how much of this he'd tell my aunt and uncle. "And I had half a beer once. Over the summer." We'd only had one, so Em and I had split it.

"That's it?"

"Yeah." I wasn't sure whether he was happy with my answer, or secretly making fun of my seriously deficient social life.

"Okay..." Dr. Nelson scribbled in the file again, then flipped up the top page, too fast for me to read. "These next questions are more specifically geared toward your problems. If you don't answer honestly, you'll be crippling us both. Got it?"

"Sure." Whatever.

"Have you ever believed you had special powers? Like the ability to control the weather?"

I laughed out loud. I couldn't help it. If that was a symptom of crazy, maybe I was sane, after all. "No, I don't think I can control the weather. Or fly, or adjust the earth's orbit around the sun. No superpowers here."

Dr. Nelson just nodded, then glanced at the file again. "Was there ever a time when people were out to get you?"

Growing more relieved by the second, I shifted onto one hip, leaning with my elbow on the arm of the chair. "Um...I'm pretty sure my chemistry teacher hates me, but she hates everyone, so I don't think it's personal."

More scribbling. "Have you ever heard voices that others could not hear?"

"Nope." That was an easy one.

Dr. Nelson scratched his bald spot with short, neat fingernails. "Have your family or friends ever suggested that your statements were unusual?"

"You mean, do I say things that don't make sense?" I asked, and he nodded, nowhere near as amused as I was by his questions. "Only in French class."

"Have you ever seen things other people couldn't see?"

My heart dropped into my stomach, and my smile melted like a Popsicle in August.

"Kaylee?"

I crossed my arms over my chest and tried to ignore the dread swirling through me, like the memory of that dark fog. "Okay, look, if I answer this honestly, I'm going to sound crazy. But the very fact that I know that means I'm not really crazy, right?"

Dr. Nelson's wiry gray eyebrows both rose. "*Crazy* isn't a diagnosis, nor is it a term we use around here."

"But you know what I mean, right?"

Instead of answering, he crossed his legs at the knee and leaned back in his chair. "Let's talk about your panic attacks. What triggered the one you had in the mall?"

I closed my eyes. *He can't help you if you lie.* But there was no guarantee he could help me if I told the truth, either.

Here goes nothin'…

"I saw a kid in a wheelchair, and I got this horrible feeling that…that he was going to die."

Dr. Nelson frowned, his pencil poised over my file. "Why did you think he was going to die?"

I shrugged and stared miserably at my hands in my lap. "I don't know. It's just this really strong feeling. Like sometimes you can tell when someone's looking at you? Or standing over your shoulder?"

He was quiet for several seconds, but for the scratching of pen against paper. Then he looked up. "So what did you see that no one else saw?"

Ah, yes. The original question. "Shadows."

"You saw shadows? How do you know no one else could see them?"

"Because if anyone else had seen what I saw, I wouldn't have been the center of attention." Even with my brain-scrambling screech. "I saw shadows wrapping around the kid in the wheel-chair, but not touching anyone else." I started to tell him the rest of it. About the fog, and the things twisting and writhing inside it.

But then Dr. Nelson's frown dissolved into a look of patient patronization—an indulgent expression I'd seen plenty of in my two days at Lakeside. He thought I was crazy.

"Kaylee, you're describing delusions and hallucinations. Now, if you're really not on any drugs—and your blood work will confirm that—there are several other possible causes for the symptoms you're experiencing—"

"Like what?" I demanded. My pulse pounded thickly in my throat, and my teeth ground together so hard my jaws ached.

"Well, it's premature to start guessing, but after—"

"Tell me. Please. If you're going to tell me I'm crazy, at least tell me what kind of crazy I am."

Dr. Nelson sighed and flipped my file closed. "Your symptoms could be secondary to depression, or even severe anxiety…"

But there was something he wasn't saying. I could see it in his eyes, and my stomach started pitching. "What else?"

"It could be some form of schizophrenia, but that's really jumping the gun. We need to run more tests and—"

But I didn't hear anything after that. He'd brought my life to a grinding halt with that one word, and hurtled my entire future into a bleak storm of uncertainty. Of impossibility. If I was crazy, how could I possibly be anything else? Ever.

"When can I go home?" That dark, sick feeling in my stomach was churning out of control, and all I wanted in that moment was to curl up in my own bed and go to sleep. For a very long time.

"Once we get a definite diagnosis and get your meds balanced…"

"How long?"

"Two weeks, at least."

I stood and was almost bowled over by the hopelessness crashing over me. Would I have any friends left, if this got out? Would I be that crazy girl at school now? The one everyone whispered about? Would I even go back to school?

If I was really crazy, did it even matter?

★ ★ ★

My next four days at Lakeside made the phrase *bored to death* seem like a distinct possibility. If not for the note from Emma that Uncle Brendon brought, I might have given up entirely. But hearing from her, knowing that she hadn't forgotten about me—or told anyone else where I was—brought relevance back to my life outside Lakeside. Made things matter again.

Em was still planning to humiliate Toby that weekend, and crossing her fingers that I'd be back at school in time to see it happen. And in case I wasn't, she'd made plans to broadcast his downfall on YouTube, just for me.

That became my new goal. Doing and saying whatever it took to get out. To get back to school, and back to my life.

Nurse Nancy started each morning with the same two questions and faithfully recorded my responses on a clipboard. I saw Dr. Nelson for a few minutes every day, but he seemed more concerned with the side effects of the medication he'd prescribed than with whether or not it was actually working. In my opinion, the fact that I hadn't had any more screaming fits was total coincidence, and not the result of any of the pills they made me take.

And the pills…

I decided early on not to ask what they were. I didn't want to know. But I couldn't ignore the side effects. I was groggy all the time, and spent half of the first two days sleeping.

The next time my aunt and uncle came, they brought two pairs of my own jeans and *Brave New World,* and I spent the next day reading it between naps. That night, Paul gave me a ballpoint pen and a legal pad, and I started writing my paper longhand, desperately missing the laptop my father had sent for my last birthday.

On my fifth night in La La Land, my aunt, uncle, and I sat on a couch in the common area. Aunt Val prattled endlessly about Sophie's dance-team routine, and the many rounds of debate with the team's faculty sponsor over the new uniforms: unitards or separate tops with hot pants.

I personally didn't care if Sophie danced in the nude. In fact, the life experience might open up some interesting career opportunities for her some day. But I listened because as dull as Aunt Val's story was, it had happened out in the real world, and I missed the real world more than I'd ever missed anything in my life.

Then, in the middle of a detailed description of the unitard in question, several simultaneous bursts of static caught my attention from the nurses' station. I couldn't make out the actual words coming over the two-way radios, but something unusual was obviously going down.

Moments later, shouting shattered the overmedicated hush from somewhere beyond the nurses' station, and the main entrance buzzed. Then the door to the unit flew open, and two large men in scrubs came in carrying a guy about my age, with a firm grip on each of his arms. He refused to walk, so his bare feet trailed on the floor behind him.

The new boy was thin and lanky, and yelling his head off, though I couldn't understand a word he said. He was also completely nude, and trying to toss off the blanket someone had draped over his shoulders.

Aunt Val leaped to her high-heeled feet, predictably shocked. Her mouth hung open, her arms limp at her sides. Uncle Brendon's scowl could have paralyzed anyone who saw it. And all over the unit, patients poured from their rooms to investigate the commotion.

I stayed on the couch, paralyzed with horror not only for what I saw, but for what I remembered. Had I looked like that when the aides had buckled me to the restraint bed? Had my eyes been so bright and distant-looking? My limbs so out of control?

I'd been dressed, of course, but I wouldn't be if my next panic attack struck while I was in the shower. Would they haul me out naked and dripping to strap me to another bed?

While I watched, spellbound and horrified as the aides half pulled the newcomer through the unit, Uncle Brendon tugged Aunt Val to one corner of the now nearly empty common room. He glanced at me once, but I pretended not to notice, knowing he wouldn't want me to hear whatever he was about to say.

"We're handling this all wrong, Val. She shouldn't be here," he whispered fiercely, and inside I cheered. Schizophrenic or not—and no diagnosis had been confirmed yet—I didn't belong at Lakeside. I had no doubt of that.

On the edge of my vision, my aunt crossed her arms over her narrow chest. "Dr. Nelson won't let her out until…"

"I can change his mind."

If anyone could, it would be Uncle Brendon. He could sell water to a fish.

One of the aides let go of his charge's arm to reposition the blanket, and the new guy shoved him backward, then tried to pull free of the other aide, now shouting a random stream of curses.

"He's not on call tonight," Aunt Val whispered, still staring nervously at the scuffle. "You won't be able to reach him until tomorrow."

My uncle's scowl deepened. "I'll call first thing in the morning. This will be her last night here, if I have to break her out myself."

If I weren't afraid of drawing attention to my eavesdropping, I would have jumped up and cheered.

"Assuming she doesn't have another…episode between now and then," Aunt Val said, effectively raining all over my parade.

And that's when I noticed Lydia curled up in a chair at the back of the room, face scrunched up in pain, watching all three of us rather than the scuffle up front. She made no effort to hide her eavesdropping, and even gave me a thin, sad little smile when she saw that I'd noticed her.

When the staff had the new guy under control and safely sedated in the closed restraint room, my aunt and uncle said a quick goodbye. And this time, when the unit door closed behind them, my usual bitter wash of loneliness and despair was flavored with a thin, sweet ribbon of hope.

Freedom was eight hours and a phone call away. I would celebrate with a designer jogging suit bonfire.

The next morning marked my seventh day at Lakeside, and my first waking thought was that I'd officially missed the homecoming dance. But it was hard to be too upset about that, because my second thought was that I would sleep in my own bed that night. Just knowing I was getting out made everything else look a little brighter.

Maybe I wasn't crazy, after all. Maybe I was just prone to anxiety attacks, and the pills the doc prescribed could keep that under control. Maybe I *could* have a normal life—once I'd put Lakeside behind me.

I woke up before dawn and had half finished a five-hundred-piece jigsaw puzzle by the time Nurse Nancy came into the common room to ask about my gastrointestinal health and my suicidal impulses. I even smiled while I bit back a suggestion about where she could shove her clipboard.

The rest of the staff seemed to find my sudden good cheer alarming, and I swear they checked on me more often than usual. Which was pointless, because all I did was work on puzzles and stare out the window, aching for fresh air. And a doughnut. I had the worst craving for doughnuts, just because I couldn't get one.

After breakfast, I packed all my stuff. Every stupid sparkly jogging suit and every fluffy pair of socks. My copy of *Brave New World,* and my handwritten, fifteen-hundred-and-twenty-two-word essay, each word counted, just to make sure. Three times.

I was ready to go.

Nurse Nancy noted my packed bag and my neatly made bed with a single raised eyebrow, but said nothing as she checked me off on her clipboard.

By lunchtime, I was fidgeting uncontrollably. I tapped my fork on the table and stared out the window, watching the visible portion of the parking lot for my uncle's car. Or my aunt's. Every time I glanced up, I found Lydia watching me, a silent frown painted on her face, along with a now constant grimace of pain. Whatever was wrong with her was getting worse; she had my sympathy. And I couldn't help wondering why they didn't give her stronger pain pills. Or if they were giving her any at all.

I'd been working on the puzzle for nearly an hour after lunch when a loud crash echoed from the boys' hall, and startled aides took off in that direction. As they ran, that familiar grim panic grabbed me like a fist around my chest, squeezing so hard I couldn't breathe.

Despair settled through me, bitter and sobering. *No! Not again! I'm getting out today...*

But not if I started screaming again. Not if they had to strap me to another bed. Not if they had to shoot me so full of drugs I slept through the next fifteen hours.

My heart pumped blood through me so fast my head spun. I stayed in my seat while the other patients stood, edging eagerly to the broad doorway. The screaming hadn't started yet. Maybe if I stayed completely still, it wouldn't. Maybe I could control it this time. Maybe the pills would work.

Down the hall, something heavy thudded against the walls, and dark panic bloomed inside me, leaving my heart swollen and heavy with a grief I didn't understand.

Lydia rose from her chair with her back to the boys' hall. Her eyes closed, and she flinched. As I watched, frozen, she fell forward, bent at the waist. Her knees slammed into the vinyl tile. She held herself off the floor with one hand—the other pressed to her gut in obvious pain—and cried out softly. But no one heard her over the splinter of wood from down the hall. No one but me.

I wanted to help her but I was afraid to move. The shriek was building inside me now, fighting its way up. My throat tightened. I gripped the arms of my chair, my knuckles white with tension. The pills weren't working. Did that mean my panic attacks were neither schizophrenia nor anxiety?

Wide-eyed, I watched as Lydia hauled herself up, using an end table for balance. One arm wrapped around her stomach, she held her free hand out to me, tears standing in her eyes. "Come on," she whispered, then swallowed thickly. "If you want out, come with me now."

If I weren't busy holding back my scream, I might have choked on surprise. She could talk?

I sucked in a deep breath through my nose, then let go of the chair and slid my hand into hers. Lydia pulled me up with surprising strength, and I followed her across the room, through a gap in the cluster of patients, and down the girls' hall, while everyone else stared in the opposite direction. She stopped once, halfway down, bent over in pain again as a horrifying screech ripped through the air from the other side of the unit.

"It's Tyler," she gasped as I pulled her up and pressed my free fist against my sealed lips, physically holding back my screams. "The new guy. He hurts so bad, but I can only take so much..."

I had no idea what she was talking about, and I couldn't ask. I could only pull her forward, moving as much for her benefit now as for mine. Whatever was wrong with her was somehow connected to Tyler, so surely distance from the commotion would be as good for her as it was for me.

At the end of the hall, we stumbled into my room as the shouting grew louder. Lydia kicked the door shut. My eyes watered. A deep keening had started at the back of my throat, and I couldn't make it stop. All I could do was hold my mouth closed and hope for the best.

Lydia dropped onto my bed and held her hands out to me, her face pale now, and damp with sweat in spite of the over-air-conditioned room. "Hurry," she said, but as I stepped forward, that terrible grayness swept into the room from nowhere. From everywhere. It was just suddenly there, leaching color from everything, thickening with each second that high-pitched squeal leaked from my throat.

I scrambled onto the bed with her and used my shirt to wipe tears from my face. It was real! The fog was *real!* But that realization brought with it a bolt of true terror. If I wasn't hallucinating, what the hell was going on?

"Give me your hands." Lydia gasped and doubled over in pain. When she looked up again, I took her hand in my empty one, but kept my mouth covered with the other. "Normally I try to block it," she whispered, pushing limp black hair from her face. "But I don't have the strength for that right now. This place is so full of pain…"

Block what? What the hell was going on? Uncertainty pitched in my stomach, almost strong enough to rival the dark fear fueling my uncontrollable keening. What was she talking about? No wonder she'd quit speaking.

Lydia closed her eyes, riding a wave of pain, then she opened them and her voice was so soft I had to strain to hear it. "I can let the pain flow naturally—that's easiest on both of us. Or I can take it from you. That way's faster, but sometimes I take too much. More than just pain." She flinched again, and her gaze shifted to something over my shoulder, as if she could see through all the walls separating us from Tyler. "And I can't give it back. But either way, it's easier if I touch you."

She waited expectantly, but I could only shrug and shake my

head to demonstrate confusion, my lips still sealed firmly against the scream battering me from the inside.

"Close your eyes and let the pain flow," she said, and I obeyed, because I didn't know what else to do.

Suddenly my hand felt both hot and cold, like I had a fever and chills at the same time. Lydia's fingers shook in mine, and I opened my eyes to find her shuddering all over. I tried to pull my hand away, but she slapped her other palm over it, holding me tight even as her teeth began to chatter. "K-keep your eyes cl-closed," she stuttered. "No m-matter what."

Terrified now, I closed my eyes and concentrated on holding my jaw shut. On not seeing the fog things in the back of my mind. On not feeling the thick current of agony and despair stirring through me.

And slowly, very slowly, the panic began to ebb. It was gradual at first, but then the discordant ribbon of sound leaking from me thinned into a strand as fragile as a human hair. Though the panic still built inside me, it was weaker now, and blessedly manageable thanks to whatever she was doing.

I dared a peek at Lydia to find her eyes closed, her face scrunched in pain, her forehead again shiny with sweat. Her free hand clutched a handful of her baggy T-shirt, pressing it into her stomach like she was hurt. But there was no blood, or any other sign of a wound; I looked closely to make sure.

She was funneling the panic from me somehow, and it was making her sick. And as badly as I wanted out of Lakeside, I would *not* take my freedom at her expense.

I still couldn't talk, so I tried to pull my hand away, but Lydia's eyes popped open at the first tug. "No!" She clung to my fingers, tears standing in her eyes. "I can't stop it, and fighting only makes it hurt worse."

The pain wouldn't kill me, but from the looks of it, whatever she was doing might kill her. I tugged again and she swallowed thickly, then shook her head sharply.

"It hurts *me,* Kaylee. If you let go, I hurt worse."

She was lying. I could see it in her eyes. She'd heard my aunt and uncle and knew that if I had another screaming fit, Uncle Brendon wouldn't be able to get me out. Lydia was lying so I wouldn't pull away, even though she was hurting herself worse— maybe killing herself—with every bit of panic she took from me.

At first I let her, because she seemed determined to do it. She obviously had her reasons, even if I didn't understand them. But when the guilt became too much and I tried to pull away again, she squeezed my hand so hard it hurt.

"He's cresting…" she whispered, and I searched her eyes in vain for a translation. I still had no idea what she was talking about. "It's going to shift. Tyler's pain will end, and yours will begin."

Begin? *Because it's all been fun and games so far…*

But before I could finish that thought, Lydia's hands went limp around mine, and she relaxed so suddenly and thoroughly she almost seemed to deflate. For a precious half second, she smiled, obviously pain-free, and I started to think it was over.

"He's gone," Lydia said softly.

Then the panic *truly* hit me.

What I'd felt before had only been a preview. This was the main event. The real deal. Like at the mall.

Anguish exploded inside me, a shock to my entire system. My lungs ached. My throat burned. Tears poured from my eyes. The scream bounced around in my head so fast and hard I couldn't think.

I couldn't hold it in. The keening started up again, more urgent than ever, and my jaws—already sore from being clenched—were no match for the renewed pressure.

"Give it to me…" Lydia said, and I opened my eyes to see her staring at me earnestly. She looked a little better. A little stronger. Not quite so pale. But if she took any more of my pain, she'd backslide. Fast and hard.

Unfortunately, I was beyond the ability to focus by then. I didn't know whether or not to give her what she wanted, much less how to do it. I could only ride the scream jolting through me like a bolt of electricity and hope it stayed contained.

But it wouldn't. The keening grew stronger. It thickened, until I thought I'd choke on it. My teeth vibrated beneath the relentless power of it, and I chattered like I was cold. I couldn't hold it back.

Yet I couldn't afford to let it go.

"There's too much. It's too slow," Lydia moaned. She was tense, like every little movement hurt. Her hands shook again, and her face had become one continuous grimace. "I'm sorry. I have to take it."

What? What does that mean? Her pain was obvious, and she wanted more? I pulled my hand away, but she snatched it back just as my mouth flew open. I couldn't fight it anymore.

The scream exploded from my throat with an agonizing burst of pain, like I was vomiting nails. Yet there was no sound.

An instant after the scream began—before the sound had a chance to be heard—it was sucked back inside me by a vicious pull from deep in my gut. My mouth snapped shut. Those nails shredded my throat again on the way down. It whipped around inside me, my unheard screech, being steadily pulled out of me and into...

Lydia.

She began to convulse, but I couldn't pry her fingers from my hand. Her eyes rolled up so high only the lower arc of her green irises showed, yet still she clung to me, pulling the last of the scream from me and into her. Pulling my pain with it.

Gone was the agony of my bruised lungs, my raw throat and my pounding head. Gone was that awful grief, that despair so encompassing I couldn't think about anything else. Gone was the gray fog; it faded all around us while I tried to free my hand.

Then, suddenly, it was over. Her fingers fell away from mine.

Her eyes closed. She fell over backward—still convulsing—before I could catch her. She hit her head on the footboard, and when I fumbled for a pillow to put under her, I realized her nose was bleeding. Dripping steadily on the blanket.

"Help!" I shouted, the first sound I'd made since the whole thing started, several endless minutes earlier. "Somebody help me!" My voice sounded funny. Slurred. Why was it so hard to talk? Why did I feel so weird? Like everything was moving in slow motion? Like my brain was packed with cotton.

Footsteps pounded down the hall toward me, then the door flew open. "What happened?" Nurse Nancy demanded, two taller female aides peering over her shoulder.

"She..." I blinked, trying to focus in a thick cloud of confusion. "She took too much..." Too much of what? The answer was right there, but it was so blurry... I could see it, but couldn't quite bring it into focus.

"What?" Nurse Nancy knelt over the girl on my bed—Lisa? Leah?—and pulled back her eyelids. "Get her out of here!" she yelled at one of the aids, gesturing toward me with one hand. "And bring a stretcher. She's seizing."

A woman in bright blue scrubs led me into the hall by one arm. "Go sit in the common room," she said, then jogged past me.

I wandered down the hall slowly, one hand on the cold, rough wall for balance. Trying to stay above water as wave after wave of confusion crashed over me. I sank into the first empty chair I found and buried my face in my hands. I couldn't think. Couldn't quite remember...

People were talking all around me, whispering phrases I couldn't make sense of. Names I didn't quite recognize. So I latched on to the first familiar thing I saw: a jigsaw puzzle spread out on a table by the window. That was my puzzle. I'd been working it before something bad happened. Before...

Cold hands. Dark fog. Screaming. Bleeding.

I'd placed three puzzle pieces when two aides rolled a stretcher past the nurses' station and out the main door of the unit. "Another one?" the security guard asked, as he held the door open.

"This one's still breathing," the aide in purple said.

This one? But the harder I tried to remember, the blurrier the images got.

I'd only placed two more pieces when someone called my name. I looked up from my puzzle to see another aide—her name was Judy; I remembered that—standing next to my uncle. Who stood next to my suitcase.

"Kaylee?" Uncle Brendon frowned at me in concern. "Ready to go home?"

Yes. That much was clear. But my relief came with a bitter aftertaste of guilt and sadness. Something bad had happened. Something to do with the girl on my bed. But I couldn't remember what.

I followed Uncle Brendon through the main door—the one you had to be buzzed through—then stopped. Two men leaned over a stretcher in front of the elevator, where a girl with dark hair lay motionless. One man was steadily squeezing a bag attached to a mask over her face. A smear of blood stained her cheek. Her eyes were closed, but in my fractured memory, they were bright green.

"Do you know her?" Uncle Brendon asked. "What happened to her?"

I shuddered as the answer surfaced from the haze in my head. Maybe someday I would know what it meant, but in that moment, I only knew that it was true.

"She took too much."

★ ★ ★ ★ ★

MY SOUL TO TAKE

For Number 1, who knows that fajitas will fix any plot hole.

"Come on!" Emma whispered from my right, her words floating from her mouth in a thin white cloud. She glared at the battered steel panel in front of us, as if her own impatience would make the door open. "She forgot, Kaylee. I should have known she would." More white puffs drifted from Emma's perfectly painted mouth as she bounced to stay warm, her curves barely contained in the low-cut shimmery red blouse she'd "borrowed" from one of her sisters.

Yes, I was a little envious; I had few curves and no sister from whom to borrow hot clothes. But I did have the time, and one glance at my cell phone told me it was still four minutes to nine. "She'll be here." I smoothed the front of my own shirt and slid my phone into my pocket as Emma knocked for the third time. "We're early. Just give her a minute."

My own puff of breath had yet to fade when metal creaked and the door swung slowly toward us, leaking rhythmic flashes of smoky light and a low thumping beat into the cold, dark alley. Traci Marshall—Emma's youngest older sister—stood with one palm flat against the door, holding it open. She wore a snug, low-cut black tee, readily displaying the family resemblance, as if the long blond hair wasn't enough.

"'Bout time!" Emma snapped, stepping forward to brush past her sister. But Traci slapped her free hand against the door frame, blocking our entrance.

She returned my smile briefly, then frowned at her sister. "Nice to see you too. Tell me the rules."

Emma rolled wide-set brown eyes and rubbed her bare, goose-pimpled arms—we'd left our jackets in my car. "No alcohol, no chemicals. No fun of any sort." She mumbled that last part, and I stifled a smile.

"What else?" Traci demanded, obviously struggling to maintain a rare scowl.

"Come together, stay together, leave together," I supplied, reciting the same lines we'd repeated each time she snuck us in—only twice before. The rules were lame, but I knew from experience that we wouldn't get in without them.

"And..."

Emma stamped her feet for warmth, chunky heels clacking on the concrete. "If we get caught, we don't know you."

As if anyone would believe that. The Marshall girls were all cast from the same mold: a tall, voluptuous mold that put my own modest curves to shame.

Traci nodded, apparently satisfied, and let her hand fall from the door frame. Emma stepped forward and her sister frowned, pulling her into the light from the hall fixture overhead. "Is that Cara's new shirt?"

Emma scowled and tugged her arm free. "She'll never know it's gone."

Traci laughed and motioned with one arm toward the front of the club, from which light and sound flooded the back rooms and offices. Now that we were all inside, she had to shout to be heard over the music. "Enjoy the rest of your life while it lasts, 'cause she's gonna *bury* you in that shirt."

Unperturbed, Emma danced her way down the hall and into the main room, hands in the air, hips swaying with the pulse of the song. I followed her, keyed up by the energy of the Saturday-night crowd from the moment I saw the first cluster of bodies in motion.

We worked our way into the throng and were swallowed by it, assimilated by the beat, the heat and the casual partners pulling us close. We danced through several songs, together, alone and in random pairs, until I was breathing hard and damp with sweat. I signaled Emma that I was going for a drink, and she nodded, already moving again as I worked my way toward the edge of the crowd.

Behind the bar, Traci worked alongside another bartender, a large, dark man in a snug black tee, both oddly lit by a strip of blue neon overhead. I claimed the first abandoned bar stool, and the man in black propped both broad palms on the bar in front of me.

"I got this one," Traci said, one hand on his arm. He nodded and moved on to the next customer. "What'll it be?" Traci smoothed back a stray strand of pale, blue-tinted hair.

I grinned, leaning with both elbows on the bar. "Jack and Coke?"

She laughed. "I'll give you the Coke." She shot soda into a glass of ice and slid it toward me. I pushed a five across the bar and swiveled on my stool to watch the dance floor, scanning the multitude for Emma. She was sandwiched between two guys in matching UT Dallas fraternity tees and neon, legal-to-drink bracelets, all three grinding in unison.

Emma drew attention like wool draws static.

Still smiling, I drained my soda and set my glass on the bar.

"Kaylee Cavanaugh."

I jumped at the sound of my own name and whirled toward the stool to my left. My gaze settled on the most hypnotic set of hazel eyes I'd ever seen, and for several seconds I could only stare, lost in the most amazing swirls of deep brown and vivid green, which seemed to churn in time with my own heartbeat—though surely they were just reflecting the lights flashing overhead. My focus only returned when I had to blink, and the momentary loss of contact brought me back to myself.

That's when I realized who I was staring at.

Nash Hudson. Holy crap. I almost looked down to see if ice had anchored my feet to the floor, since hell had surely frozen over. Somehow I'd stepped off the dance floor and into some weird warp zone where irises swam with color and Nash Hudson smiled at me, and me alone.

I picked up my glass, hoping for one last drop to rewet my suddenly dry throat—and wondered fleetingly if Traci *had* spiked my Coke—but discovered it every bit as empty as I'd expected.

"Need a refill?" Nash asked, and that time I made my mouth open. After all, if I was dreaming—or in the Twilight Zone—I had nothing to lose by speaking. Right?

"I'm good. Thanks." I ventured a hesitant smile, and my heart nearly exploded when I saw my grin reflected on his upturned, perfectly formed lips.

"How'd you get in here?" He arched one brow, more in amusement than in real curiosity. "Crawl through the window?"

"Back door," I whispered, feeling my face flush. Of course he knew I was a junior—too young even for an eighteen-and-over club, like Taboo.

"What?" He grinned and leaned closer to hear me above the music. His breath brushed my neck, and my pulse pounded so hard I felt light-headed. He smelled sooo good.

"Back door," I repeated into his ear. "Emma's sister works here."

"Emma's here?"

I pointed her out on the dance floor—now swaying with three guys at once—and assumed that would be the last I saw of Nash Hudson. But to my near-fatal shock, he dismissed Em at a glance and turned back to me with a mischievous gleam in those amazing eyes.

"Aren't you gonna dance?"

My hand was suddenly sweaty around my empty glass. Did that mean he wanted to dance with me? Or that he wanted the bar stool for his girlfriend?

No, wait. He'd dumped his latest girlfriend the week before, and the sharks were already circling the fresh meat. *Though they're not circling him now...* I saw no one from Nash's usual crowd, either clustered around him or on the dance floor.

"Yeah, I'm gonna dance," I said, and again, his eyes were swirling green melting into brown and back, flashing blue occasionally in the neon glow. I could have stared at his eyes for hours. But he probably would have thought that was weird.

"Let's go!" He took my hand and stood as I slid off the bar stool, and I followed him onto the dance floor. A fresh smile bloomed on my face, and my chest seemed to tighten around my heart in anticipation. I'd known him for a while—Emma had gone out with a few of his friends—but had never been the sole object of his attention. Had never even considered the possibility.

If Eastlake High School were the universe, I would be one of the moons circling Planet Emma, constantly hidden by her shadow, and glad to be there. Nash Hudson would be one of the stars: too bright to look at, too hot to touch and at the center of his own solar system.

But on the dance floor, I forgot all that. His light was shining directly on me, and it was *sooo warm.*

We wound up only feet from Emma, but with Nash's hands on me, his body pressed into mine, I barely noticed. That first song ended, and we were moving to the next one before I even fully realized the beat had changed.

Several minutes later, I glimpsed Emma over Nash's shoulder. She stood at the bar with one of the guys she'd been grinding with, and as I watched, Traci set a drink in front of each of them. When her sister turned around, Emma grabbed her partner's drink—something dark with a wedge of lime on the rim—and drained it in three gulps. Frat boy smiled, then pulled her back into the crowd.

I made a mental note not to let Emma drive my car—ever—then let my eyes wander back to Nash, where they wanted to be in the first place. But on the way, my gaze was snagged by an unfamiliar sheet of strawberry-blond hair, crowning the head of the only girl in the building to rival Emma in beauty. This girl, too, had her choice of dance partners, and though she couldn't have been more than eighteen, she'd obviously had much more to drink than Emma.

But despite how pretty and obviously charismatic she was, watching her dance twisted something deep inside my gut and made my chest tighten, as if I couldn't quite get enough air. Something was wrong with her. I wasn't sure how I knew, but I was absolutely certain that something was *not right* with that girl.

"You okay?" Nash shouted, laying one hand on my shoulder, and suddenly I realized I'd gone still, while everyone around me was still writhing to the beat.

"Yeah!" I shook off my discomfort and was relieved to find that looking into Nash's eyes chased away that feeling of *wrongness,* leaving in its place a new calm, eerie in its depth and reach. We danced for several more songs, growing more comfortable with each other with every moment that passed. By the time we stopped for a drink, sweat was gathering on the back of my neck and my arms were damp.

I lifted the bulk of my hair to cool myself and waved to Emma with my free hand as I turned to follow Nash off the dance floor—and nearly collided with that same strawberry blonde. Not that she noticed. But the minute my eyes found her, that feeling was back in spades—that strong discomfort, like a bad taste in my mouth, only all over my body. And this time it was accompanied by an odd sadness. A general melancholy that felt specifically connected to this one person. Whom I'd never met.

"Kaylee?" Nash yelled over the music. He stood at the bar, holding two tall glasses of soda, slick with condensation. I closed the space between us and took the glass he offered, a little frightened to notice that this time, even staring straight into his eyes couldn't completely relax me. Couldn't quite loosen my throat, which threatened to close against the cold drink I so desperately craved.

"What's wrong?" We stood inches apart, thanks to the throng pressing ever closer to the bar, but he still had to lean into me to be heard.

"I don't know. Something about that girl, that redhead over there—" I nodded toward the dancer in question "—bothers me." *Well, crap.* I hadn't meant to admit that. It sounded so pathetic aloud.

But Nash only glanced at the girl, then back at me. "Seems okay to me. Assuming she has a ride home…"

"Yeah, I guess." But then the current song ended, and the girl stumbled—looking somehow graceful, even when obviously intoxicated—off the dance floor and toward the bar. Headed right for us.

My heart beat harder with every step she took. My hand curled around my glass until my knuckles went white. And that familiar sense of melancholy swelled into an overwhelming feeling of grief. Of dark foreboding.

I gasped, startled by a sudden, gruesome certainty.

Not again. Not with Nash Hudson there to watch me completely freak out. My breakdown would be all over the school on Monday, and I could kiss goodbye what little social standing I'd gained.

Nash set his glass down and peered into my face. "Kaylee? You okay?" But I could only shake my head, incapable of answering. I was *far* from okay, but couldn't articulate the problem in any way resembling coherence. And suddenly the potentially devastating rumors looked like minor blips on my disaster meter compared to the panic growing inside me.

Each breath came faster than the last, and a scream built deep within my chest. I clamped my mouth shut to hold it back, grinding my teeth painfully. The strawberry blonde stepped up to the bar on my left, and only a single stool and its occupant stood between us. The male bartender took her order and she turned sideways to wait for her drink. Her eyes met mine. She smiled briefly, then stared out onto the dance floor.

Horror washed over me in a devastating wave of intuition. My throat closed. I choked on a scream of terror. My glass slipped from my hand and shattered on the floor. The redheaded dancer squealed and jumped back as ice-cold soda splattered her, me, Nash, and the man on the stool to my left. But I barely noticed the frigid liquid, or the people staring at me.

I saw only the girl, and the dark, translucent shadow that had enveloped her.

"Kaylee?" Nash tilted my face up so that our eyes met. His were full of concern, the colors swirling almost out of control now in the flashing lights. Watching them made me dizzy.

I wanted to tell him…something. Anything. But if I opened my mouth, the scream would rip free, and then anyone who wasn't already looking at me would turn to stare. They'd think I'd lost my mind.

Maybe they'd be right.

"What's wrong?" Nash demanded, stepping closer to me now, heedless of the glass and the wet floor. "Do you have seizures?" But I could only shake my head at him, refusing passage to the wail trying to claw its way out of me, denying the existence of a narrow bed in a sterile white room, awaiting my return.

And suddenly Emma was there. Emma, with her perfect body, beautiful face and heart the size of an elephant's. "She'll be fine." Emma pulled me away from the bar as the male bartender came forward with a mop and bucket. "She just needs some air." She waved off Traci's worried look and frantic hand gestures, then tugged me through the crowd by one arm.

I clamped my free palm over my mouth and shook my head furiously when Nash tried to take that hand in his. I should have been worried about what he would think. That he would want nothing else to do with me now that I'd publicly embarrassed him. But I couldn't concentrate long enough to worry about anything but the redhead at the bar. The one who'd watched us leave through a shadow-shroud only I could see.

Emma led me past the bathrooms and into the back hall, Nash close on my heels. "What's wrong with her?" he asked.

"Nothing." Emma paused to turn and smile at us both, and gratitude broke through my dark terror for just an instant. "It's a panic attack. She just needs some fresh air and time to calm down."

But that's where she was wrong. It wasn't time I needed, so much as space. Distance, between me and the source of the panic. Unfortunately, there wasn't enough room in the whole club to get me far enough away from the girl at the bar. Even with me standing by the back door, the panic was as strong as ever. The unspoken shriek burned my throat, and if I unclenched my jaws—if I lost control—my scream would shatter eardrums all over Taboo. It would put the thumping dance beat to shame, and possibly blow out the speakers—if not the windows.

All because of some redhead I didn't even know.

Just thinking about her sent a fresh wave of devastation through me, and my knees collapsed. My fall caught Emma off guard, and I would have pulled her down if Nash hadn't caught me.

He lifted me completely off the ground, cradling me like a child, and followed Emma out the back door with me secure in his arms. The club had been dim, but the alley was *dark,* and it went quiet once the door thumped shut behind us, Emma's bank card keeping the latch from sliding home. The frigid near-silence should have calmed me, but the racket in my head had reached its zenith. The scream I refused to release slammed around in my brain, reverberating, echoing, punctuating the grief still thick in my heart.

Nash set me down in the alley, but by then my thoughts had lost all semblance of logic or comprehension. I felt something smooth and dry beneath me, and only later would I realize Emma had found a collapsed box for him to set me on.

My jeans had ridden up on my legs when Nash carried me, and the cardboard was cold and gritty with grime against my calves.

"Kaylee?" Emma knelt in front of me, her face inches from mine, but I couldn't make sense of a word she said after my name. I heard only my own thoughts. Just *one* thought, actually. A paranoid delusion, according to my former therapist, which presented itself with the absolute authority of long-held fact.

Then Emma's face disappeared and I was staring at her knees. Nash said something I couldn't make out. Something about a drink…

Music swelled back to life, then Emma was gone. She'd left me alone with the hottest guy I'd ever danced with—the last person in the world I wanted to witness my total break with reality.

Nash dropped onto his knees and looked into my eyes, the greens and browns in his still churning frantically somehow, though there were no lights overhead now.

I was imagining it. I had to be. I'd seen them dance with the light earlier, and now my traumatized mind had seized upon Nash's eyes as a focal point of my delusion. Just like the strawberry blonde. Right?

But there was no time to think through my theory. I was losing control. Successive waves of grief threatened to flatten me, crushing me into the wall with an invisible pressure, as if Nash weren't even there. I couldn't suck in a deep breath, yet a high-pitched keening leaked from my throat now, even with my lips sealed shut. My vision began to go even darker than the alley—though I wouldn't have thought that possible—like the whole world had been overlaid with an odd gray filter.

Nash frowned, still watching me, then twisted to sit beside me, his back against the wall too. On the edges of my graying vision, something scuttled past soundlessly. A rat, or some other scavenger attracted by the club's garbage bin? *No.* Whatever I'd glimpsed was too big to be a rodent—unless we'd stepped into Buttercup's fire swamp—and too indistinct for my shattered focus to settle on.

Nash took my free hand in his, and I forgot whatever I'd seen. He pushed my hair back from my right ear. I couldn't understand most of what he whispered to me, but I gradually came to realize that his actual words weren't important. What mattered was his proximity. His breath on my neck. His warmth melting into mine. His scent surrounding me. His voice swirling in my head, insulating me from the scream still ricocheting against my skull.

He was calming me with nothing more than his presence, his patience and whispered words of what sounded like a child's rhyme, based on what little I caught.

And it was working. My anxiety gradually faded, and dim, gritty color leaked back into the world. My fingers relaxed around his hand. My lungs expanded fully, and I sucked in a sharp, frigid breath, suddenly freezing as sweat from the club dried on my skin.

The panic was still there, in the shadowed corners of my mind, in the dark spots on the edge of my vision. But I could handle it now. Thanks to Nash.

"You okay?" he asked when I turned my head to face him, the bricks cold and rough against my cheek.

I nodded. And that's when a new horror descended: utter, consuming, inescapable mortification, most awful in its longevity. The panic attack was all but over, but humiliation would last a lifetime.

I'd completely lost it in front of Nash Hudson. My life was over; even my friendship with Emma wouldn't be enough to repair the damage from such a nasty wound.

Nash stretched his legs out. "Wanna talk about it?"

No. I wanted to go hide in a hole, or stick my head in a bag, or change my name and move to Peru.

But then suddenly, I *did* want to talk about it. With Nash's voice still echoing softly in my head, his words whispering faintly over my skin, I wanted to tell him what had happened. It made no sense. After knowing me for eight years and helping me through at least half a dozen previous panic attacks, Emma still had no idea what caused them. I couldn't tell her. It would scare her. Or worse, finally convince her I really was crazy.

So why did I want to tell Nash? I had no answer for that, but the urge was undeniable.

"…the strawberry blonde." There, I'd said it out loud, and committed myself to some sort of explanation.

Nash's brow furrowed in confusion. "You know her?"

"No." Fortunately. Merely sharing oxygen with her had nearly driven me out of my mind. "But something's wrong with her, Nash. She's…dark."

Kaylee, shut up! If he wasn't already convinced I was certifiable, he would be soon….

"What?" His frown deepened, but rather than bewildered or skeptical, he looked surprised. Then came vague comprehension. Comprehension, and…dread. He might not know exactly what I meant, but he didn't look completely clueless either. "What do you mean, 'dark'?"

I closed my eyes, hesitating at the last second. What if I'd misread him? What if he did think I was crazy?

Worse yet, what if he was right?

But in the end, I opened my eyes and met his gaze frankly,

because I had to tell him something, and surely I couldn't damage his opinion of me much more than I already had. Right?

"Okay, this is going to sound weird," I began, "but something's wrong with that girl at the bar. When I looked at her, she was...shadowed." I hesitated, scrounging up the courage to finish what I'd started. "She's going to die, Nash. That girl is going to die very, very soon."

≪ 2 ≫

"What?" Nash's eyebrows rose, but he didn't roll his eyes, or laugh, or pat my head and call for the men in white coats. In fact, he looked like he almost believed me. "How do you know she's gonna die?"

I rubbed both temples, trying to wipe away a familiar frustration rearing inside me. He might not be laughing on the outside, but surely he was cracking up on the inside. How could he not be? *What the hell was I thinking?*

"I don't know how I know. I don't even know that I'm right. But when I look at her, she's…darker than everyone around her. Like she's standing in the shadow of something I can't see. And I know she's going to die."

Nash frowned in concern, and I closed my eyes, barely noticing the sudden swell of music from the club. I knew that look. It was the one mothers give their kids when they fall off the slide and sit up talking about purple ponies and dancing squirrels.

"I know it sounds—" *crazy* "—weird, but…"

He took both of my hands, twisting to face me more fully on the flattened box beneath us, and again the colors in his irises seemed to pulse with my heartbeat. His mouth opened, and I held my breath, awaiting my verdict. Had I lost him with talk of creepy black shadows, or did my mistakes start all the way back with the spilled drink?

"Sounds pretty weird to me."

We both glanced up to find Emma watching us, a chilled bottle of water in one hand, dripping condensation on the grimy concrete, and I almost groaned in frustration. Whatever Nash had been about to say was gone now; I could see that in the cautious smile he shot at me, before redirecting toward Emma.

She twisted open the lid and handed me the bottle. "But then, you wouldn't be Kaylee if you didn't weird-out on me every now and then." She shrugged amiably and hauled me to my feet as Nash stood to join us. "So you had a panic attack because you think some girl in the club is going to die?"

I nodded hesitantly, waiting for her to laugh or roll her eyes, if she thought I was joking. Or to look nervous, if she knew I wasn't. Instead, her brows arched, and she cocked her head to one side. "Well, shouldn't you go tell her? Or something?"

"I..." I blinked in confusion and frowned at the brick wall over her shoulder. Somehow, that option had never occurred to me. "I don't know." I glanced at Nash, but found no answer in his now-normal eyes. "She'd probably just think I was crazy. Or she'd get all freaked out." And really, who could blame her? "Doesn't matter, anyway, because it's not true. Right? It can't be."

Nash shrugged but looked like he wanted to say something. But then Emma spoke up, never hesitant to voice her opinion. "Of course not. You had another panic attack, and your mind latched on to the first person you saw. Could've been me, or Nash, or Traci. It doesn't mean anything."

I nodded, but as badly as I wanted to believe her theory, it just didn't feel right. Yet I couldn't make myself warn the red-head. No matter what I thought I knew, the prospect of telling a perfect stranger that she was going to die felt just plain crazy, and I'd had enough of crazy for the moment.

For the rest of my life, in fact.

"All better?" Emma asked, when she read my decision on my face. "Wanna go back in?"

I was feeling better, but that dark panic still lingered on the edge of my mind, and it would only get worse if I saw the girl again. I had no doubt of that. And I would not give Nash an encore of the night's performance, if at all possible.

"I'm just gonna head home." My uncle had taken my aunt out for her fortieth birthday, and Sophie was on an overnight trip with the dance team. For once I'd have the house to myself. I smiled at Emma in apology. "But if you want to stay, you could probably catch a ride with Traci."

"Nah, I'll go with you." Emma took the water bottle from my hand and gulped from it. "She told us to leave together, remember?"

"She also told us not to drink."

Emma rolled her big brown eyes. "If she really meant that, she wouldn't have snuck us into a *bar*."

That was Emma-logic, all right. The longer you thought about it, the less sense it made.

Emma glanced from me to Nash. Then she smiled and headed down the alley toward the car lot across the street, to give us some privacy. I dug my keys from my pocket and stared at them, trying to avoid Nash's gaze until I knew what I was going to say.

He'd seen me at my worst, and rather than flipping out or making fun, he'd helped me regain control. We'd connected in a way I wouldn't have thought possible an hour earlier, especially with someone like Nash, whose one-track mind was a thing of legends. Still, I couldn't fight the certainty that this evening's dream would end in tomorrow's nightmare. That daylight would bring him to his senses, and he'd wonder what he was doing with me in the first place.

I opened my mouth, but no sound came out. My keys jangled,

the ring dangling from my index finger, and he frowned when his gaze settled on them.

"You okay to drive?" He grinned, and my pulse jumped in response. "I could take you home and walk from there. You live in the Parkview complex, right? That's just a couple of minutes from me."

He knew where I lived? I must have looked suspicious, because he rushed to explain. "I gave your sister a ride once. Last month."

My jaw tightened, and I felt my expression darken. "She's my cousin." Nash had given Sophie a ride? *Please don't let that be a euphemism…*

He frowned and shook his head in answer to my unspoken question. "Scott Carter asked me to give her a lift."

Oh. Good. I nodded, and he shrugged. "So you want me to take you guys home?" He held his hand out for my keys.

"That's okay, I'm good to drive." And I wasn't in the habit of letting people I barely knew behind the wheel of my car. Especially really hot guys who—rumor had it—had gotten two speeding tickets in his ex's Firebird.

Nash flashed a deep set of stubbly dimples and shrugged. "Then can I have a lift? I rode with Carter, and he won't be ready to go for hours."

My pulse jumped into my throat. Was he leaving early just so he could ride with me? Or had I ruined his evening with my freak-tastic hysterics?

"Um…yeah." My car was a mess, but it was too late to worry about that. "But you'll have to flip Emma for shotgun."

Fortunately, that turned out to be unnecessary. Em took the back, shooting me a meaningful glance and pointing at Nash as she slid across the seat, swiping a corn-chip bag onto the floor. I dropped her off first, a full hour and a half before her curfew, which had to be some kind of record.

As I pulled out of Emma's driveway, Nash twisted in the

passenger seat to face me, his expression somber, and my heart beat so hard it almost hurt. It was time for the easy letdown. He was too cool to say it in front of Emma, and even with her gone, he'd probably be really nice about it. But the bottom line was the same; he wasn't interested in me. At least, not after my public meltdown.

"So you've had these panic attacks before?"

What? My hands clenched the wheel in surprise as I took a left at the end of the street.

"A couple of times." *Half a dozen, at least.* I couldn't purge suspicion from my voice. My "issues" should have driven him screaming into the night, and instead he wanted details? Why?

"Do your parents know?"

I shifted in my seat, as if a new position might make me more comfortable with the question. But it would take much more than that. "My mom died when I was little, and my dad couldn't handle me on his own. He moved to Ireland, and I've been with my aunt and uncle ever since."

Nash blinked and nodded for me to go on. He gave me none of the awkward sympathy or compulsive, I'm-not-sure-what-to-say throat-clearing I usually got when people found out I'd been half-orphaned, then wholly abandoned. I liked him for that, even if I didn't like where his questions were heading.

"So your aunt and uncle know?"

Yeah. *They think I'm one egg shy of a dozen.* But the truth hurt too much to say out loud.

I turned to see him watching me closely, and my suspicion flared again, settling to burn deep in my gut. Why did he care what my family knew about my not-so-private misery? Unless he was planning to laugh with his friends later about what a freak I was.

But his interest didn't seem malicious. Especially considering what he'd done for me at Taboo. So maybe his curiosity was feigned, and he was after something else to tell his friends about. Something girls rarely denied him, if the rumors were true.

If he didn't get it, would he tell the entire school my darkest, most painful secret?

No. My stomach pitched at the thought, and I hit the brake too hard as we came to a stop sign.

My foot still wedged against the brake, I glanced in the rearview mirror at the empty street behind me, then shifted into Park and turned to face Nash, steeling my nerve for the question to come. "What do you want from me?" I spat it out before I could change my mind.

Nash's eyes widened in surprise, and he sat back hard against the passenger's side door, as if I'd shoved him. "I just... Nothing."

"You want nothing?" I wanted to see the deep greens and browns of his irises, but the beam from the nearest streetlight didn't reach my car, so only the dim light from my dashboard shone on him, and it wasn't enough to illuminate his face. To let me truly read his expression. "I can count the number of times we've really spoken before tonight on one hand." I held that hand up for emphasis. "Then you come out of nowhere and play white knight to my distressed damsel, and I'm supposed to believe you want nothing in return? Nothing to tell your friends about on Monday?"

He tried to laugh, but the sound was stilted, and he shifted uncomfortably in his seat. "I wouldn't—"

"Save it. Rumor has it you've conquered more territory than Genghis Khan."

A single dark brow rose in the shadows, challenging me. "You believe everything you hear?"

My eyebrow shot up to mirror his. "You denyin' it?"

Instead of answering, he laughed for real and propped one elbow on the door handle. "Are you always this mean to guys who sing to you in dark alleys?"

My next retort died on my lips, so surprised was I by the reminder. He had sung to me, and somehow talked me down from a brutal panic attack. He'd saved me from public humiliation. But there had to be a reason, and I wasn't that great of a conquest.

"I don't trust you," I said finally, my hands limp and worthless on my lap.

"Right now I don't trust you either." He grinned in the dark, flashing pale teeth and a single shadowed dimple, and his open-armed gesture took in the stopped car. "Are you kicking me out, or do I get door-to-door service?"

That's the only *service you get.* But I shifted into Drive and faced the road again, then turned right into his subdivision, which was definitely more than a couple of minutes from my neighborhood. Would he really have walked if I'd let him drive me home?

Would he have taken me straight home?

"Take this left, then the next right. It's the one on the corner."

His directions led me to a small frame house in an older section of the development. I pulled into the driveway behind a dusty, dented sedan. The driver's side door stood open, spilling light from the interior to illuminate a lopsided square of dry grass to the left of the pavement.

"You left your car door open," I said, shifting into Park, glad for something to focus on other than Nash, though that's where my gaze really wanted to be.

Nash sighed. "It's my mom's. She's gone through three batteries in six months."

I stifled a smile as her car light flickered. "Make that four."

He groaned, but when I glanced at him, I found him watching me rather than the car. "So…do I get a chance to earn your trust?"

My pulse jumped. Was he serious?

I should've said no. I should have thanked him for helping me at Taboo, then left with him staring after me from his front yard. But I wasn't strong enough to resist those dimples. Even knowing how many other girls had probably failed that same task.

I blame my weakness on the recent panic attack.

"How?" I asked finally, then flushed when he grinned. He'd known I'd give in.

"Come over tomorrow night?"

To his house? *No way.* I was weak-willed, not stupid. Not that I could make it anyway… "I work till nine on Sundays."

"At the Ciné?"

He knows where I work. Surprise warmed me from the inside out, and I frowned in question.

"I've seen you there."

"Oh." Of course he'd seen me there. Probably on a date. "Yeah, I'll be in the ticket booth from two on."

"Lunch, then?"

Lunch. How much could I possibly be tempted into in a public restaurant? "Fine. But I still don't trust you."

He grinned and opened his door, and the overhead light flared to life. His pupils shrank to pinpoints in the sudden glare, and as my heart raced, he leaned forward like he would kiss me. Instead, his cheek brushed mine and his warm breath skimmed my ear as he whispered, "That's half the fun."

My breath hitched in my throat, but before I could speak, the car bobbed beneath his shifting weight and suddenly the passenger seat was empty. He closed the car door, then jogged up the driveway to slam his mother's.

I backed away from his house in a daze, and when I parked in front of my own, I couldn't remember a moment of the drive home.

"Good morning, Kaylee." Aunt Val stood at the kitchen counter, bathed in late-morning sunlight, holding a steaming mug of coffee nearly as big as her head. She wore a satin robe the exact shade of blue as her eyes, and her sleek brown waves were still tousled from sleep. But they were tousled the way hair always looks in the movies, when the star wakes up in full makeup, wearing miraculously unwrinkled pajamas.

I couldn't pull my own fingers through my hair first thing in the morning.

My aunt's robe and the size of her coffee cup were the only signs that she and my uncle had had a late night. Or rather, an early morning. I'd heard them come in around 2:00 a.m., stumbling down the hall, giggling like idiots.

Then I'd stuck my earbuds in my ears so I wouldn't have to listen as he proved just how attractive he still found her, even after seventeen years of marriage. Uncle Brendon was the younger of the pair, and my aunt resented each of the four years she had on him.

The problem wasn't that she looked her age—thanks to Botox and an obsessive workout routine, she looked thirty-five at the most—but that he looked so young for his. She jokingly called him Peter Pan, but as her big 4-0 had approached, she'd ceased finding her own joke funny.

"Cereal or waffles?" Aunt Val set her coffee on the marble countertop and pulled a box of blueberry Eggos from the freezer, holding them up for my selection. My aunt didn't do big breakfasts. She said she couldn't afford to eat that many calories in one meal, and she wasn't going to cook what she couldn't eat. But we were welcome to help ourselves to all the fat and cholesterol we wanted.

Normally Uncle Brendon served up plenty of both on Saturday mornings, but I could still hear him snoring from his bedroom, halfway across the house. She'd obviously worn him out pretty good.

I crossed the dining room into the kitchen, my fuzzy socks silent on the cold tile. "Just toast. I'm going out for lunch in a couple of hours."

Aunt Val stuck the waffles back in the freezer and handed me a loaf of low-calorie whole wheat bread—the only kind she would buy. "With Emma?"

I shook my head and dropped two slices into the toaster, then tugged my pajama pants up and tightened the drawstring.

She arched her brows at me over her mug. "You have a date? Anyone I know?" Meaning, "Any of Sophie's exes?"

"I doubt it." Aunt Val was constantly disappointed that, unlike her daughter—the world's most socially ambitious sophomore—I had no interest in student council, or the dance team, or the winter carnival–planning committee. In part, because Sophie would have made my life miserable if I'd intruded on "her" territory. But mostly because I had to work to pay for my car insurance, and I'd rather spend my rare free hours with Emma than helping the dance team coordinate their glitter gel with their sequined costumes.

While Nash would no doubt have met with Aunt Val's hearty approval, I did not need her hovering over me when I got home, eyes glittering in anticipation of a social climb I had no interest in. I was happy hanging with Emma and whichever crowd she claimed at the moment.

"His name's Nash."

Aunt Val took a butter knife from the silverware drawer. "What year is he?"

I groaned inwardly. "Senior." *Here we go...*

Her smile was a little too enthusiastic. "Well, that's wonderful!"

Of course, what she really meant was "Rise from the shadows, social leper, and walk in the bright light of acceptance!" Or some crap like that. Because my aunt and overprivileged cousin only recognize two states of being: glitter and grunge. And if you weren't glitter, well, that only left one other option...

I slathered strawberry jelly on my toast and took a seat at the bar. Aunt Val poured a second cup of coffee and aimed the TV remote across the dining room and into the den, where the fifty-inch flat-screen flashed to life, signaling the end of the requisite breakfast "conversation."

"...coming to you live from Taboo, in the West End, where last night, the body of nineteen-year-old Heidi Anderson was found on the restroom floor."

Nooo...

My stomach churned around a half slice of toast, and I twisted slowly on my bar stool, dread sending a spike of adrenaline through my veins. On-screen, a too-poised reporter stood on the brick walkway in front of the club I'd snuck into twelve hours earlier, and as I watched, her image was replaced by a still shot of Heidi Anderson sitting in a lawn chair in a UT Arlington T-shirt, straight teeth gleaming, reddish-blond hair blown back by the relentless prairie wind.

It was her.

I couldn't breathe.

"Kaylee? What's wrong?"

I blinked and sucked in a quick breath, then looked up at my aunt to find her staring at my plate, where I'd dropped my toast jelly-side down. It was a miracle I hadn't lost the half I'd already eaten.

"Nothing. Can you turn that up?" I pushed my plate away and Aunt Val turned up the volume, shooting me a puzzled frown.

"No cause of death has yet been identified," the reporter said on-screen. "But according to the employee who found Ms. Anderson's body, there was no obvious sign of violence."

The picture changed again, and now Traci Marshall stared into the camera, pale with shock and hoarse, as if she'd been crying. "She was just lying there, like she was sleeping. I thought she'd passed out until I realized she wasn't breathing."

Traci disappeared and the reporter was back, but I couldn't hear her over Aunt Val. "Isn't that Emma's sister?"

"Yeah. She's a bartender at Taboo."

Aunt Val stared at the television, her expression grim. "That whole thing is so tragic…"

I nodded. *You have no idea.* But I did.

I also had chill bumps. *It really happened.*

With my previous panic attacks, my aunt and uncle had had no reason to heed my hysterical babble about looming shadows and impending death. And with no way to shush me once the screaming began, they'd taken me home—coincidently away from the source of the panic—to calm me down. Except for that last time, when they'd driven me straight to the hospital, checked me into the mental-health ward and begun looking at me with eyes full of pity. Concern. Unspoken relief that I was the one losing my mind, rather than their own, blessedly normal daughter.

But now I had proof I wasn't crazy. Right? I'd seen Heidi Anderson shrouded in shadow and known she would die. I'd told Emma and Nash. And now my premonition had come true.

I stood so fast my bar stool skidded against the tiles. I had to *tell* somebody. I needed to see confirmation in someone's eyes, assurance that I wasn't imagining the news story, because really, if I could imagine death, how much harder could it be for my poor, sick mind to make up the news story? But I couldn't tell my aunt what had happened without admitting I'd snuck into a club, and once I'd said that part, she wouldn't listen to the rest. She'd just take away my keys and call my father.

No, telling Aunt Val was out of the question. But Emma would believe me.

While my aunt stared, I dropped my plate into the sink and ran to my room, ignoring her when she called after me. I kicked the door shut, collapsed on my bed then snatched my phone from my nightstand where I'd left it charging the night before.

I called Emma's cell, and almost groaned out loud when her

mother answered. But Emma had gotten home more than an hour early for once. What could she possibly be grounded for *this* time?

"Hi, Ms. Marshall." I flopped onto my back and stared at the textured, eggshell ceiling. "Can I talk to Em? It's kind of important."

Her mom sighed. "Not today, Kaylee. Emma came home smelling like rum last night. She's grounded until further notice. I certainly hope you weren't out drinking with her."

Oh, crap. I closed my eyes, trying to come up with an answer that wouldn't make Em sound like a delinquent by comparison. I drew a total blank. "Um, no, ma'am. I was driving."

"Well, at least *one* of you has a little sense. Do me a favor and try sharing some of that with Emma next time. Assuming I ever let her out of the house again."

"Sure, Ms. Marshall." I hung up, suddenly glad I hadn't spent the night at the Marshalls', as had been my original plan. With Emma grounded and Traci probably still in shock, breakfast could *not* have been a pleasant meal.

After a minute's hesitation, and much anticipatory panic, I decided to call Nash, because in spite of his reputation and my suspicion about his motives, he hadn't laughed at me when I told him the truth about the panic attack.

And with Emma grounded, he was the only one left who knew.

I picked up my phone again—then I realized I didn't have his number.

Careful to avoid my aunt and uncle, who was now awake and frying bacon, based on the scent permeating the entire house, I snuck into the living room, snagged the phone book from an end table drawer and took it back to my room. There were four Hudsons with the right prefix, but only one on his street. Nash answered on the third ring.

My heart pounded so hard I was sure he could hear it over the phone, and for several seconds, silence was all I could manage.

"Hello?" he repeated, sounding almost as annoyed as sleepy now.

"Hey, it's Kaylee," I finally blurted, fervently hoping he re-membered me—that I hadn't imagined dancing with him the night before. Because frankly, after the night's premonition and the morning's newscast, even *I* was starting to wonder if Sophie was right about me.

Nash cleared his throat, and when he spoke, his voice was husky with sleep. "Hey. You're not calling to cancel, are you?"

I couldn't resist a smile, in spite of the reason for the call. "No. I... Have you seen the news this morning?"

He chuckled hoarsely. "I haven't even seen the *floor* yet this morning." Nash yawned, and springs creaked over the line. He was still in bed.

I stamped down the scandalous images that knowledge brought to mind and forced myself to focus on the issue at hand. "Turn on your TV."

"I'm not really into current events...." More springs squealed as he rolled over, and something whispered against his phone.

My eyes closed and I leaned against my headboard, sucking in a deep breath. "She's dead, Nash."

"What?" He sounded marginally more awake this time. "Who's dead?"

I leaned forward, and my own bed creaked. "The girl from the club. Emma's sister found her dead in the bathroom at Taboo last night."

"Are you sure it's her?" He was definitely awake now, and I pictured him sitting straight up in bed. Hopefully shirtless.

"See for yourself." I aimed my remote at the nineteen-inch set on my dresser and scrolled through the local channels until I found one still running the story. "Channel nine."

Something clicked over the phone, and canned laughter rang

out from his room. A moment later, the sounds from his television synched with mine. "Oh, shit," Nash whispered. Then his voice went deeper. Serious. "Kaylee, has this happened to you before? I mean, have you ever been right before?"

I hesitated, unsure how much to tell him. My eyes closed again, but the backs of my eyelids offered me no advice. So I sighed and told him the truth. After all, he already knew the weirdest part. "I don't know. I can't talk about it here." The last thing I needed was for my aunt and uncle to overhear. They'd either ground me for the rest of my natural life or rush me back to the psych ward.

"I'll come get you. Half an hour?"

"I'll be in my driveway."

I showered in record time, and twenty-four minutes after I hung
up the phone, I was clean, dry, clothed, and wearing just enough
makeup to hide the shock. But I was still straightening my hair
when I heard a car pull into the driveway.

Crap. If I didn't get to him first, Uncle Brendon would make
Nash come in and submit to questioning.

I pulled the plug on the flatiron, raced back to my room for
my phone, keys and wallet then sprinted down the hall and out
the front door, shouting "good morning" and "goodbye" to my
astonished uncle all in the same breath.

"It's early for lunch. How 'bout pancakes?" Nash asked as
I slid into the passenger seat of his mother's car and closed the
door.

"Um…sure." Though with death on my conscience and Nash
in my sight, food was pretty much the last thing on my mind.

The car smelled like coffee, and Nash smelled like soap,
toothpaste, and something indescribably, tantalizingly yummy.
I wanted to inhale him whole, and I couldn't stop staring at his
chin, smooth this morning where it had been deliciously rough
the night before. I remembered the texture of his cheek against

mine, and had to close my eyes and concentrate to banish the dangerous memory.

I'm not a conquest, no matter how good he smells. Or how good he tastes. And the sudden, overwhelming need to know what his lips would feel like made me shiver all over, and scramble for something safe to say. Something casual, that wouldn't hint at the dangerous direction my thoughts had taken.

"I guess the car started," I said, pulling the seat belt across my torso. Then cursed myself silently for such a stupid opening line. Of course the car had started.

His brief gaze seemed to burn through me. "I have unreasonably good luck."

I could only nod and clench the door grip while I forced my thoughts back to Heidi Anderson to keep them off Nash and… thoughts I shouldn't have been thinking.

When he glanced my way again, his focus slid down my throat to the neckline of my tee before jerking back to the road as he clenched his jaw. I counted my exhalations to keep them even.

We wound up at a booth in Jimmy's Omelet, a locally owned chain that served breakfast until three in the afternoon. Nash sat across from me, his arms resting on the table, his sleeves pushed up halfway to his elbows.

Once the waitress had taken our orders and moved on, Nash leaned forward and met my gaze boldly, intimately, as if we'd shared much more than a rhyme in a dark alley and an almost-kiss. But the teasing and flirtation were gone; he looked more serious than I'd ever seen him. Somber. Almost worried.

"Okay…" He spoke softly, in concession to the crowd talking, chewing, and clanking silverware around us. "So last night you predicted this girl's death, and this morning she showed up on the news, dead."

I nodded, swallowing thickly. Hearing it like that—so matter-of-fact—made it sound both crazy and terrifying. And I wasn't sure which was worse.

"You said you've had these premonitions before?"

"Just a few times."

"Have any of them ever come true?"

I shook my head, then shrugged and picked up a napkin-wrapped bundle of silverware to have something to do with my hands. "Not that I know of."

"But you only know about this one because it was on the news, right?" I nodded without looking up, and he continued. "So the others could have come true too, and you might never have known about it."

"I guess." But if that were the case, I wasn't sure I wanted to know about it.

When I drew my focus from the napkin I'd half peeled from the knife and fork, I found him watching me intently, as if my every word might mean something important. His lips were pressed firmly together, his forehead wrinkled in concentration.

I shifted on the vinyl-padded bench, uneasy under such scrutiny. Now he probably really thought I was a freak. A girl who thinks she knows when someone's going to die—that might be interesting in certain circles; it definitely presented a certain morbid cachet.

But a girl who really could predict death? That was just scary.

Nash frowned, and his focus shifted back and forth between my eyes, like he was looking for something specific. "Kaylee, do you know why this is happening? What it means?"

My heart thumped painfully, and I clutched the shredded napkin. "How do you know it means anything?"

"I...don't." He sighed and leaned back in the booth, dropping his gaze to the table as he picked up a mini-jar of strawberry preserves from the jelly carousel. "But don't you think it should mean something? I mean, we're not talking about lottery numbers and horse-race winners. Don't you want to know why you can do this? Or what the limits are? Or—"

"No." I looked up sharply, irritated by the familiar, sick dread settling into my stomach, killing what little appetite I'd managed to hold on to. "I don't want to know why or how. All I want to know is how to make it stop."

Nash leaned forward again, pinning me with a gaze so intense, so thoroughly invasive, that I caught my breath. "What if you can't?"

My mood darkened at the very thought. I shook my head, denying the possibility.

He glanced down at the jelly again, spinning it on the table, and when he looked back up, his gaze had gone soft. Sympathetic. "Kaylee, you need help with this."

My eyes narrowed and a spike of anger and betrayal shot through me. "You think I need counseling?" Each breath came faster than the last as I fought off memories of brightly colored scrubs, and needles and padded wrist restraints. "I'm not crazy." I stood and dropped the knife on the table, but when I tried to march past him, his hand wrapped firmly around my wrist and he twisted to look up at me.

"Kaylee, wait, that's not what I—"

"Let go." I wanted to tug my arm free, but I was afraid that if he didn't let go, I'd lose it. Four-point restraints or an unyielding hand, it was all the same if I couldn't get free. Panic clawed slowly up from my gut as I struggled not to pull against his grip. My chest constricted, and I went stiff in my desperation to stay calm.

"People are looking..." he whispered urgently.

"Then let me go." Each breath came short and fast now, and sweat gathered in the crooks of my elbows. "Please."

He let go.

I exhaled, and my eyes closed as sluggish relief sifted through me. But I couldn't make myself move. Not yet. Not without running.

When I realized I was rubbing my wrist, I clenched my hands into fists until my nails cut into my palms. Distantly, I noticed that the restaurant had gone quiet around us.

"Kaylee, please sit down. That's not what I meant." His voice was soft. Soothing.

My hands began to relax, and I inhaled deeply.

"Please," he repeated, and it took every bit of self-control I had to make myself back up and sink onto the padded bench. With my hands in my lap.

We sat in silence until conversation picked up around us, me staring at the table, him staring at me, if I had to guess.

"Are you okay?" he asked finally, as the waitress set food on the table behind me, and I felt the tension in my shoulders ease as I leaned against the wooden back of the booth.

"I don't need a doctor." I made myself look up, ready to stand firm against his argument to the contrary. But it never came.

He sighed, a sound heavy with reluctance. "I know. You need to tell your aunt and uncle."

"Nash…"

"They might be able to help you, Kaylee. You have to tell someone—"

"They know, okay?" I glanced at the table to find that my fingers were tearing the shredded napkin into even smaller pieces. Shoving them to the side, I met Nash's gaze, suddenly, recklessly determined to tell him the truth. How much worse could he possibly think of me?

"Last time this happened, I freaked out and started screaming. And I couldn't stop. They put me in the hospital, and strapped me to a bed, and shot me full of drugs, and didn't let me out until we all agreed that I'd gotten over my 'delusions and hysteria' and wouldn't need to talk about them anymore. Okay? So

I don't think telling them is going to do much good, unless I want to spend fall break in the mental-health unit."

Nash blinked, and in the span of a single second, his expression cycled through disbelief, disgust, and outrage before finally settling on fury, his brows low, arms bulging, like he wanted to hit something.

It took me a moment to understand that none of that was directed at me. That he wasn't angry and embarrassed to be seen out with the school psycho. Probably because no one else knew. No one but Sophie, and her parents had threatened her with social ostracism—total house arrest—if she ever let the family secret out of the proverbial bag.

"How long?" Nash asked, his gaze boring into mine so deeply I wondered if he could see right through my eyes and into my brain.

I sighed and picked at the label on a small bottle of sugar-free syrup. "After a week, I said all the right things, and my uncle took me out against doctor's orders. They told the school I had the flu." I was a sophomore then, and nearly a year away from meeting Nash, when Emma started dating a series of his teammates.

Nash closed his eyes and exhaled heavily. "That never should have happened. You're not crazy. Last night proves that."

I nodded, numb. If I'd misread him, I'd never be able to walk tall in my own school again. But I couldn't even work up any irritation over that possibility at the moment. Not with my secrets exposed, my heart laid open and latent terror lurking in the drug-hazy memories I'd hoped to bury.

"You have to tell them again, and—"

"No."

But he continued, as if I'd never spoken. "—if they don't believe you, call your dad."

"No, Nash."

Before he could argue again, a smooth, pale arm appeared

across my field of vision, and the waitress set a plate on the table in front of me, and one in front of him. I hadn't even heard her approach that time, and based on Nash's wide eyes, he hadn't either.

"Okay, you kids dig in. And let me know if I can get you somethin' else, 'kay?"

We both nodded as she walked off. But I could only cut my pancakes into neat triangles and push them around in the syrup. I had no appetite. Even Nash only picked at his food.

Finally, he put his fork down and cleared his throat until I looked up. "I'm not going to talk you into this, am I?"

I shook my head. He frowned, then sighed and worked up a small smile. "How do you feel about geese?"

After a breakfast I didn't eat, and Nash didn't enjoy, we stopped at a sandwich shop, where he bought a bag of day-old bread. Then we headed to White Rock Lake to feed a honking, pecking flock of geese, a couple of which were gutsy little demons. One snatched a piece of bread right out of my hand, nearly taking my finger with it, and another nipped Nash's shoe when he didn't pull food from the bag fast enough.

When the bread was gone, we escaped from the geese— barely—for a walk around the lake. The wind whipped my hair into knots and I tripped over a loose board in the pier, but when Nash took my hand, I let him keep it, and the silence between us was comfortable. How could it not be, when he'd now seen every shadow in my soul and every corner in my mind, and hadn't once called me crazy—or tried to feel me up.

And why not? I wondered, sneaking a glimpse at his profile as he squinted at the sun across the lake. Was I not pretty enough?

No, I didn't want to be the latest on his rumored list of conquests, but I wouldn't mind knowing I was worthy.

Nash smiled when he noticed me watching him. His eyes were more green than brown in the sunlight, and they seemed to be churning softly, probably reflecting the motion of the water. "Kaylee, can I ask you something personal?"

Like death and mental illness weren't personal?

"Only if I get to ask you something."

He seemed to consider that for a moment, then grinned, flashing a single deep dimple, and squeezed my hand as we walked. "You first."

"Did you sleep with Laura Bell?"

Nash pulled me to an abrupt halt and arched both brows dramatically over long, beautiful boy-lashes. "That's not fair. I didn't ask you who you've been with."

I shrugged, enjoying his discomfort. "Ask away." I wouldn't even need any fingers to tick off my list.

He scowled; he obviously had another question in mind. "If I say yes, are you going to get mad?"

I shrugged. "It's none of my business."

"Then why do you care?"

Grrr… "Okay, new question." I tugged him into step again, working up the nerve to ask something I wasn't sure I really wanted the answer to. But I had to know, before things went any further. "What are you doing here?" I held our joined hands up for emphasis. "What's in this for you?"

"Your trust, hopefully."

My head spun just a little bit at that, and I stifled a dazed grin. "That's it?" I blinked up at him as we stepped onto the pier. Even if that was true, that couldn't be all of it. I donned a mock frown. "You sure you're not trying to get laid?"

His grin that time was real as he pulled me close and pressed me gently against the old wooden railing, his lips inches from my nose. "You offering?"

My heart raced and I let my hands linger on his back, tracing the hard planes through his long-sleeved tee. Feeling him pressed against me. Smelling him up close. Considering, just for a single, pulse-tripping moment…

Then I landed back on earth with a fantasy-shattering thud. The last thing I needed was to be listed among Nash Hudson's past castoffs. But before I could figure out how to say that without pissing him off or sounding like a total prude, his eyes flashed with amusement and he leaned forward and kissed the tip of my nose.

I gasped, and he laughed. "I'm kidding, Kaylee. I just didn't expect you to think about it for so long." He grinned, then stepped back and took my hand again, while I stared at him in astonishment, my cheeks flaming.

"Ask your question before I change my mind."

His smile faded; the teasing was over. What else could he possibly want to know? What they served for lunch in the psych ward?

"What happened to your mom?"

Oh.

"You don't have to tell me." He stopped and turned to face me, backpedaling when he mistook my relief for discomfort. "I was just curious. About what she was like."

I pushed tangled strands of brown hair back from my face. "I don't mind." I wished my mother was still alive, of course, and I really wished I could live with my own family, rather than Sophie's. But my mom had been gone so long I barely remembered her, and I was used to the question. "She died in a car wreck when I was three."

"Do you ever see your dad?"

I shrugged and kicked a pebble off the pier. "He used to come several times a year." Then it was just Christmas and my birthday. And now I hadn't seen him in more than a year. Not that I cared. He had his life—presumably—and I had mine.

Judging from the flash of sympathy in Nash's eyes, he'd heard even the parts I hadn't said out loud. Then there was a subtle shift in his expression, which I couldn't quite interpret. "I still think you should tell your dad about last night."

I scowled and headed back down the pier with my arms crossed over my chest, pleased when the wind shifted to blow my hair away from my face for once.

Nash jogged after me. "Kaylee..."

"You know what the worst part of this is?" I demanded when he pulled even with me and slowed to a walk.

"What?" He looked surprised by my willingness to talk about it at all. But I wasn't talking about my dad.

My eyes closed, and when the wind died down, the sun felt warm on my face, in startling contrast to the chill building inside me. "I feel like I should have done something to stop it. I mean, I knew she was going to die, and I did nothing. I didn't even tell her. I just tucked my tail and ran home. I let her die, Nash."

"No." His voice was firm. My eyes flew open when he turned me to face him, wooden slats creaking beneath us. "You didn't do anything wrong, Kaylee. Knowing it was going to happen doesn't mean you could have stopped it."

"Maybe it does. I didn't even try!" And I'd been so caught up on what her death meant for me that I'd barely stopped to think about what I should have done for her.

His gaze bored into mine, his expression fierce. "It's not that easy. Death doesn't strike at random. If it was her time to go, there's nothing either of us could have done to stop that."

How could he be so sure? "I should have at least told her...."

"No!" His harsh tone startled us both, and when he reached out to grab my arms, I took a step back. Nash let his head dip and held his hands out to show that he wouldn't touch me, then shoved them in his pockets. "She wouldn't have believed you. And, anyway, it's dangerous to mess with stuff you don't understand, and you don't understand this yet. Swear that if this happens again and I'm not there, you won't do anything. Or say anything. Just turn around and walk away. Okay?"

"Okay," I agreed. He was starting to scare me, his eyes wide and earnest, the line of his beautiful mouth tight and thin.

"Swear," Nash insisted, irises flashing and whirling fiercely in the bright sunlight. "You have to swear."

"I swear." And I meant it, because in that moment, with the sun painting his face in a harsh relief of light and shadow, Nash looked both scared and scary.

But even worse, he looked like he knew exactly what he was talking about.

‹ 4 ›

Nash took me home two hours before I had to be at work, and when I walked through the door, the scent of freesia gave me an instant headache. Sophie was home.

My cousin stood from the couch, where she'd obviously been peeking through the curtains, and propped thin, manicured hands on the hipbones poking out above low-cut, skinny jeans. "Who was that?" she asked, though her narrowed eyes said she already had a suspect in mind.

I smiled sweetly and walked past her into the hall. "A guy."

"And his name would be...?" She followed me into my room, where she sat on my unmade bed as if it were hers. Or as if we were friends. Sophie only played that game when she wanted something from me, usually money or a ride. This time, she was obviously hunting information. Gossip to fuel the rumor bonfire she and her friends kept burning bright at school.

But I wasn't about to fan her flames.

I turned my back on her to empty my pockets onto my dresser. "None of your business." In the mirror, I saw a scowl flit across her face, pulling her pixie features out of shape.

The problem with getting everything you want in life is that you're not prepared for disappointment when it comes.

I considered it my pleasure to acquaint Sophie with that concept.

"Mom said he's a senior." She pulled her legs onto my bed and crossed them beneath her, shoes and all. When I didn't answer, she glared at my reflection. "I can find out who he is in, like, two seconds."

"Then you obviously need nothing from me." I pulled my hair into a high ponytail. "Welcome to the party, Nancy Drew."

Tiny lines formed around her mouth when she frowned, and I crossed the room to pull my uniform shirt from a hanger, leaving it swinging on the closet rod. "Out. I have to go to work. So I can pay for my car insurance." Sophie wouldn't be eligible for her license for another five months, and it drove her nuts that I could drive and she couldn't.

My car was the best thing my father had ever given me, even if it was used. And even if he'd never actually seen it.

"Speaking of cars, your mystery date's looked familiar. Little silver Saab, with leather upholstery, right?" Sophie stood, ambling toward the door slowly, narrow hips swaying, cocking her head as if in thought. "The backseat's pretty comfortable, even with that little rip on the passenger side."

Pain shot through my jaw, and I realized I was grinding my teeth.

"Say hi to Nash for me," she purred, one hand wrapped around my door. Then her expression morphed from vicious vixen to Good Samaritan, in the space of a single second. "I'm not trying to hurt your feelings here, Kaylee, but I think you should know the truth." Her pale green eyes went wide in faux innocence. "He's using you to get to me."

My temper flared and I slammed the door. Sophie yelped and jerked her hand out of the way just in time to avoid four broken fingers. My fist clenched my uniform shirt, and I tossed it over the dancer's-butt dent she'd left in my comforter.

She's wrong. But I studied my reflection anyway, trying

to see myself as everyone else did. As Nash did. No, I didn't have Sophie's lean dancer's build, or Emma's abundant curves, but I wasn't hideous. Still, Nash could do much better than not-hideous.

Was that why he hadn't kissed me? Was I a convenience between girlfriends? Or a pity date? Some kind of social outreach program for kindhearted jocks?

No. He wouldn't spend so much time talking to someone he had no real interest in, even if he was looking for a casual hookup. There were easier scores elsewhere.

But I could use a qualified second opinion. Phone in hand, I plopped down on the bed and held my breath while I typed, hoping Emma's mom had given her back her phone.

No such luck. Two very long minutes after I sent the text message—Can u talk?—the reply came.

She is still grounded. Talk to Emma at work.

She should never have taught her mother to text. I told her no good could come of that.

Em and I were scheduled for the same shift, so that afternoon I filled her in on my date with Nash as we sold tickets to the latest computer-animated cartoon and the inevitable romantic comedy. On our dinner break, we sat in one corner of the snack bar, sharing a soft pretzel and cheese fries while I told her about Heidi Anderson—what she hadn't heard from her sister—where no one could overhear.

Emma was fascinated by the accuracy of my prediction, and she agreed with Nash that I should tell my aunt and uncle, though her motive had more to do with shooting them a big I-told-you-so than with helping me figure out what to do with my morbid talent.

But again, I declined the advice. I had no interest in any future meetings with Dr. Nelson—he of the medical restraints and the zombie pills. In fact, I was clinging to the hope that the next prediction—if there was another—would be months, or even years down the road. After all, there had been nearly nine months between the past two.

The last part of my shift dragged on at half the normal speed because less than fifteen minutes in, the manager moved Emma to the snack bar, leaving me alone in the ticket booth with an A&M computer science major whose undershirt—which he lifted his uniform to show me—read: *My other shirt is a storm trooper uniform.*

When the day was finally over, I clocked out and waited for Emma in the employee snack room. As I was zipping my jacket, Emma pushed through the door and stood with her body holding it open, a dark frown shadowing her entire face.

"What's wrong?" My hand hovered over the hook where her jacket still hung.

"Come on. You have to hear this." She pushed the door open wider and stood to the side, so I could pass through. But I hesitated. Her news obviously wasn't good, and I was all full up on creepy and depressing for the moment. "Seriously. This is weird."

I sighed, then shoved my hands into my jacket pockets and followed her over eight feet of sticky linoleum tile and across the theater lobby toward the snack counter.

Jimmy Barnes was busy with a customer, but once he saw Emma waiting to talk to him, he rushed through the order so quickly he almost forgot to squirt butter on the popcorn. He had a bit of a crush on Emma.

He wasn't the only one.

"Back already?" Jimmy nodded at me, then leaned with both plump arms on the glass countertop, staring at Em as if the meaning of life lay buried in her eyes. His fingers were stained yellow with butter-flavored oil and he smelled like popcorn and the root beer he'd dribbled down the front of his black apron.

"Can you tell Kaylee what Mike said?"

Jimmy's goofy, puppy-love smile faded, and he stood, angling his body to face us both. "Creepiest thing I ever heard." He reached below the counter to grab a plastic-wrapped stack of sixteen-ounce paper cups, and began refilling the dispenser as he spoke.

"You know Mike Powell, right?" he asked.

"Yeah." I glanced at Emma with both brows raised in question, but she only nodded toward Jimmy, silently telling me to pay attention.

Jimmy pressed on an inverted stack of cups, which sank into a hole in the countertop to make room for more. "Mike took a shift at the snack bar at the Arlington branch today, filling in for some guy who got fired for spittin' in someone's Coke."

"Hey, can I get some popcorn over here?"

I looked up to see a middle-aged man waiting in front of the cash register, flanked by a little girl with her thumb in her mouth and an older boy with his gaze—and his thumbs—glued to a PSP.

"Will that be a jumbo, sir?" Jimmy held up one just-a-minute finger for us and veered toward the closest of several popcorn machines while I dug my phone from my pocket to check the time. It was after nine and I was starving. And not exactly eager for whatever weird, creepy story Jimmy had to tell.

When the customers left with a cardboard tray full of junk food and soda, Jimmy turned back to us. "Anyway, Mike called about half an hour ago, totally freaked out. He said some girl died right in front of his register this afternoon. Just fell over dead, still holding her popcorn."

Shock pinged through me, chilling me from the inside out. I glanced at Emma, and she gave me a single grim nod. As I turned back to Jimmy, a dark unease unfurled deep inside me, spiraling up my spine like tendrils of ice. "You're serious?"

"Totally." He twisted the end of the plastic sleeve around the remaining cups. "Mike said the whole thing was unreal. The ambulance took her away in a freakin' body bag, and the manager closed the place down and handed out vouchers to all the customers. And the cops kept asking Mike questions, trying to figure out what happened."

Emma watched me for my reaction, but I could only stare, my hands gripping the edge of the counter, unable to force my scattered thoughts into any logical order. The similarity to Heidi Anderson was obvious, but I had no concrete reason to connect the two deaths.

"Do they know how she died?" I asked finally, grasping at the first coherent thought to form.

Jimmy shrugged. "Mike said she was fine one minute, and flat on her back the next. No coughing, no choking, no grabbing her heart or her head."

A vague, heavy dread was building inside me, a slow simmer of foreboding, compared to the rapid boil of panic I'd felt when I saw Heidi's shadow-shroud. The deaths were connected. They had to be.

Emma was watching me again, and I must have looked as sick as I felt because she put one hand on my shoulder. "Thanks, Jimmy. See ya Wednesday."

On the way home, Emma loosened her seat belt and twisted in the passenger seat to frown at me in the dark, her face a mask of grim fascination. "How weird was that? First you predict that girl's death at Taboo. Then tonight, *another* girl falls down dead at the theater, just like last night."

I flicked on my blinker to pass a car in the right lane. "They're not the same," I insisted, in spite of my own similar thoughts. "Heidi Anderson was drunk. She probably died of alcohol poisoning."

"Nuh-uh." Emma shook her head, blond hair bouncing in the corner of my vision. "The news said they tested her blood. She was drunk, but not that drunk."

I shrugged, uncomfortable with the turn of the conversation. "So she passed out and hit her head when she fell."

"If she did, don't you think the cops would have figured that out by now?" When I didn't answer, Emma continued, shielding her eyes from the glare of a passing highway light. "I don't think they know what killed her. I bet that's why they haven't scheduled her funeral yet."

My hands tightened on the wheel, and I glanced at her in surprise. "What are you, spying on the dead girl?"

She shrugged. "Just watching the news. I'm grounded—what else is there to do? Besides, this is the weirdest thing that ever happened around here. And the fact that you predicted one of them is beyond bizarre."

I flicked on my blinker again and swerved off the highway at our exit, forcing my hand to relax around the wheel. I didn't even want to think about my premonition anymore, much less talk about it. "You don't know the deaths are connected. It's not like they were murdered. At least not the girl in Arlington. Mike *saw* her die."

"She could have been poisoned…." Emma insisted, but I continued, ignoring her as I slowed to make the turn onto her street.

"And even if they are connected, they have nothing to do with us."

"You knew the first one was going to die."

"Yeah, and I hope it never happens again."

Emma frowned but let the subject go. After I dropped her off, I pulled into an empty lot down the street from her house and called Nash.

"Hello?" In the background, I heard gunfire and shouting, until he turned down the volume on his TV.

"Hey, it's Kaylee. Are you busy?"

"Just avoiding homework. What's up?"

I stared out the windshield at the dark parking lot, and my heart seemed to stumble over the next few beats while I worked up my nerve.

"Kaylee? You there?"

"Yeah." I closed my eyes and forced the next words out before my throat froze up. "Can I use your computer? I need to look something up, but I can't do it at home without Sophie snooping." And I did not want my aunt to bring me laundry without knocking—as was her habit—and see what I was looking up online.

"No problem."

But second thoughts came fast and hard. I should not be alone with Nash in his house—that whole willpower thing again.

He laughed as if he knew what I was thinking. Or heard it in my nervous silence. "Don't worry. My mom's here."

Relief and disappointment came in equal parts, and I fought to let neither leak into my voice. "That's fine." I started the engine, my headlights carving arcs of light across the dark gravel lot. "You hungry?"

"I was about to nuke a pizza."

"Interested in a burger?"

"Always."

Twenty minutes later, I parked on the street in front of his house and got out of the car, a fast-food bag in one hand, drink tray in the other. Again, his mother's Saab was in the driveway, but this time the door was closed.

I crossed the small, neat yard and stepped onto the porch, but Nash opened the front door before I could knock. "Hey, come on in." He took the drinks and held the door open, and I stepped past him into a clean, sparsely decorated living room.

Nash set the cups on an end table and stuffed his hands in his pockets while I looked around. His mother's furniture wasn't new or as upscale as Aunt Val's, but it looked much more comfortable. The hardwood floor was worn but spotless, and the entire house smelled like chocolate-chip cookies.

At first I assumed the scent was from a candle like the ones Aunt Val lit at Christmas, to give the impression that she knows how to bake. But then I heard an oven door creak open to the left of the living room, and that cookie-scent swelled. Mrs. Hudson was *actually* baking.

When my gaze returned to Nash, I found him looking at my shirt, but in amusement, rather than real interest. Which is when I realized I was still wearing my Ciné uniform. *Way to dress the part, Kaylee…*

Nash laughed when he saw my surprise, then gestured toward a narrow hallway branching off the living room. "Come on…" But before he'd taken two steps, the swinging door into the kitchen opened, and a slim, well-proportioned woman appeared in the doorway, barefoot, in snug jeans and a blue-ribbed tee.

I'm not sure what I'd expected Nash's mom to look like, but this woman did *not* fit the bill. She was young. Like, thirty. But that couldn't be right, because Nash was eighteen. She wore her long, dark blond curls pulled into a simple ponytail, except for a few ringlets that had fallen to frame her face.

She could have been his older sister. His very hot older sister. *Aunt Val would* hate *her.…*

When Mrs. Hudson's eyes found mine, the world seemed to stop moving. Or rather, she stopped moving. Completely. As if she weren't even breathing. I guess I wasn't what she'd expected either. Nash's exes were all beautiful, and I bet none of them had ever come over in a shapeless purple polo with the Ciné logo embroidered on one shoulder.

Regardless, the intense way she stared at me unnerved me, like she was trying to read my thoughts in my eyes, and I had an unbearable urge to close them in case that's exactly what she was doing. Instead, I clutched the fast-food bag in both hands and returned her look with a frank one of my own, because she didn't look angry. Only very curious.

After several uncomfortable seconds, she flashed a beautiful, un-motherly smile and nodded, as if she approved of whatever she'd seen in me. "Hi, Kaylee, I'm Harmony." Nash's mom wiped her right hand on the front of her jeans, leaving a faint, palm-shaped smudge of flour, then stepped forward and reached out for mine. I shook her hand hesitantly. "I've heard so much about you."

She'd heard about me?

I glanced up to see Nash scowling at his mother, and had the distinct impression I'd just missed him shaking his head, or shooting her some other silent "shut up!" signal.

What was I missing?

"It's nice to meet you too, Mrs. Hudson." I suppressed the urge to wipe residual flour onto my work pants.

"Oh, it's not Mrs." Her smile softened, though her eyes never left mine. "It's been just me and Nash for years now. What about you, Kaylee? Tell me about your parents."

"I...um..."

Nash's fingers folded around mine and I let him pull me close. "Kaylee needs to borrow my computer." He gestured to the grease-stained bag I still held in one hand. "We're gonna eat while we work."

For a moment, Ms. Hudson looked like she might object. Then she shot Nash a stern smile. "Leave the door open."

Nash mumbled a vague acknowledgment, then headed down the short, dim hallway with the drink tray. Still speechless, I followed him, the fast-food bag clutched to my chest.

Nash's room was casual and comfortable, and I liked it instantly. His bed was unmade, and his desk was cluttered with CDs, Xbox games, and junk-food wrappers. The TV was on, but he hit the power button as he passed it, and whatever he'd been watching flashed into a silent black screen.

His desk chair was the only one in the room, and the open can of Coke on the desk said he was sitting there. For a moment, I froze like a rabbit in the crosshairs, staring at the bed, the only other place to sit, while my pulse whooshed in my ears.

Nash laughed and pushed the door to within an inch of closed, waving toward the bed with his empty hand. "It's not gonna fold up into the wall."

I was more worried about it swallowing me whole. And I couldn't help wondering how many girls had sat there before me....

Finally embarrassed into action, I shoved aside an unopened chemistry book and sat on the edge of the bed, already digging in the paper bag. "Here." I handed him a burger and a carton of fries.

He set the food on the desk and sank into the chair, jiggling the mouse until his monitor flared to life. "What are we looking for?" he asked, then folded a fry into his mouth.

I unwrapped my own burger, considering how best to phrase my answer. But there was no good way to put what I had to say. "Another girl died tonight. At the Ciné in Arlington. A guy I work with was there, and he said she just fell over dead, holding a bag of popcorn."

Nash blinked at me, frozen in mid-chew. "You're serious?" he asked after he swallowed, and I nodded. "You think it's connected to that girl in the West End?"

I shrugged. "I didn't predict this one, but it's even weirder than what happened at Taboo. I want details." So I could prove to myself that the two deaths weren't as similar as they sounded.

"Okay, hang on..." He typed something into the address bar, and a search engine appeared on the monitor. "Arlington?"

"Yeah," I said, around a bite of my burger.

Nash typed as he chewed, and links began filling the screen. He clicked on the first one. "Here it is." It was a Dallas news channel's website—the station that had aired the story about Heidi Anderson the day before.

I leaned closer to see over his shoulder, acutely aware of how good he smelled, and Nash read aloud. "Local authorities are perplexed by the death of the second metroplex teenager in as many days. Late this afternoon, fifteen-year-old Alyson Baker died in the lobby of the Ciné 9, in the Six Flags mall. Police have yet to determine her cause of death, but have ruled out drugs and alcohol as factors. According to one witness, Baker 'just fell over dead' at the concession counter. A memorial will be held tomorrow at Stephen F. Austin High School for Baker, who was a sophomore there, and a cheerleader."

Sipping from my straw, I scanned the article for a moment after he finished reading. "That's it?"

"There's a picture." He scrolled up to reveal a black-and-white yearbook photo of a pretty brunette with long, straight hair and dramatic features. "What do you think?"

I sighed and sank back onto the edge of the bed. Seeing the latest dead girl hadn't answered any of my questions, but it had given me a name and a face, and made her death infinitely, miserably more real. "I don't know. She doesn't look much like Heidi Anderson. And she's four years younger."

"And she wasn't drunk."

"And I had no idea this one was going to happen." No longer hungry, I wrapped the rest of my burger and dropped it into the bag. "The only thing they have in common is that they both died in public."

"With no obvious cause of death." Nash glanced at the bag in my lap. "Are you gonna finish that?"

I handed him the burger, but his words still echoed in my mind. He'd hit the nail on the head with that one—and driven it straight into my heart. Heidi and Alyson had both literally dropped dead with no warnings, no illness and no wounds of any kind. And I'd known Heidi's death was coming.

If I'd been there when Alyson Baker was ordering her popcorn, would I have known she was about to die?

And if I had, would telling her have done any good?

I scooted back on the bed and drew my knees up to my chest as my guilt over Heidi's death swelled within me like a sponge soaking up water. Had I *let* her die?

Nash dropped the empty burger wrapper into the bag and swiveled in the desk chair to face me. He frowned as he looked at my expression and leaned forward to gently push my legs down, so he could see my face. "There's nothing you could have done."

Were my thoughts that obvious? I couldn't summon a smile, even with his dimples and late-night stubble only inches away. "You don't know that."

His mouth formed a hard line for a moment, like he might argue, but then he smiled slyly, and his gaze locked on to mine. "What I *do* know is that you need to relax. Think about something other than death." His voice was a gentle rumble as he moved from the chair to sit next to me on the bed, and the mattress sank beneath his weight.

My breath hitched in anticipation, and my pulse raced. "What should I be thinking about?" My own voice came out lower, my words so soft I could barely hear them.

"Me," he whispered back, leaning forward so that his lips brushed my ear as he spoke. His scent enveloped me, and his cheek felt scratchy against mine. "You should be thinking about *me*." His fingers intertwined with mine in my lap, and he pulled away from my ear slowly, his lips skimming my cheek, deliciously soft in contrast to the sharp stubble. He dropped a trail of small kisses along my jaw, and my heart beat harder with every single one.

When he reached my chin, the kisses trailed up until his mouth met mine, gently sucking my lower lip between his. Teasing without making full contact. My chest rose and fell quickly, my breaths shallow, my pulse racing.

More…

He heard me. He must have. Nash pulled back just long enough to meet my gaze, heat blazing behind his eyes, and I realized that he was breathing hard too. His fingers tightened around mine and his free hand slid into the hair at the base of my skull.

Then he kissed me for real.

My mouth opened beneath his, and the kiss went deeper as I drew him in, suddenly ravenous for something I'd never even tasted. My fingers tightened around his, and my free hand found his arm, exploring the hard planes, reveling in the potential of such restrained strength.

Nash pulled back then and looked at me, deep need smoldering behind his eyes. The intensity of that need—the staggering depth of his longing—slammed into me like a wave on the side of a ship, threatening to knock me overboard. To toss me into that turbulent sea, where the current would surely carry me away.

His finger traced my lower lip, his gaze locked on to mine, and my mouth opened, ready for his again.

His hesitance was a terrible mercy. I could barely breathe with him touching me, so overwhelmed was I by...everything. But he smelled so good, and felt so good, I didn't want him to stop, even if I never breathed again.

This time I kissed him, taking what I wanted, delighted and astonished by his willingness to let me. My head was so full of Nash I wasn't sure I'd ever think about anything else again....

Until the bedroom door opened.

Nash jerked back so fast he left me gasping in surprise. I blinked, slowly struggling up from the wave of sensations I wanted to ride again. My cheeks flamed as I smoothed my ponytail.

"Dinner, huh?" Ms. Hudson stood in the doorway, arms crossed over her chest, a fresh smear of chocolate on the hem of her shirt. She frowned at us, but didn't look particularly angry or surprised.

Nash rubbed his face with both hands. I sat there, speechless, and more embarrassed than I'd ever been in my life. But at least we'd been caught by his mother, rather than my uncle. That, I would never have recovered from.

"Let's leave the door open for real this time, huh?" She turned to leave, but then her gaze caught on the computer screen, where Alyson Baker's picture still stared out at the room. Something dark flickered across her face—fear, or concern?—then her expression hardened as she leveled it at her son.

"What are you two doing?" she demanded softly, obviously no longer referring to our social interaction.

"Nothing." Nash's expression carried just as much weight as his mother's had, but I couldn't read anything specific in his, though the tension in the room spiked noticeably.

"I should go." I stood, already digging my keys from my pocket.

"No." Nash took my hand.

Ms. Hudson's expression softened. "You really don't have to," she said. "Stay and have some cookies. Just leave the door open." She eyed Nash on that last part, and tension drained from the air as her frown melted.

Nash rolled his eyes but nodded. Then they both turned to me, waiting for my answer.

"Thanks, but I have some homework to finish...." And Nash's mother had just caught us making out on his bed, which felt very much like the end of the night to me.

Nash walked me to my car and kissed me again, his body pressing mine into the driver's side door, our hands intertwined. Then I drove home in a daze and floated straight to my room, ignoring every less-than-subtle hint for information Sophie tossed my way. And only later would I realize that I had, in fact, forgotten all about the dead girls and was still thinking about Nash when I fell asleep.

5

"Inside or out?" Nash set his tray on the nearest table and dug in his pocket. Coins jingled, barely audible over the clatter of silverware and the buzz of several dozen simultaneous conversations, and he pulled out a handful of change, already turning toward the soda machine.

The autumn morning had dawned clear and cool, but by third period, it was warm enough for my biology teacher to open the windows in the lab and vent the acrid scent of chemical preservatives. "Out." Lunch in the quad sounded good to me, especially considering the swarm of student bodies in the cafeteria, and the dozen or so people who had already noticed his fingers curled around mine in the pizza line.

Including his latest ex, who now glared at me from within a cocoon of hostile cheerleader clones.

I glanced over my shoulder at Emma, who nodded. "I'll get a table." She turned and dodged a freshman carrying three ice-cream bars, who almost knocked her tray from her hands.

"Sorry," he mumbled, then stopped to watch her, his expression a blend of blatant lust and longing. Emma didn't even notice.

Nash pulled two Cokes from the machine and set one on my tray, then we wove our way around two tables to the center aisle, headed straight for the exit. I could practically feel the eyes of my classmates trained on my back, and it was everything I could do not to squirm beneath their scrutiny. How could he stand people watching him all the time?

We were two feet from the double doors leading into the quad when they swung open, only inches from smacking into my tray. A gaggle of slim girls in matching letterman jackets brushed past us, several pausing to smile at Nash. One even ran her fingers down his sleeve, and I was startled by the sudden, irrational urge to slap her hand away. Which proved unnecessary when he walked past her with nothing but a distracted nod.

Sophie was the only one who even glanced my way, and her expression could hardly be considered friendly. Until it landed on Nash. She let her arm brush his as she passed, glancing up into his eyes, a carnal smile turning up one corner of her perfectly made-up mouth in blatant, unspoken invitation.

Seconds later, the dancers were gone, leaving behind a cloud of perfume strong enough to burn my eyes. I stomped through the still-open doors and down the steps. Nash jogged to catch up with me. He carried his tray in one hand, and his opposite arm snaked around my waist, fingers curling around my hip with an intimate familiarity that made my pulse spike. "She's just trying to piss you off."

"She says she's been in your backseat." I couldn't keep suspicion from my tone. Yes, his hand on my hip made a very public statement, and that—along with his silence on the matter of my mental health—finally put to rest my stubborn fear that he'd planned a quick hookup over the weekend, and would be done with me by Monday.

But Nash had never even tried to deny the rumors of his past exploits, and I couldn't stand the thought that Sophie had been one of them.

"What?" He stopped in the middle of the quad, frowning down at me in obvious confusion.

"The back of your car. She says there's a rip in your backseat and wants me to think she's seen it up close."

Nash chuckled softly and started walking again as he spoke, so that I had no choice but to follow. "Um…yeah. She put it there. She was wrecked the night I took her home, and she threw up all over the front floorboard. I put her in the back, and she got some stupid buckle on her shoe caught in the stitching and ripped it loose."

I laughed, and my anger melted like Sophie's makeup in July. In fact, I almost felt sorry for her—but not too sorry to dangle that little nugget of information in front of my cousin the next time she flirted with Nash in front of me.

The quad was actually a long rectangle, surrounded on three sides by various wings of the school building, with the cafeteria entrance on the end of one long wall. The fourth side opened up to the soccer and baseball practice fields at the rear of the campus.

Emma had claimed a table in the far corner, mostly sheltered from the wind by the junction of the language and science halls. I sat on the bench opposite her, and Nash slid in next to me. His leg touched mine from hip to knee, which was enough to keep me warm from the inside out, in spite of the chilly, intermittent breeze at my back.

"What's with the dance team?" Emma asked as I bit the point off my slice of pizza. "They came through here a minute ago, squealing and bouncing around like someone poured hot sauce in their leotards."

I laughed and nearly choked on a chunk of pepperoni. "They won the regional championship on Saturday. Sophie's been insufferable ever since."

"So how long will they be squeaking like squirrels?"

Holding up one finger, I chewed and swallowed another bite before answering. "The state championship is next month. After that, there will either be more irrepressible squealing, or inconsolable tears. Then it's over until May, when they audition for next year's team." Regardless, I would mourn the end of the competition season right along with Sophie. Dance-team practices took up most of her spare time for several months of the year, giving me some much-coveted peace and quiet while she was out of the house.

And, as spoiled and arrogant as she was, Sophie was totally dedicated to the team. She gave the other dancers more respect than she'd ever seen fit to waste on me, and the dedication and punctuality she showed them were the only evidence I'd seen in thirteen years that she had a single responsible bone in that infuriatingly graceful body.

Plus, most of her teammates could drive, and someone always seemed willing to give her a ride. After the state championship, Sophie would go back to daily ballet classes, and now that I had a car, I was fairly certain her parents would make me drive her to and from. Like I had nothing better to do with my time. And my gas money.

"Well, here's hoping we all go deaf either way." Emma held her bottled water aloft, and Nash and I clinked our cans into it. "So…" She screwed the lid back on her bottle. "Heard anything new about that girl from Arlington?"

Nash frowned, his brows lowered over eyes more brown than green at the moment.

"Yeah." I dropped the remains of my pizza onto my tray and picked up a bruised red apple. "Her name was Alyson Baker. Happened just like Jimmy said. She fell over dead, and the cops have no idea what killed her."

"Was she drinking?" Emma asked, obviously thinking about Heidi Anderson.

"Nope. She wasn't on anything either." Nash gestured with the crust of his first slice. "But she has nothing to do with the first, right?" He glanced my way, brows raised now in question.

"I mean, you didn't predict this one. You never even saw her, right?"

I nodded and took the first bite out of my apple. He was right, of course.

But there *was* an obvious connection between the two girls: they were both dead with no apparent cause. The local news knew that. Emma knew it. I knew it. Only Nash seemed oblivious. Or at least uninterested.

Emma pointed at him with the business end of a plastic fork, her porcelain face twisted into an equally beautiful mask of disbelief. "So you don't think it's weird that two girls have dropped dead in the past two days?"

He sighed and pulled the tab from his empty soda can, watching it, rather than either of us. "I never said it wasn't weird. But I don't get this morbid obsession you two have with those poor girls. They're gone. You didn't know either of them. Let them rest in peace."

I rolled my eyes and peeled the vendor's sticker from my apple. "We're not disturbing their rest."

"And it's not obsession—it's caution," Emma countered, aiming her water bottle at him like a conductor's baton. "No one knows how they died, and I'm not buying the coincidence angle. That could be either one of us tomorrow." Her gaze turned my way, clearly including me among the potential victims of…um… dropping dead for no reason. "Or any one of *them*." She nodded toward the cafeteria, and I turned to see Sophie and several of her friends bounce down the steps in the company of half a dozen jocks in matching green-and-white jackets.

"You're totally overreacting." Nash pushed his tray away and twisted on the bench to face us both. "It's just a weird coincidence that has nothing to do with us."

"What if it's not?" I demanded, and even I recognized the pain in my voice. I couldn't let go of the possibility that I could have helped. Could maybe have saved Heidi, if I'd only said something. "No one knows what happened to those girls, so you can't possibly know it won't happen again."

Nash closed his eyes, as if gathering his thoughts. Or maybe his patience. Then he opened them and looked at first Emma, then me. "No, I don't know what happened to either of them, but the cops will figure it out sooner or later. They probably died of totally different, completely unrelated illnesses. An aneurism, or a freak teenage heart attack. And I'll bet you my Xbox that they have nothing to do with each other."

His eyes narrowed on mine then, and he took my hand in both of his. "And they have nothing to do with you."

"Then how did she know it was going to happen?" Emma stared at us both, brown eyes wide. "Kaylee knew that first girl was going to die. I'd say that makes her pretty deeply involved."

"Okay, yes." Nash turned from me to glare at her. "Kaylee knew about Heidi. That's weird, and creepy, and sounds like the plot from some cheesy horror movie—"

"Hey!" I elbowed Nash, and he shot me a dimpled grin.

"Sorry. But she asked. My point is that your premonition is the only weird part of this. The rest is just coincidence. A total fluke. It's not going to happen again."

I pulled my hand from his grasp. "What if you're wrong?"

Nash frowned and ran his fingers through his artfully mussed hair, but before he could answer, a hand dropped onto my shoulder and I jumped.

"Trouble in paradise?" Sophie asked, and I looked up to find her beaming at Nash over my head.

"Nope. We're all shiny and happy here, thanks," Emma said when I couldn't unclench my teeth long enough to reply.

"Hey, Hudson." A green-sleeved arm slid around Sophie's shoulders, and I found myself staring at Scott Carter, the first-string quarterback and my cousin's current plaything. "Makin' new friends?"

Nash nodded. "You know Emma, right?"

Carter's jaw tightened as his eyes settled on my best friend. He knew her, all right. Emma had turned him down cold over the summer, then dumped a Slushie on his shirt at the Cinemark when he refused to take the hint. If anyone other than Jimmy had been working with her, she'd probably have been reported and fired.

Nash's hand curled around mine. "And this is Kaylee."

Carter's eyes turned my way, for probably the first time ever, and his smile returned as his gaze traveled from my face to the front of my shirt. Which he could probably see straight down, since he was standing. "Sophie's sister, right?"

"Cousin," Sophie and I said in unison. It was the only thing we agreed on.

"Hey, we're taking my dad's boat out on White Rock Lake Friday night. You two should come."

"She can't." Sophie sneered at me, curling her arm through Carter's. "She has to *work*."

As if it were a dirty word. Though personally, after what Emma had to say about him, I'd rather spend all night scraping gum from the underside of theater chairs than spend one minute on Carter's father's boat.

"We'll catch you next time," Nash said, and Carter nodded as Sophie tugged him toward a table at the front of the quad, already swarming with green-and-white jackets.

"Wow." Emma whistled softly. "He is such a dick. He just looked down your shirt with Sophie and Nash both standing there. That's a jock for you."

"We're not all bad," Nash said, but he looked distinctly una-mused by both Carter's optical invasion and Emma's commentary on it.

Without his teammates around, it was easy to forget that Nash played football. Baseball too. What could he possibly want with me, while girls like Sophie were standing in line to drool all over him?

"Don't you usually sit over there?" I asked, nodding toward the green-and-white bee swarm. We'd sat with the jocks earlier in the year, when Emma was going out with one of the linebackers, but honestly, the noise and constant posturing got on my nerves.

"You two are much better company." Nash grinned, pulling me closer, but for once, I barely noticed. Something in that crowd of matching jackets had snagged my attention. Something felt…wrong.

Nooo…! It couldn't happen again! Nash had said it wouldn't!

But already the first tendrils of panic were prickling the inside of my flesh.

The edges of my vision went dark, as if death hovered just out of sight. My heart hammered. My skin tingled, and my hands curled into fists. Nash flinched and pulled his hand from mine. I'd forgotten I was holding it and had drawn blood from his palm.

"Kaylee?" His voice was thick with concern, but I couldn't look away from the green-and-white crowd. Couldn't concentrate on him while panic thundered through my head and guilt clawed at my heart. Someone was going to die. I could feel it, but I couldn't tell who yet. The jackets blended into one another, like a herd of Technicolor zebras, individuals hiding among the mingling multitude.

But social camouflage wouldn't work. Death would find the one it wanted, and I couldn't warn the victim if I couldn't find him. Or her.

And it was a her. I could feel that much.

"She's doing it again."

I heard Emma as if she were speaking from far away, though I knew dimly that she'd moved to sit next to me. I couldn't look at her. I had eyes only for the crowd hiding the soon-to-be-dead girl. I needed to see who she was. I had to see….

Then the crowd parted and the applause began. Music played;

someone had brought out a small stereo. Girls were tossing their jackets onto a pile on the ground. They lined up in the grass, forming a zigzag formation I recognized from the competitions my aunt and uncle had dragged me to. The dance team was doing a demonstration. Showing off the routine that had captured the regional trophy.

And then I saw her. Second from the left, three down from Sophie. A tall, slender girl with honey-brown hair and heavily lashed eyes.

Meredith Cole. The team captain. Shrouded in a shadow so thick I could barely make out her features.

As soon as my eyes found her, my throat began to burn, like I'd inhaled bleach fumes. Devastation drenched me, threatening to pull me beneath the surface of despair. And that familiar dark knowledge left me shivering where I sat. Meredith Cole would die very, very soon.

"Kaylee, come on." Nash stood, tugging on my arm, trying to pull me up. "Let's go."

My throat tightened, and my breaths grew short. My head swam with the bitter chaos building inside me, and my heart felt swollen and heavy with grief. But I couldn't go. I had to tell her. I'd let Heidi die, but I could save Meredith. I could warn her, and everything would be okay.

My mouth fell open, but the words didn't come. Instead, a scream clawed at my throat, announcing its arrival with the usual burst of panic, and this time there was nothing I could do to stop it. I couldn't speak; I could only scream. But that wouldn't be enough. I needed *words* to warn Meredith, not inarticulate shrieking. What good was my "gift" if I couldn't use it? If all I could do was scream uselessly?

The keening began deep in my throat, so low it felt like my lungs were on fire. Yet the sound was soft at first. Like a whisper I felt more than heard. I clamped my jaws shut in horror as

Nash's eyes widened, his irises seeming to churn again in the bright sunlight.

My vision darkened and went dull, as if that same foggy gray filter had been draped over the entire world. The day was dimmer now, the shadows thicker, the air hazy. My own hands looked fuzzy, as if I couldn't quite bring them into focus. Tables, students, and the school building itself were suddenly leached of their vibrancy, like someone had opened a drain at the base of a rainbow and let all the color out.

I stood and clamped a hand over my mouth, begging an oddly faded-looking Nash with my eyes for help. The keening sound rolled up my throat now and stuck there, like a growl, offering no release.

Nash wrapped one arm around my waist and nodded for Emma to take my other side. "Calm down, Kaylee," he whispered into my ear, his breath warm against my neck, stirring the fine hairs there. "Just relax and listen to—"

My legs collapsed, even as my gaze was drawn back to Meredith, now dancing between Sophie and a petite blonde I knew only by sight.

Nash scooped me into his arms and held me tight to his chest, still whispering something in my ear. Something familiar. Something that rhymed. His words fell on me with an almost physical presence, soothing me everywhere they touched me, like a balm I could hear.

Yet still the scream raged inside me, demanding a way out, and apparently willing to forge an exit itself, if I offered no alternative.

Emma walked ahead of us to the end of the English hall and around the corner, out of sight of the quad. No one else noticed; they were all watching the dance squad.

Nash put me down against the short wall at the end of the building, next to a door that only worked as an exit. He sat beside me again, and this time he wrapped his arms around me while Emma knelt next to us. Nash was warm at my back, and the only sounds I could hear were his whispers and my own soft keening, persisting in spite of my struggle to suppress it.

I stared over his shoulder and past Emma's concerned face, at the weirdly gray field house in the distance, concentrating on my efforts to speak without screaming. Something rushed across the left edge of my vision, and my gaze homed in on it automatically, trying to bring it into focus. But it moved too fast, leaving me with only a vague impression of a human silhouette, out of proportion in no way I could explain with so short a glimpse. The figure was misshapen, somehow. Odd-looking. And when I blinked, I could no longer be sure of where I'd seen it.

A teacher, probably, rendered unrecognizable by the weird gray fog that had overlaid my vision. I squeezed my eyes shut to avoid any future distractions.

Then, as swiftly as it had struck, the panic faded. Tension drained from my body like air from a beach ball, leaving me limp with relief and fatigue. I opened my eyes to see that color and clarity had returned to the world. My hands relaxed, and the scream died in my throat. But an instant later it tore through the air, and it actually took me a second to realize that the shriek hadn't come from me.

It had come from the quad.

I knew what had happened without even looking. Meredith had collapsed. My urge to scream died the moment she did.

Again, I'd known someone was going to die. And again, I'd let it happen.

My eyes closed as a fresh wave of shock and grief rolled over me, followed immediately by guilt so heavy I could hardly lift my head. *My fault.* I should have been able to save her.

More shouts came from the quad, and someone yelled for someone else to call an ambulance. Doors squealed open, then crashed into the side of the brick building. Sneakers pounded on concrete steps.

Tears of shame and frustration poured down my face. I buried my head in Nash's shoulder, heedless as my tears soaked into his shirt. I might as well have killed her myself, for all the good my warning had done.

Around the corner, the buzz of chaos rose, each terrified voice blending into the next. Someone was crying. Someone else was running. And above it all, Mrs. Tucker, the girls' softball coach, blew her whistle, trying ineffectively to calm everyone down.

"Who is it?" Emma asked, still kneeling beside us, eyes wide in shock and understanding as she brushed back a strand of my hair so she could see my face.

"Meredith Cole," I whispered, wiping tears on my sleeve.

Nash squeezed me tighter, wrapping his arms around mine, where they clutched at my stomach.

Emma stood slowly, her expression a mixture of disbelief and dread. She backed away from us, legs wobbling. Then she turned carefully and peeked around the corner. "I can't see anything. There're too many people."

"Doesn't matter," I said, mildly surprised by the dazed quality of my own voice. "She's already dead."

"How do you know?" Her hand gripped the corner of the building, nails digging into the rough mortar outlining the brown bricks. "Are you sure it's Meredith?"

"Yes." I sighed, then rose and pulled Nash up, wiping more tears from my cheeks. He stood to my left, Emma to my right. Together, we turned the corner and entered the chaos.

6

Emma was right—there were people everywhere. Several class-room doors had opened into the quad, and students were pour-ing out in spite of protests from their teachers. And since there were still ten minutes left in second lunch, the cafeteria was now emptying its usual crowd onto the grass too.

I saw at least twenty students on cell phones, and the snatches of conversation I caught sounded like 911 calls, though most of the callers didn't actually know what had happened, or who was involved. They only knew someone was hurt, and there had been no gunfire.

Coach Tucker loomed on the edge of the green-and-white central throng, her sneakers spread wide for balance, pulling kids out of the way one at a time even as she shouted into a clunky, school-issue, handheld radio. Finally the crowd parted for her, revealing a motionless female form lying on the brown grass, one arm thrown out at her side. I couldn't see her face because one of the football players—number fourteen—was performing CPR.

But I knew it was Meredith Cole. And I could have told number fourteen that his efforts were wasted; he couldn't help her.

Coach Tucker pulled the football player away from the dead girl and dropped to her knees beside the body, shouting for everyone to move back. To go back into the building. Then she bent with her face close to Meredith's to see if she was breathing. A moment later, Coach Tucker tilted the dancer's head back and resumed CPR where number fourteen had left off.

Seconds later, the dance team's faculty sponsor—Mrs. Foley, one of the algebra teachers—raced across the quad from an open classroom, stunned speechless for several seconds by the chaos. After a quick word with a couple of students, she gathered her remaining dancers into a teary huddle several feet from Meredith and the softball coach. The other students stared at them all in astonishment, some crying, some whispering and others standing in silent shock.

As we watched from the fringes of the mayhem, three more adults jogged down the cafeteria steps: the principal, who looked too prim in her narrow skirt and heels to even make a dent in the pandemonium; her assistant, a small balding man who clutched a clipboard to his narrow chest like a life raft; and Coach Rundell, the head football coach.

The principal stood on her toes and whispered something into Coach Rundell's ear, and he nodded curtly. Coach wore a whistle and carried a megaphone.

He needed neither, but he used them both.

The shriek of the whistle pierced my eardrums like a railroad spike, and everyone around us froze. Coach Rundell lifted the megaphone to his mouth and began issuing orders with a speed and clarity that would have made any drill sergeant proud.

"We are now on lockdown! If you do not have second lunch, return to your classroom. If you do have second lunch, take a seat in the cafeteria."

At some signal from the principal, her assistant scuttled off to make the necessary lockdown announcements and arrangements. Teachers started herding their students inside in earnest now, and one by one, the doors closed and a tense quiet descended on the quad. Mrs. Foley, looking overwhelmed and on the verge of tears herself, gathered her sobbing dancers and led them into the building through a side entrance. The principal began ushering the lunch crowd back into the cafeteria, and when her assistant showed up again, he helped.

Nash, Emma and I fell into the stream of students right behind the huddle of green-and-white football jackets, and as we passed the last picnic table, I looked to the right, where Coach Rundell had now taken over CPR from Coach Tucker. Even sick with guilt and numb with shock, I had to see for myself. Had to prove to my head what my heart knew all along.

And there Meredith lay, long brown hair fanned out across the dead grass, her face visible only when the coach sat up for a round of chest compressions.

My eyes watered and I sniffed back more tears, and Nash stepped up on my right, blocking my view as we climbed the broad concrete steps into the building. Inside, the lights were all off because of the lockdown. But the cafeteria windows—a virtual wall of glass—had no shades and were too big to cover, so daylight streamed in, casting deep shadows and lighting the long room in a washed-out palette of colors, in contrast to the bright light usually cast from the fluorescent fixtures overhead.

At the far end of the room, the jocks had gathered in a silent, solemn huddle around one of the round tables. Several sat with their elbows propped on wide-set knees, heads either hanging or cradled in both hands. Number fourteen—who'd tried valiantly to save Meredith—held his girlfriend on his lap, her face streaked with tears and mascara, his arm around her waist, his chin resting on her shoulder.

Other students sat grouped around the rest of the tables. A few whispered questions no one had answers for, a few more cried softly, and everyone looked stunned to the point of incomprehension. There had been no warning, no violence, and no obvious cause. This lockdown didn't fit with the drills we practiced twice a semester, and everyone knew it.

The tables were all occupied, and several small groups of students sat on the floor against the long wall, holding backpacks, purses, and short stacks of textbooks. Emma looked shaken and pale as we made our way toward an empty corner, and I could feel my legs wobbling, left almost totally numb by the accuracy of my second prediction in three days. Only Nash seemed relatively steady, his bruising grip on my hand the sole indication that he might not be as calm as he looked.

We sat in a row on the floor, Em on my left, Nash still clutching my right hand, each too stunned to speak. My thoughts were chaotic, a never-ending furor of guilt, shock, and utter incredulity. A private cacophony in absolute contrast to the hushed, somber room around me. And I couldn't make it stop. Could not slow the torrent long enough to wallow in any single emotion, or puzzle out any one question.

I could only sit, and stare, and wait.

Minutes later, sirens blared to life down the street, warbling softly at first, but growing in volume with each passing second. The ambulance came to an earsplitting halt at the front of the school, but by the time it rolled carefully around the building and past the cafeteria windows, the electronic screeching had gone silent, though it still echoed in my head, a fitting sound track to the mayhem within.

The ambulance stopped out of sight of the windows, but its lights flashed an angry red against the dull brown brick, declaring an optimistic urgency I knew to be unnecessary.

Meredith Cole was dead, and no matter how long they worked on her, she wasn't coming back. That bitter certainty ate at me, consuming me from the inside out until I felt hollow enough to echo with each aching thump of my heart.

While the medics worked outside, teachers came and went from the cafeteria, occasionally answering questions from anyone brave enough to speak up, and at some point, the senior guidance counselor pulled up a chair at the jocks' table and began speaking softly to those who'd been close enough to actually see Meredith fall.

Eventually, the vice principal came over the intercom and declared that the school day had been officially suspended, and that we would all be dismissed individually, once our legal guardians had been contacted. By that time, the red lights had stopped flashing, and though no one had yet made the announcement, it echoed around us like all-important truths, unvoiced, and unwanted, and unavoidable.

After that, the first group of students was called to the office and Emma leaned against me while I leaned against Nash, letting his scent and his warmth soothe me as I settled in for the wait. But minutes later, Coach Tucker stopped in the cafeteria doorway and scanned the faces until her gaze landed on me. I sat up as she navigated the maze of tables, heading right for us, and stood when she reached out a hand to pull me up, barely sparing a glance for Nash and Emma when they rose. "The dancers are understandably upset, and we're calling their parents first. Sophie's not taking it well. Her sponsor spoke to your mother, and they'd like you to go ahead and take your sister home."

I sighed, grateful when Nash's hand slid into mine again. "She's my cousin."

Coach Tucker frowned, as if details like that shouldn't matter under the circumstances. She was right, but I couldn't bring myself to apologize.

"Don't worry about your books." She eyed me sternly now. "Just get her home."

I nodded, and the coach headed back through the cafeteria, motioning for me to follow. "I'll talk to you guys later," I said, glancing from Emma to Nash as I squeezed his hand. She smiled weakly, and he nodded, digging his phone from his pocket.

I'd just stepped into the hall, heading toward the office, when my own phone buzzed. A glance at the screen showed a blinking text message icon. It was from Nash.

Don't tell anyone. Will explain soon.

A moment later, a follow-up message arrived. It was one word: Please.

I didn't reply, because I didn't know what to say. No one would believe me if I tried to explain what had happened. But the premonitions were real, and they were accurate. Silence no longer seemed like an option, especially if there was any chance I could stop the next one from coming true.

If I could at least give the next victim a warning—and maybe a fighting chance—wasn't I morally obligated to do just that?

Besides, hadn't Nash suggested I tell my aunt and uncle the day before?

"Kaitlin! Over here." I glanced up to find Mrs. Foley waving me forward from the atrium outside the front office. Sophie sat on the floor behind her, beneath the foliage of a huge potted plant, surrounded by half a dozen other red, mascara-smeared faces.

"It's Kaylee," I muttered, coming to a stop in front of the stunned dancers.

"Of course." But the sponsor didn't look like she cared what my name was. "I've spoken to your mother—" but I didn't bother to tell her that would be impossible without a Ouija board "—and she wants you to take Sophie straight home. She's going to meet you there."

I nodded, and ignored the sympathetic hand the dance-team sponsor placed momentarily on my shoulder, as if to thank me for sharing some venerable burden. "You ready?" I asked in my cousin's general direction, and to my surprise, she bobbed her head in assent, stood with her purse in hand, and followed me across the quad without betraying a single syllable of malicious intent.

She must have been in shock.

In the parking lot, I unlocked the passenger's side door, then went around to let myself in. Sophie slid into her seat and pulled the door closed, then turned to face me slowly, her normally arrogant expression giving way to what could only be described as abject grief.

"Did you see it?" she asked, full lower lip quivering, and for once absent of lip gloss. She must have wiped it all off, along with the tears and most of her makeup. She looked almost...normal. And I couldn't help the pang of sympathy her misery drew from me, in spite of the bitch-itude she radiated every other day of my life. For now, she was just scared, confused, and hurting, looking for a compassionate ear.

Just like me.

And it kind of stung that I couldn't totally let my guard down with her, because I had no doubt that once her grief had passed, Sophie would go all *Mean Girls* on me again, and use against me whatever I'd shown her. "See what?" I sighed, adjusting the rearview mirror so I could watch her indirectly.

My cousin rolled her eyes, and for a moment her usual intolerance peeked through the fresh layer of raw sorrow. "Meredith. Did you see what happened?"

I turned the key in the ignition, and my little Sunfire hummed to life, the steering wheel vibrating beneath my hands. "No." I felt no great loss over having missed the show; the preview was quite enough to deal with.

"It was horrible." She stared straight out the windshield as I buckled my seat belt and pulled the car from the parking lot, but she obviously saw nothing. "We were dancing, just showing off for Scott and the guys. We'd made it through all the hard parts, including that step where Laura usually skips a beat in practice...."

I had no idea what step she was talking about, but I let her ramble on, because it seemed to make her feel better without putting me on the figurative chopping block.

"…and were nearly done. Then Meredith just…collapsed. She crumpled up like a doll and fell flat on the ground."

My hands clenched the steering wheel, and I had to force them loose to flick on my blinker. I turned right at the stoplight, exhaling only once the school—and thus the source of my latest premonition—was out of sight. And still Sophie prattled on, airing her grief in the name of therapy, completely oblivious to my discomfort.

"I thought she'd passed out. She doesn't eat enough to keep a hamster alive, you know."

I hadn't known, of course. I didn't typically concern myself with the eating habits of the varsity dance squad. But if Meredith's appetite was anything like my cousin's—or my aunt's, for that matter—Sophie's assumption was perfectly plausible.

"But then we realized she wasn't moving. She wasn't even breathing." Sophie paused for a moment, and I treasured the silence like that first gulp of air after a deep dive. I didn't want to hear any more about the death I'd been unable to prevent. I felt guilty enough already. But she wasn't done. "Peyton thinks she had a heart attack. Mrs. Rushing told us in health last year that if you work your body too hard and don't fuel it up right, your heart will eventually stop working. Just like that." She snapped her fingers, and the glitter in her nail polish flashed in the bright sunlight. "Do you think that's what happened?"

It took me a moment to realize her question wasn't rhetorical. She was actually asking my opinion about something, and there was no sarcasm involved.

"I don't know." I glanced in the rearview mirror as I turned onto our street, and wasn't surprised to see Aunt Val's car on the road behind us. "Maybe." But that was an outright lie. Meredith Cole was the third teenage girl to drop dead with no warning in the past three days, and while I wasn't about to voice my suspicions out loud—at least not yet—I could no longer tell myself the deaths weren't connected.

Nash's coincidence theory had hit an iceberg and was sink-ing fast.

I parked in the driveway, and Aunt Val drove past us into her spot in the garage. Sophie was out of the car before I'd even turned the engine off, and the minute she saw her mother, she burst into tears again, as if her inner floodgates couldn't with-stand the assault of sympathetic eyes and a shoulder to cry on.

Aunt Val ushered her sobbing daughter through the garage and into the kitchen, then guided her gently to a stool at the bar. I came behind them both, carrying Sophie's purse, and punched the button to close the garage bay door. Inside, I dropped my cousin's handbag on the counter while Sophie sniffed, and blub-bered, and hiccupped, spitting out half-coherent details as she wiped first her cheeks, then her already reddened nose with a tissue from the box on the counter.

But Aunt Val didn't seem very interested in the specifics, which she'd probably already heard from the dance-team spon-sor. While I sat at the table with a can of Coke and a wish for silence, she bustled around the kitchen making hot tea and wip-ing down countertops, and only once she'd run out of things to do did she settle onto the stool next to her daughter. Aunt Val made Sophie drink her tea slowly, until the sobs slowed and the hiccupping stopped. But even then Sophie wouldn't stop talking.

Meredith's death was the first spear of tragedy to pierce my cousin's fairy tale of a world, and she had no idea how to deal with it. When she was still sobbing and dripping snot into her lukewarm tea twenty minutes later, Aunt Val disappeared into the bathroom. She came back carrying a small brown pill bottle I recognized immediately: leftover zombie pills from my last visit with Dr. Nelson, from the mental-health unit.

I twisted in my chair and arched my brows at my aunt, but she only smiled half regretfully, then shrugged. "It will calm her down and help her sleep. She needs to rest."

Yes, but she needed a natural sleep, not the virtual coma

induced by those stupid sedatives. Not that either of them would have listened to me, even if I'd offered my opinion on the subject of chemical oblivion.

For a moment, I envied my cousin her innocence, even as I watched it die. I'd learned about death early in life, and as inconsolable as Sophie was at the moment, she'd had fifteen years to prance around in her plastic-wrapped, padded, gaily colored, armor-plated existence, where darkness dared not tread. No matter what happened next, no one could take away her happy childhood.

Aunt Val watched Sophie swallow a single, tiny white pill, then walked her daughter down the hall into her room, where the bedsprings soon creaked beneath her slight weight. Ten minutes later, she was snoring obnoxiously enough to leave no doubt in my mind that my cousin had inherited just as much from her father as from her mother.

While my aunt put Sophie to bed, I grabbed a second Coke from Uncle Brendon's shelf in the fridge—the one realm Aunt Val's sugar-free, nonfat, tasteless regime had yet to conquer—and took it into the living room, where I checked the local TV station. But there was no news on at two-thirty in the afternoon. I'd have to wait for the five o'clock broadcast.

I turned off the TV, and my thoughts wandered to the Coles, whom I'd only met once, at a dance-team competition the year before. My eyes watered as I imagined Meredith's mother trying to explain to her young son that his big sister wouldn't be coming home from school. Ever.

Glass clinked in the kitchen, momentarily pulling me from the mire of guilt and grief I was sinking into, and I twisted on the couch to see my aunt pouring hot tea into a huge latte mug. My brows furrowed in confusion for a moment—maybe Aunt Val needed a sedative too?—until she stood on her toes to open the top cabinet. Where she and Uncle Brendon kept the alcohol.

My aunt pulled down a bottle of brandy and unscrewed the

lid. Then she dumped a generous shot into her mug. And left the bottle on the countertop, clearly planning on a second helping.

She took a sip of her "tea," then turned toward the living room, remote control in hand. The moment her gaze met mine, she froze, and her cheeks flushed.

"It hasn't hit the news yet," I said, and couldn't help noticing how tired and heavy her steps looked as she crossed the tiles into the living room. Aunt Val and Mrs. Cole had been gym buddies for years. Maybe Meredith's death had hit her harder than I'd realized. Or maybe she was unnerved by how upset Sophie was. Or maybe she'd connected Meredith's death to Heidi Anderson's—to my knowledge, she hadn't yet heard about Alyson Baker—and had started to suspect something was wrong. As I had.

Either way, her skin was pale and her hands were shaking. She looked so fragile I hesitated to add to her troubles. But the premonitions had gone too far. I needed help, or advice, or… something.

What I really needed was for someone to tell me what good premonitions of death were if they didn't help me warn people. What was the point of knowing someone was going to die, if I couldn't stop it from happening?

Aunt Val wouldn't know any of that, but neither would anyone else. And in the absence of my own parents, I had no one else to talk to.

My fingers tangled around one another in my lap as she sank wearily onto the other end of the couch, her knees together, ankles crossed primly. The frown lines around her mouth and the tremor in her hand said she was not as composed as she clearly wanted to appear.

That, and the not-tea scent wafting from her mug.

The last time I'd tried to tell her I knew someone was going to die, she and Uncle Brendon had driven me straight to the hospital and left me there. Of course, at the time, I'd been screaming hysterically in the middle of the mall and lashing out at anyone who tried to touch me.

Presumably, they'd had no choice.

Surely it would go better this time, because I was calm and rational, and not currently in the grip of an irrepressible screaming fit. And because she was already one shot into a bottle of brandy.

My nerves pinged out of control, and I reached absently for the scent diffuser on the end table to my left, stirring the vanilla-scented oil with a thin wooden reed. "Aunt Val?"

She jumped, sloshing "tea" onto her lap. "Sorry, hon." She set her mug on a coaster on the end table, then rushed into the kitchen to blot at her pants with a clean, wet rag. "This thing with Meredith has me on edge."

I knew exactly how she felt.

I exhaled smoothly, then took a deep breath as my aunt returned to the living room, the wet spot on her slacks now covering half of one slim thigh. "Yeah, it was pretty…scary."

"Oh?" She stopped several feet from her chair, eyes narrowed at me in concern laced with…suspicion? "Were you there?" Had she already guessed what I was going to say?

Maybe Nash was right. Maybe I should keep my secret a little longer….

I shook my head slowly, and my gaze flicked back to the sticks protruding from the tiny oil bottle. "No, I didn't actually see it—" she exhaled in relief, and I almost hated to ruin it with the rest of what I had to say "—but… You know the girl who died at Taboo the other day?"

"Of course. How sad!" She returned to her chair and took a slow sip from her tea, eyes closed, as if she were thinking. Or maybe praying. Then she took a much longer drink and lowered her mug, eyes wide and wary. "Kaylee, that girl had nothing to do with what happened today. According to the news, she was drunk, and may have been on something stronger than alcohol."

I hadn't heard that last tidbit, but I got no chance to question it because she was talking again. Like mother, like daughter.

My aunt gestured with her mug as she spoke, but nothing sloshed out this time. It was already empty. "Sophie said Meredith collapsed while she was dancing. That poor child ate almost nothing and lived on caffeine. It was really only a matter of time before her body cried 'enough.'"

"I know, and Sophie may be right." I let go of the scent sticks and bent the tab on my Coke can back and forth, carefully working it free from its anchor to avoid seeing the pity and skepticism surely lurking behind her cautious sympathy. "The way they died may have nothing to do with anything." Though I certainly had my doubts. "But, Aunt Val, I think *I'm* the connection between them."

"What?"

I made myself look up just in time to see my aunt's eyes narrow in confusion. But then her forehead actually relaxed, tension lines smoothing as if she'd just figured out what I was talking about, and it came as a relief.

If the return of my "delusions" put her at ease, what on earth had she expected me to say?

Her expression softened, and the familiar, patronizing mask of sympathy stung my pride. "Kaylee, is this about your *panic attacks?*" She leaned forward and whispered that last part, as if she were afraid someone would overhear.

Anger zinged through me like tiny bolts of lightning, and I made myself set down my half-empty drink can before I crushed it. "It's not a joke, Aunt Val. And I'm not crazy. I knew Meredith was going to die before it happened."

For an instant—less than a single breath—my aunt looked terrified. Like she'd just seen her own ghost. Then she shook her head—literally shaking off her fear of my relapse—and donned a stoic, determined mask. I'd been right all along. She wasn't going to listen. Ever.

"Kaylee, don't do this again," she begged, a frown etching deep lines around her mouth as she stood and carried her empty mug into the kitchen. I followed her, watching in mounting irritation as she lifted the teakettle from the stove. "I know you're upset about Meredith, but this won't bring her back. This isn't the way to deal with your grief."

"This has nothing to do with grief," I insisted through gritted teeth, dropping my half-full can into the recycling bin. It landed with a thud, followed by the fizz and gurgle of the contents emptying into the plastic tub.

I read frustration in my aunt's narrowed gaze. Desperation in the death grip she had on the teakettle. She probably wished she could knock me out as easily as she had Sophie. And some part of me knew that talking to her would do no more good than trying to warn Meredith had. But another, more stubborn part of me refused to give up. I was done with secrets and sympathetic looks. And I was definitely done with hospitals and those little white pills. I was not going to let anyone else call me crazy. Not ever again.

Aunt Val must have seen my determination, because she set the teakettle back on the stove, then planted both palms flat on the countertop, eyeing me from across the bar. "Think about Sophie. She's already traumatized. What do you think a selfish, attention-seeking story like this would do to her?"

My jaw tightened, and tears burned behind my eyes. "Screw Sophie!" My fists slammed into the bar, and the blow reverberated up my arms like a bruising shock wave of anger.

My aunt flinched, and I felt a momentary surge of satisfaction. Then I stepped deliberately back from the bar, my hands propped on my hips. "I'm sorry," I said, well aware that I didn't sound very sorry. "But this isn't about her. I'm trying to tell you I have a serious problem, and you're not even listening!"

Aunt Val closed her eyes and took a deep breath, like she was practicing yoga. Or searching for patience. "We all know you have problems, Kaylee," she said when her eyes opened, and her quiet, composed tone infuriated me. "Calm down and—"

"I knew, Aunt Val." I planted both hands on the countertop again and stared at the granite. Then I looked up and made myself say the rest of it. "And I knew about the girl at Taboo too."

My aunt's eyes narrowed drastically, showcasing two sets of crow's feet, and her voice dropped dramatically. "How could you, unless you were there?"

I shrugged and crossed my arms over my chest. "I snuck in." I wasn't about to rat on Emma or her sister. "Ground me if you want, but that won't change anything. I was there, and I saw Heidi Anderson. And I knew she was going to die. Just like I knew about Meredith."

Aunt Val's eyes closed again, and she turned to stare out the window over the sink, gripping the countertop with white-knuckled hands. Then she exhaled deeply and turned back to me. "Okay, this other girl aside…" Though we both knew she'd readdress the clubbing issue later. "If you knew Meredith was going to die, why didn't you tell someone?"

A fresh pang of guilt shuddered through me like a psychological aftershock, and I sank onto one of the cushioned bar stools facing her, my arms crossed on the countertop. "I tried." Tears filled my eyes, blurring my aunt's face, and I swiped at them with my sleeve before they could fall. "But when I opened my mouth, all I could do was scream. And it happened so fast! By the time I could talk again, she was dead." I looked up, searching her face for some sign of understanding. Or belief. But there was nothing I recognized in her expression, and that scared me almost as badly as listening to Meredith die.

"I'm not even sure that saying something would have helped," I said, feeling my courage flounder. "But I swear I tried."

Aunt Val rubbed her forehead, then picked up her mug and started to take a drink—until she realized she hadn't poured one. "Kaylee, surely you know how all this sounds."

I nodded and dropped my gaze. "I sound crazy." I knew that better than anyone.

She shook her head and leaned across the bar for my hand. "Not crazy, hon. Delusional. There's a difference. You're probably just really upset about what happened to Meredith, and your brain is dealing with that by making up stories to distract you from the truth. I understand. It's scary to think that anyone anywhere can just drop dead with no warning. If it could happen to her, it could happen to any of us, right?"

I pulled my hand from hers, gaping at my aunt in disbelief. What would it take to make her believe me? Proof was pretty hard to come by when the premonitions only came a few minutes in advance.

I slid off the stool and backed up a step, eager to put a little space between us. "I barely knew Meredith. I'm not scared because I think it can happen to me. I'm scared because I knew it was going to happen to her, and I couldn't stop it." I sucked in a deep breath, trying to breathe beyond the guilt and grief threatening to suffocate me. "I almost wish I *were* going crazy. At least then I wouldn't feel so guilty about letting someone die. But I'm not crazy. This is real."

For several seconds, my aunt just stared at me, her expression a mixture of confusion, relief, and pity, like she wasn't sure what she should feel.

I sighed, my shoulders fell. "You still don't believe me."

My aunt's expression softened, and her posture wilted almost imperceptibly. "Oh, hon, I believe that you believe what you're saying." She hesitated, then shrugged, but the gesture looked more calculated than casual. "Maybe you should take a sedative too. It will help you sleep. I'm sure everything will make more sense when you wake up."

"Sleep won't help me." I sounded acerbic, even to my own ears. "Neither will those stupid pills." I grabbed the bottle from the bar where she'd left it and hurled it at the refrigerator as hard as I could. The plastic cracked and the lid fell off, scattering small white pills all over the floor.

Aunt Val jumped, then stared at me like I'd just broken her heart. When she knelt to clean up the mess, I jogged down the hall and into my room, then slammed the door and leaned against it. I'd done the best I could with my aunt; I'd try again with Uncle Brendon when he came home.

Or maybe not.

Maybe Nash knew what he was talking about when he said not to tell anyone.

7

For several minutes, I stood still in my room, so angry, and scared, and confused, I didn't know whether to scream, or cry, or hit something. I tried to read the novel on my nightstand to distract myself from the disaster my life had become, and when that didn't work, I turned on the TV. But nothing on television held my attention and all the songs on my iPod only seemed to magnify my anger and frustration.

My mind was so full of chaos, my thoughts coming much too fast for me to grasp, that no matter what I did or where I stood, I couldn't escape the miserable roar of half-formed thoughts my head spun with. I was starting to seriously reconsider that sedative—desperate to just be *nowhere* for a little while—when my phone buzzed in my pocket.

Another text message from Nash. U OK?

Fine. I lied. U? I almost told him he'd been right. That I shouldn't have told my aunt. But that was a lot of information to fit into a text.

Yeah. With Carter, he replied. Call U soon.

I thought about texting Emma, but she was still grounded. And knowing her mother, she stood no chance of a commuted sentence, even after practically seeing a classmate drop dead.

Frustrated and mentally exhausted, I finally fell asleep in the middle of the movie I wasn't really watching in the first place. Less than an hour later, according to my alarm clock, I woke up and turned the TV off. And that's when I realized I'd almost slept through something important.

Or at least something interesting.

In the sudden silence, I heard my aunt and uncle arguing fiercely, but too softly to understand from my room at the back of the house. I eased my bedroom door open several inches, holding my breath until I was sure the hinges wouldn't squeal. Then I stuck my head through the gap and peered down the hall.

They were in the kitchen; my aunt's slim shadow paced back and forth across the only visible wall. Then I heard her whisper my name—even lower in pitch than the rest of the argument—and I swallowed thickly. She was probably trying to convince Uncle Brendon to take me back to the hospital.

That was *not* going to happen.

Angry now, I eased the door open farther and slipped into the hall. If my uncle gave in, I'd simply step up and tell them I wasn't going. Or maybe I'd just jump in my car and leave until they came to their senses. I could go to Emma's. No, wait. She was grounded. So I'd go to Nash's.

Where I wound up didn't matter, so long as it wasn't the mental-health ward.

I inched down the hall, grateful for my silent socks and the tile floor, which didn't creak. But I froze several feet from the kitchen doorway when my uncle spoke, his words still low but now perfectly audible.

"You're overreacting, Valerie. She got through it last time, and she'll get through it this time. I see no reason to bother him while he's working."

While I appreciated my uncle standing up for me, even if he didn't believe in my premonitions either, I seriously doubted Dr.

Nelson would consider himself "bothered" by a phone call about a patient. Not considering what he was probably getting paid.

"I don't know what else to do." Aunt Val sighed, and a chair scraped the floor as my uncle's shadow stood. "She's really upset, and I think I made it worse. She knows something's going on. I tried to get her to take a sedative, but she busted the bottle on the refrigerator."

Uncle Brendon chuckled, from across the kitchen now. "She knows she doesn't need those damn pills."

Yeah! I was starting to wonder if my uncle wore chain mail beneath his clothes, because he sounded eager to slay the dragon Skepticism. And I was ready to ride into battle with him....

"Of course she doesn't," Aunt Val conceded wearily, and her shadow folded its arms across its chest. "The pills are a temporary solution, like sticking your finger in a crack in a dam. What she really needs is your brother, and if you're not going to call him, I will."

My father? Aunt Val wanted him to call my dad? Not Dr. Nelson?

My uncle sighed. "I hate to start all this now if we could possibly put it off awhile longer." The refrigerator door squealed open, and a soda can popped, then hissed. "It was just coincidence that this happened twice in one week. It may not happen for another year, or even longer."

Aunt Val huffed in exasperation. "Brendon, you didn't see her. Didn't *hear* her. She thinks she's losing her mind. She's already living on borrowed time, and she should not have to spend whatever she has left of it thinking she's crazy."

Borrowed time?

A jolt of shock shot through me, settling finally into my heart, which seemed reluctant to beat again for a moment. What did that mean? I was sick? Dying? How could they not have told me? And how could I be dying if I felt fine? Except for knowing when other people are going to die...

And if that were true, wouldn't I know if I were going to die?

Uncle Brendon sighed, and a chair scraped across the floor again, then groaned as he sank into it. "Fine. Call him if you want to. You're probably right. I just really hoped we'd have another year or two. At least until she's out of high school."

"That was never a certainty." Aunt Val's silhouette shrank as it came closer, and I scuttled toward my room, my spine still pressed against the cold wall. But then she stopped, and her shadow turned around. "Where's the number?"

"Here, use my phone. He's second in the contacts list."

My aunt's shadow elongated as she moved farther away, presumably taking the phone from my uncle. "You sure you don't want to do it?"

"Positive."

Another chair scraped the tiles as my aunt sat, and her shadow became an amorphous blob on the wall. A series of high-pitched beeps told me she was already pressing buttons. A moment later she spoke, and I held my breath, desperate to hear every single word of whatever they'd been keeping from me.

"Aiden? It's Valerie." She paused, but I couldn't hear my father's response. "We're fine. Brendon's right here. Listen, though, I'm calling about Kaylee." Another pause, and this time I heard a low-pitched, indistinct rumble, barely recognizable as my father's voice.

Aunt Val sighed again, and her shadow shifted as she slumped in her chair. "I know, but it's happening again." Pause. "Of course I'm sure. Twice in the last three days. She didn't tell us the first time, or I would have called sooner. I'm not sure how she's kept quiet about it, as it is."

My father said something else I couldn't make out.

"I did, but she won't take them, and I'm not going to force her. I think we've moved beyond the pills, Aiden. It's time to tell her the truth. You owe her that much."

He owed me? Of course he owed me the truth—whatever that was. They all owed me.

"Yes, but I really think it should come from her father." She sounded angry now.

My father spoke again, and this time it sounded like he was arguing. But I could have told him how futile it was to argue with Aunt Val. Once she'd made up her mind, nothing could change it.

"Aiden Cavanaugh, you put your butt on a plane today, or I'll send your daughter to you. She deserves the truth, and you're going to give it to her, one way or another."

I snuck back to my room, shocked, confused, and more than a little proud of my aunt. Whatever this mysterious truth was, she wanted me to have it. And she didn't think I was losing my mind. Neither of them did.

Though they apparently thought I was dying.

I think I'd rather be crazy.

I'd never really contemplated my own death before, but I would have thought the very idea would leave me too frightened to function. Especially having very nearly witnessed someone else's death only hours earlier. Instead, however, I found myself more numb than terrified.

There was a substantial fear building inside me, tightening my throat and making my heart pound almost audibly inside my chest. But it was a very distant fear, as if I couldn't quite wrap my mind around the concept of my own demise. Of simply not existing one day.

Maybe the news just hadn't sunk in yet. Or maybe I couldn't quite believe it. Either way, I desperately needed to talk it through with someone who wasn't busy keeping vital secrets from me. So I texted Emma, in case her mother had lifted the cell phone ban.

Ms. Marshall replied a few minutes later, telling me that

Emma was still grounded, but she'd see me the next day for Meredith's memorial, if I was planning to go.

I wrote back to tell her I'd be there, then dropped my phone on my bed in disgust. What good is technology if your friends are always grounded from it? Or hanging out with teammates?

For lack of anything better to do, I turned the TV on again, but I couldn't concentrate because what I'd just overheard kept playing through my mind. I analyzed every word, trying to figure out what I'd missed. What they'd been keeping from me.

I was sick; that much was clear. What else could "living on borrowed time" mean? So what did I have? What kind of twisted illness had "premonitions of death" as the primary symptom, and death itself as the eventual result?

Nothing, unless we were still considering adolescent dementia. Which we were not, based on the fact that they didn't think I needed the zombie pills.

So what kind of illness could make me *think* I was crazy?

Ignoring the television now, I slid into my desk chair and fired up the Gateway notebook my father had sent me for my last birthday. Each second it took to load sent fresh waves of agitation through me, fortifying my unease until that fear I'd expected earlier finally began to take root in earnest.

I'm going to die.

Just thinking the words sent terror skittering through me. I couldn't sit still, even for the few minutes it took Windows to load. When my leg began to jiggle with nerves, I stood in front of my dresser to peer in the mirror. Surely if I were ready to kick the proverbial bucket, I would know the minute I saw myself. That's how it seemed to work when someone else was going to die.

But I felt nothing when I looked at my reflection, except the usual fleeting annoyance that, unlike my cousin, my skin was pale, my features completely unremarkable.

Maybe it didn't work with reflections. I'd never seen Heidi

in the mirror, nor Meredith. Holding my breath, and barely resisting the absurd urge to cross my fingers, I glanced down at myself, unsure whether I was more afraid of feeling the urge to scream, or of not feeling it.

Again, I felt nothing.

Did that mean I wasn't dying, after all? Or that my gruesome gift didn't work on myself? Or merely that my death wasn't yet imminent? *Aaagggghhh! This was pointless!*

My computer chimed to tell me it was up and running, and I dropped into my desk chair. I pulled up my internet browser and typed "leading cause of death among teenagers" into the search engine, my chest tight and aching with morbid anticipation.

The first hit contained a list of the top ten causes of death in individuals fifteen through nineteen years of age. Unintentional injury, homicide, and suicide were the top three entries. But I had no plans to end my own life, and accidents couldn't be predicted. Neither could murder, unless my aunt and uncle were planning to take me out themselves.

Lower on the list were several equally scary entries, like heart disease, respiratory infection, and diabetes, among others. However, those all included symptoms I couldn't possibly have overlooked.

That left only the fourth leading cause of death for people my age: malignant neoplasms.

I had to look that one up.

The description from a separate, respected medical site was dense and nearly impossible to comprehend. But the layman's definition under that was too clear for comfort. "Malignant neoplasm" was doctor-talk for cancer.

Cancer.

And suddenly every hope I'd ever harbored, every dream I'd ever entertained, seemed too fragile a possibility to survive.

I had a tumor. What else could it be? And it had to be brain cancer to affect the things I felt and knew, didn't it? Or the things I thought I knew.

Did that mean the premonitions weren't real? Were brain tumors giving me delusions? Some sort of sensory hallucinations? Had I imagined predicting Heidi's and Meredith's deaths, after the fact?

No. It couldn't be. I refused to believe that any mere illness—short of Alzheimer's—could rewrite my memories.

Hovering on the sharp, hot edge of panic now, I returned to the search engine and typed "symptoms of brain cancer." The first hit was an oncology website that listed seven kinds of brain cancer along with the leading symptoms of each. But I had none of them. No nausea, seizures, or hearing loss. I had no impaired speech or motor function, and no spatial disorders. I wasn't dizzy, had no headaches, and no muscle weakness. I wasn't incontinent—thank goodness—nor did I have any unexplained bleeding or swelling, nor any impaired judgment.

Okay, some might say sneaking into a nightclub was a sign of impaired judgment, but I was pretty sure my decision-making skills were right on target for someone my age, and miles above the judgment of others. Such as certain spoiled, vomit-prone cousins, who shall remain nameless.

I was tempted to rule out brain cancer based on the symptoms alone, until I noticed the section on tumors in the temporal lobe. According to the website, while temporal-lobe "neoplasms" sometimes impaired speech and caused seizures, they were just as often asymptomatic.

As was I.

That was it. I had a tumor in my temporal lobe. But if so, how did Aunt Val and Uncle Brendon know? More important, how long had they known? And how long did I have?

My fingers shook on the keys, and a nonsense word appeared in the address bar. I pushed my chair away from the desk and closed my laptop without bothering to shut it down. I had to talk to someone. Now.

I shoved my chair aside and crawled onto my bed on my hands and knees, snatching my phone from the comforter on the way to my headboard. At the top of the bed, I leaned back and pulled my knees up to my chest. My eyes watered as I scrolled through my contacts for Nash's number. I was wiping tears from my face with my sleeves by the time he answered.

"Hello?" He sounded distracted, and in the background, I heard canned fight sounds, then several guys groaned in unison.

"Hey, it's me." I sniffed to keep my nose from running.

"Kaylee?" Couch springs creaked as he sat up—I had his attention now. "What's wrong?" He switched to an urgent whisper. "Did it happen again?"

"No, um… Are you still at Scott's?"

"Yeah. Hang on." Something brushed against the phone, and dimly I heard Nash say, "Here, man, take over for me." Then footsteps clomped, and the background noise gradually softened until a door creaked closed, and the racket stopped altogether. "What's up?"

I hesitated, rolling onto my stomach on my bed. He hadn't signed on for this kind of drama. But he hadn't run from the death predictions, and I had to talk to someone, and it was either Nash or Emma's mother. "Okay, this is going to sound stupid, but I don't know what else to think. I heard my aunt and uncle arguing, then my aunt called my dad." I swallowed back a sob and wiped more moisture from my face. "Nash…I think I'm dying."

There was silence over the line, then engine noise as a car drove past him. He must have been in Scott's front yard. "Wait, I don't get it. Why do you think you're dying?"

I folded my lumpy feather pillow in half and lay with one cheek on it, treasuring the coolness against my tear-flushed face. "My uncle said he thought I'd have more time, then my aunt told my dad that he needed to tell me the truth, so I wouldn't think I was crazy. I think it's a brain tumor."

"Kaylee, you're adding two and two and coming up with seven. You must have missed something." He paused and footsteps clomped on concrete, like he was on the sidewalk. "What did they say, exactly?"

I sat up and made myself inhale slowly, trying to calm down. The words weren't coming out right. No wonder he had no idea what I was talking about. "Um…Aunt Val said I was living on borrowed time, and that I shouldn't have to spend any of it thinking I was crazy. She told my dad it was time to tell me the truth." I stood and found myself pacing nervously back and forth across my fuzzy purple throw rug. "That means I'm dying, right? And she wants him to tell me?"

"Well, they obviously have *something* important to tell you, but I seriously doubt you have a brain tumor. Shouldn't you have some symptoms, or something, if you're sick?"

I dropped into my desk chair again and ran my finger over the mouse pad to wake up the monitor. "I looked it up, and—"

"You researched brain tumors? This afternoon?" Nash hesitated, and the footsteps paused. "Kaylee, is this because of Meredith?"

"No!" I shoved off against the desk so hard my wheeled chair hit the side of the bed. "I'm not a hypochondriac! I'm just trying to figure out why this is happening to me, and nothing else makes sense." Frustrated, I scrubbed one hand over my face and made myself take another deep breath. "They don't think I'm crazy, so it's not psychological." And my relief at knowing that was big enough to swallow the Pacific Ocean. "So it has to be physical."

"And you think it's brain cancer…."

"I don't know what else to think. There's one kind of brain cancer that sometimes doesn't have any symptoms. Maybe I have that kind."

"Wait…" He paused as a gust of wind whistled over the line. "You think you have a tumor because you have *no* symptoms?"

Okay, I still wasn't making any sense. I closed my eyes and let my head fall against the back of the chair. "Or maybe the premonitions *are* my symptom. Some kind of hallucination."

Nash laughed. "You're not hallucinating, Kaylee. Not unless Emma and I have tumors too. We both saw you predict two deaths, and we saw one of them actually happen. You weren't imagining that."

I sat up in my chair, and this time my long, soft exhalation was in relief. "I was seriously hoping you'd say that." It helped—albeit a tiny little bit—to know that if I was dying, at least I was going out with my mind intact.

"Glad I could help." I could hear the smile in his voice, which drew one from me in response.

I swiveled in my chair and propped my feet up on my night-stand. "Okay, so maybe I'm having premonitions because of the tumor. Like, it's activating some part of my brain most people can't access. Like John Travolta in that old movie."

"Saturday Night Fever?"

"Not that old." My smile grew a little, in spite of what should have been a very somber conversation. I loved how easily Nash calmed me, even over the phone. His voice was hypnotic, like some kind of auditory tranquilizer. One I could easily get hooked on. "The one where he can move stuff with his mind, and learn whole languages by reading one book. And it all turns out to be because he has brain cancer and he's dying."

"I don't think I've seen that one."

"He gets all kinds of freaky abilities, then he dies. It's tragic. I don't want to be tragic, Nash. I want to be alive." And suddenly the tears were back. I couldn't help it. I'd had more than enough of death in the past few days, without adding my own to the list.

"Okay, you're going to have to trust me on this, Kaylee." The footsteps were back, and then a door closed, cutting off the bluster of wind on his end of the call. Then his voice got softer. "Your premonitions don't come from brain cancer. Whatever your aunt and uncle were talking about, that's not it."

"How do you know?" I blinked the moisture from my eyes, irritated with how emotional I was becoming. Wasn't that another symptom of brain cancer?

Nash sighed, but he sounded more worried than exasperated. "I have to tell you something. I'll pick you up in ten minutes."

8

Seven minutes later, I sat on the living-room couch, my keys in my pocket, my phone in my lap, my fingernails rasping anxiously across the satin upholstery. I was angled to face both the television—muted, but tuned to the local evening news—and the front window, hoping no one would realize I was expecting company. "No one," meaning my aunt and uncle. Sophie was still out cold, and I was starting to wonder how many of those pills her mother had given her.

Aunt Val was in the kitchen, banging pots, pans, and cabinet doors as she made spaghetti, her favorite comfort food. Normally she wouldn't indulge in so many carbs in a single meal, but she was obviously having a rough day. A very rough day, if the scent of garlic bread was any indication.

"Hey, Kay-Bear, how you holdin' up?"

I glanced up to find my uncle leaning against the plaster column separating the dining room from the living room. He hadn't called me that in nearly a decade, and the fact that he was using my old nickname probably meant he thought I was… fragile.

"I'm not crazy." I met his clear green eyes, daring him to argue.

He smiled, and the resulting smile lines somehow made him look even younger than usual. "I never said you were."

I huffed and shot a glare toward the kitchen, where Aunt Val was stirring noodles in a huge aluminum pot. "She thinks I am." I knew better than that now, of course, but wasn't about to let on that I'd heard their argument.

Uncle Brendon shook his head and crossed the eggshell carpet toward me, arms folded over the faded tee he'd changed into after work. "She's just worried about you. We both are." He sank into the floral-print armchair opposite me. He always sat there, rather than on the solid white chair or sofa, hoping that if he spilled something, Aunt Val would never notice the stain on such a busy pattern.

"Why aren't you worried about Sophie?"

"We are." He paused, then seemed to consider his answer. "But Sophie's…resilient. She'll be fine once she's had a chance to grieve."

"And I won't?"

My uncle raised one brow at me. "Val said you barely knew Meredith Cole." And just like that, he'd sidestepped the real question—that of my future well-being.

And we both knew it.

Before I could answer—and I was in no hurry—an engine purred outside, and I glanced through the sheers to see an un-familiar blue convertible pull into the driveway beside my car, glittering in the late-afternoon sun. Behind the wheel was a very familiar face, crowned by an equally familiar head of thick brown hair.

I stood, stuffing my phone into my empty pocket.

"Who's that?" Uncle Brendon twisted to look out the window.

"A friend. I gotta go."

He stood, but I was already halfway across the room. "Val's making dinner!" he called after me.

"I'm not hungry." Actually, I was starving, but I had to get out of the house. I couldn't possibly suck down spaghetti like it was a regular Monday night. Not knowing that my entire family had been lying to me for who knows how long.

"Kaylee, get back here!" Uncle Brendon roared, following me through the front door onto the porch. I'd rarely heard him raise his voice, and had never heard him yell like that.

I took off at a trot, slid into the passenger seat, then slammed the door and locked it.

"Is that your uncle?" Nash asked, right hand hovering over the gearshift. "Maybe I should meet—"

"Go!" I shouted, louder than I'd meant to. "I'll introduce you later." Assuming I lived that long.

Nash slammed the car into Reverse and swerved backward out of the driveway, twisting in his seat to peer out the rear windshield. As we pulled away from the house, I took one last look at my uncle, who stared after us from the middle of the driveway, thick arms crossed over his chest. Behind him, Aunt Val stood on the porch holding a dishrag, her perfect mouth hanging open in surprise.

When we turned the corner, I let myself melt into the car seat, only then noticing how posh it was. "Please tell me you didn't pick me up in a stolen car."

Nash laughed and glanced away from the road to smile at me, and my pulse sped up when our gazes met, in spite of the circumstances. "It's Carter's. I've got it till midnight."

"Why would Scott Carter let you take his car?"

He shrugged. "He's a friend."

I just blinked at him. His questionable choice of companions aside, Emma was my best friend, and I would never let her take my car. And I didn't drive a brand-new Mustang convertible.

Nash grinned when I didn't seem convinced, and his next glance lingered longer than it should have, then roamed south of my face. "He might be under the impression that you… um… need some serious comfort."

My heart leaped into my throat, and I had to speak around it. "And you think you're up for the challenge?" Flirting should have felt weird, considering the day I'd had. But instead, it made me feel alive, especially with the possibility of my own death hanging over me like a black cloud, casting its malignant shadow over my life. Over everything but Nash, and the way I felt when he looked at me. Touched me…

Nash shrugged again. "Carter offered to pick you up himself…."

Of course he had. Because he was Nash's best friend, and Sophie's boyfriend. And my cousin had seriously bad taste in guys. As, apparently, did Nash. "Why do you hang out with him?"

"We're teammates."

Ahhh. And if blood was thicker than water, then football, evidently, would congeal in one's veins.

"And that makes you friends?" I twisted to peer briefly into the tiny backseat, which was empty and still smelled like leather. And like Sophie's freesia-scented lotion.

Nash shrugged and frowned, like he didn't understand what I was getting at. Or like he wanted to change the subject. "We have stuff in common. He knows how to have a good time. And he goes after what he wants."

He could easily have been describing my father's German shepherd. As could I, when I replied, "Yeah, but once he gets it, he'll just want something else."

Nash's hands tightened around the wheel, and he glanced at me with his eyes wide in comprehension, his forehead furrowed in disappointment. "Is that what you think I'm doing?"

I shrugged. "Your record kind of speaks for itself." And why else had he put up with so much from me? Why would a guy like Nash Hudson stick around through freaky death premonitions and possible brain cancer, if he didn't want something?

Or even if he did, for that matter? He could have put in a lot less work for a lot more payoff somewhere else.

"This isn't like that, Kaylee," he insisted, and I wasn't sure I wanted to know what "that" was. "This is… We're different." He didn't look at me when he said it, but I felt myself flush anyway.

"What does that mean?"

He sighed, and his hands loosened around the wheel. "You hungry?"

Half an hour later, we sat in Scott Carter's car with the front seats pushed back as far as they would go. The setting sun took up the entire windshield, painting White Rock Lake a dozen deep hues of red and purple.

I was well into a six-inch turkey sub, and Nash was half done with some combination of provolone, ham, pepperoni, and a couple of meats I didn't recognize. But it smelled good.

I'd already dripped mustard on Carter's gearshift, and vinegar on the front seat. Nash had just laughed and helped me mop it all up.

If I was dying, I'd decided to spend every single day I had left eating at least one meal with Nash. Talking to him made me feel good, even when everything else in my life was totally falling apart.

I swallowed a big bite, then washed it down with a gulp from my soda. "Promise me that if I do have a brain tumor, you'll bring me sandwiches in the hospital."

He eyed me almost sternly, peeling paper away from his bread. "You don't have cancer, Kaylee. At least, that's not why you're having premonitions."

"How do you know?" I bit another chunk from my sandwich, chewing as I waited for an answer he seemed reluctant to provide.

Finally, after three more bites and two false starts, Nash

wrapped the remains of his sandwich and stuffed it between our drinks on the console, then took a deep breath and met my gaze. His forehead was wrinkled like he was nervous, but his gaze held steady. Strong.

"I have to tell you something, and you're not going to believe me. But I can prove it to you. So don't freak out on me, okay? At least not until you've heard the whole thing."

I swallowed another bite, then wrapped the rest of my sandwich and set it in my lap. This didn't sound like the kind of news I should get with food in my mouth. Not unless I wanted to check out earlier than I'd expected, with a chunk of turkey wedged in my throat. "Okaaay… Whatever it is, it can't be worse than brain cancer, right?"

"Exactly." He ran his fingers through deliberately messy hair, then met my gaze with an intensity that was almost frightening. "You're not human."

"What?" Confusion was a calm white noise in my head, where I'd expected fear or even anger to rage. I'd been prepared to hear something weird. I was intimately acquainted with weird. But I had no idea what to say to "not human."

"Either your aunt and uncle don't know, or they don't want you to know for some reason, which is why I didn't tell you yesterday at breakfast. But you're killing me with this whole brain cancer thing." He was watching me carefully, probably judging from my expression how close I was to flipping out on him.

And honestly, if I'd had any idea what he was talking about, I might have been pretty close.

"I think if they knew you thought you were dying, they'd tell you the truth," he continued. "It sounds like they're going to tell you soon anyway, but I didn't want you to think I was lying to you too." He flashed deep dimples with a small grin. "Or that you have cancer."

For a moment, I could only stare at him, struck numb and dumb by an outpouring of words that contained no real information. And I have to admit there were a couple of seconds there when I wondered if maybe I wasn't the one in need of a straitjacket.

But he'd believed me when I told him about Heidi, as crazy as the whole thing sounded, and had talked me through two different premonitions. The least I could do was hear him out.

"What am I?" The very question—and my willingness to ask it—made my heart pound so hard and so fast I felt like the car was spinning. My arms were covered in goose bumps.

Fading daylight cast shadows defining the planes of his face as he squinted through the windshield into the sun, now a heavy scarlet ball on the edge of the horizon. But his focus never left my eyes. "You're a *bean sidhe,* Kaylee. The death premonitions are normal. They're part of who you are."

Another moment of stunned silence, which I clung to—a brief respite from the madness that each new word seemed to bring. Then I forced the pertinent question to my lips, fighting to keep my jaw from falling off my face as my mouth dropped open. "Sorry, what?"

He grinned and ran one hand over the short stubble on his jaw. "I know, this is the part where you start thinking I'm the crazy one."

As a matter of fact…

"But I swear this is the truth. You're a *bean sidhe.* And so are your parents. At least one of them, anyway."

I shook my head and pushed my hair back from my face, trying to clear away the confusion and make sense of what he'd said. "Banshee? Like, from mythology?" We'd done a mythology unit in sophomore English the year before, but it was mostly Greek and Roman stuff. Gods, goddesses, demigods, and monsters.

"Yeah. Only the real thing." He took a drink from his cup, then set it in the holder. "There's a bunch they don't teach you in school. Things they don't even know about, because they think it's all just a bunch of old stories."

"And you're saying it's not?" I found myself scooting closer to the door, until the handle cut into my back, trying to put some space between myself and the only guy in the world who could make me sound normal.

"No. Kaylee, it's you!" He watched me intently, expectantly, and while I wanted to wallow in denial, I couldn't. Even if Nash was one grape short of a bunch, there was something compelling about him. Something irresistible, even beyond the sculpted arms, gorgeous eyes, and adorable dimples. He made me feel... content. Relaxed. Like everything would be okay, one way or another. Which was quite a feat, considering his claim that I was unqualified to run in the human race.

"Think about it," he insisted. "What do you know about *bean sidhes?*"

I shrugged. "They're women in long, wispy gowns who walk around during funerals, wailing over the dead. Sometimes they wail over the dying, announcing that the end is near." I sipped watered-down soda, then gestured with my cup. "But, Nash, banshees are just stories. Old European legends."

He nodded. "Most of it, yes. They spell it wrong, for starters. The Gaelic is B-E-A-N S-I-D-H-E. Two words. Literally, it means 'woman of the faeries.'"

My eyebrows shot halfway up my forehead as I dropped my cup back into the drink holder. "Wait, you think I'm a faerie? Like, with little glittery wings and magic wands?"

Nash frowned. "This isn't Disney, Kaylee. 'Faerie' is a very broad term. It basically means 'other than human.' And forget about the wispy gowns and following funerals. All that went out of style a long time ago. But the rest of it? Women as death heralds? Sound familiar?"

Okay, there was a *slight* similarity to my morbid predictions, but... "There's no such thing as *bean sidhes,* no matter how you spell it."

"There are no premonitions either, right?" His hazel eyes

sparkled in the fading light when he grinned, refusing to be derailed by my cynicism. "Okay, let's see how much of this I can get right. Your dad… He looks really young, right? Too young to have a sixteen-year-old daughter? Your uncle too. They're brothers, right?"

Unimpressed, I rolled my eyes and folded one leg beneath me on the narrow leather car seat. "You saw my uncle an hour ago—you know he's young. And I haven't seen my dad in a year and a half." Though as a child, I'd always thought he looked young and handsome. But that was a long time ago….

"I know your uncle looks young, but that means nothing to a *bean sidhe*. He could be a hundred."

That time I laughed. "Right. My uncle's a senior citizen." Wouldn't it piss Aunt Val off to think he could be more than twice her age and still look younger!

Nash frowned at my skepticism, his face darkening as the last rays of daylight slowly bled from the sky. "Okay, what about the rest of your family? Your ancestors are Irish, right?"

I rolled my eyes and crossed my arms over my chest. "My name's Cavanaugh. That's not a big leap." Plus, he already knew my dad lived in Ireland.

"*Bean sidhes* are native to Ireland. That's why the stories all stem from old Irish folktales."

Oh. Now that was quite a coincidence. But nothing more. "Got anything else, Houdini?"

Nash reached across the center console and took my hand again, and this time I didn't pull away. "Kaylee, I knew what you were the minute you told me Heidi Anderson was going to die. But I probably would have known earlier if I'd been paying attention. I just never expected to run into a *bean sidhe* at my own school."

"How would you have known earlier?"

"Your voice."

"Huh?" But my heart began to beat harder, as if it knew something my head hadn't quite caught on to.

"Last Friday at lunch, I heard you and Emma talking about sneaking into Taboo, and couldn't get you out of my head. Your voice stuck with me, like after I truly heard you that first time, I couldn't stop hearing you. Your voice carries above everything else. I can find you in a crowd even if I can't see you, so long as you're talking. But I didn't know why. I just knew I needed to talk to you outside of school, and that you'd be at the club on Saturday night."

Suddenly I couldn't catch my breath. My lungs seemed too big for my chest, and I couldn't make them fully expand. "You followed me to Taboo?" His admission made my head spin, questions and confessions both battling for the right to speak first. But I couldn't think clearly enough to focus on them.

"Yeah." He sounded so matter-of-fact, as if it should be no big surprise that a hot, out-of-my-league guy would go to a club on a Saturday night just to see me. "I wanted to talk to you."

I swallowed thickly and stared at my hands. I could hardly believe what I was about to tell him. "When you talk to me, I feel like everything's okay, even when things are really falling apart. Why?" I looked up then and met his gaze, searching for the truth even if I wouldn't understand it. "What did you do to me?"

"Nothing. Nothing on purpose, anyway." He squeezed my hand, threading his fingers through mine. "We truly hear each other because we're the same. I'm a *bean sidhe*, Kaylee. Just like my mom and dad, and at least one of your parents. Just like you."

Just like me. Was it possible? My instinct was to say no. To shake my head and squeeze my eyes shut until I was sure the crazy dream was over. Really, though, was being a *bean sidhe* any weirder than being plagued with premonitions of death?

But even if it was true, something didn't fit....

"In the stories there are no male *bean sidhes*."

"I know." Nash scowled and let go of my hand to cross his arms over his chest. "The stories come from what humans know about us, and they only seem to know about the ladies. You girls are pretty hard to miss, with all the screaming and wailing."

"Ha ha." I started to shove him, then froze in the act of raising my arm. I'd just defended—albeit jokingly—a species I claimed not to belong to. Or even believe in.

And that's when it hit me. When the whole thing sank in.

Yes, it sounded crazy. But it felt *right*. And little pieces of it actually made sense, in a way that was more intuitive than logical.

My throat felt swollen, and my eyes began to burn with tears of relief. Being not-human was better than being crazy. And infinitely better than dying of cancer. But most important, having answers—even weird answers—was better than not knowing. Than doubting myself.

"I'm a *bean sidhe?*" Two tears fell before I could banish them, and I wiped the rest away with my sleeve. Nash nodded solemnly, and I repeated it, just to get used to the idea. "I'm a *bean sidhe.*"

Saying it out loud helped that last little bit of certainty slip into place, and I felt my chest loosen. One long breath slipped from my throat, and I sank into the car seat, staring out the windshield at a sunset I barely noticed. A tension I hadn't even felt began to ease through my body.

Nash had given me one answer, but he'd brought to mind dozens of others, and I needed more information. Immediately.

"So why doesn't anyone know about male *bean sidhes?* And if you're a guy, wouldn't that make you more of a male *sidhe?*"

He reached for his drink, and the muscles in his arm shifted beneath skin tinted red in the last rays of sunlight. "Unfortunately, the term was coined by humans, who don't know male *bean sidhes* exist, because we don't wail. We don't get the premonitions."

I frowned. "So what makes you a *bean sidhe?* I mean, how are you different from…humans?" Even having accepted my new identity, it felt weird to refer to myself as other than human.

He leaned against Carter's car-door handle and took another long drink before answering. "We have other abilities. But what I can do won't make much sense to you until you know what you can do."

I shook my head, uncomprehending. "I thought I was a death herald."

"That's what you are, not what you can do. At least, that's not all you can do."

I leaned forward, angling my knee to avoid the gearshift, more curious than I wanted to admit as I waited for the rest of it. But he twisted to peer out his window. "My legs are getting stiff. Let's walk." He pushed his door open without waiting for my reply.

"What?" I demanded, leaning over the console to watch as he stretched in the parking lot, muscles bunching and shifting as he pulled both arms over his head. "You're going to keep me in suspense?"

"No, just in motion." I groaned with impatience, and he ducked into the car to grin at me. "What, you can't walk and talk at the same time?" Then his grin widened and he slammed the door in my face. I had no choice but to follow.

Automatic lights flared to life as I stepped onto the concrete, bathing the entire lot, the adjacent, deserted playground, and part of the pier in a soft yellow glow. I circled the car and gave him my hand when he reached for it. "Fine, I'm walking. Start—"

Nash kissed me, one hand gripping the curve of my left hip, and the rest of my sentence was lost forever. When he finally pulled away, he left me breathing hard and craving things I could barely conceptualize. His gaze met mine from inches away, and

I noticed that his irises were still swirling in the soft yellow light overhead. Or maybe they were swirling again.

Suddenly his eyes didn't seem so strange. And neither did my fascination with them. "So...your eyes?" I whispered when I could speak again, making no move to step back. "Is that part of what male *bean sidhes* do?"

"My eyes?" He frowned and blinked. "The colors are swirling, aren't they?"

"Yeah." I leaned closer for a better look, and since I was so close, anyway, I kissed him back, sucking lightly on his lower lip, then delving deeper. Exhilaration shot through me when he groaned and gripped my waist with both hands. His hands started to slide lower, and I only stepped back when I got scared by the realization that I didn't want him to stop.

"Um..." I cleared my throat and shoved my hands in my pockets, then finally looked up to find him watching me. "Your eyes are beautiful," I said, desperate to bring the conversation back on track. "But don't they kind of clue people in? That you're...not human?"

"Nah." He brushed a chunk of dark hair from his forehead and grinned. "It only happens when I'm experiencing something...um...really intense." I felt myself flush, but he continued as if he hadn't noticed. "A *bean sidhe's* eyes are like a mood ring you can't take off. But you can't read your own, and humans can't see it at all. Just other *bean sidhes*." His held my gaze with an intense look of his own. "Yours are doing it too. More shades of blue than the ocean, swirling like a Caribbean whirlpool."

Oh, lovely. My flush deepened until I thought my cheeks would combust. He could see what I was thinking—what I wanted—in my eyes. But I could see what he wanted too....

"Tell me the rest of it." I turned toward the park with my hands still in my pockets. I wanted to know everything—but mostly I wanted to change the subject.

Nash stepped over a parking bumper and caught up with me

in two strides. "Human lore says that when a *bean sidhe* wails, she's mourning the dead, or the soon-to-be dead, but that's not the whole story." He glanced up to study my profile. "I've seen you hold back your wail twice. What do you remember about the time you let it go?"

I flinched at the memory, reluctant to revisit the event that landed me in the hospital. "It was horrible. Once I let it go, I couldn't pull it back. And I couldn't think about anything else. There was this feeling of total despair, then this awful noise that felt like it just erupted from my throat." I stepped over a landscape timber, then onto the thick bed of wood chips carpeting the playground, and Nash followed. "The scream was in control of me, rather than the other way around. People were staring, and dropping purses and shopping bags to cover their ears. This little girl started crying and clinging to her mom, but I couldn't make it stop. It was the worst day of my life. Seriously."

"My mom says the first time's always rough. Though it doesn't usually get you locked up."

That's right; his mother was a *bean sidhe* too. No wonder she'd stared at me. She probably knew I had no idea what I was.

When we got to the heart of the playground—a massive wooden castle full of towers, and tunnels, and slides—Nash stepped beneath a piece of equipment and reached up for the first monkey bar beam. "Were you watching the pre-departed when he actually…departed?"

I raised an eyebrow in dark amusement, trying not to stare at the triceps clearly displayed beneath the snug, short sleeves of his tee. "Pre-departed?"

He grinned. "It's a technical term."

"Aah. No, I wasn't looking at anything." I sank onto a low tire swing held up by three chains, rocking back and forth slowly, trying to forget the words even as I spoke them. "I was trying to make the screeching stop. Mall Security called my aunt and uncle, and when I couldn't stop crying, they took me to the hospital."

Nash let go of the bar and settled onto the rubber-coated steps of a nearby slide, watching me from a couple of feet away. "Well, if you'd looked at the other guy, you would have seen the deceased's soul. Hovering."

"Hovering?"

"Yeah. Souls are fundamentally attracted to a *bean sidhe's* wail, and as long as it lasts, they can't move on. They just kind of hang there, suspended. You remember sirens in mythology? How their song could draw a sailor to his death?"

"Yeah…?" And that image did nothing to ease the apprehension now swelling inside me like heartburn.

"It's like that. Except the people are already dead. And they aren't usually sailors."

"Wow." I put my feet down to stop the tire from rocking. "I'm like flypaper for the soul. That's…weird. Why would anyone want to do that? Suspend some poor guy's soul?"

Nash shrugged and stood to pull me up. "Lots of reasons. A *bean sidhe* who knows what she's doing can hold on to a soul long enough for him to prepare for the afterlife. Let him make his peace."

I frowned, unable to picture it. "Okay, but how peaceful can it possibly be, with me screaming bloody murder?"

He laughed again, and I followed him up the steps to a wobbly bridge made of wooden planks chained loosely together. "It doesn't sound like screaming to the soul. Or to me either. Your wail is beautiful to male *bean sidhes*." Nash turned to look at me from the top step, his gaze soft, and almost reflective. "More like a wistful, haunting song. I wish you could hear it the way we hear it."

"Me too." Anything would be better than the earsplitting screech I heard. "What else can I do? Tell me the parts that don't make me want to dig my own ears out of my skull."

Nash pulled me onto the bridge, which rocked beneath us until I sat in the middle with my legs dangling over the side. "You can keep a soul around long enough for him to hear the thoughts and condolences of his friends. Or say goodbye to his family, though they can't hear him."

"So I'm…useful?" My pitch rose in earnest hope.

"Totally." He settled onto the next plank, facing my profile with one leg hanging over the edge of the bridge and the other arching behind me.

My smile swelled, as did the warmth spreading throughout my chest, slowly overtaking my unease at the very thought of suspending a human soul. I wasn't sure whether this blossoming peace stemmed from my newfound purpose in life—and in death—or from the way Nash watched me, like he'd do anything to make me smile.

"So what can you do?"

"Well, my vocal cords aren't as powerful as yours, but a male *bean sidhe's* voice does carry a kind of…Influence. A strong power of suggestion, or projection of emotion." He shrugged and draped one arm over the rope railing, leaning back to see me better. "We can project confidence, or excitement. Or any other emotion. A bunch of us together can urge groups into action, or pacify a mob. That one was big during the witch trials, and public panics of old." He grinned. "But mostly, we just relax people when they're nervous, or upset." Nash shot me a meaningful look, and I sucked in a startled breath so big I nearly choked on it.

"You calmed me, didn't you? In the alley behind Taboo."

"And behind the school, this afternoon. With Meredith…"

How could I not have realized? I'd never been able to control the panic before, without putting distance between myself and… the pre-deceased.

I blinked back grateful tears and started to thank him, but he spoke before I could get the words out. "Don't worry about it. It was cool to finally get to show off."

"And there's more, other than the Influence?"

He nodded, and the bridge rocked as he leaned forward, eyeing me dramatically. "I can direct souls."

"What?" Chill bumps popped up beneath my sleeves, in spite of the unseasonably warm evening.

Nash shrugged, like it was no big deal. "You can suspend a soul, and I can manipulate it. Tell it where to go."

"Seriously? Where do you send it?" I couldn't wrap my mind around the concept.

"Nowhere." He leaned back against the rope and frowned. "That's the problem. Your skills are useful. Altruistic, even. Mine…? Not so much."

"Why not?"

"Because there's only one place to send a disembodied soul."

"The afterlife?" I folded one leg beneath the other and twisted to face him, trying not to be completely overwhelmed by the possibilities he was throwing at me.

He shook his head as a cicada's song began in the distance. "A soul doesn't need me for that."

And suddenly I understood. "You can put it back! Into the *body*." I sat up straight and the bridge swayed. "You can bring someone back to life!"

Nash shook his head, still somber in spite of my growing enthusiasm, and stood to pull me up. "It takes two of us. A female to capture the soul, and a male to reinstate it." His hand found my hip again, and the heat behind his gaze nearly scorched me. "We could be amazing together, Kaylee."

My cheeks blazed.

Then the reality of what he was saying truly hit me, like a blast of cold air to the face.

"We can save people? Reverse death? You should have told

me that part first!" A tingly exhilaration blossomed in my chest, and at first I didn't understand when he shook his head.

But then my excitement withered, replaced by a cold, heavy feeling of regret. Of mounting guilt. "So not only did I fail to warn Meredith, I let her die, when we could have saved her. Why didn't you tell me?" I couldn't stop the flash of anger that realization brought. Meredith would still be alive if I'd known how to help her!

"No, Kaylee." Nash tilted my chin up until I saw the dark regret swirling in his eyes. "We can't just go around shoving souls back into dead bodies. It doesn't work like that. You can't even warn someone of his own death. It's physically impossible, because you can't do anything else while you're singing a soul's song. Right?"

I nodded miserably. "It's completely consuming…." Though I still couldn't imagine that horrible screech sounding like the song he'd described. "But there has to be a way around that." I sidestepped him on the wobbly bridge and took the steps two at a time. My mind was racing and I needed to move. "We could work out some kind of signal or something. When I get a pre-monition, I could point, and you could go warn the… um… pre-deceased."

Nash caught up with me, already shaking his head again. He caught my arm and pulled me to a halt, but let go when I stiffened. "Even if you could warn someone, it wouldn't change anything. It would just make the poor guy's last moments terrifying." I started to shake my head, but he rushed on. "That's what I've been trying to tell you, Kaylee. You can't stop death."

"But you just said we could." I leaned against the side of a green plastic twisty-slide, frowning up at him. "Together, we could have saved Meredith. Maybe even Heidi Anderson. Doesn't it bother you that we didn't even try?"

"Of course it does, but saving Meredith wouldn't have stopped her death. It would only have prolonged her life. And reanimating someone whose time has come carries serious consequences. And believe me, the price isn't worth paying."

"What does that mean?" How could saving someone not be worth the price?

Nash's gaze burned into me, as if to underline the importance of what he was going to say. "A life for a life, Kaylee. If we'd saved Meredith, someone else would have been taken instead. Could be one of us, or anyone nearby."

Ouch.

I sank onto the rubber mat at the base of the slide, my eyes closed in horror. Okay, that was a high price. And even if I'd been willing to pay it myself, I had no right to make that decision for an innocent bystander. Or for Nash. Yet I couldn't let the issue go. No matter what he said, no matter how logical the arguments, letting Meredith die felt wrong, and I couldn't stand the thought of ever having to do that again.

Nash sighed and sank onto the mat with me, his arms propped on his knees. "Kaylee, I know how you feel, but that's the way death works. When someone's time comes, he has to go, and you'll only drive yourself crazy looking for loopholes in the system. Trust me." The anguish in Nash's voice resonated in my heart, and I ached to touch him. To ease whatever grief lent such pain to his words.

"You've tried, haven't you?" I whispered. He nodded, and I leaned over to let my mouth meet his, lingering when the contact shot sparks through my veins. I wanted to hold him, to somehow make it all better. "Who was it?"

"My dad."

Stunned, I leaned back to see his face, and the hurt I found there seemed to leach through me, leaving me cold with dread. "What happened?"

Nash exhaled slowly and leaned back against the side of the slide. Light from the streetlamp above played on his hand when he rubbed his forehead, as if to fend off the memory. "He fell off a ladder trying to paint the shutters on a second-story window and hit his head on some bricks bordering my mom's flower bed. She was pruning the bushes when he fell, so she saw it happen."

"Where were you?" I spoke softly, afraid he'd stop talking if my voice shattered his memories.

"In the backyard, but I came running when she screamed. When I got there, she was crying, holding his head on her lap. There was blood all over her legs. Then my dad stopped breathing, and she started singing.

"It was beautiful, Kaylee." His words grew urgent and he sat straighter, like he was trying to convince me. "Eerie and sad. And there was his soul, just kind of hanging above them both. I tried to guide it. I didn't really know what I was doing, but I had to try to save him. But he made me stop. His soul… I could hear it. He said he had to go, and I should take care of my mom. He said she would need me, and he was right. She felt guilty because she'd asked him to paint the shutters. She hasn't been the same since."

I didn't realize I was holding my breath until I had to take the next one. "How old were you?"

"Ten." His eyes closed. "My dad's was the first soul I ever saw, and I couldn't save him. Not without killing someone else, and he wouldn't let me risk my own life. Or my mom's." He opened his eyes to stare at me intently. "And he was right about that too, Kaylee. We can't take an innocent life to spare someone who's supposed to die."

He'd get no argument from me there. But… "What if Meredith wasn't supposed to die? What if it wasn't her time?"

"It was. That's how it works." Nash's voice held the conviction of a child professing belief in Santa Claus. He was a little too sure, as if the strength of his assertion could make up for some secret doubt.

"How do you know?"

"Because there are schedules. Official lists. There are people who make sure death is carried out the way it's supposed to be."

I blinked at him, eyes narrowed in surprise. "Are you serious?"

"Unfortunately." A breeze of bitterness swept across his face, but it was gone before I was even sure it was there in the first place.

"That sounds so…bureaucratic."

He shrugged. "It's a very well-organized system."

"Every system has flaws, Nash." He started to disagree, but I rushed on. "Think about it. Three girls have died in the same area in the past three days, each with no known cause. They all just fell over dead. That's not the natural order of things. It's the very definition of 'unnatural.' Or at least 'suspicious.'"

"It's definitely unusual," he admitted. Nash rubbed his temples again and suddenly sounded very tired. "But even if they weren't supposed to die, there's nothing we can do about it without getting someone else killed."

"Okay…" I couldn't argue with that logic. "But if someone isn't meant to die, does the penalty for saving him still apply?"

Nash looked shocked suddenly, as if that possibility had never occurred to him. "I don't know. But I know someone who might."

10

"So who's this Tod?" I slurped the last of my soda, watching as passing headlights briefly illuminated his features, then abandoned him to short stretches of shadow. It was like rediscovering him with each beam of light that found his face, and I couldn't stop watching.

"He works second shift at the hospital." Nash flicked his blinker on as he made a left-hand turn.

"Doing what?"

"Tod's…an intern." He took another left, and Arlington Memorial lay before us on the right, the mirrored windows of the new surgical tower reflecting the streetlights back at us.

I gathered the wrappers from our meal and shoved them into the paper sack on the floorboard between my feet. "I didn't know interns had set schedules."

Nash turned into the dimly lit parking garage and glanced in both directions, looking for an empty spot near the entrance. But he was also obviously avoiding my eyes. "He's not exactly a medical intern."

"What is he, then? Exactly."

An empty space appeared at the end of the first level, and he pulled into it, taking more care with Carter's car than he had with his mother's. Then he shifted into Park and killed the engine before turning to face me fully. "Kaylee, Tod isn't human either. And he's not exactly a friend, so he may not be eager to answer our questions."

I crossed my arms over my chest and tried to look irritated, which wasn't easy, considering that every time he looked at me like that, like there was nothing else in the world worth looking at, my heart beat harder and my breath caught in my throat. "A non-human non-friend? Who works at the hospital as a non-medical intern?" At least it wasn't another football player. "Now that we're clear on what he's *not,* care to tell me what he *is?*"

Nash sighed, and I knew from the sound that I wasn't going to like whatever he had to say. "He's a grim reaper."

"He's a what?" Surely I'd heard him wrong. "Did you just say Tod's the Grim Reaper?"

Nash shook his head slowly, and I exhaled in relief. *Bean sidhes* were one thing—we could actually help people—but I was not ready to face the walking, talking personification of Death. Much less ask him questions.

"He's not *the* Grim Reaper," Nash said, watching me closely. "He's only *a* reaper. One of thousands. It's just a job."

"Just a job? Death is just a job! Wait…" I sucked in a deep breath and closed my eyes. Then I counted to ten. When that wasn't enough, I counted to thirty. Then I met Nash's gaze, hoping panic didn't show in the probably swirling depths of mine. "So…when you said you can't stop death, what you really meant is that you can't stop Tod?"

"Not him specifically, but yes, that's the general idea. Reapers have a job to do, just like everyone else. And as a whole, they're not very fond of *bean sidhes.*"

"Do I even want to know why not?"

Nash smiled sympathetically and took my hand, and my pulse jumped at even such small contact. *Crap.* I could already see that any future anger at him was going to be very hard to sustain. "Most reapers don't like us because we have the potential to seriously screw up their workday. Even if we don't actually restore a person's soul, a reaper can't touch it so long as you hold it. So every second you spend singing means a one-second delay in the delivery of that soul. In a busy district, that could throw him disastrously behind schedule. Also, it just plain pisses them off. Reapers don't like anyone else playing with their toys."

Great. "So not only am I not-human, but Death is my arch foe?" *Who, me? Panic?* "Anything else you want to tell me, while we're confessing?"

Nash tried to stifle a chuckle, but failed. "Reapers aren't our enemies, Kaylee. They just don't particularly enjoy our company."

Something told me the feeling would be mutual. I gave him a shaky nod, and Nash opened the driver's side door and stepped into the dark parking garage. I got out on the other side, and as I closed the door, he clicked a button on Carter's key chain to lock the car. Both sounds reverberated around us, and by all appearances, we were alone in the garage. Which was good, considering the discussion we were in the middle of.

"So what does Tod look like? Whitewashed skeleton skulking around in a black cape and hood? Carrying a scythe? 'Cause I'm thinking that would cause mass panic in the hospital."

He took my hand as we made our way down the aisle toward the garage entrance, footsteps echoing eerily. "Do you chase after funeral processions in a long, dirty dress, hair trailing behind you in the wind?"

I shot him a mock frown. "Have you been following me again?"

Nash rolled his eyes. "He looks normal—not that it matters. You can't see a reaper unless he wants to be seen."

A warm, late-September wind blew through the garage

entrance, fluttering flyers stuck to windshields and fast-food wrappers scattered across the concrete. "Will Tod want us to see him?"

"Depends on what kind of mood he's in." Nash walked past the huge revolving door in favor of the heavy glass pane, which he pulled open for me to pass through into the tiny vestibule. I held the next door for him, and we stepped into a small, quiet lobby lined with empty, uncomfortable-looking armchairs. The warmth of the building was a relief, and my goose bumps faded with each step we took away from the door.

Nash ignored the volunteer at the help desk—not that it mattered; she was asleep at her post—and guided me toward a bank of elevators at the end of the hall.

My shoes squeaked on the polished floor, and each breath brought with it a whiff of antiseptic and pine-scented air freshener. Either would have been bad enough on its own, and together they threatened to overwhelm both my nose and my lungs. Fortunately the elevator on the left stood empty and open.

Inside, Nash pushed the button for the third floor. When the doors closed, the "welcome" scent faded, replaced immediately by the generic hospital smell, a combination of stale air, cafeteria meat loaf, and bleach.

"Tod works on the third level?" I asked as gears grinded overhead and the elevator began to rise.

"He works all over the hospital, but Intensive Care is on three, and that's where we're most likely to find him. Assuming he wants to be found."

A new chill went through me as his statement sank in. We were most likely to find Tod in Intensive Care—where people were most likely to be dying.

My palms began to sweat, and my heart pounded so hard I was sure Nash could hear it echo in the elevator. What were the chances I'd make it through the ICU without finding a soul to sing for?

Slim to none, I was betting. And since we were already in the hospital, if I freaked out this time, they'd probably put me on the express gurney to the mental-health ward. Do not pass Go. Do not collect two hundred dollars.

I was *not* going back there.

My hand clenched Nash's, and he stroked my fingers with his thumb. "If you feel it starting, just squeeze my hand and I'll get you out." I started to shake my head, and he ran the fingers of his free hand down the side of my face, staring into my eyes. "I promise."

I sighed. "Okay." He'd already helped me through two panic attacks—I couldn't stop thinking of them as such—and I had no doubt he could do it again. And, anyway, I didn't really have any choice. I couldn't help the next victim of an untimely death without finding Tod-the-reaper, and I couldn't find Tod without checking all his favorite haunts.

The elevator dinged, and the door slid open with a soft *shhh* sound. I glanced at Nash, bolstering my courage as I straightened my spine. "Let's get this over with."

The third floor stretched out to either side of us, and one long, sterile white hall opened up directly across from the elevator doors, where a man and a woman in matching blue scrubs sat behind a big circular nurses' station. The man looked up when my shoes squeaked on the floor, but the woman didn't notice us.

Nash nodded toward the left-hand hallway, and we headed that way, walking slowly, pretending to read the names written on disposable nameplates outside each door. We were just two kids hoping to pay respects to our grandfather one last time. Except that we didn't "find" him on the chosen hallway, or anywhere else on the third floor, which was almost a letdown after my initial fear of entering the ICU. Fortunately, Arlington wasn't that big of a town, and only three of the beds in Intensive Care were actually occupied. And none of those occupants was in any immediate danger of meeting a reaper.

Tod was also absent from the fourth, fifth, and sixth floors, at least as far as we could tell. The only places left to look were the surgical tower, the emergency room on the first floor, and the maternity ward, on two.

I did *not* want to find a grim reaper—even if he didn't carry a scythe—in the maternity ward, and we would definitely be noticed in the surgical tower. So we checked the ER first.

During my one previous trip to Arlington Memorial, my aunt and uncle had called ahead, and the mental-health ward had been expecting us, which meant we didn't have to stop in the ER. So I'd never seen one in person until Nash and I crossed the front lobby and pushed through the double doors into the emergency waiting area. I have, however, spent plenty of time in the psychiatric unit, which is no trip to Disneyland. It's populated with nurses who look at you with either pity or contempt, and patients in slippers who either won't meet your eyes or won't look away. But the ER holds its own special brand of misery.

Far from the energetic rush of adrenaline I'd expected based on certain television hospital dramas, the actual emergency room was quiet and somber. Patients waited in thinly cushioned chairs lining the walls and grouped in the middle of the long room, their faces twisted into grimaces of pain, fear, or impatience.

One old woman languished in a wheelchair beneath a thread-bare blanket, and several feverish children shivered in their mothers' arms. Men in work clothes pressed crusted gauze bandages to wounds seeping blood, or ice packs to purple lumps on their heads. At the far end of the room near the triage desk, a teenager moaned and clutched one arm to her chest as her mother thumbed through an old tabloid, blatantly ignoring her.

Every few minutes, employees in scrubs entered through one end of the room, crossed the faded, dingy vinyl tile, and pushed through a set of double doors on the other end. Those alone read from charts or stared straight ahead, while those in pairs broke the grim near-silence with incongruous snatches of casual conversation. Regardless, the employees went out of their way to avoid eye contact with the people waiting, while the patients eyed them in hope so transparent it was uncomfortable for me to watch.

"Do you see him?" I whispered to Nash, skipping over the sick women and children to scan the faces of the men.

"No, and we won't until he's ready to be seen."

I stuffed my hands in my pockets, physically resisting the urge to take his hand for comfort, just because the ER creeped me out. If I couldn't handle the huddled masses staring into space like zombies, how could I hope to face the Grim Reaper? Or even *a* grim reaper? "So how are we supposed to find him?"

"The plan was for him to find us," he whispered back. "Two *bean sidhes* walking around while he's trying to work should have drawn him out pretty quickly, if for no other reason than to run us off."

"Then I'm guessing he's decided not to show."

"Looks that way." Nash's gaze settled on a sign on the wall, which pointed the way to the gift shop, the cafeteria, and the radiology lab. "You thirsty?"

"Not really." I'd polished off a thirty-two-ounce soda in the car, and would have to find a bathroom soon as it was.

"Then come sit with me. If we make it clear we have all night to wait, he'll probably show up to hurry us along."

"But we don't have all—"

"Shh." Smiling, he slid one arm around my waist and whispered into my ear. "Don't tip our hand." Pleasant chills rushed down my neck and throughout my body, originating where his breath brushed my earlobe.

We followed the signs down the hall, around the corner, and into the cafeteria, which was still serving dinner at seven-thirty in the evening. Nash bought a huge slice of chocolate cake and a school-size carton of milk. I got a Coke. Then we chose a small square table in one corner of the nearly empty room.

Nash sat with his back to the wall, eating as if nothing were wrong. As if he went looking for an agent of death every evening. But I couldn't sit still. My gaze roamed the room, skimming over a custodian emptying a trash can and a woman in a hairnet inspecting the salad bar for wilted lettuce. My feet bounced on the floor, my knees hitting the underside of the table over and over. Nash's milk sloshed with each impact, but he didn't seem to notice.

He was halfway through his cake—minus the bite or two I'd found room for—when a shadow fell across our table. I looked up to find a young man standing in front of the empty chair on my right. He wore faded, baggy jeans and a short-sleeved white tee with no sign of a coat, in spite of the temperature outside. And his fierce expression did nothing to harden cherubic lips and bright blue eyes, crowned by a mop of blond curls.

Nash didn't even look up.

I glanced at the blond guy, then followed his gaze to the disposable salt-and-pepper shakers in the center of the table. Assuming he wanted to borrow them, I was reaching for the salt when he pulled the empty chair out and dropped into it, crossing bare forearms on the table in front of him.

"What do you want?" he growled in a pitch so low and gravelly I would have sworn it could never have come from such an angelic face.

Nash took his time chewing, then finally swallowed and pushed his plate back. "Answers."

I frowned, gaping at the blond in disbelief. "You're the grim reaper?"

Tod glanced at me for the first time, his frown practically etched into place. "You were expecting someone older? Taller? Maybe kind of gaunt and skeletal?" Contempt dripped from his words like acid, and his focus snapped back to Nash in annoyance. "See? That's the problem with the old title. I should start calling myself a 'collections agent' or something like that."

"Then they'd just make you wear a suit and tie," I said, amused by the mental image.

The corner of Nash's mouth twitched.

"Who's the sidekick?" Tod tossed his head my way, but his attention—and irritation—remained focused on Nash.

"We need to know about the exchange rate," Nash said, cutting me off before I could introduce myself.

Tod's brows gathered low over shadowed blue eyes, and in the gleam from the fluorescent bulbs overhead, I noticed a short, pale goatee on the end of his strong, square chin. "Do I look like the information desk to you?"

"You look...bored." A mischievous look spread over Nash's face as Tod's scowl deepened, and I wondered what I was missing. "The hospital not keeping you busy? Hey, I hear there's an opening at Colonial Manor. You liked it there, didn't you?"

"The nursing home?" I asked, but neither of them even glanced at me; they were too busy glaring at each other. "Why would a nursing home hire someone to kill its patients? For that matter, why would a hospital?"

Nash chuckled and ran one hand through his head full of messy brown spikes, but Tod's eyes flicked my way, and his jaw tightened. "Does she come with a mute button?"

"He doesn't work *for* the hospital," Nash said, ignoring the reaper's hopefully rhetorical question. "He works *in* the hospital. And at this rate, he'll be stuck here for the next century, at least. Right, Tod?"

The reaper didn't answer, but I could hear his teeth grinding.

"You know, if you keep bottling up your anger like that, you're not going to be anywhere a century from now, much less still working full-time." Wait, was I needling an agent of death? *Probably not the best idea, Kaylee...*

"Reapers don't age," Tod snapped at me, while still glaring at Nash. "It's one of the fringe benefits."

"Like us, right?" I glanced at Nash just in time to see him flinch, and knew I'd said something wrong. And when I looked at Tod again, I found him staring at me in surprise, an impish grin highlighting his angelic features like light from above.

"Where'd you find her?"

"We do age," Nash said, but the last word was clipped short, like he'd almost said my name, then left it out at the last minute. And that's when I understood: he didn't want Tod to know who I was.

I was fine with that. The very idea of Death knowing my name made my skin crawl. Even if this particular Death was only one of many, and almost too pretty to look at.

"We just age very slowly," Nash continued.

By then I was blushing furiously; I'd just painted myself as a complete fool. What kind of idiot doesn't know the lifespan of her own species?

Nash hooked his foot around my ankle beneath the table, rubbing my leg in sympathy and comfort. I shot him a grateful smile and made myself meet Tod's eyes boldly. The best way to even the playing field was to knock him down a peg. "Why are you stuck here?" I asked, hoping I'd correctly assessed that as his sore spot.

"Because he's a rookie." Nash smirked. "And there isn't much opportunity for advancement in a line of work where the employees never die."

"You're a rookie?" I looked at Tod again, and again his jaw bulged with irritation. "How old are you?" I'd assumed, based on that "ageless" comment, that he was much older than he looked.

"He's seventeen," Nash said, his smirk still firmly in place.

"I was seventeen when I started this job," the reaper snapped. "But that was two years ago."

"You've been doing this for two years and you're still a rookie?"

Tod looked insulted, and I wasn't sure whether to laugh or apologize. "Yeah, well, my recruiter wasn't very concerned with truth in advertising. And your boyfriend here is right about the turnover rate—it's nonexistent. The senior reapers in this district are edging up on two hundred years old. If we hadn't lost one last year, I'd still be sitting in the TV room at Colonial Manor, waiting for old men to keel over into their oatmeal."

"Wait, how do you lose a reaper?" I couldn't help but ask. "Freak sickle accident?" But no one else looked amused by my joke.

"The less you know about reaper business, the better," Nash whispered, and Tod nodded arrogantly.

Oh. I held both hands up in defense and leaned back in my chair. "Sorry. So…old men keeling into their oatmeal…?"

Tod shrugged. "Yeah. But at least here I get the occasional gunshot victim or unexpected relapse. Life's all about the surprises, right?"

"I guess." But surprises had kind of lost their novelty for me with the discovery that I wasn't human. Except for that whole fatal premonition thing. I'd love to be caught off guard by death again, like normal people.

Well, not by my own death, of course.

"Speaking of surprises…" Twisting the lid off my Coke, I glanced at Nash for a signal, and he nodded, telling me to continue. Evidently I wasn't imagining Tod's willingness to talk to me, rather than to him. "We need your help avoiding a really nasty one."

Tod made a show of glancing at his wrist, conspicuously absent of a watch. "You two have already wasted my whole break. I have an aneurism on the fourth floor in ten minutes, and I can't be late. I hate the ones that linger."

"This won't take long." I pinned him with my gaze, refusing to break contact once I saw him hesitate. "Please."

The reaper sighed, running one hand through his mop of short curls. "You have five minutes."

I breathed softly in relief. Until the reality of the situation sank in.

Had I just begged for an audience with Death?

11

"This is about the exchange rate?" the reaper asked, drawing me out of my own head, where shock over the events of the past couple of hours was finally catching up with me.

When I didn't answer, Nash nodded.

The reaper shrugged and slouched back into his chair. "You know as much as I do about that. A life for a life."

Nash glanced at me with both brows raised, to ask if I was okay. I nodded, drawing my thoughts back into focus, and he leaned forward with his arms crossed on the table. "But that's the penalty for saving someone on your list, right? Someone who's *supposed* to die."

"You're not 'saving' anyone." Tod scowled—we'd obviously found his hot button. "You're stealing souls, which only delays the inevitable. And throws my whole shift off schedule. And hurls my boss into all new realms of pissed-off. And you don't even want to know about the paperwork involved in even a simple, equal exchange."

"I'm not—" Nash started, but Tod cut him off.

"But beyond all that, it's illegal. Thus the penalty."

I screwed the lid back onto my bottle and pushed it toward

the middle of the table. "But does the penalty still apply if we save someone who wasn't supposed to die?"

Tod's forehead wrinkled in confusion, then his expression went suddenly blank, leaving a cold comprehension shining in his eyes. "Shit like that doesn't happen here—"

"Come off it, Tod." Nash eyed the reaper intently, old pain etched into the lines of his frown. "You owe me the truth."

But Tod went on as if he hadn't been interrupted. "—and even if it did, you'd never know it, because no reaper could afford to admit he accidently took the wrong soul."

"We're not talking about an accident." I glanced up when the cafeteria doors flew open and a woman entered with three kids in tow, reminding me for the first time since Tod had joined us that we were discussing very odd things in a very public place.

"What about the list? Wouldn't that prove it if someone wasn't supposed to die?" Nash whispered now in concession to our new company.

Tod scrubbed his face with both hands, clearly frustrated and losing patience with our questions. "Probably, but you'd never get your hands on the list. And even if you could, it'd be too late. The penalty would already have been applied."

"Are you seriously saying a reaper would take an innocent life in exchange for a soul he shouldn't have claimed in the first place?" Indignation burned hot in my veins. If any process in the world was free from corruption, it should have been death. After all, wasn't death the great equalizer?

Or was that taxes?

"No, you're right." Tod gave me a halfhearted nod. "In theory, the penalty shouldn't apply in a case like that. But theory and reality don't always coexist where death is concerned. So even if you could get your hands on the right list, and even if you were right about the reaper's…mistake, chances are that an innocent soul would already have been taken. Or one of your own."

I couldn't help noticing he didn't put us in the "innocent" category.

"So we're screwed either way." Exasperated, I tossed my hands into the air and leaned back in my chair, closing my eyes.

"What's this about, anyway?" Tod asked, and I opened my eyes to find him watching me in…was that interest? "Who are you trying to save?"

"We don't know. Probably no one." Nash poked at the last bite of cake with his fork, smearing chocolate frosting across the paper plate. "Several girls have died in our area recently, and Ka—" He stopped, omitting my name from the sentence at the last second. "She—" he nodded in my direction "—thinks their deaths are suspicious."

"'She' does, huh?" A grin tugged at the corner of the young reaper's mouth, and I could practically hear the gears turning in his head. "What's suspicious about them?"

"They were all teenagers. They were all very pretty. They all died the same way. They were all in good health. They each died a day apart." I ticked the facts off on my fingers as I spoke, and when I'd used up one hand, I showed it to him. "Take your pick. But either way, that's too many coincidences. There's *no* way all three of them were supposed to die, and I don't care whose list they were on."

The gleam of interest in Tod's eyes told me I'd recaptured his attention. "You think they were killed?"

I tapped one foot on the sticky floor, trying to sort out my thoughts. "I don't know. Maybe, but if so, I have no idea how. All but the first one died in front of witnesses, who saw nothing suspicious. Other than a beautiful girl keeling over with no warning."

"There are ways to make that happen, of course." Tod half stood and walked his chair closer to the table, then sank back into it. "But even if they were killed, that doesn't change anything. Murder victims are on the master list every day. I've only had one in two years, but the senior reapers get them on a weekly basis."

I felt my eyes go wide, and a heavy, tight feeling gripped my chest. "You mean people are *supposed* to be killed?" For a moment, true horror eclipsed the determination and fear already warring inside me. How could murder be a part of the natural order?

Tod shook his head. "People are supposed to die, and the specifics vary widely. Including murder."

I turned on Nash, blinking back the angry tears burning my eyes. "So what's the point of all this? If I can't change it, why do I have to know about it?"

Nash took my hand. "She's having trouble letting them go," he said, and Tod nodded as if he understood.

"What do you know about it?" I snapped, beyond caring that none of this was the reaper's fault. Or that I probably should have been scared of him. "You take lives for a living." As ironic as that sounded... "Death is an everyday occurrence for you."

Nash huffed, and a satisfied look hovered on the edge of his expression. "Yeah, and you'd never know from listening to him now that he had so much trouble with it at first."

"Watch it, Hudson," Tod growled, bright blue eyes going icy.

A new look flitted across Nash's features—some combination of amusement and mischief. "Tell her about the little girl."

"Do you have some kind of disorder? Some synapse misfiring up there—" he gestured vaguely toward Nash's head "—that makes you incapable of keeping your mouth shut? Or are you just a garden-variety fool?"

"What girl?" I ignored both the reaper's outburst and the *bean sidhe's* satisfied half smile.

"It'll help her understand," Nash said when it became clear that Tod wasn't going to respond.

"Understand what?" I demanded, glancing from one to the other. And finally Tod sighed, still glaring at Nash.

"He's just trying to make me look like an idiot," the reaper snapped. "But I have stories that make him look even worse, so keep that in mind, soul snatcher, next time you go shooting off your mouth."

Nash shrugged, obviously unbothered by the threat, and Tod twisted in his chair to face me fully. "At first, I wasn't too fond of my job. The whole thing seemed pointless and sad, and just plain wrong at times. Once I actually refused an assignment and nearly got myself terminated. I'm guessing that's what he wants you to hear."

Nash nodded on the edge of my vision, but I kept my focus on the reaper. "Why would you refuse an assignment?"

Tod exhaled in frustration. Or maybe embarrassment. "I was working at the nursing home, and this little girl came with her parents to visit her grandmother. She choked on a peppermint her grandma's roommate gave her, and she was supposed to die. She was on the list—all official. But when the time came, I couldn't do it. She was only three. So when a nurse showed up and gave her the Heimlich, I let her live."

"What happened?" My heart ached for the little girl, and for Tod, whose job conflicted with every ounce of compassion in my body. And in his, evidently.

"My boss got pissed when I came back without her soul. He took her grandmother's instead, and when a shift opened up at the hospital, he passed me over and gave it to someone else." Anger darkened his eyes. "I was stuck at the nursing home for nearly three more years before he finally moved me over here. And there's no telling how long it'll be before I move up again."

"But don't you think it was worth it?" I couldn't help asking. "The grandmother had already lived her life, but the little girl was just starting. You saved her life!"

The reaper shook his head slowly, blond curls glimmering in the light overhead. "It wasn't an even exchange. From the moment she was supposed to die, that little girl was living on borrowed time. Her grandmother's time. When you make an exchange, what you're really doing is trading one person's death date for another's. That little girl died six months later, on the day her grandmother was originally scheduled to go."

That time I couldn't stop the tears. "How can you stand it?" I wiped at my eyes angrily with the napkin Nash handed me, glad I wasn't wearing much mascara.

Tod glanced at Nash, then his expression softened when he turned back to me. "It's easier now that I'm used to it. But at the time, I had to learn to trust the list. The master list is like the script from a play—it shows every word spoken by every actor, and the show keeps going so long as no one deviates from it."

"But that does happen, right?" I wadded the napkin into a tight ball. "Even if the list is infallible, the people aren't. A reaper could deviate from the list, like you did with the little girl, right?"

Nash shifted in his seat, drawing our attention before Tod could answer. "You think those girls died in place of people who were actually on the list? That they were exchanges?"

I shook my head. "Three in three days? It's still too much of a coincidence. But if Tod can deviate by not taking a soul, couldn't another reaper deviate by taking an extra one? Or three?"

"No." Tod shook his head firmly. "No way. The boss would notice if someone turned in three extra souls."

I arched one brow at him. "What makes you think he turned them in?"

The reaper's scowl deepened. "You don't know what you're talking about. It's impossible."

"There's a way to find out." Nash eyed me somberly before turning his penetrating gaze on Tod. "You're right—we can't get our hands on the list. But you can."

"No." Tod shoved his chair back and stood. Across the cafeteria, the mother and children looked up, one little boy smeared from ear to ear with chocolate ice cream.

"Sit down!" Nash hissed, glaring up at him.

Tod shook his head and started to turn away from us, so I grabbed his hand. He froze the minute my flesh touched his and turned back to me gradually, as if every movement hurt. "Please." I begged him with my eyes. "Just hear him out."

The reaper slowly pulled his fingers from my grasp, until my hand hung in the air, empty and abandoned. He looked both angry and terrified when he sank back into his seat, now more than a foot from the table.

"We don't need to see the whole thing," Nash began. "Just the part from this weekend. Saturday, Sunday, and today."

"I can't do it." He shook his head again, blond curls bouncing. "You don't understand what you're asking for."

"So tell us." I folded my hands on the table, making it clear that I had time for a long story. Even if I didn't.

Tod exhaled heavily and aimed his answer at me, pointedly ignoring Nash. "You're not talking about just one list. 'Master list' is a misnomer. It's actually lots of lists. There's a new master for every day, and my boss splits that up into zone, then shift. I only see the part for this hospital, from noon to midnight. There's another reaper who works here the other half of the day, and I never see anything on his lists, much less the lists for other zones. It's not like I can just walk up to a coworker and ask to see his old lists. Especially if he's actually reaping 'independently.'"

"He's right. That's too complicated." Nash sighed, closing his eyes. Then he opened them again and looked at me resolutely. "We need the master list."

Tod groaned and opened his mouth to argue, but I beat him to it. "No, we don't. We don't even need to see it."

"What?" Nash frowned, and I raised one finger, asking him silently to wait as I turned back to the reaper.

"I understand that you don't work off the master list, but you've seen it, right? You said there are murder victims on it every week…?"

"Yeah, I see it every now and then." Tod shrugged. "It's all digital now, and my boss keeps it running on his computer all the time, in case he has to adjust anything. I glance at it when I go in his office."

"Okay, that's good." I couldn't resist a small smile. "We don't need to see it. We just need you to look at it and tell us whether or not these three names were there."

Tod leaned forward with his elbows on his knees, cradling his head in his hands. He rubbed his forehead, then took a deep, resigned breath and finally looked up at me. "Where did they die?"

"The first one was in the West End, at Taboo. Heidi…?" Nash glanced at me with his brows arched.

"Anderson," I supplied. "The second was Alyson Baker, at the Cinemark in Arlington, and the third was at East Lake High School, just this afternoon."

"Wait, those are all in different zones." Tod frowned, and the well-defined muscles of his arms tensed as he leaned against the table. "If you really think none of them were supposed to die, you're talking about three different reapers involved in this little conspiracy. Which is starting to sound pretty complicated, by the way."

"Hmm…" I didn't know enough about reapers to know how far-fetched a theory we were talking about, but I did know that the more people who were in on a secret, the harder it was to keep quiet. Tod was right. So…maybe we were only looking for one reaper, after all. "Is there anything keeping one of you guys from operating in someone else's zone?"

"Other than integrity and fear of being caught? No."

Grim reaper integrity…?

"So if a reaper has neither integrity nor fear, there's nothing to stop him from taking out half the state of Texas next time he gets road rage in rush-hour traffic?" I heard my pitch rising, and made myself lower my voice as I screwed the lid off my

Coke. "Don't you guys have to turn in your…um…death ray, or whatever, when you're off the clock?"

Tod's perfect lips quirked up in a quick smile. "Um, no. There's no death ray, though that would be really cool. Reapers don't use any equipment. All we have is an ability to extinguish life and take possession of the soul. But trust me, that's more than enough."

With that, his expression darkened. "In theory, you should never find a reaper without integrity. It's not like we apply for this job to satisfy some kind of massive power hunger. We're recruited, and screened for every psychological condition known to man. No one capable of something like you're talking about should ever find work as a reaper."

"You sound less than confident in the system," I said, watching his face carefully.

He shrugged. "You said it yourself. People aren't infallible, and the system is run by people."

"So can you get a look at the lists?" Nash said, watching Tod almost as closely as I did.

Tod bit his lower lip in thought. "You're talking about three different zones, for three different days—and none of them on the current master list."

"So can you do it?" I repeated, leaning forward in anticipation.

Tod nodded slowly. "It won't be easy, but I like a challenge. So long as it pays off." His blue-eyed gaze zeroed in on me, and something told me he was no longer talking about poking around in his boss's office. "I'll get you what you want to know—in exchange for your name."

"No." Nash didn't even hesitate. "You'll do it because if you don't, we'll hang out here and she'll suspend every soul you try to take until you're so far behind schedule your boss sends you back to the nursing home. If you're lucky."

"Right." Tod smirked now as his gaze shifted from me to

Nash. "She's so green her roots are showing. I bet she's never even seen a soul."

"He's right," I said. Nash snatched my hand from the table and squeezed it hard, begging me silently not to give Tod what he wanted. But I saw no reason not to. My name would be easy to figure out, which made it a cheap price for the information we needed. "My first name is Kaylee. You can have my last name when you give us what we want."

"Deal." Tod stood, beaming as if his face gave off its own glow. "I'll let you know what I find out, but I can't promise it'll be tonight. I'm already late for that aneurism."

I nodded, disappointed but not really surprised.

"Now, if you'll excuse me, I have to go make some poor woman a widow." And with that, he disappeared.

There was no chiming of bells, no twinkling of light. No signal at all that he was about to vanish. He was simply there one moment, and gone the next, with no special—or sound—effects of any kind.

"You didn't tell me he could do that!" I glanced at Nash to find him frowning at the table. "What's wrong?"

"Nothing." He stood and picked up the paper plate still holding his last bite of cake. "Let's go." We threw our trash away on our way out of the cafeteria, and I followed him across the hospital and through the parking garage in silence. *Guess he really didn't want Tod to know my name…*

When we reached the car, Nash followed me to the passenger's side door, where he unlocked and opened it for me. But instead of getting in, I turned to face him and put one hand flat on his chest. "You're mad at me." My heart beat so hard my chest ached. I could feel his heart thumping beneath my palm, and for one horrifying moment, I was sure I'd never get to feel it again. That he would simply drive me home, then vanish from my life like Tod had vanished from the cafeteria.

But Nash shook his head slowly. He was backlit by an

overhead light near the entrance, and his dark hair seemed to glow around the edges. "I'm mad at him. I should have come by myself, but I didn't think he'd be interested in you."

My eyebrows shot up and I stepped to the side to see him better. "Because I'm a shrieking hag?"

Nash pulled me close again and pressed me into the car, then kissed me so deeply I wasn't sure if I was actually breathing. "You have no idea how beautiful you are," he said. "But Tod's been hung up on someone else for a long time, so I thought you'd be safe. I should have known better."

"Why didn't you want him to know my name?"

Nash leaned back to see me better, and the line of his jaw went hard. "Because he's Death, Kaylee. No matter how innocent he looks, or how desperately he clings to the notion that he's some kind of afterlife hero, carting helpless souls from point A to point B, he's still a reaper. One day he might find your name on his list. And while I know that keeping your name a secret won't save you if that happens, I'm not just going to hand over your identity to one of Death's gophers."

"He knows your name." I let my hand trail from his chest down his arm until my fingers curled around his.

"I knew him before he was a reaper."

"You did?" It hadn't occurred to me until then that Tod might have had a normal life once. What were reapers like before they surrounded themselves with death and the dying?

Nash nodded, and I opened my mouth to ask another question, but he laid one finger against my lips. "I don't want to talk about Tod anymore."

"Fair enough," I mumbled against his finger. Then I removed his hand and stepped up on my toes. "I don't want to talk about him either." I kissed him, and my pulse went crazy when he responded. His tongue met mine briefly, then his lips trailed over my chin and down my neck.

"Mmm…" I murmured into his hair, as his tongue flicked

in the hollow of my collarbone. Chill bumps popped up on my arms, and my hands went around his back. My fingers splayed over the material of his shirt. "That feels good."

"You taste good," he whispered against my skin. But before I could respond, an engine growled to life a row away, and light washed over us both, momentarily blinding me. Nash straightened, moaning in frustration as the car across the aisle pulled toward us before turning toward the exit. "I guess I should take you home," he said, shading his face with one hand while the other remained on my arm.

I blinked, trying to clear floating circles of light from my eyes. "I don't want to go home. My entire family has been lying to me my whole life. I don't have anything to say to them."

"Don't you want to know why they've been lying to you?"

I blinked at him, taken by surprise for a moment. I hadn't considered simply confronting them with the truth. They'd *never* see that coming.

A slow smile spread across my face, and I saw it reflected in Nash's. "Let's go."

12

"You're coming in, right?" I asked when Nash shifted into Park but left the engine running.

There wasn't enough light in the driveway for me to truly see his eyes, but I knew he was watching me. "You want me to?"

Did I?

A slim silhouette appeared in the front window: Aunt Val, one hand on her narrow hip, the other holding an oversize mug. They were waiting to talk to me. Or more likely *at* me, because they probably had no intention of telling me the truth, since they didn't know someone else already had.

"Yeah, I do."

It wasn't that I needed him to fight my battles. I was actually looking forward to demanding some long-overdue answers, now that the big lie—aka my entire life—had been exposed.

But I could certainly have used a little moral support.

Nash smiled, his teeth a dim white wedge among shadows, and twisted the key to shut down the engine.

We met at the front of the car and he took my hand, then leaned forward to brush a kiss against the back of my jaw, just below my left ear. Even as I stood in my driveway, knowing my aunt and uncle were waiting, his touch made me shiver in anticipation of more.

I'm not crazy. I knew that now. And I wasn't alone—Nash was like me. Even so, dread was a plastic spork slowly digging out my insides as I pulled open the front door, then the screen. I stepped into the tiled entry and tugged Nash in after me.

My aunt stood in the middle of the floor, a frail mask of reproach poorly disguising whatever stronger, more urgent sentiment peeked out around the edges. My uncle rose from the couch immediately, taking us both in with a single glance. To his credit, the first expression to flit across his features was relief. He'd been worried, probably because I hadn't answered any of the twelve messages he'd left on my silenced cell.

But his relief didn't last long. Now that he knew I was alive, he looked ready to kill me himself.

Uncle Brendon's anger lingered on me, then more than a bit of it transferred when his focus shifted to Nash. "It's late. I'm sure Kaylee will see you at the memorial tomorrow."

Aunt Val only sipped her coffee—or maybe "coffee"—offering me no help.

Nash looked to me for a decision, and my tight grip on his hand demonstrated my resolve. "Uncle Brendon, this is Nash Hudson. I need to ask you some questions, and he's going to stay. Or else I go with him."

My uncle's dark brows drew low and his gaze hardened—but then his eyes went wide in surprise. "Hudson?" He studied Nash more carefully now, and sudden recognition lit his face. "You're Trevor and Harmony's boy?"

What? My gaze bounced between them in confusion. On my left, Aunt Val coughed violently and pounded on her own chest. She'd choked on her "coffee."

"You know each other?" I asked, but Nash looked as clueless as I felt.

"I knew your parents years ago," Uncle Brendon said to Nash. "But I had no idea your mother was back in the area." He shoved both hands into the pockets of his jeans, and the uncertain gesture made my uncle look even younger than usual. "I was so sorry to hear about your father."

"Thank you, sir." Nash nodded, his jaw tense, both his motion and words well practiced.

Uncle Brendon turned back to me. "Your friend's father was…" And that's when it hit him. His face flushed, and his expression seemed to darken. "You told her."

Nash nodded again, holding his gaze boldly. "She has a right to know."

"And obviously neither of you were going to tell me." Aunt Val sank into the nearest armchair and drained her mug, then almost dropped it onto a coaster.

"Well, I can't say this is entirely unexpected. Your dad's already on his way here to explain everything." My uncle's hands hovered at his sides, as if he didn't quite know what to do with them. Then he sighed and nodded to himself, like he'd come to some kind of decision. "Sit down. Please. I'm sure you both have questions."

"Can I get anyone a drink?" Aunt Val rose unsteadily, her empty mug in hand.

"Yeah." I gave her a saccharine smile. "I'll have whatever you're having."

She frowned—for once unconcerned with the wrinkles etched into her forehead—then made her way slowly into the kitchen.

"I'd love some coffee," Uncle Brendon called after her as he sank into the floral-print armchair, but his wife disappeared around the corner with no reply.

I dropped onto the sofa and Nash sat next to me, and in the sudden silence I realized my cousin hadn't come out to interrogate me or flirt with him. And no music came from her room. No sound at all, in fact. "Where's Sophie?"

Uncle Brendon sighed heavily and seemed to sink deeper into the chair. "She doesn't know about any of this. She's asleep."

"Still?"

"Again. Val woke her up for dinner, but she hardly ate anything. Then she took another of those damned pills and went back to bed. I ought to flush the rest of them." He mumbled the last part beneath his breath, but we both heard him.

And I agreed with him wholeheartedly on that one, if on little else at the moment.

Fueling bravado with my smoldering anger, I pinned my uncle with the boldest stare I could manage. "So I'm not human?"

He sighed. "You never were one to beat around the bush."

I only stared at him, unwilling to be distracted by pointless chatter. And when my uncle began to speak, I clutched Nash's hand harder than ever.

"No, technically we're not human," he said. "But the distinction is very minor."

"Right." I rolled my eyes. "Except for all the death and screaming."

"So you're a *bean sidhe* too, right?" Nash interjected, oiling the wheels of discourse with more civility than I could have mustered in that moment. At least one of us was calm….

"Yes. As is Kaylee's father, my brother." Uncle Brendon met my eyes again then, and I knew what he was going to say from the cautious sympathy shining in his eyes. "As was your mother."

This wasn't about my mom. So far as I knew, she'd never lied to me. "What about Aunt Val?"

"Human." She answered for herself, stepping into the living room with a steaming cup of coffee in each hand. She crossed the carpet cautiously and handed one mug to my uncle before sinking carefully into the armchair across from his. "And so is Sophie."

"Are you sure?" Nash frowned. "Maybe she just hasn't had an opportunity for any premonitions yet."

"She was there with Meredith this afternoon," I reminded him.

"Oh, yeah."

"We've known from the moment she was born," my aunt said, as if neither of us had spoken.

"How?" I asked, as she slowly, carefully crossed one leg over the other.

Aunt Val lifted the mug to her lips, then spoke over it. "She cried." She sipped her coffee, her eyes not quite focused on the wall over my head. "Female *bean sidhes* don't cry at birth."

"Seriously?" I glanced at Nash for confirmation, but he only shrugged, apparently as surprised as I was.

Uncle Brendon eyed his wife in mounting concern, then turned back to us. "They may have tears, but a *bean sidhe* never truly screams until she sings for her first soul."

"Wait, that can't be right." I'd cried plenty as a child, hadn't I? Surely at my mother's funeral…?

Okay, I couldn't actually remember much from that age, but I knew for a fact that I'd screamed bloody murder when I rode my bike off the sidewalk and into a rose bush, at eight years old. And again at eleven, when I accidentally ripped a hoop earring through my earlobe with a hairbrush. And again when I'd been dumped for the first time, at fourteen.

How long had I been making fatal predictions, without even knowing it? Had I thrown inconsolable fits in preschool? Or had my youth largely kept me away from death? How long had they been treating me like I was crazy, when they knew what was wrong with me all along?

My spine stiffened, and I felt my cheeks flush in anger. Every answer my uncle provided only brought up more questions, about things I should have known all along. "Why didn't you tell me?" I demanded, teeth clenched to keep me from yelling and waking Sophie up. I'd missed so much. Wasted countless hours doubting my own sanity.

When what I really should have been doubting was my humanity!

"I'm so sorry, Kaylee. I wanted to." Uncle Brendon closed his eyes as if he were gathering his thoughts, then met mine again, and to my surprise, I realized I believed him. "I started to tell you last year, when you were…in the hospital. But your dad asked me not to. The damage was already done, and he hoped we could wait a little longer. At least until you finished high school."

That's what they'd hoped I'd have more time for! Not life, but a normal, human adolescence. A noble thought, but somewhat lacking in the execution…

"I'm surprised your little farce held up this long!" I found myself on the edge of the couch as I spoke, Nash's hand still grasped in mine. He was the only thing keeping me seated as I vented the geyser of anger and resentment threatening to burst through the top of my skull. "How long did you think it would be before I'd run into someone on the verge of death?"

Uncle Brendon shrugged miserably but held my gaze. "Most teenagers never see anyone die. We were hoping you'd be that fortunate, and we could wait and let your dad explain all this… later. When you were ready."

"When I was ready? I was ready last year, when I saw a bald kid in a wheelchair being pushed through the mall in his own private death shroud! You were waiting for *him* to be ready." For my father to finally step up and earn his title.

"She's right, Brendon," Aunt Val slurred, now slumped in her chair, her linen-clad legs splayed gracelessly. I watched her, waiting for more, but turned back to my uncle when she lifted her mug to her mouth instead of speaking.

"Why keep it a secret in the first place?"

"Because you—" Aunt Val began again, gesturing in grand sweeps with her half-empty mug. But my uncle cut her off with a stern look.

"That's for your father to explain."

"It's not like he hasn't had time!" I snapped. "He's had sixteen years."

Uncle Brendon nodded, and I read regret on his face. "I know—we all have. And considering how you wound up figuring it out—" he glanced apologetically at Nash "—I think we were wrong to wait so long. But your dad will be here in the morning, and I'm not going to step on his toes with the rest of it. It's his story to tell."

There was a story? Not just a simple explanation, but an actual story?

"He's really coming?" I'd believe that when I saw him.

Yet my chest tightened, shot through with a jolt of adrenaline at the thought: my dad had answers no one else seemed willing to give me. But I might have known it would take an all-out catastrophe to get him stateside again. He wasn't coming to see me. He was coming to do damage control, before my aunt reversed the charges.

Uncle Brendon frowned at my obvious skepticism—he could probably see it swirling in my eyes. "We called him this afternoon—"

"*I* called him," Aunt Val corrected. "I told him to put his ass on a plane, or I'd…"

"You've had enough." My uncle was on his feet before I could blink, and an instant later he held his wife's mug. She slouched in her chair, eyes wide in sluggish surprise, hand still curved, as if around the cup handle. "I'll get you some fresh coffee." He stopped in the threshold between the living room and dining room, Aunt Val's mug gripped so tightly his knuckles were white. "I'm sorry," he said to Nash. "My wife isn't taking any of this well. She's worried about the girls, and she's a friend of Meredith Cole's mother."

Yeah, but she and Mrs. Cole were gym buddies, not conjoined

twins. And I'd hardly ever seen my aunt drink more than a single glass of wine at a time—she said alcohol had too many calories.

Nash nodded. "My mother would be upset too."

Yeah, but I bet she wouldn't be drowning in brandy....

"How is your mother?"

"She still misses him." Nash glanced at our entwined hands, obviously uncomfortable talking about his own family.

Uncle Brendon's expression softened in sympathy. "Of course she does." Then he turned into the kitchen and let the subject rest.

For a moment, we stared at the carpet in silence, not quite sure what to say next. We'd hit a lull in the single most awkward conversation of my life, and I wasn't exactly eager to pick it back up.

But Aunt Val obviously was. "She wouldn't have liked this." Her gaze was focused on the floor several feet in front of her chair, her arms draped over the sides, hands dangling. I'd never seen her look so...aimless. Limp.

"My mom?" Nash asked, confused, but I knew what she meant. She was talking about *my* mother.

"Wouldn't have liked what?" I asked, curious in spite of my lingering anger. No one ever seemed willing to talk about my mom in front of me.

"If it had gone the other way, she would have told you the truth. But Aiden couldn't face it. He was never as strong as she was." Aunt Val's gaze found me, and I was startled by the sudden clarity in her eyes. The unexpected intensity shining through a glaze of intoxication. "I never met anyone stronger than Darby. I wanted to be just like her until—"

"Valerie!" Uncle Brendon stood frozen in the doorway, a fresh—presumably un-spiked—mug of coffee in one hand.

"Until what?" I glanced from one to the other.

"Nothing. She doesn't know what she's saying." He set the mug on the nearest end table—without a coaster—and crossed the room in a blur of denim, practically exhaling frustration and anxiety. Uncle Brendon lifted his wife from her chair with an arm around her shoulders, and she tottered unsteadily, lending credence to his claim.

Yet despite her wobbly legs, her eyes were steady when they met his, and his silent censure did not escape her notice. But neither did it make her retract her statement. Whatever had just passed between them, it was crystal clear that Aunt Val did in fact know what she was saying.

Uncle Brendon half carried his wife toward the hallway. "I'm going to get her settled in for the night. It was good to meet you, Nash, and please give my best to your mother." He glanced pointedly at me, then at the door.

Evidently visiting hours were over.

"Uncle Brendon?" I had one question that couldn't wait for my father, and I wanted to be holding Nash's hand when I heard the answer, just in case.

My uncle hesitated in the doorway, and Aunt Val laid her head on his shoulder, her eyes already closed. "Yeah?"

I took a deep breath. "What did Aunt Val mean when she said I'm living on borrowed time?"

Comprehension washed over him like waves smoothing out sand on the beach. "You heard us this afternoon?"

I nodded, and my hand tightened around Nash's.

A pained look chased his smile away, and he pulled Aunt Val straighter against him. "That's part of your father's story. Have a little patience and let him tell it. And try to trust me—Val really doesn't know what she's talking about."

I exhaled in disappointment. "Fine." That was the best I was going to get; I could already tell. Fortunately, my father would be there in the morning, and this time I wouldn't let him leave without answering every one of my questions.

"Get some sleep, Kaylee. You too, Nash. With the memorial, tomorrow probably won't be any easier than today was."

We both nodded, and Uncle Brendon lifted Aunt Val into his arms—she was snoring lightly now—and carried her down the hall.

"Wow." Nash whistled as I fell back against the arm of the couch facing him. "How much has she had?"

"No telling. She doesn't drink much, though, so it probably doesn't take much to lay her out cold, and she started this afternoon."

"My mom just bakes when she gets upset. Some weeks I live on brownies and chocolate milk."

I grinned. "Trade ya." Aunt Val would rather shoot herself than touch a stick of real butter, much less a bag of chocolate chips. Her theory was that not knowing how to bake saved her thousands of calories a month.

My theory was that for all the brandy she'd had in the past eight hours, she could have had a whole pan of brownies.

"I like brownies. You're stuck with your aunt."

"Yeah, I figured."

Nash stood, and I followed him to the door, my arm threaded through his. "I gotta get Scott's car back before he calls the cops," he said. I walked him out, and when we stopped by the driver's side door, I wrapped my arms around his waist as his went around my back. He felt sooo good, and the thought that I could touch him anytime I wanted sent a whole flock of butterflies fluttering around in my stomach.

I leaned back against the car, and Nash leaned into me. His mouth met mine, and my lips opened, welcoming him. Feeding from him. When his kisses trailed down my chin to my neck, I let my head fall back, grateful for the night air cooling the heat he brought off me in waves. His lips were hot, and the trail of his kisses burned down my throat and over my collarbone.

Each breath came faster than the last. Every kiss, every flick of his tongue against my skin, scalded me in the most delicious way. His fingers trailed up from my waist as his lips dipped lower, pushing aside the neckline of my shirt.

Whoa... "Nash." I put my hands on his shoulders.

"Mmm?"

"Hey..." I pushed against him, and he rose to meet my own heated gaze, his irises churning furiously in the light from the porch. Was this because we were two of a kind? This irresistible urge to touch each other?

My racing pulse slowed as my heart began to ache. Was it really me he wanted, or did our mutual species throw our hormones into overdrive? Would he want me if I were human?

Did that even matter? I *wasn't* human. Neither was he.

"You want me to pick you up for the memorial?"

His eyes narrowed in confusion over my abrupt subject change. Then he inhaled deeply, slowed the churning in his eyes, and settled against the car next to me. "What about your dad?"

"He can drive himself."

Nash rolled his eyes. "I didn't think you'd want to go, with your dad in town."

"I'm going. And I'm going to drag my dad and uncle along too."

He arched his brows, sliding one arm around my waist. "Why?"

"Because if some vigilante reaper is after teenage girls, I figure he'll find an auditorium full of us pretty hard to resist. And the more *bean sidhes* that are present, the greater the chance one of us will get a look at him, right?"

"In theory." Nash frowned down at me, and I could feel a "but" coming. "But, Kaylee—" I grinned, mildly amused at having predicted something other than death "—it'not going to happen again. Not this soon. Not in the same place."

"It's happened for the past three days in a row, Nash, and it's always happened where there are large groups of teenagers. The memorial will have the highest concentration of us in one room since graduation last year. There's just as much chance he'll pick someone there as anywhere else."

"So what if he does? What are you going to do?" Nash demanded in a harsh whisper. He glanced over my shoulder to make sure no one had appeared on the porch, then met my eyes again, and I realized that behind his sudden anger lay true fear.

I knew I should have been scared too, and in truth, I was. The very concept of reapers running around harvesting their metaphysical crop from empty human husks made my stomach pitch and my chest tighten. And the idea of actually looking for one of those reapers... Well, that was crazy.

But not as crazy as letting another innocent girl die. Not if we could stop it.

I watched Nash, letting my intent show on my face. Letting determination churn slowly in my eyes.

"No!" He looked toward the house again, then back at me, his irises roiling. "You heard what Tod said," he whispered fiercely. "Any reaper willing to steal unauthorized souls won't hesitate to take one of ours instead."

"We can't just let him kill someone else," I hissed, just as urgently. I resisted the urge to step back, half-afraid that any physical space I put between us during an argument would translate into an emotional distance.

"We don't have any choice," he said. I started to argue, but he cut me off, running one hand through his chunky brown hair. "Okay, look, I didn't want to have to go into this right now—I figured finding out you're not human was enough to deal with in one day. But there's a lot you still don't understand, and your uncle's probably going to explain all this soon, anyway." He sighed and leaned back against the car, his eyes closed as if he were gathering his thoughts. And when he met my gaze again, I saw that his determination now matched my own.

"What we can do together?" He gestured back and forth

between us with one hand. "Restoring a soul? It's more complicated than it sounds, and there are risks beyond the exchange rate."

"What risks?" Wasn't the exchange rate bad enough? A new thread of unease wound its way up my spine, and I leaned against the car beside him, watching light from the porch illuminate one half of his face while rendering the other side a shadowy compilation of vague, strong features. I was pretty sure that if whatever he was about to say was as weird as finding out I was a *bean sidhe,* I'd need Carter's car at my back to hold me up.

Nash's gaze captured mine, his eyes churning in what could only be fear. "*Bean sidhes* and reapers aren't the only ones out there, Kaylee. There are other things. Things I don't have names for. Things that you don't ever want to see, much less be seen by."

My skin crawled at his phrasing. *Well,* that's *more than a little scary.* Yet incredibly vague. "Okay, so where are these phantom creepies?"

"Most of them are in the Netherworld."

"And where is that?" I crossed my arms over my chest, and my elbow bumped Carter's side-view mirror. "Because it sounds like a Peter Pan ride." Yet my sarcasm was a thin veil for the icy fingers of unease now crawling inside my flesh. It might have been easy to dismiss claims of this other world as horror movie fodder—if I hadn't just discovered I wasn't human.

"This isn't funny, Kaylee. The Netherworld is here with us, but not really *here.* It's anchored to our world, but deeper than humans can see. If that makes sense."

"Not much," I said, but with the skepticism gone, my voice sounded thin and felt empty. "How do we know this Netherworld and its…Nether-people are there, if we can't see them?"

Nash frowned. "We *can* see them—we're not human." Like I needed another reminder of that. "But only when you're singing for someone's soul. And that's the only time they can see you."

And suddenly I remembered. The dark thing scuttling in the alley when I was keening for Heidi Anderson. The movement on the edge of my vision when Meredith's soul song threatened to leak out. I had seen something, even without actually giving in to the wail.

That's why Uncle Brendon had told me to hold it in. He was afraid I would see too much.

And maybe that too much would see me.

13

Nash must have seen understanding on my face—and near panic—because he wrapped one arm around my waist and pulled me closer across the waxed surface of Carter's car. "It's not as bad as it sounds. An experienced *bean sidhe* knows how to stay safe. But we're not experienced, Kaylee." It was nice of him to include himself in that statement, but we both knew I was the newbie. "Besides, we don't even know for sure that those girls weren't on the list. This is all still theory. A very unlikely, dangerous theory."

"We'll know once Tod calls," I insisted, the new information spinning around in my head, complicating what I'd thought I was prepared to do, should intervention prove necessary.

"That might not be tonight."

"It will be." He'd find out for us. Soon. Whether we'd actually gotten through to him, or he just really wanted my last name, I'd known in the instant before he'd disappeared that he would get us the information. "Call me as soon as you hear from him. Please."

He hesitated, then nodded. "But you have to promise you won't do anything dangerous, no matter what he says. No soul singing by yourself."

Like I'd admit it if I were planning something risky. Besides… "I have no desire to see this Netherworld on my own. And my little talent's no good without yours anyway, right?"

"Good point." He relaxed a little then, and kissed me good-night. I held him tight when he started to pull away, clinging to the taste and the feel of all things good and safe. Nash had become a shining tower of sanity in this new world of unprecedented chaos and unseen peril. And I didn't want to let him go.

Unfortunately, in the world of curfews and alarm clocks, he couldn't stay.

I closed and locked the door behind him, and watched through the front window until he backed out of the driveway and drove out of sight. I was pulling the curtains closed when something creaked behind me. "Kaylee?" I jumped and whirled to find my uncle standing in the hallway threshold, watching me.

"Jeez, Uncle Brendon, you scared the crap out of me!"

His smile was more of a grimace. "You're not the only one around here with big ears."

"Yeah, well it's not the big ears that worry me so much as the big *mouths*," I said, grateful that I could hear Sophie snoring again, now that the rest of the house was quiet. I padded across the carpet toward my uncle, then stepped around him and into the hall, desperately hoping he was bluffing. That he hadn't actually heard my little argument with Nash.

He followed me to my room, and when I tried to swing the door shut behind me, his palm smacked into the hollow wood panel, holding it firmly open. "What's going on, Kaylee?"

"Nothing." Going for nonchalance, I kicked first one sneaker then the other onto the floor of my closet.

"I heard you two talking." He leaned against the door frame, thick arms crossed over a broad chest, still well defined after who-knows-how-many years of life. "What are you planning at the memorial, and who's Tod?"

Well, crap. I shoved aside a pile of clean, unfolded clothes Aunt Val had dumped on my bed at some point and sank onto the comforter, my mind whirling in search of an answer that was at least as much truth as it was fabrication. But I came up empty. Nothing I made up would ring true to him, especially considering he knew more about *bean sidhes* than I knew about... anything.

So maybe I should just tell him the truth.... That way, if the rogue reaper *did* show up at the memorial and Nash refused to help me out of some misguided attempt to protect me, surely Uncle Brendon would step in. He might act tough, but inside he was a big teddy bear, and he could no more watch an innocent girl die before her time than I could.

"You sure you want to hear this?" I pulled my legs beneath me on the bed, fiddling with the frayed hem of my jeans.

Uncle Brendon shook his head. "I'm pretty sure I *don't* want to. But go ahead."

"You might want to sit," I warned him, reaching to pluck my iPod from my pillow. The earbuds had gotten tangled again; I guess that's what I get for falling asleep wearing them.

My uncle shrugged, then settled into my desk chair, waiting with his arms still crossed over his chest.

"Okay, here's the deal. And I'm only telling you this because I know you'll do the right thing. So technically, I think my voluntary disclosure exempts me from any penalty for what I'm about to admit."

His lips quirked, as if a smile had been vetoed at the last minute. "Go on..."

I inhaled and held the next breath for a moment, wondering where best to begin. But there *was* no good place to start, so I dove in, hoping my good intentions would bail me out during the less altruistic parts of the story. "Meredith Cole wasn't the first one."

"She wasn't your first premonition?" He didn't look surprised.

Of course, he *couldn't* have forgotten the other times—including the incident preceding my trip to the hospital.

"That too. But, I mean, she wasn't the first girl to die *this week*. There was one Saturday night and one yesterday afternoon. It happened the same way with all three girls."

"And you predicted them all?" *Now* he looked surprised, his forehead crinkled, brows furrowed.

"No, I never even saw the second one." I glanced at my lap, avoiding his eyes while my fingers worked nervously at the earbuds, trying to produce two separate wires from a knot any sailor would have been proud of. "But I saw the girl who died on Saturday, and knew it was going to happen. Same thing with Meredith this afternoon." Which I assumed Aunt Val had told him.

"Wait, Saturday night?" The ladder-backed chair creaked and I looked up as he leaned forward to eye me in growing suspicion. "I thought you stayed home."

I shrugged and raised one brow at him. "I thought I was human."

My uncle frowned but nodded, as if to say he'd earned that one. Still, I couldn't believe Aunt Val hadn't ratted on me. As cool as that was of her, I couldn't help wondering *why*. Had all the "coffee" made her forget my indiscretion?

"So where did this first girl die?" He leaned back again, crossing thick arms over his chest. "Where did you go?"

Suddenly the wires now tangled around my fingers seemed fascinating… "Taboo, this dance club in the West End. But—"

He scowled, and even with thick brown brows casting shadows across his eyes, I thought I saw some movement of the green in his irises. *I know that never happened before. I would have noticed.* "How did you even get into a nightclub?" he demanded. "Do you have a fake ID?"

I rolled my eyes. "No, I just snuck in through the back." Sort of… "But that's not really the point," I rushed on, hoping he'd be distracted by the next part. "One of the girls in the club was...*dark*. Like she was wearing shadows no one else could see. And when I looked at her, I knew she was going to die, and that panic—or premonition, or whatever it is—came on hard and fast, just like last time. It was horrible. But I didn't know I'd been right—that she'd actually died—until I saw the story on the news yesterday morning." Speaking of which... "Are the others dead too? The ones I saw last year?" My fingers stilled in my lap as I stared at my uncle, begging him, *daring* him to tell me the truth.

He looked sad, like he didn't want to have to say it, but there was no doubt in his eyes. Nor any hesitation. "Yes."

"How do you know?"

He smiled almost bitterly. "Because you girls are never wrong."

Great. Morbid *and* accurate. *Sounds like the sales pitch for a county-fair fortune-teller...*

"Anyway, after I saw the news yesterday morning, I kind of freaked. And then it happened again that afternoon, and things got *really* weird."

"But you didn't predict that one, right?"

I nodded and dropped my hopelessly knotted earbuds in my lap. "I heard about that one secondhand, but had to look up the story online. This girl in Arlington died exactly like the girl at Taboo. And like Meredith. They all three just fell over dead, with no warning. Does that sound normal to you?"

"No." To his credit, my uncle didn't even hesitate. "But that doesn't rule out coincidence. How much did Nash tell you about what we can do?"

"Everything important, I hope." And even if he'd left some gaps, that was much better than the *canyons* my own family had created in my self-awareness. Not to mention my psyche.

Uncle Brendon's eyes narrowed in doubt, and he crossed one ankle over the opposite knee. "Did he mention what happens to a person's soul when he dies?"

"Yeah. That's where Tod comes in."

"Who's Tod?"

"The reaper who works at the hospital. He's stuck there because he let this little girl live once when she was supposed to die, and his boss killed the girl's grandmother instead. But anyway—"

Uncle Brendon shot out of the chair, his face flushed so red I thought he might be having an aneurism. Did *bean sidhes* have aneurisms?

"Nash took you to see a *reaper?*" He stomped across my rug, gesturing angrily with both arms. "Do you have any *idea* how dangerous that is?" I tried to answer, but he barreled forward, stopping at the end of my bed to stare down at me as he ranted. "Reapers don't like *bean sidhes*. Our abilities are at odds with theirs, and most of them feel very threatened by us. Going to see a reaper is like walking into a police station waving a loaded *shotgun.*"

"I know." I shrugged, trying to placate him. "But Nash knew this guy before he was a reaper. They're friends—sort of."

"That may be what *he* thinks, but somehow I doubt Tod agrees." And he was pacing again, as if the faster he walked, the faster he could think. Though my doubts about that technique stemmed from personal experience.

"Well, he must, 'cause he's going to help us." No need to mention that his help stemmed more from my involvement in the matter than from Nash's.

"Help you with *what?*" Uncle Brendon froze halfway across the room, facing me, and this time his eyes were definitely swirling.

"Help us figure out what's going on. He's getting some information for us."

My uncle's expression darkened, and my breath hitched in my throat as the green in his irises churned so fast it made me dizzy. "What kind of information? Kaylee, what are you doing? I want the truth, and I want it right now or I swear you won't leave this house again until you turn twenty-one."

I had to smile at the irony of Uncle Brendon asking *me* for the truth. I sighed and sat straighter on the bed. "Okay, I'll tell you, but don't freak out. It's not as dangerous as it sounds—" *I hope* "—because there's this loophole in the exchange rate, and—"

"The exchange rate?" Uncle Brendon's face went from tomato-red to nuclear countdown in less than a second. And then there was more pacing. *"This* is why we wanted your father to be the one to explain everything. Or at least me. That way we'd know how much you understand and what you're still clueless about."

"I'm not clueless." My temper spiked, and I stretched to drop my iPod on my nightstand before I accidentally crimped the cord.

"You are if you think you have any business even *contemplating* the exchange rate. You have no idea how dangerous messing in reaper business can be!"

"Ignorance is dangerous, Uncle Brendon. Don't you get it?" Standing, I grabbed a clean pair of jeans and shook them out harshly, pleased when the material snapped against itself, sharply accenting my anger. "Eventually, if the premonitions kept up, I would have been unable to hold back my song. I'd have wound up delaying some random reaper's schedule and really pissing him off—not to mention whatever *other* invisible creepies are out there—with no idea what I was doing. See? The longer you all keep me bumbling around in the dark, the greater the chance that I'll stumble into something I don't understand. Nash knows that. He explained the possibilities *and* the consequences. He's arming me with knowledge because he understands that the best offense is knowing how to avoid trouble."

"From what I heard, it sounds more like you're out *looking* for trouble."

"Not trouble. The truth." I dropped the folded jeans on the

end of the bed. "There's been precious little of that around here, and even now that I know what I am, you and Aunt Val are still keeping secrets."

He exhaled heavily and sat on the edge of my dresser, scruffing one hand through unkempt hair. "We're not keeping secrets from you. We're giving your dad a chance to act like a real father."

"Ha!" I stomped around the bed to put it between us, then snatched a long-sleeved tee from the pile. "He's had sixteen years. What makes you think he'll start now?"

"Give him a chance, Kaylee. He might surprise you."

"Not likely." I folded the shirt in several short, sharp motions, then tossed it on top of the jeans, where one arm flopped free to dangle over the side. "If Nash knew what my dad had to say, he'd tell me."

Uncle Brendon leaned forward and flipped the sleeve back on top of my shirt. "Nash should *never* have taken you to see a reaper, Kaylee. *Bean sidhes* have no natural defenses against most of the other things out there. That's why we live here, with the humans. The key to longevity lies in staying out of sight. In only meeting a reaper once in your life—at the very end."

"That's ridiculous!" I tossed another folded shirt onto the stack and tugged a pair of pajama pants from the pile. "A reaper can't touch you unless your name shows up on his list, and when that happens, there's nothing you can do to stop it. Avoiding reapers is pointless. Especially when they can *help* you." In theory. But wasn't my theory about the dead girls based on the suspicion that at least one reaper *had* strayed from his purpose?

"What truth is this reaper helping you look for?" Uncle Brendon sank back into the desk chair with a defeated-sounding sigh. He rubbed his temple as if his head ached, but I was *not* taking the blame for that. If every adult in my life hadn't been lying to me for thirteen years, none of this would have happened.

"He's sneaking a peek at the master list for the past three days, to find out if the dead girls were on it."

"He's *what?*" Uncle Brendon went totally, frighteningly still, and the only movement in the room was the tic developing on the outer edge of his left eyelid.

"Don't worry. He's not taking it. He's just going to look at it."

"Kaylee, that's not the point. What he's doing is dangerous, for all three of you. Reapers take their lists very seriously. People aren't supposed to know when they're going to die. That's why you can't warn them. Once you get a premonition, you can't speak, right?"

"Yeah." I plucked at some fuzz on the flannel pants, distinctly uncomfortable with the direction the discussion was now headed, and the guilt it brought on. "I tried to warn Meredith, but I knew if I opened my mouth, I'd only be able to scream."

Uncle Brendon nodded somberly. "There's a good reason for that. Grief consumes people. Imminent death *obsesses* people. It's bad enough for a person to know he's dying of terminal cancer, or something like that. But to know the exact moment? To have the date and time stamped on your brain, looming closer to you as life slips away? That would drive people crazy."

I gaped at him, pants clenched tightly in both hands. "You think I don't know that?"

"Of course you do." He ran one hand through thick brown hair, exhaling through his mouth in frustration. "You know it much better than I ever could, and it got you hospitalized."

"No, *you* and *Aunt Val* got me hospitalized." I couldn't let that one slide.

"Ultimately, yes." Uncle Brendon conceded the point with a single crisp nod. "But only because we couldn't help you on our own. We couldn't even calm you down. You screamed for more than an hour, long after the premonition passed, though I was probably the only one who could tell when that happened."

I turned and pulled open the top drawer of my dresser, then dropped the pj's inside. "How could you tell?"

"Male *bean sidhes* hear a female's wail as it truly sounds. After a while, yours changed from the soul song to regular screaming. You were terrified—hysterical—and we were afraid you'd hurt yourself. We didn't know what else to do."

"It didn't occur to you to talk to me? Tell me the truth?" I plucked several pairs of underwear from the pile and stuffed them into another drawer, then slammed it shut.

"I wanted to. I even *tried* to at one point, but you wouldn't listen. I doubt you could even hear me over your own screaming. I couldn't calm you down, even when I tried to Influence you."

"Nash could. He's done it twice now." I sank onto my bed at the memory, absently pulling another bundle of cloth onto my lap, placated by just thinking about Nash.

"He has?" A strange look passed over my uncle's face—some odd combination of surprise, wistfulness, and concern. "He's *Influenced* you?"

"Only to calm me during those two premonitions. Why?" And suddenly I understood what he was really asking. "No! He would never try to Influence me into doing something. He's not like that."

He seemed to consider my point for a moment, then finally nodded. "Good. I'm glad he can help you control your wail, even if he has to use his Influence. That's certainly better than the alternative." He smiled as if to set me at ease, but instead, the tense line of his mouth set me on edge. "But we've strayed from the point. Kaylee, you can't get involved in reaper business. And you certainly shouldn't have asked a reaper to spy on a coworker like that. If he gets caught, it won't be pretty. They'll probably fire him."

"So what?" What was one lost job compared to an innocent girl's *life?* Besides, losing a job wasn't the end of the world; Emma was proof of that. She'd lost one every couple of months for nearly a year until I'd gotten her hired at the Ciné. "Soul-snatching seems like a pretty specialized skill, and Nash says there are reapers all over the world. Surely he can find another job somewhere else. He doesn't like the hospital much, anyway."

Uncle Brendon closed his eyes and took a deep breath before meeting my gaze again. "Kaylee, you don't understand. There's no coming back once a reaper loses his position."

"Coming back? What does that mean? Coming back from what?"

"From the dead. Reapers are dead, Kaylee. The only thing keeping their bodies functioning and their souls inside is the job. Once a reaper loses that, it's all over."

"*Nooo.*" The socks I'd been pairing dropped into my lap as I tried to wrap my mind around what he was saying.

So when Tod said he'd almost lost his job for letting the little girl live, what he meant was that he'd almost lost his *life*. And if he got caught spying for me, that's exactly what would happen. *Not cool. Not cool at* all.

Why on earth had he said he'd do it? Surely not just for my name? I wasn't *that* interesting, and my name couldn't be too hard to find on his own. He already knew where I went to school.

"But we had to do it." I met Uncle Brendon's eyes, speaking the truth as soon as I recognized it. "We *had* to know if those girls were on the list. I don't think they were supposed to die, and we won't know for sure without a peek at the list."

However, my resolve wavered even as I spoke. It was the same old moral dilemma. Did I have the right to decide whether one life was worth risking another? A girl I might not even know, for a guy I'd only met once? An *already dead* guy, who'd surely known the risk when he agreed to it.

Suddenly nothing made sense. I knew in my heart that these girls weren't supposed to be dying, but trying to save the next one would expose me to creatures I couldn't even begin to imagine in a world I couldn't see, and put several other lives in danger. Including my own.

My shoulders fell and I stared at my uncle in almost paralyzing confusion. "So what am I supposed to do?" I hated how young and clueless I sounded, but he was right. I really had no idea what was going on, and all the good intentions in the world wouldn't mean a thing if I didn't know what to do with them.

"I don't think there's anything you can do, Kaylee." Uncle Brendon looked just as frustrated as I felt. "But we don't know there's anything actually wrong yet, and until we know for sure, you're just borrowing trouble."

I tried really hard to keep an open mind. Not to jump to conclusions. After all, I wasn't exactly rolling in evidence. All I had was a bad feeling and some soul-searing guilt. And even if I turned out to be right, my options were few and far between. Not to mention far-*fetched*. I'd just found out I was a *bean sidhe* and had yet to try out a single one of my purported skills. There was no guarantee I could do anything to save the next girl's life, even if it *was* wrongly endangered.

Maybe I should just stay out of reaper business. After all, it didn't really involve me.

Yet.

But what if it did soon? One girl from my school had already died, and there was no guarantee that wouldn't happen again. And it could happen to anyone. It could be me, or any one of my friends.

"But what if I am right? If these girls are dying before their time, I can't just stand by and let it happen again if I can possibly stop it. But I can't save anyone on my own, and pulling someone else into it will just put more people in danger." Like I'd risked Tod. And Nash.

"Well then, I think you have your answer. Even if you're willing to risk yourself—and for the record, I will not let you do that so long as you're in my care—you have no right to risk anyone else."

I abandoned the laundry for my pillow, plucking anxiously at a feather sticking out through the pillowcase. "So I should just let an innocent girl die before her time?"

Uncle Brendon exhaled heavily. "No." He leaned forward with his elbows on his knees and took a long, deep breath. "I'll tell you what. When you hear back from this reaper, if it turns out that these girls weren't on the list, I'll look into it. With your father. On one condition. You swear to *stay out of it*."

"But—"

"No buts. Do we have a deal?" I opened my mouth to answer, but he interrupted. "And before you answer, think about Nash, and Tod, and whoever else you might be putting in danger if you try to handle this yourself."

I sighed. He knew he had me with that last bit. "Fine. I'll let you know what Tod finds out as soon as I know something."

"Thank you. I know none of this is easy for you." He stood and shoved his hands into his pockets as I dropped my socks into the open drawer behind me.

"Yeah, well, what's a little mental illness and pathological screaming among family?"

My uncle laughed, leaning against the door frame. "It could be worse. You could be an oracle."

"There are oracles?"

"Not many anymore, and most of those are truly certifiable. If you think predicting one death at a time is hard on your sanity, try knowing what's going to happen to everyone you meet, and being unable to turn the visions off."

I could only shudder at the thought. How could there be so much out there that I'd never known about? How could I not realize that half of my own family wasn't even human? Shouldn't the swirly eyes have clued me in?

"How come I never saw your eyes swirl before tonight?"

Uncle Brendon gave me a wistful smile. "Because I'm very old and have learned how to control my emotions, for the most part. Though that gets harder to do around you every day. I think that's part of why your dad stays away. When he looks at you, he sees your mother, and he can't hide his reaction. And if you saw his eyes, you'd have questions he wasn't ready to answer."

Well, not answering was no longer an option…. "So how old are you? For real."

Uncle Brendon chuckled and glanced at the ground, and for a moment I thought he wouldn't answer—that I'd broken some kind of *bean sidhe* code of conduct by asking. But then he met my eyes, still smiling faintly. "I wondered how long that one would take you. I turned one hundred twenty-four last spring."

"Holy crap!" I felt my eyes go wide as his smile deepened. "You could have retired sixty years ago. Does Aunt Val know?"

"Of course. And she teases me mercilessly. The children from my first marriage are older than she is."

"You were married before?" I couldn't keep shock from my voice.

That longing smile was back. "In Ireland, half a century ago. We had to move every couple of decades to keep people from noticing that we didn't seem to age. My first wife died in Illinois twenty-four years ago, and our children—both *bean sidhes*—now have grandchildren of their own. Remind me and I'll show you pictures sometime."

I nodded, numb with surprise. "Wow. So are those kids any nicer than Sophie?" I couldn't help but ask.

Uncle Brendon gave me a halfhearted frown, which smoothed into a sympathetic smile. "Frankly, yes. But Sophie's still young. She'll grow into her attitude."

Somehow, I had my doubts.

But then something else occurred to me. "Ironic, isn't it?"

I took another step back, assessing him from a better vantage point—and an all-new perspective. "You're three times Aunt Val's age, but you look so much younger."

He winked, one hand on the doorknob as he turned to leave. "Well, Kaylee, I can tell you right now that 'ironic' isn't quite how she describes it."

14

Music rang out from the dark, the heavy, crunchy beat throbbing near my ear. I blinked and pulled the blanket over my shoulder, irritated by the interruption in my sleep, even as I was relieved by the end of my dream. Which was really more of a nightmare.

In my sleep, I'd been navigating a dark landscape dotted with peculiar, hazy landmarks. Misshapen, shadowy figures scurried and slithered all around me, always just out of sight when I whirled to face them. Farther out, larger shapes lumbered, and though they never came close enough to focus on, I knew they were following me. In the dream, I was looking for something. Or maybe looking for my way out of something. But I couldn't find it.

In my room, the music played on, and I groaned when I realized it was coming from my phone. Still groggy, I flopped over, tangling my leg in the comforter, and reached toward my nightstand. My right hand grazed the phone, still bouncing around on the varnished surface, and the vibrations tickled my fingertips.

Blinking slowly, I held the phone up and glanced at the display, surprised to realize it cast a soft green glow over half the room. The number was unfamiliar, and no name was available.

Probably a wrong number, but I flipped the phone open anyway, because of the time of day displayed on the screen. It was 1:33 a.m. No one calls in the middle of the night unless something's wrong.

"Hello?" I croaked, sounding as alert as a bear in January. And almost as friendly.

"Kaylee?"

So much for a wrong number. "Mmm, yeah?"

"It's Tod."

I sat up so quickly my head spun, and I had to rub my eyes to make the lights on the back of my eyelids stop flashing. "Nash gave you my number?" That sounded suspicious even with sleep shrouding my brain like mist over a cold lake.

"No, I haven't called him yet. I wanted to tell you first."

"Okaaay…" Yet even with important information practically hanging from his lips, I couldn't dismiss the hows and whys. "Where did you get my number?"

"It's programmed into Nash's phone."

"And how did you get his phone?"

"He left it on his dresser." Tod's voice was smooth and nonchalant, and I could almost picture him shrugging as he spoke.

"You went into his room? How did you get in?" But then I remembered him disappearing from plain sight in the hospital dining room. "Never mind."

"Don't worry, he has no idea."

"That's not the point!" I groaned and leaned over to tap the base of my touch lamp once. It flared to life on the dimmest setting. "You can't just sneak into people's houses without permission. That's trespassing. It's an invasion of privacy. It's… creepy."

Tod huffed over the line. "I work twelve hours a day. I don't have to eat or sleep. What else am I supposed to do with the other half of my afterlife?"

I leaned against the headboard and shoved tangled hair back from my face. "I don't know. Go see a movie. Sign up for some classes. But stay out of—" I sat straighter, glancing at my own surroundings in suspicion as something occurred to me. "Have you been in my room?"

A soft, genuine laugh rang over the line. "If I knew where your room is, we'd be talking in person. Unfortunately, Nash doesn't have your address in his phone. Or written down anywhere I could find without waking him up."

"Small miracle," I mumbled.

"He does have your last name, though. Ms. Cavanaugh."

Crap. With my last name, and his convenient pooflike travel method, it wouldn't take him long to find out where I lived. Maybe Uncle Brendon was right about reapers.

"Don't you want to know why I called, Kaylee Cavanaugh?" he taunted.

"Um…yeah." But I was no longer sure the information was worth dealing with Tod-the-reaper, who seemed more and more "grim" with each word he spoke.

"Good. But I should probably tell you that the terms of our agreement have changed."

I bit my lower lip, cutting off a groan of frustration. "What does that mean?"

Springs creaked over the line as he settled deeper into whatever he was sitting on, and I could almost taste his satisfaction seeping through the earpiece. "I agreed to look at the list in exchange for your last name. I've done my part but no longer need the agreed-upon reimbursement. Fortunately for you, I'm willing to renegotiate."

"What do you want?" I asked, pleased to hear that suspicion was just as thick in my voice as delight was in his.

"Your address."

"No." I didn't even have to think about it. "I don't want you sneaking around here spying on me." Or revealing himself to Sophie, whose parents didn't want her exposed to this brave new Netherworld.

"Oh, come on, Kaylee. I wouldn't do that."

I rolled my eyes, though he couldn't see me. "How do I know that? You were in Nash's house tonight."

"That's different."

"How is that different?" I tugged my covers up to my waist and let my head fall back against my headboard.

"It…doesn't matter."

"Tell me."

He hesitated, and hinges squealed softly again on his end of the connection. "I knew Nash a long time ago. And sometimes I just…don't want to be alone." The vulnerability in his voice resonated in my heart, only further confusing me. But then his actual words sank in.

"You've done this before? What, do you hang out there?"

"No. It's not like that. Kaylee…you can't tell him!" In spite of the earnestness of his plea, I knew Tod wasn't afraid of Nash. He was afraid of embarrassment. I guess some things don't change in the afterlife.

"I can't *not* tell him. Tod, he's supposed to be your friend." At least he used to be. "He has a right to know you've been spying on him."

"I'm not spying on him. I don't care what he's doing, and I've never—" He stopped, and his voice grew hard. "Look, swear you won't tell him, and I'll tell you what I found out about the list."

Surprise lifted my eyebrows halfway up my forehead. He was willing to pay me to keep his little secret? Terrific. But… "Why would you trust me not to tell?"

"Because Nash said you don't lie."

Great. A grim reaper was holding me to my honor. "Fine. I swear I won't tell him in exchange for what you found out about the list. But you have to swear to stay out of his house."

For a moment, there was only silence over the line—Tod obviously wrestling with his decision. What could be so important about hanging out at Nash's house? Why on earth would he need to go back?

"Deal," he said finally, and I exhaled silently in relief. For some reason, I was sure he would keep his word too.

"Good." I tossed back my covers. I was awake, so I might as well be up. "So did you get a look at the lists?"

"I caught a bit of a break there. My boss was out of the office for nearly an hour dealing with some kind of complication in the northern end of the district. And since I happen to know his password—"

"How do you 'happen' to know his password?" I sank into my desk chair and plucked a blue metallic pen from a clay jar I'd made in Girl Scouts a decade earlier, then began doodling on a purple sticky pad.

"Last month he accidentally locked himself out of the system, and as the only reaper in the office who actually lived during the digital age, I'm kind of the de facto tech guy."

Oh. Weird, but I'd take it. "So what about the lists?"

"They weren't there."

"What?" I dropped the pen, anger blazing a white-hot trail up my spine, splintering to burn down to the tips of my fingers. I'd just bargained for nothing? Sworn to keep a secret from Nash only to find out that Tod couldn't get a look at the lists?

"The names. They weren't there," he clarified, and relief drenched most of my irritation. Followed quickly by renewed fear on behalf of every girl I knew. "You were right," Tod continued. "Not one of those girls was supposed to die."

After talking to Tod, I couldn't sleep. I needed to tell my uncle that my suspicion had been confirmed: one of Tod's fellow reapers was working overtime on some unauthorized soul-snatching. But I saw no reason to wake him after two hours of sleep, even for news of this magnitude. None of the other girls had died before noon, so if the pattern persisted, we had a while before the next one would die.

I would tell my uncle and father at the same time, so I wouldn't have to say it twice. And in the morning, so that hopefully I could avoid having to explain how a grim reaper got my phone number and why he'd called me in the middle of the night.

But telling Nash couldn't wait.

My pulse thudded as I scrolled through my contacts list for his name, my heart heavy with what I had to tell him and with what I'd sworn not to tell him. I firmly believed that keeping secrets wasn't good for any relationship; my family was living proof of that. But Tod had sworn not to go back to Nash's house, so his secret was now harmless, and thus more than worth the lives that might be saved by me keeping it to myself.

Right?

The phone rang three times in my ear, with agonizing slowness. Yet part of me hoped he wouldn't answer. That I could put off telling Nash for a few more hours too.

He answered in the middle of the fourth ring.

"Hello?" Nash sounded as tired as I felt.

"Hey, it's me." Too nervous to sit now, I stood to pace the length of my bed.

"Kaylee?" He was instantly alert, an ability I truly envied. "What's wrong?"

I plucked a round glass paperweight from my dresser and rolled it between my palms as I talked, my head crooked at a painful angle with the slim phone pinched between my shoulder and my ear. "The girls weren't on the list."

"They weren't? How do you know—" His breath hissed in angrily, and I closed my eyes, waiting for the explosion. "That bastard! He found you?"

"Just my phone number."

"How?"

"I…you'll have to ask him." I'd sworn not to tell Nash, but I wasn't going to lie.

"No problem." Something scratched against the mouthpiece as he covered it, but I still heard him shout. "Come on out, Tod!"

"You knew he was there?" I couldn't quite squelch a smile, even knowing how angry he was.

"He's not half as stealthy as he thinks he is," Nash growled.

I set the glass ball on my dresser and took my phone back in my hand, turning to avoid a glimpse of my bed-head in the mirror. "Neither are you. Your mom's going to wake up if you don't quit yelling."

"She's working eleven to seven at the hospital tonight."

"Well, I'm sure Tod's gone now." Surely he hadn't called me from Nash's house….

A door squealed open over the line, and floorboards creaked beneath Nash's feet. "He's still here."

"How do you know?"

"I just do." Another pause, and this time he didn't bother to cover the phone, because he was done shouting. "I'm not playing, Tod. If you don't show yourself in five seconds, I'm calling your boss."

"You don't have the number." Tod's voice was unmistakable, even at a whisper. He *had* called me from Nash's house!

Why? Just to rub my boyfriend's face in it?

"I told you to stay away from her." Nash's voice was so deep with anger it was almost unrecognizable.

By contrast, Tod sounded as calm as ever, which probably pissed Nash off even further. "And I haven't been anywhere near her, but that's not because of anything you said. She just hasn't invited me over." *Yet…* We all three heard the unspoken qualifier, and even through the phone I could feel Nash's rage.

Then I heard it.

"What the hell do you think you're doing?" he demanded, and his voice had gone soft and dangerous.

"I don't answer to you, Nash."

"Get out of my room, get out of this house, and stay away from Kaylee. Or I swear we'll show up at the hospital tomorrow and make your entire shift a living hell."

I froze in the middle of my fuzzy purple rug, horrified by the very thought of standing between a reaper and his intended harvest. "Nash, he was doing us a favor." But they both ignored me.

"You come to my work again, and I'll haunt your ass like the ghost of Christmas past!" Tod snapped.

"That was a one-night haunting," Nash mumbled, but the reaper made no reply, and finally Nash sighed. Then springs squeaked as he dropped onto what I assumed was his couch. "He's gone."

"Why didn't you tell me he was dead?"

"Because I was already throwing information at you left and right, and I was afraid one more supernatural fact of life might really freak you out."

"No more secrets, Nash." Irritated now, I sank onto the rug and plucked at the twisty purple threads in the dim glow of my lamp. "I'm not fragile. From now on, tell me everything."

"Okay. I'm sorry. You want to know about Tod?" His voice went distant, as if he regretted offering before he'd even finished speaking the words.

I crawled onto my bed and turned off the touch lamp, then lay with one cheek on the cool surface of my pillow. "Not everything. But at least what's relevant to me."

Nash exhaled deeply, and I could almost feel his reluctance. Part of me wanted to take it back, to tell him he didn't owe me any answers. But I didn't, because the other half of me insisted I needed those answers. Tod's behavior scared me, and if Nash had information that could help me understand what I was getting into, I wanted it.

"I've known him forever," Nash began, and I went still to

make sure I didn't miss anything. It was weird in the best possible way, talking to him in the middle of the night, in the dark, in my bed. His voice was intimate, almost like he was whispering in my ear. And that very thought made my pulse whoosh harder and warmed me all over.

"We used to be close. Then he died a few years ago, and the reapers recruited him. He took the job because that's the only way to stay here. With the living. But he had a hard time adjusting to the work." Nash paused, then his voice became almost wistful. "That's why I thought he'd be able to help you understand death—that it's a necessary part of life. Because he went through the same thing, wanting to save everyone. But he got over it, Kaylee, and his adjustment came with serious consequences. He doesn't think about things the way we do anymore. Doesn't have the same values and concerns. He's truly a reaper now. Dangerous."

I frowned, thinking of what I now knew about Tod that Nash didn't. "Maybe he's not as dangerous as you think. Maybe he just needs…company."

"He broke into my house to find your phone number. If he were human, I'd have him arrested. As it is, there isn't much I can do, short of ratting on him to his boss." Which was as good as killing Tod. "I swear, if he wasn't already dead, I'd kill him myself. I'm sorry, Kaylee. I should never have taken you to him."

Alone in my room, I sighed and turned onto my left side, holding the phone at my right ear. "He got the information for us."

"Plus a little, it sounds like." Nash exhaled heavily, and seemed to be calming down.

I sat up in my bed and slid my cold feet beneath the blankets. "He was trying to help."

"That's the thing—he's not a bad guy. But since the… change…he only helps on his own terms, and won't do anything that doesn't benefit him. Putting yourself in debt to someone like that—especially to a reaper—is a very bad idea. We should have figured it out without his help."

I had no idea what to say. Yes, Tod had crossed a very important line. Several lines, in fact. But by Nash's own admission, the reaper wasn't a bad person. And he'd come through for us—in a manner of speaking.

Springs groaned as Nash shifted in his seat. "So what's the plan? We still don't know who the next girl will be, or if there will even be one."

I squeezed my eyes shut, unsure how he'd react to my news. "I called in the cavalry."

"The what?"

"My uncle. And my dad." Feeling mostly awake now, I touched my lamp again, and the room got brighter. "Uncle Brendon said they'd find out what was going on if I promised to stay out of it."

Nash gave a gravelly chuckle that sent a bolt of heat blazing through me. "I knew I liked your uncle."

I smiled. "He's not bad. All the lying aside. I'll tell them about the list in the morning."

"Fill me in at the memorial?"

"On the drive, assuming you still want a ride." A warm feeling trickled through me at the thought of seeing him again.

"I would love a ride."

15

In the morning, I woke to find daylight streaming into my room between the slats of the blinds, and my bedroom door shaking and thumping beneath someone's fist. "Kaylee, get your lazy butt out of bed!" Sophie shouted. "Your dad's on the phone."

I rolled over, pulling the covers askew, and glanced at the alarm clock on my nightstand. 8:45 a.m. Why would my father call when he'd see me in less than an hour? To tell me he'd landed? Or that he *hadn't* landed.

He wasn't coming. I should have known.

For a moment, I ignored my cousin and stared at the thick crown molding along the edge of the tiered ceiling, letting my temper simmer just beneath the surface. I hadn't seen my father in more than eighteen months, and now he wasn't even going to come explain why he'd never told me I wasn't *human*.

Not that I needed him. Thanks to his cowardice, I had a perfectly good set of guardians at my disposal. But he owed me an explanation, and if I wasn't going to get it in person, I could at least demand it over the phone.

I tossed the covers back and stepped into the pajama pants pooled on the floor, and when I opened my door, there stood Sophie, completely dressed and in full makeup, looking as fresh and well-put-together as I'd ever seen her. The only sign that her night's slumber had been chemically induced was the slight puffiness around her eyes, which would probably be gone within the hour.

The last time *I'd* taken one of the zombie pills, I'd woken up looking like roadkill.

"Thanks." I took the home phone from Sophie, and she only nodded, then turned and plodded down the hall with none of her usual watch-me-prance energy.

I kicked my door shut and held the cordless phone to my ear. It felt huge and cumbersome after my cell, and I couldn't remember the last time I'd actually held the home phone.

"You could have called my cell," I said into the receiver.

"I know."

My father's voice was just like I remembered—deep, and smooth, and distant. He probably looked exactly the same too, which meant my appearance would likely come as a bit of a shock to him, despite his understanding of the passage of time. I was almost fifteen the last time he'd seen me. Things had changed. *I* had changed.

"I have this number memorized, so it was just easier," he continued. That was absentee-father-speak for *I'm too embarrassed to admit I don't remember your cell-phone number. Even though I pay the bill.*

"So let me guess." I pulled out my desk chair and plopped into it, punching the power button on my computer just to keep my hands busy. "You're not coming."

"Of course I'm coming." I could practically hear him frowning over the line, and that's when I realized I could also hear actual background noise. An official-sounding voice over a loudspeaker. Random snatches of conversation. Echoing footsteps.

He was at the airport.

"My flight's been delayed by engine trouble in Chicago. But

with any luck, I'll be in this evening. I just wanted to let you know I'd be late."

"Oh. Okay." *Soooo glad I didn't start by demanding he tell me everything over the phone.* "I guess I'll see you tonight."

"Yeah." Silence settled over the line then, because he didn't know what to say, and I was *not* going to make it easier on him by speaking first. Finally, he cleared his throat. "Are you okay?" His voice felt…heavy, as if he wanted to say more, but left the unspoken words hanging.

"Fine." *Not that you could fix it if I weren't,* I thought, jiggling my mouse to find the cursor on-screen. "It's all taken some getting used to, but I'm ready to have all the secrets out in the open."

"I'm so sorry about all this, Kaylee. I know I owe you the truth—about everything—but some of this won't be easy for me to say, so I need you to bear with me. Please."

"Like I have a choice." But as furious as I was over the massive lie that was my life, I was desperate to know why they'd all lied in the first place. Surely they had a good reason for letting me think I was crazy, rather than telling me the truth.

My father sighed. "Can I take you out for dinner when I get in?"

"Well, I'll have to eat *something*." I double-clicked on my internet browser and typed the name of a local news station into the search bar, hoping for an update.

He hesitated for another long moment, as if waiting for more, and as badly as part of me wanted to speak, wanted to spare him the awful silence I'd suffered, I resisted. Birthday visits and Christmas cards weren't enough to hold his place in my life. Especially since they'd stopped coming… "I'll see you tonight, then."

"Okay." I hung up and set the phone on the desktop, staring at it blankly for several seconds. Then I released the breath I hadn't realized I was holding and scrolled through the day's headlines online, hoping to purge my father from my thoughts. At least until he showed up on the porch.

There was nothing new about Alyson Baker or Meredith Cole, but the coroner had officially declared a cause of death for Heidi Anderson. Heart failure. But wasn't that ultimately what everyone died of? However, in Heidi's case, there was no cause listed for her heart failure. As I'd known all along, she'd simply died. Period.

Frustrated all over again, I turned off the computer and dropped the home phone into its cradle on my way to the bathroom. Twenty minutes later, showered, blow-dried, and dressed, I sat at the bar in the kitchen with a glass of juice and a granola bar. I'd just ripped open the wrapper when Aunt Val wandered in, wrapped in my uncle's terry-cloth robe, rather than her usual silky one. Her hair was one big blond tangle, yesterday's styling gel spiking random strands in odd places, like a leftover punk rocker's. Eyeliner was smeared below her eyes, and her skin was pale beneath lingering blotches of blush and foundation.

She shuffled straight to the coffeepot, which was already full and steaming. For several minutes, I chewed in silence as she sipped, but by the time she brought her second mug to the counter, the caffeine had kicked in.

"I'm sorry about last night, hon." She combed one hand over her hair, trying to smooth it. "I didn't mean to embarrass you in front of your boyfriend."

"It's fine." I wadded my wrapper and tossed it into the trash can on the other side of the room. "There was too much else going wrong to worry about one drunk aunt."

She grimaced, then nodded. "I guess I deserved that."

But watching her wince over every movement—as if contact with the very air hurt—made me feel guilty. "No, you don't. I'm sorry."

"So am I." Aunt Val forced a smile. "I can't *begin* to explain how sorry I am. None of this is your fault...." She stared down into her coffee, as if she had more to say, but the words had fallen into the mug and were now too soggy to use.

"Don't worry about it." I finished my orange juice and set my glass in the sink, then headed back to my room, where I texted Emma to make sure she was still coming to the memorial.

Her mom said she'd meet me there fifteen minutes early—at a quarter to one.

The rest of the morning passed in one endless stretch of mindless television and internet surfing. I tried twice to get my uncle alone so I could pass along Tod's information, but every time I found him, he was with a very somber, clingy Sophie, who seemed to be dreading the memorial as badly as I was.

After an early lunch I could only pick at, I changed out of my T-shirt, hoping my long-sleeved black blouse was appropriate attire for the memorial service for someone I'd failed to save. On my way out the door, I saw Sophie sitting on the bench in the hall, her hands folded on the skirt of a slim black dress, her head hanging so that her long blond hair fell nearly to her chest. She looked so pitiful, so lost, that as badly as I hated to spoil the drive alone with Nash, I offered her a ride to school.

"Mom's taking me," she said, briefly meeting my gaze with her own huge, sad eyes.

"Okay." *Just as well.*

I pulled into Nash's driveway five minutes later and waited nervously for him to get into the car. I was afraid talking to him would be weird after his middle-of-the-night fight with Tod, and his reluctant discussion of it with me. But he leaned over to kiss me as soon as his door was closed, and from the depth of that kiss—and the fact that neither of us seemed willing to end it—I was guessing he was over the awkwardness.

The school parking lot was packed. Overflowing. Lots of parents had come, as well as some city officials, and according to the morning paper, the school had called in extra counselors to help the students learn to deal with their grief. We had to park on the side of the road nearest the gym and walk nearly a quarter of a mile. Nash took my hand on the way, and we met Emma at the front door, where one of her sisters had dropped her off. I'd promised to give her a ride home.

Emma looked like crap. She wore her hair pulled into a tight, no-frills ponytail, along with the bare minimum of makeup. And if her reddened eyes were any indication, she'd been crying. But she didn't know Meredith any better than I did.

"You okay?" I slipped my free arm around her waist as we made our way through a set of double doors, pushed along with the crowd.

"Yeah. This whole thing's just so weird. First that girl at the club, then the one at the movies. Now one from our own school. Everyone's talking about it. And they don't even know about *you*," she said, whispering the last word.

"Well, it gets even weirder than that." Nash and I guided her toward an empty alcove near the restrooms. I hadn't had a chance to tell her any of the latest developments, and for once I was glad she was grounded from her phone. If she hadn't been, I might have blurted out the whole story—*bean sidhes,* grim reapers, and death lists—before I'd thought any of it through. Which probably would have scared her even more.

"How could it get any weirder than this?" Emma spread her arms to take in the somber crowd milling around the lobby.

"Something's wrong. They weren't supposed to die," I whispered, standing on my toes to get closer to her ear, as Nash pressed in close on my other side.

Emma's eyes went wide. "What does that mean? Who's ever supposed to die?"

I glanced at Nash, and he gave me a tiny shake of his head. *We* really *should have discussed how much to tell Emma.* "Um. Some people *have* to die, or the world would be overpopulated. Like… old people. They've lived full lives. Some of them are ready to go, even. But teenagers are too young. Meredith should have still had most of her life in front of her."

Emma frowned at me like I'd lost my mind. Or at least several IQ points. No, I'm not a very good liar. Though technically, I wasn't lying to her.

With Emma still trying to puzzle out my odd editorial on death, Nash guided us through the crowd toward the gym, where we found seats on the bleachers near the middle of the visitors' side and smooshed in with several hundred other people. A temporary stage had been set up beneath one of the baskets, and several school officials were seated there with Meredith's family, beneath the school's banner and the state and national flag.

For the next hour and a half, we listened to Meredith's friends and family come forward to tell us all how nice she was, and how pretty, and smart, and kind. Not all of their praise would really have applied to Meredith, had she been there with us, but the dead have a way of becoming saints in the eyes of their survivors, and Ms. Cole was no exception.

And to be fair, other than being beautiful and popular, she was no different from most of the rest of us. Which was precisely why everyone was so upset. If Meredith could die, so could any one of us. Emma's eyes watered several times, and my own vision blurred with tears when Mrs. Cole came up to the podium, already crying freely.

Sophie sat in the bottom row, surrounded by sobbing dancers blotting streaks of mascara with tissues pulled from small, tasteful handbags. Several of them spoke, mostly Meredith's fellow seniors, reciting stale platitudes with fresh earnestness. Meredith would have wanted us to move on. She loved life, and dancing, and would want neither to stop in her absence. She wouldn't want to see us cry.

After the last of her classmates spoke, an automated white screen was rolled down from the ceiling, and someone played a video of still photographs of Meredith from birth to death, set to some of her favorite songs.

During the film, several students stood and made their way to the lobby, where counselors waited to counsel them. Sniffles and quiet sobs echoed all around us, a community in mourning, and all I could think about was that if we couldn't find the reaper responsible for the unauthorized reaping of Meredith's soul, it would happen all over again.

After the memorial, Nash, Emma, and I made our way slowly down the bleachers, caught up in the gradual current of people more interested in comforting one another than in actually vacating the building.

Eventually we made it to the gym floor, where more groups had clustered, gravitating en masse toward one of the four exits. Since we'd parked in front of the school, we headed for the main doors, shuffling forward inches at a time.

Nash had just taken my hand, his arm brushing the entire length of mine, when a sudden, devastating wave of sorrow crashed over me, settling heavily into my chest and stomach. My lungs tightened, and an unbearable itch began at the base of my throat. But this time, rather than silently bemoaning the onset of my dark forecast and the imminent death of another classmate, I welcomed it.

The reaper was here; we would have our chance to stop him.

16

My hand grasped Nash's. He glanced my way, and his eyes went wide. "Again?" he whispered, leaning down so that his lips brushed my ear, but I could only nod. "Who is it?"

I shook my head, each breath coming quickly now. I hadn't pinpointed the source yet. There were too many people, in too many tightly formed groups. All the bodies in dark colors were blending together in a virtual camouflage of funeral attire, and in some cases I couldn't distinguish one form from another.

A bolt of uncertainty shot through my heart, piercing my determination like a spear through flesh. *What if I can't do this? What if I can't find the victim, much less save her…?*

"Okay, Kaylee, relax." His whispered words flowed over me with an almost physical sliding sensation, trying to calm me even as his eyes churned in slow, steady fear. "Look around slowly. We can save the next one. But you have to find her first."

I tried to follow his directions, but the panic was too loud, a private, frenzied buzzing as the scream built inside my head. It interrupted thought. Rendered logic an abstract concept.

Nash seemed to understand. He stepped in front of me so that we were facing, his nose inches from my forehead. He stared into my eyes and took both my hands in his. The crowd shuffled by, parting to flow around us like water around a river outcropping. Several people glanced our way, but no one stopped—I wasn't the only young woman having a public breakdown in the gym, and most of the others were much louder than mine. For the moment, anyway.

I clenched my jaw shut, holding back the strongest soul song I'd ever felt as I let my gaze rove the crowd, passing over the boys and adults and lingering on the girls. She was here somewhere, and she was going to die. There was nothing I could do to stop that. But if I found her in time, and if I was truly capable of doing what Nash had explained to me, I could bring her back. *We* could bring her back.

Then all we'd have to worry about was avoiding the rogue reaper fury.

It may have been coincidence, or maybe my very real need, despite our strained relationship, to see that my cousin was safe, but my gaze settled first on Sophie. She stood beneath the basket at the far end of the gym with a group of teary-eyed friends, arms linked in a huddle of sorrow. But none of those red, damp faces intensified my panic, and not one of them was dimmed by a veil of shadows that only I could see. The girls were fine, but for their grief. Fortunately, I would not have to add to it.

Next my focus found another cluster of young women—freshmen, if I had to guess. Everywhere I turned there were more girls, some in dresses, some in dark pants, others in jeans, the official uniform of adolescence. It was like the boys and adults no longer existed. My eyes were drawn only to the girls.

But of all the faces—freckled, tear-streaked, thin, round, pale, dark, and tanned—none held my gaze. Not one cried out to my soul.

Finally, after what seemed like forever, but couldn't have been more than a minute, my gaze found Nash again. My jaws ached from being clenched, my throat was raw from holding back the scream, and my fingernails had left impressions in his hands. I shook my head and blinked away the tears forming in my eyes. She was still there somewhere—based on the unprecedented strength of the cry building inside me—but I couldn't find her.

"Try again." Nash squeezed my hands. "One more time." I nodded and made myself swallow the rising sound—an agony like gulping broken glass—but this time the consequences of repressing it were very real. Pressure built in my chest and throat, and I was increasingly certain that if I couldn't release it soon or remove myself from the source, my body would rupture into one gaping wound of grief.

Desperate now, I looked over his shoulder, where people still pressed slowly toward the exit. Everyone in that direction faced away from me, identities obscured by the anonymous backs of their heads. A thin redhead, with long, loose curls. Two heavyset girls with identical black waves. A brunette with thin, fine hair as straight as a ruler. She turned, and I saw her profile, but the panic didn't escalate.

Then one head caught my attention—another blonde, about fifteen feet away, her entire form dark with a thick, ominous shadow that somehow fell on no one else. The moment my gaze found her, my throat convulsed, fighting to release the wail my jaws held back. My chest ached for fresh air, but I was scared to take it in, afraid that would fuel the scream I wasn't yet ready to release. The blonde was tall and curvy, her hair cut straight across the middle of her back. If she'd had a ponytail, I'd have sworn it was Emma.

But whoever she was, she was about to die.

I couldn't speak to warn Nash, so I squeezed his hand, harder than I'd meant to. He started to pull away, but then comprehension widened his eyes and made a firm line of his mouth.

"Where?" he whispered urgently. "Who is it?"

Now weak from resisting the song, I could only nod in the blonde's direction, but that was little help. My gesture took in at least fifty people, more than half of them young women.

"Show me." He let go of my left hand but still clung to my right. "Can you walk?"

I nodded but wasn't sure that I actually could. My head rang with the echo of screams unvoiced, my legs wobbled, and my free hand grasped the air. A soft, high-pitched mewling leaked from me now, the song seeping through my imperfectly sealed lips. And with it came a familiar darkness, that odd gray filter overlaying my vision. The world felt like it was closing in on me, while something else—anomalous forms and a world no one else could see—seemed to unfold before my eyes.

Nash pulled me forward. I staggered and gasped, and my jaw fell open. But he righted me quickly, and I clamped my mouth shut, biting my tongue in a hasty effort to keep from screaming. Blood flowed into my mouth, but the next step I took was under my own volition. Pain had cleared my head. My vision was back to normal.

I stumbled on, Nash guiding me, adjusting our slow course when I shook my head. It only took twelve steps—I counted to help myself focus—then the blonde was within reach, temporarily stalled in her progress toward the door by the crowd. I stopped behind her and nodded to Nash.

He looked sick. His face went suddenly pale, and his throat worked too hard to swallow back something he obviously didn't want to say. "You sure?" he whispered, and I nodded again, my jaw creaking now with the effort to hold back my wail. I was sure. This was the one.

Nash reached out, his fingers trembling as they passed into the eerie shadow shroud, and glanced at me one last time. Then he laid his hand on the girl's right shoulder.

She turned, and my heart stopped.

Emma.

She'd pulled her ponytail loose at some point and had shuffled ahead of us when I'd lagged behind, fighting the panic.

I had to make myself breathe, force my lungs to expand with

my teeth still clenched together. And again my vision darkened. Went fuzzy. That eerie, dusky haze slipped over everything, so that I saw the world through a thin, colorless fog.

Emma stared at me through the gloom, wide eyes dimmed by their own private shadow. Her expression was full of understanding, yet missing that vital piece of the puzzle. "It's happening again, isn't it?" she whispered, taking my free hand in hers. "Who is it? Can you tell yet?"

I nodded, and when I blinked, two tears slid down my face, scalding me with thin, hot trails. As I watched, a boy from my biology class brushed Emma's arm, passing into and out of her personal shade without the slightest flicker of awareness in his eyes. All around us students and parents moved with slow, aimless steps, edging gradually toward the doors. Oblivious to the Netherworld murk they walked through. To what the next few moments would bring.

On the periphery of my vision, something rushed through the grayness. Something large, and dark, and *fast*. My heart thumped painfully. A spike of adrenaline tightened my chest. My gaze darted to follow the odd form, but it was gone before I could focus on it, moving easily through the crowd without bumping a single body. But it walked like nothing I'd ever seen, with a peculiar, lopsided grace, as if it had too many limbs. Or maybe too few.

And no one else saw it.

My eyes slammed shut in horror. My mind rebelled against what I'd seen, dismissing it as impossible. I knew there were other things out there. I'd been warned. I'd even caught glimpses before. But this was too much; only a thin stream of sound leaked from my tightly locked throat!

"We have to wait," Nash whispered, and my eyes opened, my attention snapping back to Emma and the terrible matter at hand. Yet the misshapen form lingered in my mind, its odd bulk imprinted indistinctly on the backs of my eyelids. "She has to die before we can bring her back, and singing too soon would be wasting your energy."

No. My hair slapped my face as I shook my head, fervently denying what I already knew to be true. I couldn't let Emma die. I *wouldn't.* But there was nothing I could do to stop it, and we all knew that. Except for Emma.

"What?" She glanced from me to Nash, confusion lining her forehead. "What's he talking about?"

Sweat gathered on my palms, and for once I was glad I couldn't talk. Couldn't answer her. Instead, I swallowed thickly, my throat tightening around the cry scalding me from the inside. The gray haze was darker now, though no thicker. I could see through it easily, yet it tainted everything my terrified gaze landed on, as if the entire gym had been draped in a translucent cloud of smog. And still things moved on the edge of my vision, drawing my eyes in first one direction, then another.

I would have given anything to be able to speak in that moment, not just to warn Emma—because that was evidently a moot point—but to ask Nash what the hell was going on. Could he see what I saw? More important, could they already see us?

My head swiveled quickly, my eyes following an eerie burst of motion, but I was too late. I spun in the opposite direction, squinting into the ghostly gloom as I tracked another movement. My jaws ached, my head pounded, and the keening deep in my throat rose in volume. Those closest to us stared at me now, only looking away when Nash drew me into an embrace, pulling my head down onto his shoulder as if to comfort me. Which was, in part, what he was doing.

"Kaylee, no," he whispered into my hair, but this time his Influence was little help. The urge to wail was too strong, the death coming too fast—distantly I saw Emma watching us, still wrapped in an almost solid sheet of shadow. "Don't look at them."

He sees them too? That answered one of my questions....

"Focus on holding it back," he said. "Your keening breaches the gap, but I don't think they can see us yet. They will when you sing, but they're not here with us, no matter what it looks like."

Gap? Gap between what and what? Our world and the Netherworld? *Not good. Not good at all…*

I stepped out of his arms to see his face, looking for answers in his expression, but there were none to be found. Probably because I couldn't ask the right questions.

Fine. I would ignore the weird gray reality-veil, as impossible as that seemed. But what about the reaper? If Emma was going to die—even if only temporarily—I would *not* let it be for nothing.

I glanced pointedly at Emma for effect, my heart breaking a little more at the alarm clear on her face, then exaggerated shrugging my shoulders for Nash, all the while choking back the scream that now felt immediate.

By some miracle, he understood.

"You can't see him until he wants to be seen," Nash reminded me gently, stepping close to murmur against my forehead. His very words, the almost-physical satin-soft glide of his Influenced voice against my skin, made the panic abate a bit. Not enough to offer much relief, but enough to hold back the screaming for a few more seconds. "And I'd bet my life savings he doesn't want to be seen. You have to wait. Just hold it in a little longer."

"What?" Emma repeated, squeezing my hand now to get my attention. "Can't see who? Where—"

Then, in midsentence, she simply collapsed.

Emma's legs folded beneath her with my hand still clenched in hers. Her head hit the person behind her. He stumbled and almost went down. I fell forward with her, tears flowing freely now. Nash's hand was ripped from my grip as my knees slammed into the floor and the blow reverberated throughout my body. And Emma's eyes stared up at nothing, the windows to her soul thrown wide open, though it was obvious no one was home.

"Kaylee!" Nash dropped to the ground on Emma's other side. He stared at me imploringly as people turned to look, eyes wide, mouths hanging open.

I barely heard him. I no longer noticed the dimness or the odd movement creeping back into the edges of my vision. I couldn't think about anything but Emma, and how she lay there, unmoving, staring at the ceiling as if she could see through it.

"Let it go, Kaylee. Sing for her. Call her soul so I can see it. Hold it as long as you can."

I looked down at Emma, beautiful even in death. Her fingers were still warm in mine. Her hair had fallen over her shoulder, and the soft ends of it brushed my arm. I let my head fall back and my mouth fall open.

Then I screamed.

The shriek poured from me in an agonizing torrent of discordant, abrasive notes that scraped my throat raw and seemed to empty me, from my toes all the way to the top of my head. It hurt like hell. But beyond the pain, I felt overwhelming relief to no longer be the physical vessel for such an unearthly din and agonizing grief over having lost my best friend. The cousin I should have had. My confidante and, at times, my sanity.

The entire gymnasium went still in an instant. People froze, then turned to stare, most slapping hands over their ears and grimacing in pain. Someone else screamed—I could tell because her mouth was wide open, though I couldn't hear her over the much more powerful noise coming from my own mouth.

And then, before I could even process all the gawking stares aimed my way, the whole world seemed to *shift*.

That fine gray mist settled into place all around me, *over* everything normal, though that was more a feeling than a physical fact. The strange, misshapen creatures I couldn't focus on before were suddenly everywhere, interspersed with and in some cases overlaying the human crowd, ogling me just like the students and parents, but from the far side of the grayness. They were drab, as if the haze had somehow stolen their color, and they looked distant, as if I were watching them through some kind of formless, tinted glass.

Was that what Nash meant, when he said they wouldn't actually be with us? Because if so, I didn't quite understand the distinction. They were entirely too close for comfort, and drawing nearer every second.

On my left, a strange, headless creature stood between two boys in wrinkled khakis, blinking at me with eyes set into his bare chest, between small, colorless nipples. An odd, narrow nose protruded from the hollow below his sternum, and thin lips opened just above his navel.

No need to *mention* how I knew it was a he....

Horrified, I closed my eyes, and my scream faltered. But then I remembered Emma. Em needed me.

They're not here with us. They're not here with us. Nash's voice seemed to chant from inside my head. I let the song loose again, marveling at the capacity of my lungs, and opened my eyes. I was determined to look only at Nash. He could get me through this; he'd done it before.

But my gaze snagged instead on a beautiful man and woman slinking their way toward me through the crowd. They looked almost normal, except for their hazy gray coloring and the odd, elongated proportion of their limbs—and the tail curled around the female's slim ankle. As I watched, spellbound, the man walked *through* my science teacher, who didn't so much as flinch.

That's it. Enough. I couldn't handle any more weird gray monsters. This time I would look at Nash, or at nothing.

My throat burned. My ears rang. My head pounded. But finally Nash's face came into focus directly across from me. But to my complete dismay, his gaze did not meet mine. He stared, rapt, at the space over Emma's body, eyes narrowed in concentration, face damp with sweat.

I looked up, and suddenly I understood. There was Emma. Not the body cooling slowly on the floor in front of me. The real Emma. Her soul hung in the air between us, the most amazing thing I'd ever seen. If a soul can be called a thing.

She wasn't beautiful, like I'd expected. No glowing ball of heatless light. No Emma-shaped ghost fluttering in an ethereal breeze. She was dark and formless, yet translucent, like a clear, slowly undulating shadow of…nothing. But what her soul lacked in form, it made up for in feel. It felt important. Vital.

Cold fingers touched my arm and I jumped, sure one of the Nether-creatures had come for me. But it was only the principal, kneeling next to me, saying something I couldn't hear. She was asking me what had happened, but I couldn't talk. She tried to pull me away from Emma, but I wouldn't be budged. Nor would I be silenced.

A short, round woman in a sacklike dress burst into the circle that had formed around us, shoving people out of her way. The gray creatures took no note of her, and I realized they probably couldn't see her. Or any of the other humans.

The woman squatted by Nash and said something, but he didn't answer. His eyes had glazed over; his hands lay limp on his lap. When she couldn't get through to Nash, she tossed an odd glance my way and shot to her feet. She wobbled for a moment, then dashed around him and knelt at Emma's head to check her pulse.

More people knelt on the ground, hands covering their ears, their mouths moving frantically, uselessly. They were oblivious to the creatures peppered throughout their midst, a condition which was apparently mutual. A tall, thin man made frantic motions with both arms, and the humans behind him backed up. The gray creatures seemed to press even closer, but I saw it all distantly, as the scream still tore from my throat, burning like razors biting into my flesh.

Then my eyes were drawn back to Emma's soul, which had

begun to twist and writhe frenetically. One smoky end of it trailed toward the corner of the gym, as if struggling in that direction, while the rest wrapped around itself, sinking toward Emma's body like the heavy end of a raindrop.

Transfixed, I glanced at Nash to see sweat dripping down his face. His eyes were open but unfocused, his hands now clenching handfuls of his pressed khaki pants. And as I watched, the soul descended a little more, as if the gravity over Emma's body had been somehow boosted.

People rushed all around us, staring in my direction, shouting to be heard over me. Human hands touched my arms, tugged at my clothing, some trying to comfort me and silence my cry, others trying to pull me away. Odd colorless forms gathered in groups of two or three, watching boldly, murmuring words I couldn't hear and probably wouldn't have understood. And Emma's soul moved slowly toward her body, that one smoky tendril still winding off toward the corner.

Nash almost had her. But if he couldn't do it quickly, it would be too late. My voice was already losing volume, my throat throbbing in agony now, my lungs burning with the need for fresh oxygen.

Then, at last, the lucent shadow settled over Emma's body and seemed to melt into it. In less than a second, it was completely absorbed.

Nash exhaled forcefully, and blinked, wiping sweat from his forehead with one sleeve. My voice finally gave out, and my mouth closed with a sharp snap, loud in the sudden silence. And every single gray being, every last wisp of fog, simply winked out of existence.

For a moment, no one moved. The hands on me went still. The human onlookers were frozen in place as if they could feel the difference, though they clearly had no idea what had happened, other than that I'd stopped screaming.

My gaze settled on Emma, searching out some sign of life.

Rising chest, jiggling pulse. I would even have taken a wet, snotty sneeze. But for several torturous seconds, we got nothing, and I was convinced we'd failed. Something had gone wrong. The unseen reaper was too strong. I was too weak. Nash was out of practice.

Then Emma breathed. I almost missed it, because there was no Oscar-worthy gasp for air. No panting, no wheezing, and no choking cough to clear sluggish lungs. She simply inhaled.

My head fell into my hands, tears of relief overflowing. I laughed, but no sound came out. I had truly lost my voice.

Emma opened her eyes, and the spell was broken. Someone in the crowd gasped, and suddenly everyone was in motion, leaning closer, whispering to companions, covering gaping mouths with shaking hands.

Emma blinked up at me, and her forehead furrowed in confusion. "Why am I…on the floor?"

I opened my mouth to answer, but the residual pain in my throat reminded me I'd lost my voice. Nash shot me a grin of total, exhilarating triumph and answered for me. "You're fine. I think you passed out."

"She had no pulse." The round woman sat back from Emma, her face flushed in bewilderment. "She was… I checked. She should be…"

"She passed out," Nash repeated firmly. "She probably hit her head when she fell, but she's fine now." To demonstrate, he held out his hand for one of hers, then pulled her upright, her legs stretched out on the floor in front of her.

"You shouldn't move her!" the principal scolded from my side. "She could have broken something."

"I'm fine." Emma's voice was thick with confusion. "Nothing hurts."

A quiet murmur rose around us, as the news spread to those too far back to have seen the show. Whispered words, like "died" and "no pulse" set me on edge, but when Nash reached across Emma's lap to take my hand, the anxiety receded.

Until a second scream shattered the growing calm.

Heads turned and people gasped. Emma and Nash stared in horror over my shoulder, and I twisted to follow their gaze.

The crowd still surrounded us, but through gaps between the bodies, I saw enough to piece together what had happened.

Someone else was down.

I couldn't see who it was, because someone was already bent over her, performing CPR. But I knew by the straight black skirt and slim, smooth calves that it was a girl, and I knew from the pattern that she would be young and beautiful.

Nash's hand tightened around mine, and I glanced up to find his face as tense with regret as mine surely was. We'd done the unthinkable. We'd saved Emma at the expense of someone else's life. Not one of ours—an innocent, uninvolved girl's.

I arched both eyebrows at him, asking silently if he was willing to try it again. He nodded gravely but looked less than confident that we could carry it off. And in the back of my mind, tragic certainty lingered: if we saved another one, the reaper would simply strike again. And again. Or he'd take one of us. Either way, we couldn't afford to play his game.

But I couldn't let someone else die for no reason.

I opened my mouth to scream—and nothing came out. I'd forgotten my voice was gone, and this time so was the urge to wail. There was no panic. No fresh pain clawing up the inside of my throat.

Horrified, I looked to Nash for advice, but he only frowned back at me. "If you can't sing, she's already gone," he whispered. "The urge ends once the reaper has her soul."

Which was why my song for Meredith had ended as soon as she'd died—we'd made no bid for her soul.

Devastated, I could only watch as people scurried around the dead girl, trying to help, trying to see, trying to understand. And in the middle of the confusion, one of the onlookers caught my eye. Because she wasn't looking on. While everyone else was focused on the girl lying on the gym floor, one slim arm thrown across the green three-point line, one woman stood against the back corner, staring at…me.

She didn't move, and in fact seemed eerily frozen against all the commotion surrounding us. As I watched, she smiled at me slowly, intimately, as if we'd shared some kind of secret.

And we had. She was the reaper.

"Nash…" I croaked, and groped for his hand, hesitant to take my eyes from the oddly motionless woman.

"I see her." But he'd barely spoken the last word before she was gone. She blinked out of existence, as silently and suddenly as Tod had, and in the bedlam, no one else seemed to notice.

Frustration and fury blazed through me, singeing me from the inside out. The reaper was taunting us.

We'd known the possible consequence and had taken the risk anyway, and now someone had died to pay for our decision. And the reaper had probably known all along that we couldn't stop her.

And the worst part was that when I looked at Emma, who had no idea what her life had cost, I didn't regret my choice. Not even a little bit.

17

Over the next few minutes, details filtered back to us through the crowd, now thankfully focused on the other side of the room. The girl was a junior. A cheerleader named Julie Duke. I knew the name and could call up a vague image of her face. She was pretty and well liked, and if memory served, more friendly and accepting than most of the other pom-pom-wavers.

When Julie still had no pulse several minutes after she collapsed, adults began herding the students toward the doors, almost as one. Nash and I were allowed to stay because we were Emma's ride, but the teachers wouldn't let her leave until the EMTs had checked her out. However, Julie was the top priority, so when the medics arrived, the principal led them directly to the cluster of people around her.

But it was too late. Even if I hadn't already known that, it would have been obvious by their posture alone, and the unhurried way they went about their business, and eventually wheeled her out on a sheet-draped gurney. Then a single EMT in black pants and a pressed uniform shirt walked across the gym toward us, first-aid kit in hand. He examined Emma thoroughly, but found nothing that could have caused her collapse. Her pulse, blood pressure, and breathing were all fine. Her skin was flushed and healthy, her eyes were dilating, and her reflexes were... reflexing.

The medic concluded that she'd simply fainted, but said she should come to the hospital for a more thorough exam, just in case. Emma tried to decline, but the principal trumped her decision with a call to Ms. Marshall, who said she'd meet her daughter there.

When I was sure Sophie had a ride home, Nash and I followed the ambulance to the hospital, where the triage nurse put Emma in a small, bright room to await examination. And her mother. As soon as the nurse left, closing the door on his way out, Emma turned to face us both, her expression a mixture of fear and confusion.

"What happened?" she demanded, ignoring the pillows to sit straight on the hospital bed, legs crossed yoga-style. "The truth."

I glanced at Nash, who'd pulled a rubber glove from a box mounted on the wall, but he only shrugged and nodded in her direction, giving me the clear go-ahead. "Um..." I croaked, unsure how much to tell her. Or how to phrase it. Or whether my still-froggy voice would hold out. "You died."

"I *died?*" Emma's eyes went huge and round. Whatever she'd expected to hear, I hadn't said it.

I nodded hesitantly. "You died, and we brought you back."

She swallowed thickly, glancing from me to Nash—who was now blowing up the disposable glove—and back. "You guys saved me? Like, you did CPR?" Her arms relaxed, and her shoulders fell in relief—she'd obviously been expecting something... weirder. I considered simply nodding, but no one else would corroborate our story. We had to tell her the truth—or at least one version of it.

"Not exactly." I faltered, raising one brow at Nash, asking him silently for help.

He sighed and let the air out of the glove, then sank onto the edge of Emma's bed. I sat in front of him and leaned back against

his chest. I'd barely broken physical contact with him since singing to Emma's soul, and I wasn't looking to do it anytime soon.
"Okay, we're going to tell you what's going on—" However, I
knew when he squeezed my hand that he wasn't going to tell
her *every*thing, and he didn't want me to either. "But first I need
you to swear you won't tell anyone else. No one. Ever. Even if
you're still living ninety years from now and itching to make a
deathbed confession."

Emma grinned and rolled her eyes. "Yeah, like I'll be thinking about the two of you when I'm a hundred and six and
breathing my last."

Nash chuckled and wrapped his arms around my waist. I
leaned into his chest, and his heart beat against my back. When
he spoke, his breath stirred the hair over my ear, softly soothing
me, though I knew that part was meant for Emma. Just in case.

"So you swear?" he asked, and she nodded. "You know how
Kaylee can tell when someone's going to die?" Emma nodded
again, her eyes narrowed now, fresh curiosity shining in them,
edged with fear she probably didn't want us to see. "Well, sometimes, under certain circumstances…she can bring them back."

"With his help," I added hoarsely, then immediately wondered
if his own involvement was one of the parts Nash wanted to keep
to himself. But he kissed the back of my head to tell me it was
okay.

"Yes, with my help." His fingers curled around mine, where
my hand lay in my lap. "Together, we…woke you up. Sort of.
You'll be fine now. There's absolutely nothing wrong with you,
and the doctor will probably decide you passed out from stress,
or grief, or something. Just like the EMT did."

For nearly a minute, Emma was silent, taking it all in. I was
afraid that even under Nash's careful Influence, she might freak
out, or start laughing at us. But she only blinked and shook her
head. "I died?" she asked again. "And you guys brought me back.

I *knew* I should have had that little digital health meter installed over my head, so I know when I'm about to drop."

I smiled, relieved that she could see the humor in the situation, and Nash laughed out loud, his whole body quaking against my back. "Well, with any luck, we've unlocked infinite health for you," he said.

Emma smiled back briefly, then her face grew serious. "Was it like the others? I just collapsed?"

"Yeah." I hated having to tell her about her own death. "In midsentence."

"Why?"

"We don't know," Nash said before I could answer. I let his response stand, because technically it was the truth, even if it wasn't the whole truth. And because I didn't want Emma mixed up in anything that involved a psychotic, extra-grim, female reaper.

She thought for a moment, her fingers skimming the white hospital blanket. When her hand bumped the bed's controller, she picked it up, glancing at the buttons briefly before meeting my gaze again. "How did you do it?"

"That's…complicated." I searched for the right words, but they wouldn't come. "I don't know how to explain it, and it's not really important." At least as far as Emma was concerned. "What matters is that you're okay."

She pressed a button on the controller, and the head of the bed rose several inches beneath her. "So what happened with Julie?"

That was the question I'd been dreading. I glanced at my lap, where my fingers were twisting one another into knots. Then I shifted to look at Nash, hoping he had a better, less traumatizing way to explain it than simply "She died for you."

But evidently he did not. "We saved your life, and we'd do it again if we had to. But death is just like life in some ways, Em. Everything has a price."

"A price?" Emma flinched, and her hand clenched the

controller. The bed lowered beneath her, but she didn't even notice. "You killed Julie to save me?"

"No!" I reached out for Emma, but she scooted backward into the pillow, horrified. "We had nothing to do with Julie dying! But when we brought you back, we created a sort of vacuum, and something had to fill it." Which wasn't exactly true. But I couldn't explain that there shouldn't have been a price for her life without telling her about *bean sidhes,* and reapers, and other, darker things I didn't even understand yet myself.

Emma relaxed a little but didn't move any closer to us. "Did you know that when you saved me?" she asked, and again I was surprised by how insightful her questions were. *She'd probably make a much better* bean sidhe *than I will.*

Nash cleared his throat behind me, ready to field the question. "We knew it was a possibility. But your case was an exception, of sorts, so we hoped it wouldn't happen. And we had no idea who would go instead."

Emma frowned. "So you didn't get a premonition about her death?"

"No, I..." *Didn't.* I hadn't even thought about it until she asked. "Why didn't I know about her?" I asked, twisting to look at Nash.

"Because the reason for her death—" meaning the reaper's decision to take her "—didn't exist until we brought Emma back. Which proves Julie wasn't supposed to die either."

"She wasn't supposed to die?" Emma hugged a hospital pillow to her chest.

"No." I leaned into Nash's embrace and immediately felt guilty because she'd just died, yet had no one to lean on. So I sat up again, but couldn't bring myself to let go of his hand. "Something's wrong. We're trying to figure it out, but we're not really sure where to start."

"Was *I* supposed to die?" Her gaze burned into me. I'd never seen my best friend look so vulnerable and scared.

Nash shook his head firmly on the edge of my vision. "That's why we brought you back. I wish we could have helped Julie."

Emma frowned. "Why couldn't you?"

"We...weren't fast enough." I grimaced as frustration and anger over my own failure twisted at my gut. "And I sort of used it all up on you."

"What does that mean—" But before she could finish the question, the door opened, and a middle-aged woman in scrubs and a lab coat entered. She carried a clipboard and led a very flustered Ms. Marshall.

"Emma, I believe this woman belongs to you?" The doctor tucked her clipboard under one arm, and Ms. Marshall brushed past her and rushed to the bed, where she nearly crushed her youngest daughter in a hug.

Suddenly the bed lurched beneath us, and Nash and I jumped off the mattress, startled. "Sorry." Emma dug the controller from beneath her leg, where it had fallen.

"Um, we're gonna go," I said, backing toward the door. "My dad's supposed to get in tonight, and I really need to talk to him."

"Your dad's coming home?" Still tight within the embrace, Emma pushed a poof of her mother's hair aside so she could see me, and I nodded.

"I'll call you tomorrow. 'Kay?"

Emma frowned as her mother settled onto the bed, but nodded when the doctor held the door open for us. She would be fine. For better or worse, we'd saved her life, at least for now. And with any luck, she wouldn't catch another reaper's eye for a very, very long time.

Ms. Marshall waved to me as the door closed in front of us, and the last thing I heard was Emma insisting that she *would* have called, if she still had her phone.

Our footsteps clomped on the dingy vinyl tile as we passed the nurses' station, heading for the heavy double doors leading into the ER waiting room. It was only four o'clock in the afternoon, and I was exhausted. And the tickle in my throat reminded me that I still sounded like a bullfrog.

I'd barely finished that thought when a familiar voice called my name from the broad, white corridor behind us. I froze in midstep, but Nash only stopped when he noticed I had.

"I thought you might want something warm for your throat. Sounds like you really wore it out today."

I turned to find Tod holding a steaming paper cup, his other hand wrapped around an empty IV stand.

Nash tensed at my side. "What's wrong?" he asked. But he was looking at me rather than at Tod.

I glanced at the reaper with my brows raised. Tod shrugged and grinned. "He can't see me. Or hear me unless I want him to." Then he turned to Nash, and I understood that whatever he said next, Nash would hear. "And until he apologizes, you and I will carry on all of our conversations without him."

Nash went stiff, following my gaze to what he apparently saw as an empty hallway. "Damn it, Tod," he whispered angrily. "Leave her alone."

Tod grinned, like we'd shared a private joke. "I'm not even touching her."

Nash ground his teeth together, but I rolled my eyes and spoke up before he could say something we'd all regret. "This is ridiculous. Nash, be nice. Tod, show yourself. Or I'm leaving you both here."

Nash remained silent but did manage to unclench his jaws. And I knew the moment Tod appeared to him, because his focus narrowed on the reaper's face. "What are you doing here?"

"I work here." Tod let go of the IV stand and ambled forward, holding the steaming cup out for me. I took it without thinking—my throat did hurt, and something hot would feel good going down. I sipped from a tiny slit in the lid and was surprised to taste sweet, rich hot chocolate, with just a bit of cinnamon.

I gave him a grateful smile. "I love cocoa."

Tod shrugged and slid his hands into the pockets of his baggy jeans, but a momentary flash in his eyes gave away his satisfaction. "I wasn't sure you'd like coffee, but I figured chocolate was a sure thing."

A soft gnashing sound met my ears as Nash tried to grind his teeth into stubs, and his hand tightened around mine. "Let's go, Kaylee."

I nodded, then shrugged apologetically at Tod. "Yeah, I should get home."

"To see your dad?" The reaper grinned slyly, and whatever points he'd gained with the hot chocolate he lost instantly for invading my privacy.

"You were spying on me?"

A door opened on the right side of the hallway and an orderly emerged, pushing an elderly man in a wheelchair. They both glanced our way briefly before continuing down the hall in the opposite direction. But just in case, Tod lowered his voice and stepped closer. "Not spying. Listening. I'm stuck here twelve hours a day, and it's ridiculous for me to pretend I don't hear stuff."

"What did you hear?" I demanded.

Tod looked from me to Nash, then glanced at the nurses' station at the end of the hall, at the juncture of two other corridors. Then he nodded toward a closed, unnumbered door on the left and motioned for me and Nash to join him.

I went, and Nash followed me reluctantly. Tod made an "after you" gesture at the door, but when I tried to open it, the knob wouldn't turn. "It's locked."

"Oops." Tod disappeared, and a moment later the door opened from the inside. The reaper stood in a small, dark storage closet lined with shelves stacked with medication, syringes, and assorted medical supplies.

I hesitated, afraid someone might walk in and catch us. A

reaper could blink himself out of trouble, but *bean sidhes* could not. But then light footsteps squeaked toward us from one of the other hallways, and Nash suddenly shoved me inside and closed the door behind us.

There was a second of darkness, then something clicked and light bathed us from a bare bulb overhead. Nash had found the switch. "Okay, spit it out," he snapped. "I do not want to explain to Kaylee's father why we were caught in a locked hospital storage room full of controlled substances."

"Fair enough." Tod leaned with one shoulder against a shelf along the back wall, giving me and Nash as much room as possible—which was about a square foot apiece. "I was waiting on a guy with a knife wound to the chest. Should have been short and simple, but I stepped out to take a call from my boss, and by the time I got back inside, the doc had brought him back three times. You know, with those shock paddle things?"

"So you let him live?" Nash sounded nearly as surprised as I was.

"Um…no." Tod frowned, blond curls gleaming in the unfiltered light. "He was on my list. Anyway, when I finished with the stab victim, I came out to the lobby for a cup of coffee and heard you talking." He was looking at me now, and completely ignoring Nash. "So I followed you into your friend's room. She's hot."

"Stay away from…her," I finished lamely, remembering at the last minute that it wasn't wise to give out my friends' names to the agents of death. Not that the reaper couldn't find it on his own anyway. And not that Death didn't already have Emma's name on file, after that afternoon.

Tod rolled his eyes. "What kind of reaper do you think I am? And anyway, what fun would killing her be?"

"Leave her alone," Nash snapped. "Let's go." He turned and grabbed the handle, then threw the door open fast enough that if anyone from the nurses' station had been looking, we'd have been caught for sure. Surprised, I hurried after him and barely heard the storage closet close behind me. We were nearly to the double doors when Tod spoke again.

"Don't you want to know about the phone call?" He only whispered, but somehow his voice carried as if he'd spoken from an inch away.

I stopped, pulling Nash to a sudden halt. He glanced at me in confusion, then in mounting irritation, and I realized with a jolt of shock that once again he hadn't heard Tod—and that I shouldn't have either. The reaper was at least twenty feet away, still in front of the closet.

"The call from your boss?" I whispered experimentally, to see if Tod could hear me.

The reaper nodded, smiling smugly.

"What did he say?" Nash growled softly, angrily.

"Come on." After a quick look to make sure none of the nurses were watching, I nearly dragged him down the hall and back into the closet behind Tod. "Why should we care about your communication issues with your boss?" I asked aloud, to catch Nash up on the discussion.

"Because he has a theory about the off-list reaping." Tod's grin grew as he leaned against the left-hand shelf, and a small dimple appeared in his right cheek, highlighted by the stark light from overhead. How could I not have noticed that before?

"What theory?" Nash asked. Apparently he could hear Tod again.

"Everything costs something. You should know that by now."

"Fine." I huffed in frustration and ignored Nash when his hand tightened around mine. "Tell us what you know, and we'll tell you what we know."

Tod laughed and pulled a plastic bedpan from the shelf, peering into it as if he expected a magician's rabbit to hop out. "You're bluffing. You don't know anything about this."

"We saw the reaper when Emma died," I said, and his smile

faded instantly. He dropped the bedpan back onto the shelf and I knew I had his attention. "Start talking."

"You better be telling the truth." Tod's gaze shifted between me and Nash repeatedly.

"I told you, Kaylee doesn't lie," Nash said, and I couldn't help noticing he didn't include himself in that statement.

Tod hesitated for a moment, as if considering. Then he nodded. "My boss is this really old reaper named Levi. He's been around for a while. Like, a hundred fifty years." He crossed his arms over his chest, getting comfortable against the back wall of shelves. "Levi said something like this happened when he first became a reaper. Everything was a lot less organized back then, and by the time they figured out someone was taking people not on the list—they wrote the whole thing by hand back then, can you imagine?—they'd already lost six souls from his region."

"You're serious?" Nash wrapped one arm around my waist, and I let him pull me close. "Or are you just making all this up to impress Kaylee?"

Tod shot him a dark scowl, but I thought it was a totally valid question. "Every word of this came straight from Levi. If you don't believe me, you can ask him yourself."

Nash stiffened, and muttered something about that not being necessary.

"So why were they dying?" I asked, drawing us back on subject.

The reaper's eyes settled on me again, and he lowered his voice conspiratorially, blue eyes gleaming. "Their souls were being poached."

"Poached?" I twisted to glance at Nash with one brow raised, but he only shrugged, his mouth set in a hard line. "Why would anyone steal souls?"

"Good question." Tod fingered a box of disposable thermometer covers. His grin widened, and I was reminded of the way movie-goers sometimes cheer during murder scenes, secure in the knowledge that they're seeing fake blood and movie magic. "There's not much use for detached souls in *this* world…." The reaper left his last word hanging, and a sick feeling twisted deep in my stomach.

"But there is in the Netherworld?" I finished for him, and Tod nodded, evidently impressed that my newbie roots were no longer showing.

"Souls are a rarity on the deeper plane. Something between a delicacy and a luxury. They're in very high demand, and every now and then a shipment goes missing in transit."

"A shipment of souls?" A bolt of dread shot through me at the very thought. "In transit from where? To where?"

Nash answered, looking simultaneously pleased to know the answer and annoyed at having to provide it. "From here to where they're…recycled."

"Reincarnated?"

"Yeah." Tod stood straighter and bumped his head on an upper shelf, then rubbed it as he spoke. "But sometimes a shipment doesn't make it, so those souls aren't passed on. They're replaced with new ones, which is one of the reasons you'll run into a brand-new soul sometimes."

I made a mental note to ask later how one might identify a new soul. "So these poached souls are going to the Netherworld?" I asked, trying to simply stay afloat in the current of new information. "You mean Meredith, and Julie, and the others were killed so some monster in another realm could make a midnight snack out of their souls?" I gripped a shoulder-height shelf for balance as my head spun. I couldn't quite wrap my mind around what I'd just said.

"That's Levi's theory." Tod picked up a roll of sterile gauze and tossed it into the air, then caught it. "He said the last time this happened, they were being collected as payment to a hellion."

My hand clutched the shelf and a protruding screw cut my

finger, but I barely noticed because of the dark dread swirling in me like a dense fog. "A hellion?"

Nash exhaled heavily. "Humans would call them demons, but that's not exactly right, because they have no association with any religion. They feed on pain and chaos. But they can't leave the Netherworld."

"Okay…" My pulse raced, and I flashed back to the gray creatures I'd seen during Emma's soul song. Were those hellions? "Payment for what?"

The reaper shrugged. "Could be anything. Sometimes deals are struck. Under the table, of course. Levi'll take care of it, as soon as he finds the reaper responsible." He caught the gauze one more time and shrugged, having evidently given us everything he knew. Which was much more than I'd expected. "So…what about this reaper you saw?"

"Tell Levi he's looking for a woman." I shifted closer to Nash and accidentally bumped a shelf. Several boxes of medical tubing fell over, spilling their contents like clear plastic worms.

"A woman?" Tod's eyes widened, and I nodded.

"Tall and thin, with wavy brown hair," Nash said. "Sound like someone you know?"

Tod shook his head. "But Levi knows every reaper in the state. He'll take care of it." He hesitated, as if unsure whether or not to say the next part. "But he thinks you're going to get your own souls poached before he can get everything back under control."

"Is that what *you* think?" I wasn't sure why his opinion mattered to me, but it did.

Tod shrugged, fingering his makeshift ball. "I'd say that's a very real possibility. Especially if you keep wiggling your fingers in front of the tiger's mouth."

"We had no choice." I bent to restack the boxes I'd spilled. "The tiger was about to eat my best friend."

"You're something else, Kaylee Cavanaugh," Tod whispered,

and I knew from Nash's blank, angry expression that he hadn't heard that part either, though he'd clearly seen the reaper's lips move. "It could have been you, instead of that cheerleader. It might be, next time. Or it might be him." His gaze flicked to Nash and back, and his irreverent expression darkened.

"Let Levi handle it," he said. "If you won't do it for me, or even for yourself, do it for Nash. Please."

Tod looked truly scared, and I didn't know what to make of fear coming from a grim reaper. So I nodded. "We're out of it. I already promised my uncle." I reached back for Nash's hand as Tod nodded. Then he disappeared, still holding the gauze, and I was alone with Nash in the cramped closet.

"What did he say?" Nash shifted in his seat, staring out the passenger's side window at the passing streetlights. We were almost to my house, and those were the first words he'd spoken since we'd pulled out of the hospital parking garage.

"Is there anything else I should know about reapers?" I couldn't keep annoyance out of my voice; I was tired of being left in the dark. "Can they read my thoughts or see through my clothes?" *Which would actually explain a lot…* "Or make me stand on my head and squawk like a chicken?"

Nash sighed and finally turned to face me. "Reapers are like a supernatural jack-of-all-trades. They can appear wherever they want and can choose who sees and hears them. If they want to be seen or heard at all. They have other minor abilities, but nothing else as infuriating as the whole selective-hearing thing." He wrapped one hand around the armrest, his knuckles white with tension. "So what did he say?"

I hesitated to answer; if Tod had wanted Nash to hear, he'd have broadcast on all frequencies. *Then again, he didn't make me promise….* "He asked me not to get you killed. He's trying to protect you."

I glanced away from the road in time to see Nash roll his eyes.

"No, he's trying to protect *you,* and he knows you'll be more cautious for my sake than for your own."

"How do you know that's what he's doing?"

"Because that's what I would have done."

An adrenaline-soaked warmth spread through my chest, even though I knew Nash was wrong. Tod was looking out for him, at least in part.

Squinting into the late-afternoon sun, I turned into my neighborhood. Two lefts later, my aunt's car came into sight, parked in the driveway next to the empty spot mine usually occupied. My uncle had taken the day off, expecting my father to arrive around midmorning. And surely Sophie had already made it back from the memorial. *The gang's all here....*

Nash followed me into the living room, where my uncle sat in the floral-print armchair, angled so that he could see both the television—tuned to the local news—and the front window. He stood when we came in, stuffing his hands into his pockets, his anxious gaze searching my expression immediately for any sign of trouble.

"Sophie told us what happened. Are you okay?"

"Fine." I collapsed onto one end of the couch and pulled Nash down with me.

Uncle Brendon's gaze captured mine and held it. "Val...isn't feeling well today. I just put her back in bed."

Now? I glanced out the front window to see the last rays of afternoon light just then sinking below the rooftops across the street. It wasn't even five-thirty.

"This may not be the best time for company," he continued, glancing briefly at Nash.

"I want him to meet Dad," I insisted, and my uncle looked like he wanted to argue. But then he nodded in resignation and sank into his chair. "What did Sophie tell you?" I asked. I was surprised he hadn't called me, but I'd checked my phone in the car, and there were no messages or missed calls.

But then again, he was probably pretty busy dealing with my aunt.

Uncle Brendon leaned back in his chair and lifted a sweating can of Coke from the end table. "She said Emma fainted, and while everyone was fussing over her, one of the cheerleaders fell over dead. The whole school's in complete shock. It's already been on the news."

I swallowed thickly and glanced at Nash. And naturally, Uncle Brendon caught the look.

"Emma died, didn't she?" His expression was pained, as if he wasn't sure he really wanted to hear the truth. "She died, and you two brought her back."

At his words, horror and a stunned incredulity washed over me in a devastating wave—the culmination of every terrifying thing I'd seen and done over the past few days, and I could only nod, holding back tears through sheer will.

Anger rolled across my uncle's face like fog before a storm, and he stood, his hand fisted around the can. If it had been full, he'd have been wearing most of his soda. "I told you to stay out of it. I said your father and I would look into it. You could have *died,* and as it stands now, you got someone *else* killed."

I shot to my feet, anger eclipsing my weaker emotions. "That's not fair. None of this was our fault!"

"There's nothing fair about this," Uncle Brendon roared, and I knew from his volume alone that Sophie wasn't at home. "If you don't believe me, go ask that poor cheerleader's parents."

Nash stood at my side, his stance steady and strong, his gaze unyielding. "Mr. Cavanaugh, we had nothing to do with Julie's death. In fact, we tried to save her too, but—"

We all seemed to realize simultaneously that he'd said the wrong thing. I squeezed Nash's hand to silence him, but it was too late.

"You tried to do it again?" Uncle Brendon's fury was surpassed only by his fear.

"We had to!" I was shouting now, and the entire living room swam with the tears filling my eyes. "I couldn't let the reaper steal another soul without at least trying to stop it."

A glimpse of sympathy flashed through his anger, but then it was gone, stamped out by fear born of caution. "You have to. You can't go sticking your nose into reaper business every time someone you know dies, unless you want to die with them!" He turned to Nash then, anger still spinning in his eyes. "If you're going to tell her what she can do, you have a responsibility to also tell her what she can't do."

"He did," I said before Nash could answer. "But Emma wasn't supposed to die."

My uncle's eyes narrowed in suspicion. "How do you know that?"

Nash spoke before I could, probably to keep me from digging my hole any deeper. "Tod got a look at the list. The reaper is a rogue, and none of those girls were supposed to die."

"See?" I demanded, when Nash went silent without revealing the rest of Tod's information. "We had to save her. She wasn't meant to die yet." *Plus, she's my best friend.* "Tell me you wouldn't have done the same thing."

"He wouldn't have." The new voice came from the entry, carried on a soft September breeze, and we all whirled toward it in unison. My dad stood in the doorway, a suitcase in each hand. "But I would."

I should have said something. I should have had some kind of greeting for the father I hadn't seen in a year and a half. But my mouth wouldn't open, and the longer I stood there in silence, the better I came to understand the problem. It wasn't that I had nothing to say to him. It was that I had too much to say.

Why did you lie? Where have you been? What makes you think coming back now will make any difference? But I couldn't decide what to say first.

Nash didn't have that problem. "I'm guessing this is your dad?" he whispered, leaning closer so that our shoulders touched.

My father nodded, thick brown waves bobbing with the movement. His hair was longer than I remembered it, and nearly brushed his shoulders. I couldn't help wondering how different I looked to him.

"You must be Harmony's boy," my father said, his deep voice rumbling. "Brendon said you'd probably be here."

"Yes, sir," Nash said. Then, to me, he said, "He doesn't sound like he's from Ireland."

My father dropped his bags in the entryway. "I'm not. I just live there." He reached back to pull the front door closed, then scuffed his boots on the mat before stepping into the living room. My dad took a long look at me, from head to toe, and his jaw hardened when his eyes lingered on my right hand, still clasped in Nash's. Then his gaze landed on my face, and a series of emotions passed over his.

Grief, first of all. I'd expected that one. The older I got, the more I looked like my mother. She was only twenty-three when she died—at least that's what they'd told me—and sometimes even I was freaked out by the resemblance in old pictures. He also looked sad and a little worried, as if he dreaded our upcoming conversation.

But the last expression—the part that kept me from storming out of the house and taking off in the car he'd paid for—was pride. My father's eyes gleamed with it, even as old pain etched lines into his otherwise youthful face.

"Hey, kiddo." He took a deep breath, and his entire chest fell as he exhaled. "Think I could get a hug?"

I'd had no intention of hugging my father. I was still so mad at him I could hardly think about anything else, even with everything else going on. Yet I disentangled my hand from Nash's and stepped forward on autopilot. My father crossed the rest of the floor toward me. He wrapped his huge arms around me and my head found his chest, just like it had when I was little.

He might have looked different, but he smelled exactly the same. Like coffee, and the wool in his coat, and whatever cologne he'd been wearing as long as I could remember. Hugging my father brought back the ghosts of memories so old I couldn't quite bring them into focus.

"I missed you," he said into my hair, as if I were still a child.

I stepped back and crossed my arms over my chest. Hugs wouldn't fix everything. "You could have visited."

"I should have." It wasn't quite an apology, but at least we agreed on something.

"Well, you're here now." Uncle Brendon turned toward the kitchen. "Sit, Aiden. What can I get you to drink?"

"Coffee, thanks." My dad shrugged out of his black wool coat and draped it over the back of an armchair. "So…" He sank into the chair, and I sat opposite him, beside Nash on the couch. "I hear you've discovered your heritage. And tried it out, evidently. You restored a friend?"

I met his eyes boldly, daring him to criticize my decision when he'd already admitted he'd have done the same. "Emma wasn't supposed to die. None of them were."

"None of *them?*" My father frowned toward the kitchen; obviously Uncle Brendon hadn't yet given him the details of my discovery. "Who else are we talking about?"

"There were three others. One a day, three days in a row." Nash's thumb stroked the back of mine until my father scowled at him, and he dropped my hand and leaned back on the couch. "Then the reaper took someone else today when we saved Emma."

Irritated—yet amused—I reclaimed his hand and let them both rest on my lap. Absentee fathers had no right to disapprove of boyfriends. "All four of them—five if you count Emma—just fell over dead with no warning. It wasn't their time to go."

"How do you know?"

I leaned into Nash, smiling innocently as my father's jaw tightened. "Nash's friend Tod is a reaper."

My father's brows rose in surprise, and for a moment he forgot to scowl. "Your friend's a reaper?"

Nash shrugged. "I knew him before he…died."

Dad leaned forward, elbows propped on his knees, eyes narrowed. "And this reaper told you the girls weren't on his list?"

"They weren't on *any* list," I said, drawing his scrutiny from Nash. "Tod's boss thinks there's a reaper out there poaching souls to be sold in the Netherworld. Or something like that."

Uncle Brendon froze in the doorway, holding two steaming, fragrant mugs. "Someone's selling souls in the Netherworld?" He and my father exchanged twin looks of horror and dread before turning back to us. "What do you know about the Netherworld?"

"Just that there *is* one, and that some of the locals are hot for human souls." I shrugged, trying to set them both at ease. "But that doesn't really matter to us, right? Tod's boss said he would take care of it."

The relief on my uncle's face was as thick as the tension in Nash's posture. "Good. The reapers should take care of their own problems. It really isn't *bean sidhe* business."

Frowning, I scuffed the toe of my shoe into the carpet. "Except that this psycho reaper tried to take a *bean sidhe's* best friend. That kind of makes it my business."

Uncle Brendon scowled and looked ready to argue, but my father spoke before he could. "Did people see you bring Emma back?" he asked, cradling his steaming mug as if for warmth.

Nash sat straighter, eager to defend me. "No one knew what was happening. Em had just collapsed, and everyone thought Kaylee was freaked out over that. And once Emma sat up, they all thought she'd just fainted."

That was mostly true, though rumors were already circulating that Emma's heart had actually stopped for a minute. The lady who took her pulse had probably started them. Not that I could blame her. The poor woman would probably need therapy.

But then, so might I. And maybe Emma.

My father shrugged, eyeing his brother sternly. "Sounds like no harm was done."

"Except for Julie," I muttered, and immediately wished I'd kept my mouth shut.

My father paused with his mug halfway to his mouth. "She's the exchange?"

"Yeah." And though I knew in my heart that Julie's death wasn't our fault, I couldn't escape the guilt that tightened my chest and made my whole body feel heavy.

Uncle Brendon sank into the other armchair and shook his head in regret. "This is why you have to stay out of reaper business. That poor girl would be alive right now if you two had just left things alone."

"Yeah, but Emma wouldn't." My free hand gripped the arm of the couch. "And we had no way of knowing for sure she'd take another one. Tod said there shouldn't be any penalty for saving a life that shouldn't have been taken in the first place."

"She?" My father slowly lowered his mug onto its coaster. "Do I even want to know how you know the reaper is a woman?"

I shifted uncomfortably on the couch and glanced at Nash, but he shrugged, leaving it up to me. So I made myself meet my father's gaze. "We...kind of saw her."

Uncle Brendon sat straight in his chair, every muscle in his body tense. "How?"

"She just showed up." I shrugged. "When they were doing CPR on Julie. She was at the back of the gym, behind most of the crowd, and she smiled at us."

"She smiled at you?" My father frowned. "Why would she show herself on purpose?"

"It doesn't matter," my uncle said. "The reapers will take care of their own. We should stay out of it."

For a moment, I thought my father would argue. He looked almost as angry as I was. But then he nodded decisively. "I agree."

"But what if they can't find her?" I demanded, Nash's hand still clasped in mine.

My father shook his head and leaned back in his chair, crossing both arms over the front of his sweater. "If you two can find her, the reapers can find her."

"But—"

"They're right, Kaylee," Nash said only inches from my ear. "We don't even know who the reaper will go after next. If she does it again at all."

She *would*. The moment she'd smiled at me, I'd known she wasn't finished. She would take another girl soon, unless someone stopped her. But no one else seemed willing to try.

My father turned to his brother, his thoughts hidden by a calm facade. "How are your girls?" he asked, and just like that, the subject was closed.

"They aren't taking this very well." My uncle heaved a heavy sigh. "Sophie's out with her friends. The girl who died yesterday was on her dance team, and the rest of the squad is spending every waking moment together, like some sort of perpetual wake. And Val… She got a quarter of the way through a bottle of brandy this afternoon, before I even knew she'd opened it. I put her to bed about an hour ago to let her sleep it off."

Wow. Maybe Aunt Val needed to go see Dr. Nelson.

"I'm sorry, Bren."

Uncle Brendon shrugged, as if it didn't matter, but the tense line of his shoulders said otherwise. "She was always pretty high-strung. Sophie's the same way. They'll be fine once this all blows over."

But it wasn't going to blow over, and I couldn't be the only one who knew that.

Uncle Brendon stood and picked up his mug. His every movement spoke of exhaustion and dread. "I'm going to check on my wife. Val got the guest room ready for you this morning. If you need anything else, just ask Kaylee."

"Thanks." When Uncle Brendon's bedroom door closed, my father stood and faced Nash, obviously expecting him to stand too. "Nash, I can't tell you how grateful I am for how you've helped my daughter."

Still stubbornly seated, Nash shook his head. "I couldn't have done anything without her there to hold the soul."

"I mean what you did for Kaylee. Brendon says your dose of truth probably saved her from a serious breakdown." He held his hand out, and Nash floundered for one awkward moment, then stood and accepted it.

"Dad…" I started, but he shook his head.

"I messed up, and Nash picked up the slack. He deserves to be thanked." He shook Nash's hand firmly, then let go and stepped back, clearing an obvious path to the front door.

I rolled my eyes at his less-than-subtle hint. "I agree. But Nash is staying. He knows more about this than I do anyway." I slipped my hand into his and stood as close to him as I could get.

To my surprise, though he looked irritated, my father didn't argue. His gaze shifted from me to Nash, then back to me, and he simply nodded, evidently resigned. "Fine. If you trust him, so do I." He backed slowly toward his chair and sat facing us. Then he inhaled deeply and met my steady gaze. I was ready to hear whatever he had to say.

But the real question was whether or not he was ready to say it.

"I know this all should have come out years ago," he began. "But the truth is that every time I decided it was time to tell you about your mother—about yourself—I couldn't do it. You look so much like her...."

His voice cracked, and he glanced down, and when he looked at me again, his eyes were shiny with unshed tears.

"You look so much like her that every time I see you, my heart jumps for joy, then breaks all over again. Maybe it would have been easier if I'd kept you with me. If I'd seen you every day and watched you develop into your own person. But as it is, I look at you and I see her, and it's so damn *hard*..."

Nash squirmed, and I stared at my hands as my father looked around the living room, avoiding our eyes until he had himself under control. Then he sighed and swiped one arm across his eyes, blotting tears on a sweater too thick to be truly necessary in September.

Crap. He was actually crying. I didn't know how to deal with a crying father. I barely knew how to deal with a normal one.

"Um, anyone else hungry? I didn't get any supper."

"I could eat," Nash said, and I was sure he'd picked up on my need to break the tension.

Or maybe he was just hungry.

"Is macaroni and cheese okay?" I asked, already halfway out of the room by the time he nodded. Nash and my dad followed me through the dining room and into the kitchen, where I knelt to dig a bag of elbow pasta from the back of a bottom cabinet.

I'd thought I was ready. That I could deal with whatever he had to say. But the truth was that I couldn't just sit there and watch my father cry. I needed something to keep my hands busy while my heart broke.

"You can cook?" My father eyed me in surprise as I pulled a pot from another cabinet, and a block of Velveeta from my uncle's shelf in the fridge.

"It's just pasta. Uncle Brendon taught me." He'd also taught me to hide the occasional bag of chocolate behind his stash of pork rinds, which Aunt Val would never touch, even to throw away in a frenzied junk food purge.

My father sat on one of the bar stools, still watching as I turned the burner on and sprinkled salt into the water. Nash settled on a stool two down from him and crossed his arms on the countertop.

"So what do you want to know first?" My dad met my gaze over the cheese I was unwrapping on a cutting board.

I shrugged and pulled a knife from a drawer on my left. "I think I have a pretty good handle on the whole *bean sidhe* thing, thanks to Nash." My father cringed, and I might have felt guilty if he'd ever made any attempt to explain things himself. "But why did Aunt Val say I was living on borrowed time? What does that mean?"

This time he flinched like I'd slapped him. He'd obviously been expecting something else—probably a technical question from the *How to Be a* Bean Sidhe handbook, my copy of which had probably gotten lost in the mail.

My father sighed and suddenly looked very tired. "That's a long story, Kaylee, and one I'd rather tell in private."

"No." I shook my head firmly and ripped open the bag of pasta. "You flew halfway around the world because you owe me an explanation." *Not to mention an apology.* "I want to hear it now."

My father's brow rose in surprise, and more than a hint of irritation. Then he frowned. "You sound just like your mother."

Yeah, well, I had to inherit a backbone from someone. "Wouldn't she want you to tell me whatever it is you have to say?"

He couldn't have looked more shocked if I'd punched him. "I honestly don't know. But you're right. You're entitled to all the facts." He closed his eyes briefly, as if gathering his thoughts.

"It all started the night you died."

19

"What?" My hand fisted around a cube of cheese, and it squished between my fingers. My pulse pounded so hard in my throat I thought it would explode. "You mean the night Mom died."

My father nodded. "She died that night too. But you went first."

"Whoa…" Nash leaned forward on his stool, glancing back and forth between me and my father. "Kaylee died?"

My dad sighed, settling in for a long story. "It was February, the year you were three. The roads were icy. We don't get much winter weather in Texas, so when it does come, no one quite knows how to handle it. Including me."

"Wait, I've heard all this before." I dumped the pasta into the now-boiling water, and a puff of steam wafted into my face, coating my skin in a layer of instant dampness and warmth. "You were driving, and we were broadsided by another car on an icy road. I broke my right arm and leg, and Mom died."

My father nodded miserably, then swallowed thickly and continued. "We were on our way here, for Sophie's birthday party. Your mother thought the weather was too bad, but I said we'd be fine. It was a short trip, and your cousin adored you. The whole thing was my fault."

"What happened?" I asked, my cheesy hand forgotten.

My father blinked slowly, as if warding off tears. "There was a deer in the road. I wasn't going that fast, but the road was icy, and the deer was huge. I swerved to avoid it, and the car slid on the ice. We wound up sideways in the road. An oncoming car smashed into us. Near the rear on the passenger's side. Your car seat was crushed."

I closed my eyes and gripped the countertop as a wave of vertigo threatened to knock me over. *No.* My mother had died in that accident, not me. I'd been pretty banged up, but I'd lived.

I was living proof of that!

My eyes opened, focusing on my father instantly. "Dad, I remember parts of that. I was in the hospital for weeks. I had two casts. We still have pictures. But I'm alive. See?" I spread my arms across the countertop to demonstrate my point. "So what happened? The paramedics brought me back?"

The truth was looming, a great, dark cloud on my mind's horizon. I could almost see it, but I refused to bring it into focus. Refused to acknowledge the coming storm until it broke over my head, drenching me with a cold, cruel wash of the answers I'd thought I wanted.

I no longer wanted them.

But my father only shook his head. "They didn't get there in time. The man driving the other car was a doctor, but his wife hit her head on something, and he was trying to wake her up. By the time he came to help us, it was all over."

"No." I stirred the pasta so hard boiling water slopped onto the stovetop, hissing on the flat burner.

Nash's hand landed softly on mine, though I hadn't heard him move, and I looked up to meet his sympathetic gaze. "You died, Kaylee. You know it's true."

My father nodded again, and when his eyes squeezed shut, two silent tears trailed down his stubbly cheeks. "I had to go in through the driver's side and pull the whole car seat out. When

I picked you up, you didn't make a sound, even though your right arm and leg were bent all out of shape." His eyes opened, and the pain swirling there held me captive. "I held you like a baby, and you just looked at me. Then your mom crawled out of the car and took your good hand. She was crying, and she couldn't talk, and I could see the truth on her face. I knew we were going to lose you."

He sniffled and I stood still, afraid that if I moved, he'd stop talking. And even more frightened because part of me really wanted him to stop. "You died, right there on the side of the road, with snow melting in your hair."

"Then why am I still here?" I whispered, but I already knew the answer. "It was my time, wasn't it?" I flicked on the faucet and held my hands under the warm water, scrubbing cheese from between my fingers as I eyed my father. "I was supposed to die, and you brought me back."

"Yes." His voice cracked on that one syllable, and his face was starting to flush with the effort to hold back more tears. "We couldn't stand it. She sang for you, and it was the most beautiful thing I've ever heard. I could barely see, I was crying so hard. But then I saw you. Your soul. So small and white in the dark. It was too soon. I couldn't let you go."

I turned off the water and grabbed a towel from a drawer near my hip, dripping on the floor as I dried my hands, then leaned over the bar and stared at him. "Tell me how it happened."

He didn't hesitate this time. "I made your mother look at me, to make sure she understood. I told her to take care of you. That I was going to bring you back. She was crying, but she nodded, still singing. So I guided your soul back into your tiny little body. You blinked at me. Then, with your first breath, you sang."

"I...*sang?*" The towel slipped from my fingers and landed silently on the tiles, but I barely noticed.

"The soul song." My father pressed the heels of his hands

to his eyes, as if to physically hold back tears, but his face was still wet when he looked at me again. "I thought it was for me. You needed your mother more than you needed me, and I was ready to go. But as I stood there holding you, the reaper showed himself."

"He let you see him?" Nash interrupted from my side. I'd almost forgotten he was there.

My father nodded. "He stood in the grass, on the shoulder of the road. He smiled at me, with this creepy little grin, like he knew what I was thinking. I told him I was ready to go. I gave you to your mother, and you were still singing this beautiful, high-pitched song, like a bird. I felt so peaceful, thinking that the last thing I would hear was you singing my soul song." He paused, and this time the tears actually fell. "But I should have known better, because your mother wasn't singing with you."

I stared across the countertop at my dad, mesmerized, my supper forgotten.

"The bastard took her instead." My father's fist hit the tile hard enough to shake the whole bar, and his jaw bulged with fresh fury. "He just looked at Darby, and she collapsed. I had to lunge for you, to keep you from hitting the ground when she fell."

"Kaylee, breathe," Nash said, rubbing my back. At some point during the story, I'd stopped inhaling, and didn't even realize it until Nash spoke.

"She died because of me?" My hands fisted, and my fingernails bit into my palms.

"No. Baby, no." My dad leaned forward then, to look directly into my eyes. "She died because of *me*." He took my hands and wouldn't let them go, even when I tugged halfheartedly. "Because I insisted on going out. Because I swerved to avoid the deer. Because I wasn't strong enough to make him take me instead. None of it was your fault."

But nothing he said could make me feel better. I was supposed to die, and because I hadn't, my mother had. And even if *she* hadn't, my father would have. Or maybe one of the people in the other car. The bottom line was that I was alive when I should have been dead, and my mother had paid the price.

"So…borrowed time?" I twisted the knob on the stove to turn it off, and moved the pot onto a cold burner, acting out of habit, because I was numb with shock. "I'm living my mother's life now? Is that what Aunt Val meant?"

"Yes." My father sat back on his stool, giving me plenty of space. "You'll live until she was supposed to die. But don't worry about that. I'm sure she would have had a very long life."

And that's when I burst into tears.

I'd held back until then, my sorrow eclipsed by overwhelming guilt over being the cause of my mother's death. But thinking about how long her life should have been… *That* I couldn't handle.

Nash cleared his throat, drawing our attention. "She knew the risk, right, Mr. Cavanaugh?" He stared at my father with a blatantly expectant look on his face. "Kaylee's mom knew what she was doing, right?"

"Of course." My dad nodded firmly. "She probably didn't even realize I'd planned to make the exchange myself. She was willing to pay the price, or she would never have sung for you. I just…wanted to save her too. It was supposed to be me, but I lost you both that night. And I never really got you back, did I?"

I forced back my next sob, rubbing spent tears from my cheeks with my palms. I was getting really good at not-crying. "I'm right here, Dad." I set the strainer in the sink and dumped the pasta into it, then slammed the empty pot down on the counter-top. "You left."

"I had to." He sighed and shook his head. "At least, I *thought* I did. He came after you again, Kaylee. The reaper was furious that we saved you. He took your mother, but then he came back for you, two nights later. In the hospital. I would never have known it was coming if your grandmother hadn't come in from Ireland after the wreck. She practically lived in your room with me, and she got a premonition of your death."

"Wait, I was supposed to die again?" My hand hesitated over the strainer.

"No." My father shook his head vehemently. "No. Your mother and I angered the reaper when we saved you. He came back for you out of spite. Your mother wasn't hurt in the accident, and you were living on her time. There's *no way* she should have died two days after you would have. So when he came for you the second time, I called him on it."

"Did he show himself?" Nash asked, and I glanced to my right to see him staring at my father, as fascinated as I was.

My dad nodded. "He was an arrogant little demon."

"So what happened?" I asked.

"I punched him."

For a moment, we stared at him in silence. "You punched the reaper?" I asked, and my hand fell from the strainer onto the edge of the sink.

"Yeah." He chuckled at the memory, and his grin brought out one of my own. I couldn't remember the last time I'd seen my father smile. "Broke his nose."

"How is that possible?" I asked Nash, thinking of his sort-of-friendship with Tod.

"They have to take on physical form to interact with any physical object," he said, fiddling with the long cardboard box the cheese had come in. "They can't be killed, but they can definitely feel pain."

"And you know this how...?" I asked, pretty sure I knew the answer to that one too.

Nash grinned. "Tod and I don't always get along." But then he turned back to my dad, serious again. "Why did the reaper come after Kaylee a second time?"

"I don't know, but I was afraid he'd do it again." My father paused, and his half grin faded into a somber look of regret. "I sent you to Brendon to keep you safe. I was worried that if I stayed with you, he'd end up taking you too. So I sent you away. I'm sorry, Kaylee."

"I know." I wasn't quite up to accepting his apology yet, though the fact that he clearly meant it helped quite a bit. I dumped the pasta back into the empty pot and followed it with two fistfuls of cheese cubes. Then I turned the burner on medium heat and added salt, a little milk, and a spoonful of Aunt Val's low-calorie margarine.

I stared into the pot as I stirred. "How long are you staying?"

"As long as you want me here," he said, and something in his voice made me look up. Did that mean what I thought it meant?

"What about your job?"

He shrugged. "There are jobs here. Or, if you want, you could come back to Ireland with me. I'm sure your grandparents would love to see you."

I hadn't seen them since the last time I'd seen my father, and I'd never been out of the country. But...

My gaze was drawn to Nash. When he saw me looking, he nodded, but I wasn't fooled. He didn't want me to go, and that was enough for me.

"I'd love to visit Ireland, but I live here, Dad." I sprinkled some pepper into the pot and kept stirring. "I don't want to leave." The disappointment on his face nearly killed me. "But you're welcome to stay here. If you want."

"I—"

I'd like to think he would have said yes. That he was considering a house for the two of us, hopefully not too far from Nash's, but plenty far from Sophie and her fluffy pink melodrama. But I'd never know for sure. He didn't get to finish because the front door opened, and something thumped to the floor, then Sophie groaned.

"Who left these stupid bags right in front of the door?" she demanded.

Amused by her ungainly entrance, I craned my neck to see over Nash's shoulder. My cousin knelt on the floor, one hand propping her up over an old, worn suitcase. I started to laugh, but when my gaze settled on hers, all amusement drained from me instantly, leaving me cold and empty. Her face was shadowed, her features so dark I could barely make them out, even with light drenching her from overhead.

The reaper had come for its next victim.

Sophie was about to die.

20

"Sophie?" My father stood and turned toward her without a single glance my way. "Wow, you look just like your mother, except for your eyes. Those are Brendon's eyes—I'd lay my life on it." If he'd looked at me, he'd have seen her fate. I was sure of it. But he didn't look.

Even Nash was watching my cousin.

Fear and adrenaline sent a painful jolt through my chest, and I gripped the edge of the countertop. "Sophie…" I whispered with as much volume as I could muster, desperate to warn her before the panic kicked in for real. But no one heard me.

Sophie picked herself up with more grace than I'd ever wielded in my life, brushing off the front of the dark, slim dress she'd worn to the memorial. "Uncle Aiden." She pasted on a weary smile, to match red-rimmed eyes, polite even in the grip of grief. "And Nash. Two of my favorite men in the same room."

For once, I barely registered the flames of jealousy her claim should have lit within me, because the inside of my throat had begun to burn viciously. Yes, I often wanted to shut her up, but not *permanently*.

"Dad!" I rasped, still clinging to the countertop for support, but again, no one noticed me.

Except Sophie.

"What's wrong with her?" My cousin clacked into the dining room in her dress shoes, hands propped on narrow, pointy hips. "Kaylee, you look like you're gonna throw up in your… What is that?" She eyed the half-used brick of Velveeta. "Mac and cheese?"

Nash turned to me so fast he nearly lost his balance. "Kaylee?" But I could only watch him, my jaws already clenched against the wail for my cousin's soul. "Again?" I nodded, and he pulled me close, already whispering words I couldn't concentrate on, his rough cheek scratchy against mine.

"Kay?" My father whirled toward me a second behind Nash, and a look of horror slid over his features when he recognized the look on mine. He followed my gaze to my cousin slowly, as if afraid of what he'd see. "Sophie?" he asked, and I nodded, gritting my teeth so hard pain shot through my temples. "How long?"

I shook my head. I'd had no idea my ability came with a built-in time gauge, much less how to use it.

"Brendon!" my father shouted, his focus locked on me.

Sophie flinched, then stepped forward to see me better, leaning over the back of a dining-room chair, her eerily shadowed forehead wrinkled in confusion.

Nash was still whispering to me, holding me tight with his back to the stove. His lips brushed my ear, his words gliding over me with a soothing breath of Influence, helping me hold the panic in check. I breathed deeply, trying to hold back the looming wail as I stared over his shoulder, my focus glued to my oddly darkened cousin.

"What's going on?" Sophie gripped the high back of the chair in both hands, and her gaze met mine. "She's freaking out again, isn't she? Mom keeps that shrink's number around here somewhere." She started toward the kitchen, but my father put out one arm to stop her.

"No, Sophie." He glanced toward the hall and shouted, "Brendon! Get out here!" Then he turned back to his niece. "Kaylee will be fine."

"No, she won't." Sophie shook her head and tugged her arm from his grasp, green eyes wide. Her concern felt genuine. I think she was actually afraid for me. Or maybe afraid *of* me. "I know you're worried about her, but she needs serious help, Uncle Aiden. Something's wrong with her. I told them this would happen again, but no one ever listens to me. They should have let that doctor give her shock therapy."

"Sophie…" My dad's shoulders tensed, his expression caught between fear and anger. He was going to set her straight—except that Nash beat him to it.

"Damn it, Sophie, she's trying to help you, and you…" He whirled on her, eyes churning furiously. But the moment he stepped away from me, the panic descended in full force. I pulled him back by one arm, and Nash's look of surprise melted into understanding, and he resumed whispering, as if he'd never stopped.

Footsteps pounded down the hall and I opened my eyes to see Uncle Brendon stumble to a halt in the middle of the living room. He looked from me to my dad, then followed my father's gaze to Sophie. As I watched, my uncle's features crumpled in an agony so complete, so encompassing, that I could barely stand to see it.

For several seconds, no one moved, as if afraid that the slightest twitch would draw the reaper out of hiding and bring about the inevitable conclusion. Sophie glanced from one of us to the next in total confusion. Then my father sighed, and the soft sound seemed to reach every corner of the wide-open living area. "Are you okay?" he asked, and I nodded unsteadily. I wasn't the one facing death. Not yet, anyway.

"What's going on?" Sophie demanded, shattering the quiet like a gunshot at a funeral. But no one answered. She was the source of all the trouble, yet no one even looked at her. For once, everyone was looking at me.

"Is it Sophie?" Uncle Brendon asked, walking slowly toward us, as if it hurt to move. His voice was barely audible over the unvoiced scream already reverberating in my head. I nodded, and his eyes closed as he inhaled deeply, then exhaled. "Are you sure?" He had to open his eyes to see me nod again, then the line of his jaw hardened. "Will you help me?" he asked, pain twisting his features into a mask I barely recognized. "I swear I won't let her take you."

Unfortunately, after my father's story, I wasn't sure Uncle Brendon would have any control over who the reaper took instead. Any reaper who would reap a soul not on the list wouldn't think twice about taking the *bean sidhe* who got in her way. Or everyone else in the room, for that matter.

But I couldn't just let Sophie die, even if she was a royal pain in the butt most of the time.

"What are you all talking about?" My cousin glanced at each of us in turn, like we'd all lost our minds, and sanity was getting lonely. "What's going on?"

Uncle Brendon crossed the living room in four huge steps and motioned to his daughter to join him on the couch. She went reluctantly, and he pulled her down onto the center cushion. "Honey, I have to tell you something, and I don't have time for the long, gentle version." He took Sophie's hands, and my chest ached with what could only be the splintering of my heart.

"You're going to die in a few minutes," he said. Sophie frowned, but her father rushed on before she could interrupt. "But I don't want you to worry, because Kaylee and I are going to bring you right back. You'll be fine. I'm not sure what'll happen after that, but what I need you to know is that you're going to be *just fine.*"

"I don't know what you're talking about." Confusion pinched Sophie's fine features into a scowl, and I could see panic lurking on the edge of her expression. Her world had just ceased making sense, and she didn't know what to do with information she couldn't understand. I knew exactly how she felt. "Why would I die? And what on earth can Kaylee do about it?"

Uncle Brendon shook his head. "We don't have time for all that now. I don't know how long we have, so I need you to trust me. I *will* bring you back."

Sophie nodded, but she looked terrified, as much for her father as for herself. She probably thought he'd gone over the proverbial deep end and was now drowning in it. She glared at me over his shoulder, as if I'd somehow contaminated him with my mental defect, but I couldn't summon any irritation toward my cousin—not with her moments from death.

"Noooo."

Every head in the room swiveled toward the hall, where Aunt Val now stood, clutching the door frame as if that were the only thing holding her up. "It wasn't supposed to be Sophie."

"What?" Uncle Brendon stood so fast the motion made *me* dizzy. He stared at his wife in dawning horror. "Valerie, what did you *do?*"

Aunt Val? What did she have to do with grim reapers and *bean sidhes?* She was human!

Before my aunt could answer, a fresh wave of grief rolled over me and I staggered on my feet. Nash caught me before I hit the dining-room table and lowered me carefully into one of the chairs. It wouldn't be long now.

Sophie started to tremble then, and the very sight of her sent tremors through my own limbs. Anguish racked me from the inside out. My heart felt too big for my chest. My throat burned like I was breathing flames.

But beyond the physical pain of holding back Sophie's soul song, I felt my cousin's loss intensely, though the reaper had yet to strike. It was like watching my own hand laid out on a chopping block, knowing the woodsman was coming for it. Knowing

I'd never get it back. And it didn't matter that we'd never been close. I wasn't in love with my feet either, but I didn't want to lose them.

"Mom?" Sophie squeaked, shifting her weight from one side to the other as she hugged herself. "What's going on?"

"Don't worry, honey," Aunt Val said from the middle of the living-room carpet, her focus darting all over the place, like a junkie on a bad trip. "I won't let her take you." She paused, without ever looking at her daughter, and threw her head back as far as it would go, blond waves cascading down her back almost to her waist.

"Marg!" she shouted, and I flinched. My hands gripped the chair arms as I tried to regain my control after she'd nearly shaken it lose. "I know you're here, Marg!"

Marg? I hadn't told Aunt Val about seeing the reaper, or that she was, in fact, female. And I hadn't even known the reaper's name. Until now.

And suddenly I understood. Aunt Val knew the reaper's name because she had hired her.

No! Denial and devastation pinged through me. I couldn't believe it. Aunt Val was the only mother I'd known for the past thirteen years. She loved me, and she certainly loved Sophie and Uncle Brendon. She would never do business with a reaper, much less bargain with the souls of the innocent.

But the drinking, and the questions… She'd known all along why the girls were dying!

"This wasn't part of the deal!" my aunt screamed, hands clenched into fists, shaking in either fear or fury. Or both. "Show yourself, you coward! You can't *do* this!"

But that's where she was so very wrong.

21

Aunt Val's shriek had yet to fade from my ears when Sophie's legs collapsed beneath her. As she fell, she smacked the back of her head on the edge of an end table. She hit the floor with a muffled thud, and blood trickled from her hair to stain the white carpet.

Neither of her parents saw. Uncle Brendon was scanning the bright room obsessively, as if the reaper might be hiding behind an armchair, or in one of the potted plants. Aunt Val still stared at the ceiling, shouting for Marg to appear and explain herself.

As if reapers hailed from above.

But the moment Sophie died, her soul song forced itself from my throat, and I nearly choked, trying to hold it back out of habit.

Aunt Val noticed me retching and whirled around to look for her daughter. "No!" she screamed, and I'd never heard a human voice come so close to my own screech until that moment.

She dropped to her knees on the floor. "Wake up, Sophie." She stroked loose blond curls back from her daughter's face, and her fingers came away smeared with blood. "Marg, *fix this!* This wasn't the deal!"

"Sophie!" Uncle Brendon joined his wife beside his daughter's

lifeless body, as Nash and I looked on in horror, too shocked to
move. Then my uncle looked at me over his wife's shoulder, but
I couldn't understand what he wanted. I was too busy holding
back the scream.

Nash dropped into a squat by my chair and took my hands,
his gaze piercing mine with quiet strength and intensity. "Let it
out," he whispered. "Show us her soul so we can guide it."

So I sang for Sophie.

I sang for a soul taken before its time, for a young life lost. For
childless parents, and for a girl who would never get to decide
who and what she wanted to be. For my cousin, my surrogate
sister, whose quick tongue would never be tempered by age and
experience.

As I screamed, the lights dimmed, though I could see no
noticeable difference in any one bulb. The entire room began to
gray, like the gym had earlier, and I glanced hesitantly around
the room, suddenly terrified of finding dark, misshapen creatures
skulking around my own house.

There were none to be found. I was clearly seeing the Netherworld, but it was…empty, somehow.

But even more disconcerting than that was the sound. Or
rather, the *absence* of sound. While I sang, I heard nothing else
around me, as if someone had pushed the mute button on some
cosmic remote control. After a few seconds, I couldn't even hear
myself scream, though I knew from the fire in my throat and
lungs that I was, in fact, still screeching at the top of my inhu-
man lungs.

Nash stayed with me, his fingers linked through mine on the
arm of the dining-room chair, completely unbothered by the un-
godly screech clawing its way from my mouth. My father stood
still, staring at my cousin's soul, a pale, pink-tinged amorphous
shape hovering several feet above her body, bobbing like a kite
tethered to the ground in a brisk wind.

Her soul had risen higher than Emma's had, and some part

of me understood that that was my fault. Because Nash had to prompt me to release the wail for Sophie.

Uncle Brendon stood with his arms stiff at his sides, his hands fisted, exposed forearms bulging with great effort. I couldn't see his face, but I imagined it looked like Nash's, when he'd guided Emma's soul: red and tense, and damp with sweat.

Aunt Val had collapsed over her daughter, crying inconsolably now. She was the only one in the room who couldn't see Sophie's soul, and some distant part of me found that unbearably tragic.

Uncle Brendon's shoulders fell, and he turned to me in exhaustion. "Hold her," he mouthed, and I nodded, still screaming. I would do my best, but my throat was still sore from singing Emma's song that afternoon, and I wasn't sure how long I could hold on to Sophie.

My uncle gestured to my father. I didn't catch all of what he said, but the gist of it was clear: he couldn't do it alone. For some reason, he couldn't budge his daughter's soul.

My dad nodded, and they both turned back to Sophie, working together now.

Aunt Val knelt with her hand on her daughter's sternum, facing the rest of the room. But she wasn't looking at any of us. She was talking, evidently, to the room in general. Her face was splotched with tears, and flushed with both grief and guilt. I couldn't understand much of what she said, but I made out two words based on the familiar motion of her lips.

"Take me."

And then I got it. She was talking to the reaper—Marg— begging her to spare Sophie's life in exchange for her own.

And that's when everything changed. The feel of the room abruptly *shifted,* as if all the angles had changed, the proportions recalibrated. It was like watching a movie with the screen ratio all messed up.

A slim, dark figure appeared in the middle of the weird-looking living room, only feet from my father and uncle, across the room from Sophie's body.

I recognized her instantly from Meredith's memorial. Marg. She still wore the same long black sweater, cut to accentuate her slight figure, and soft ballet-style slippers, now half-sunk into my aunt's thick pile carpet.

The reaper spared me a glance and frowned, then dismissed me and turned toward Aunt Val. I could see only a sliver of the reaper's face now, but that was plenty. "Are you sure?" she asked, her voice like molten metal, smooth and slow-flowing, but hot enough to singe at a touch.

I was so surprised to hear her that I almost stopped singing, and Sophie's soul began to drift toward Marg. Then Nash squeezed my hand and my voice strengthened. Sophie's soul steadied once more.

The reaper didn't seem to notice. She was watching my aunt, who was saying something else I couldn't hear. I could only hear Marg, which meant the reaper hadn't forgotten about me—that for some reason, she wanted me to hear what she was saying.

Aunt Val nodded firmly in response to the reaper's question, her lips moving rapidly.

The reaper studied her for a moment, then shook her head, and what little I could see of her mouth curved into a slow, malicious smile. "Your soul will not suffice," Marg said, her voice trailing over me with an almost physical presence. "You promised Belphegore young, beautiful souls, and like your body, your soul is aging and blemished. She will not accept it."

My aunt was speaking again, gesturing angrily, and her husband flinched all over at something she said, fists still clenched in effort. Again I desperately wished I could hear both sides of the argument.

"We reached no agreement on the specific souls to be harvested," the reaper said, and chills popped up on my arms. Just listening to her was going to kill me. "I have collected the first four, in spite of piddling interference from your young minions—"

Minions? She did *not* just call me a minion!

"—and I'll have the fifth when I tire of this game. I will have your money, Belphegore will have her souls, and you will have youth and beauty like you never imagined."

Youth? Aunt Val had hired a reaper to poach innocent souls in exchange for her youth? Could anyone truly be so vain?

Aunt Val was shouting now, the veins standing out in her slim neck. But Marg only laughed. "I am in possession of four young, strong souls, and while I hold them, half a dozen *bean sidhes* couldn't take this one from me." To demonstrate, she waved one hand in the air, palm up. Pain ripped through my chest, and Sophie's soul rose a foot higher in spite of my song and the efforts of my father and uncle to guide it.

Nash stood then, and added his best to the group effort, his face flushing with the strain.

Sophie's soul bobbed, then sank slightly, but would go no farther.

The reaper whirled around then, turning her back on my aunt to focus her fury on me and Nash. "You…"

I shook harder with each step she took toward me, and my voice began to warble. I was losing it, and once the wail faded, there would be no soul for the men to guide.

"Something is…" Her sweater flared out at the sides as she walked, giving her a larger, more intimidating presence than her small frame should have carried. Then her eyes narrowed as she studied me from mere feet away, while my heart tripped its way through a few more terrified beats. Her slow smile returned. "You live someone else's life. Belphegore would surely love a taste of your borrowed life force. If you want to see the next day's sun, shut your mouth and release that soul. Otherwise, your family will watch me feed you your own tongue before I take your soul in place of hers."

Her depraved smile broadened, and the sight of such normal, even white teeth in such a vicious face sent chills through me. "And you will die in perfect silence, little one. There is no one left to sing your soul song."

"I will sing for her." The voice was soft and lyrical, and as eerie in the odd silence as the reaper's was. My head swiveled toward the source.

Tod stood in front of the closed front door. His feet were spread for an even stance, hands fisted at his sides, jaw clenched in fury. He looked ready to do battle with the devil himself, but Tod's voice didn't match the one I'd heard.

Someone stepped out from behind him, and my pulse raced in hope. Harmony Hudson. Nash's mother. And she looked *pissed*.

"Can you hear me, hon?" she asked, and I nodded, so grateful for her presence that I didn't think to question how she'd known she was needed. "Your voice is fadin', but I can sing all night." She faced Marg then, and seemed to stand taller. "You're not leaving with her soul. Or the other one's either," she said, glancing at Sophie's soul where it still bobbed sluggishly in the air over her body.

Marg hissed like an angry cat, mouth open, teeth exposed, and for a moment I thought she'd swipe at Nash's mother with a set of retractable claws. Then she seemed to collect herself. "You'll fare no better than the child," Marg purred, slinking toward the entryway slowly. "It will take more than three of your men to steal from me while I hold four strong souls in reserve."

"How 'bout four men?" Tod said through clenched teeth. He glanced at me, then at Nash, who nodded, giving him the go-ahead for something I didn't understand. Then Tod closed his eyes in concentration, and Sophie's soul bobbed a bit lower.

My eyes widened. Tod was a reaper. Yet he was very clearly helping the others guide Sophie's soul.

Marg's eyes went dark with fury, and she whirled to face Sophie, clearly intent on taking her before she lost her chance.

And that's when my voice died.

"No!" I croaked, but no sound came out.

Yet no sooner had my scream faded from the air than true sound came roaring back to me, as if my ears had popped from a change in pressure. And the first thing to greet them was the most beautiful, ethereal music I'd ever heard in my life.

Nash's mom was singing for Sophie.

All four of the men were tugging on my cousin's soul now, with Harmony's song binding it. But Marg was pulling on it too. Sophie's soul began to rise again, and this time it edged toward the reaper, her arms spread to receive it.

"Marg, please!" Aunt Val shouted. "Take me. My soul may not be young, but it's strong, and you can't have Sophie!"

"You can't save her...." Marg sang, and, glancing around, I saw that she was right. With four souls in reserve, she was too strong for even four male *bean sidhes*. Ironic, considering how small and frail she looked....

Wait. She *was* frail. My dad had said reapers had to take on physical form to interact with their surroundings. Which meant Marg had the same physical weaknesses as the reaper who'd tried to take me. The reaper my father had *punched*...

My head spinning, throat throbbing, I ran into the kitchen. I glanced at the knife rack, then shook my head. I didn't know if I could stop her with one blow.

But I could whack the crap out of her.

I pulled open the cabinet beneath the oven and dug around for the old cast-iron skillet Uncle Brendon used for corn bread, then lugged the pan out and raced through the dining room. I passed Nash, Harmony, and Tod, and had already pulled the skillet back for a blow when I came even with my father.

Marg must have heard me coming, or seen some sign of it in my aunt's face, because she turned at the last minute. The pan hit her in the shoulder, rather than the head, so instead of knocking her unconscious, I simply knocked her down.

But she went down *hard*. Her hip hit the floor with a thud, shaking the end table two feet away.

I couldn't suppress a grin of triumph, even as a vicious ache rebounded up my arm from the blow I'd landed.

For a moment, the reaper lay stunned, glossy black waves spread around her head, arms splayed at her sides. On the edge of my vision, I saw Sophie's soul sink smoothly toward her body. Then Aunt Val let loose a shriek of rage and launched herself across the floor. I'd never seen her look less graceful or poised— and I'd never admired her more.

She landed on Marg's slim hips, straddling her, hands grasping the reaper's shoulders. Her eyes were wild, her hair nearly standing on end. She looked crazy, and I had little doubt that if she wasn't there yet, she would be soon.

"You will not take my daughter!" she shouted, inches from the reaper's face. "So you either take me now, or you're going back one soul short of the bargain!"

Marg's lips curled back in fury as I inched forward, the skillet still gripped in both hands. She glanced up at Sophie's soul, and her dark eyes blazed in fury to find that it was gone and that Sophie was now breathing, though still unconscious.

Marg stared up at my aunt then, terror fleeting across her features. Whoever this Belphegore was, Marg clearly didn't want to disappoint her. The reaper considered for less than a full second, then she nodded. "Your soul won't fulfill the deal you made, but it will pay for your arrogance and vanity." And just like that, Aunt Val slumped forward onto the reaper, her eyes already empty and glazing over.

But Aunt Val's body hit the carpet, because Marg was gone.

I blinked, staring at my aunt in shock, and carefully lowered myself to the floor, to keep from falling flat out.

"Kaylee, are you okay?" Nash's fingers curled around my left hand, reminding me that I still clutched the cast-iron skillet in my right. Startled by what I'd done with it, now that it was all over, I dropped the skillet at arm's length, and it hit the carpet with a muffled thud.

"I'm fine," I croaked. "Considering."

Uncle Brendon stomped past me to kneel at Sophie's side. He took her pulse and exhaled in relief, then felt around her head, near where she'd banged it on the end table. Then he picked her up in both arms and laid her on the couch, heedless of the blood her hair smeared across the white silk.

Aunt Val would have had a fit over the mess. But Aunt Val was dead.

With Sophie's safety assured, her father dropped to the floor beside his wife and repeated the same steps. But this time, there was no sigh of relief. Instead, my uncle scooted backward on the seat of his jeans until his back hit the side of the couch, his hair brushing Sophie's arm. Then he propped his elbows on his knees and cradled his head in his hands. His whole body shook with silent tears.

"Brendon?" my father said, laying one warm hand on my back.

"How could she do this?" his brother demanded, looking up at us with red-rimmed eyes. "What was she thinking?"

"I don't know." My dad let go of me to kneel at his brother's side.

"It's my fault. Living with us is too hard for humans. I should have known better." Uncle Brendon sobbed, swiping one sleeve across his face. "She didn't want to grow old without me."

"This is not your fault," my dad insisted, clasping his brother's shoulder. "It's not that she didn't want to get old without you, Bren. She didn't want to get old at all."

My aunt Valerie had made a deal with a hellion, and cost four innocent girls their lives. She'd lied to us all, and had nearly gotten her own daughter killed. And she had blasted a hole the size of a nuclear crater through our family's core.

But when the time came, she'd given her own life in exchange for her daughter's without a second thought, just like my mother had. Did that make her sins forgivable?

I wanted to say yes—that a mother's selfless sacrifice was enough of a good deed to erase her past sins. But the truth wasn't so pretty.

My aunt's death wouldn't bring back Heidi, or Alyson, or Meredith, or Julie. It wouldn't repair whatever psychological damage her loss caused Sophie. It wouldn't give Uncle Brendon back his wife.

The truth was that Aunt Val's sacrifice was too little, too late, and she'd left those she loved most to deal with the aftermath.

"Here, Kaylee. This will help your throat." Harmony Hudson set a small cup of honey-scented tea on the table in front of me, and I leaned over it, breathing in the fragrant steam. She started to head back into the kitchen, where the scent of homemade brownies—her favorite form of therapy—had just begun to waft from the oven, but I laid one hand on her arm.

"I would have lost Sophie if you weren't here." My voice was still hoarse, and my throat felt like I'd swallowed a pinecone. And the shock was finally starting to pass, leaving my heart heavy and my head full of the terrible details.

Harmony smiled sadly and sank into the chair next to mine. "The way I hear it, you've done more than your fair share of singing today."

I nodded and sipped carefully from the cup, grateful for the soothing warmth that trickled down my throat. "But it's over now, right? Belphegore can't leave the Netherworld, and Marg won't come back, right?"

"Not if she has any sense. The reapers know who she is now, and they'll all be looking for her." Harmony glanced to her left, and my gaze followed hers to the living room, where my aunt had died, my cousin had been restored, and I'd whacked a psychotic grim reaper with a cast-iron skillet.

Weirdest. Tuesday. Ever.

The paramedics had been gone for less than half an hour, and the thick white carpet still bore tracks from the wheels of the stretcher. They'd rolled Aunt Val out draped in a white sheet, and Uncle Brendon and Sophie followed the ambulance to the hospital, where she would get stitches in the back of her head, and her mother would be officially pronounced dead.

Sophie didn't understand what had happened; I'd known that from the moment she regained consciousness. But what I hadn't anticipated was that she would blame *me* for her mother's death. My cousin was technically dead when Aunt Val made the bargain that had saved her daughter's life, and Sophie didn't remember most of what she'd seen before that. All she knew was that her mother had died, and that I'd had something to do with it. Just like with my own mother.

She and I had more in common now than we ever had—yet we'd never been further apart.

"How did you know? About all of this?" I asked Harmony, waving toward the living room to indicate the entire disaster. But she only frowned, as if confused by the necessity for my question.

"I told her."

Startled, I looked up to find Tod sitting across from me, his arms folded on the table, a single blond curl hanging over his forehead. Harmony smiled at him, letting me know she saw him too, then rose to check on the brownies.

"How did you do it?" I brought the teacup to my mouth for another sip. "How did you guide Sophie's soul? I thought you were a reaper."

"He's both," Nash said from behind me, and I turned just as he followed my father through the front door, pulling his long sleeves down one at a time. He and my dad had just loaded Aunt Val's white silk couch into the back of my uncle's truck, so he wouldn't have to deal with the bloodstains when he and Sophie got back from the hospital. "Tod is very talented."

Tod brushed the curl back from his face and scowled.

Harmony spoke up from the kitchen as the oven door squealed open. "Both my boys are talented."

"Both?" I repeated, sure I'd heard her wrong.

Nash sighed and slid onto the chair his mother had vacated, then gestured toward the reaper with one hand. "Kaylee, meet my brother, Tod."

"Brother?" My gaze traveled back and forth between them, searching for some similarity, but the only one I could find was the dimples. Though, now that I thought about it, Tod had Harmony's blond curls....

And suddenly everything made a lot more sense. The pointless bickering. Nash knowing Tod "forever." Tod hanging out at Nash's house. Nash knowing a lot about reapers.

How could I not have seen it earlier?

"A word of warning..." Harmony gave me a soft smile, but then her focus shifted to my father. "You have to watch out for *bean sidhe* brothers. They're always more than you bargain for."

My dad cleared his throat and glanced away.

An hour later, the Hudsons had gone, and my father stood across from me at the bar, chewing the last bite of a brownie I'd had no appetite for. I set his empty saucer in the sink and ran water over it.

He slid one arm around my shoulders and pulled me close. I let him. He still knew no more about me and my life than he had an hour earlier—that much hadn't changed. But everything else had. Now he could look at me, no matter how much I resembled my mother, and see me, rather than her. He could see what he still had, rather than what he'd lost.

And he was going to stay. We'd probably fight over curfews and get on each other's nerves, but at least those things felt normal. And I needed a good dose of normal after the week I'd just had.

I sighed, staring down at the running water, too exhausted and dazed in that moment to even realize I should turn it off.

"What's wrong?" Dad reached around me to turn off the faucet.

"Nothing." I shrugged, then turned with my back to the sink. "Well, everything, really. It's just that I've only met three adult *bean sidhes* so far, and all three of you are…alone." Tragically widowed, in fact. "Do *bean sidhes* ever get happy endings?"

"Of course they do," my father insisted, wrapping one arm around my shoulders. "As much as anyone else does, at least." And to my surprise, he didn't look the least bit doubtful, even after all he'd been through. "I know that doesn't seem possible right now, considering what you saw and heard tonight. But don't judge your future based on others' mistakes. Not Valerie's, and certainly not mine. You'll have as much of a happy ending as you're willing to work for. And from what I've seen so far, you're not afraid of a little work."

I nodded, unsure how to respond.

"Besides, being a *bean sidhe* isn't all bad, Kaylee."

I gave him a skeptical frown. "That's good to hear, 'cause from where I'm standing, it looks like a lot of death and screaming."

"Yeah, there's a good bit of that. But…" My father turned me by both shoulders until I stared up at him, only dimly registering the slow, steady swirls of chocolate, copper, and caramel in his eyes. "We have a gift, and if you're willing to put up with the challenges that come with that gift, then every now and then, life will toss you a miracle." His eyes churned faster, and his hands tightened just a little on my arms.

"You're my miracle, Kaylee. Your mother's too. She knew what she was doing that night on the road. She was saving our miracle. We both were. And as much as I still miss her, I've never regretted our decision. Not even for a second." He blinked, and his eyes were full of tears. "Don't you regret it either."

"I don't." I met his gaze, hoping mine looked sincere, because the truth was that I was far from sure. What made me worthy of a life beyond what fate said I should have?

My dad frowned, like he saw the truth in my eyes, which were probably telling him more than my answer had. Stupid swirls. But before he could say anything, a familiar engine growled outside, then went silent.

Nash.

I glanced at my dad expectantly, and he scowled. "Does he always come over this late?"

I rolled my eyes. "It's nine-thirty." Though admittedly, it felt more like two in the morning.

"Fine. Go talk to him, before he comes inside and I have to pretend I'm okay with that."

"You don't like him?"

My father sighed. "After everything he's done for you, how could I not like him? But I see the way he looks at you. The way you look at each other."

I smiled, as a car door closed outside. "What are you, ancient? Don't you remember being my age?"

"I'm one hundred thirty-two, and I remember all too well. That's why I'm worried." A fleeting shadow passed over his expression, then he waved me toward the door. "Half an hour."

Irritation spiked my temper. He'd been back for all of three hours, and was already making up rules? But I stifled a retort because even my father's unreasonable curfew was better than being a long-term guest in my cousin's home. Right?

Nash glanced up in surprise when I opened the front door. He was on the bottom step, one hand on the rail. "Hey."

"Hey." I closed the door and leaned against it. "You forget something?"

He shrugged, and the slick green sleeves of his jacket shone under the porch light. "I just wanted to say goodnight without my mom looking over my shoulder. Or your dad."

"Or your brother." I couldn't resist a grin, but Nash only frowned.

"I don't want to talk about Tod."

"Fair enough." I stepped down to the middle riser and found my eyes even with his, though he stood one step below me. It was an oddly intimate pose; his body was inches from mine, but we weren't touching. "What do you want to talk about?"

He raised one brow, and his voice came out hoarse. "Who says I want to talk?"

I let him kiss me—until my dad tapped on the window at my back. Nash groaned, and I tugged him down the steps and into the driveway, out of reach of the porch light.

"So you're really okay with all this?" He spread his arms into the darkness, but the gesture included everything that had gone indescribably weird in my life over the past four days. "Most girls would have totally freaked out on me."

"What can I say? Your voice works wonders." Not to mention his hands. And his lips…

And again that ache gripped me, squeezing bitter drops of doubt from my heart. Would he be done with me in a month, once the novelty of kissing a fellow *bean sidhe* wore off?

"What's wrong?" He tilted my chin up until my gaze met his, though I couldn't see him very well in the dark.

I shoved my misgivings aside and leaned with my back against the car. "School's going to be weird after this. I mean, how am I supposed to care about trig and world history when I just brought my best friend back from the dead, and faced down a grim reaper over my cousin's poached soul?"

"You'll care, because if you get grounded for failing economics, there won't be any more of this…" He leaned into me, and his mouth teased mine until I rose onto my toes, demanding more.

"Mmm… That's pretty good motivation," I mumbled against his cheek, when I finally summoned the willpower to pull away.

"With any luck, there will be plenty of this, and no more of that." He gestured vaguely toward the house. "That was an anomaly, and it's over."

A chill shivered through me at the reminder. "What if it's not?" After all, Marg was still out there somewhere, and Belphegore was no doubt unsatisfied.

But Nash could not be shaken. "It's over. But we're just starting, Kaylee. You have no idea how special we are together. How incredible it is that we found each other." He rubbed my arms, and I knew from the earnest intensity in his voice that his eyes were probably churning. "And we have long lives ahead of us. Time to do anything we want. Be anything we want."

Time. That was the point, wasn't it? Nash's point. My father's point.

Finally, I got it. My life wasn't just my own. My mother had died to give it to me.

And no matter what happened next, I was damn well going to earn her sacrifice.

★ ★ ★ ★ ★

Acknowledgments

First of all, thanks to Rayna and Alex, for letting me pick your teenage brains, and again to Alex, for being the first reader in my target audience.

Thanks to Rinda Elliott, for showing me what I couldn't see.

Thanks to my agent, Miriam Kriss, for believing I could do this, before there was any evidence to support that claim.

Thanks to Elizabeth Mazer, and everyone else behind the scenes at Mira for making it happen.

Thanks to my editor, Mary-Theresa Hussey, for all the questions—for answering mine along the way, and knowing just which ones to ask in the margins.

And finally, thanks to Melissa, for being there.

MY SOUL TO SAVE

1

Addison Page had the world at her feet. She had the face, the body, the voice, the moves, and the money. Let's not forget the money. But advantages like that come with a price. I should have known it was all too good to be true....

"What?" I yelled, my throat already raw from shouting over the roar of the crowd and the music blasting from dozens of huge speakers. Around us, thousands of bodies bobbed in time to the beat, hands in the air, lips forming the words, shouting the lyrics along with the beautiful, glittery girl strutting across the stage, seen close-up on a pair of giant digital screens.

Nash and I had great seats, thanks to his brother, Tod, but no one was sitting. Excitement bounced off every solid surface, fed by the crowd and growing with each passing second until the auditorium seemed to swell with the communal high. Energy buzzed through me, setting my nerve endings on fire with enough kick to keep me pinging off the walls through high school and well into college.

I didn't want to know how Tod had scored seats a mere fifteen rows from the stage, but even my darkest suspicion hadn't kept me at home. I couldn't pass up a chance to see Eden live in concert, even though it meant giving up a Saturday night alone with Nash, during my dad's extra shift at work.

And this was only Eden's opening act….

Nash pulled me closer, one hand on my hip, and shouted into my ear. "I said, Tod used to date her!"

I rode the wave of adrenaline through my veins as I inhaled his scent. Six weeks together, and I still smiled every time he looked at me, and flushed every time he *really* looked at me. My lips brushed his ear as I spoke. "Tod used to date who?" There were several thousand possible suspects dancing all around us.

"Her!" Nash shouted back, nodding over the sea of concert-goers toward the main attraction, his spiky, deliberately messy brown hair momentarily highlighted by a roaming spotlight.

Addison Page, Eden's opening act, strutted across the stage in slim black boots; low-cut, ripped jeans; a tight white halter; and a sparkly silver belt, wailing a bitter yet up-tempo lament about the one who got away. The glittery blue streak in her straight, white-blond hair sparkled beneath the lights and fanned out behind her when she whirled to face the audience from center stage, her voice rising easily into the clear, resonant notes she was famous for.

I stared, suddenly still while everyone around me swayed along with the crescendo. I couldn't help it.

"Tod dated Addison Page?"

Nash couldn't have heard me. *I* barely heard me. But he nodded and leaned into me again, and I wrapped my arm around him for balance as the cowboy on my other side swung one eager, pumping fist dangerously close to my shoulder. "Three years ago. She's local, you know."

Like us, the hometown crowd had turned out as much for Texas's own rising star as for the headliner. "She's from Hurst, right?" Less than twenty minutes from my own Arlington address.

"Yeah. Addy and I were freshmen together, before we moved

back to Arlington. She and Tod dated for most of that year. He was a sophomore."

"So what happened?" I asked as the music faded and the lighting changed for the second song.

I pressed closer to Nash as he spoke into my ear, though he didn't really have to at that point; the new song was a melodic, angsty tune of regret. "Addy got cast in a pilot for the HOT network. The show took off and she moved to L.A." He shrugged. "Long distance is hard enough when you're fifteen, and impossible when your girlfriend's famous."

"So why didn't he come tonight?" I wouldn't have been able to resist watching a celebrity ex strut on stage, and hopefully fall on his face, assuming I was the dumpee.

"He's here somewhere." Nash glanced around at the crowd as it settled a bit for the softer song. "But it's not like he needs a ticket." As a grim reaper, Tod could choose whether or not he wanted to be seen or heard, and by whom. Which meant he could be standing onstage right next to Addison Page, and we'd never know it.

And knowing Tod, that's exactly where he was.

After Addison's set, there was a brief, loud intermission while the stage was set for the headliner. I expected Tod to show up during the break, but there was still no sign of him when the stadium suddenly went black.

For a moment, there was only dark silence, emphasized by surprised whispers, and glowing wristbands and cell-phone screens. Then a dark blue glow came from the stage and the crowd erupted into frenzied cheers. Another light flared to life, illuminating a new platform in the middle of the stage. Two bursts of red flames exploded near the wings. When they faded, but for the imprint behind my eyelids, *she* appeared center stage, as if she'd been there all along.

Eden.

She wore a white tailored jacket open over a pink leather bra and a short pink-fringed skirt that exaggerated every twitch of her famous hips. Her long, dark hair swung with each toss of her head, and the fevered screaming of the crowed buzzed in my head as Eden dropped into a crouch, microphone in hand.

She rose slowly, hips swaying with the rhythm of her own song. Her voice was low and throaty, a moan set to music, and no one was immune to the siren song of sex she sold.

Eden was hypnotic. Spellbinding. Her voice flowed like honey, sweet and sticky. To hear it was to crave it, whether you wanted to or not.

The sound wound through me like blood in my veins, and I knew that hours from then, when I lay awake in my bed, Eden would still sing in my mind, and that when I closed my eyes, I would still see her.

It was even stronger for Nash; I could see that at a glance. He couldn't tear his gaze from her, and we were so close to the stage that his view was virtually uninterrupted. His eyes swirled with emotion—with need—but not for me.

A violent, irrational surge of jealousy spiked in me as fresh sweat dampened his forehead. He clenched his hands at his sides, the long, tight muscles in his arms bulging beneath his sleeves. As if he were concentrating. Oblivious to everything else.

I had to pry his fingers open to lace them with mine. He turned to grin at me and squeezed my hand, beautiful hazel eyes settling into a slower churn as his gaze met mine. The yearning was still there—for me this time—but was both deeper and more coherent. What he wanted from me went beyond mindless lust, though that was there, too, thank goodness.

I'd broken the spell. For the moment. I didn't know whether to thank Tod for the tickets or ream him.

Onstage, soft lights illuminated dancers strutting out to join Eden as the huge screen tracked her every movement. The dancers closed in on her, writhing in sync, hands gliding lightly over her arms, shoulders, and bare stomach. Then they paired off so she could strut down the catwalk stretching several rows into the crowd.

Suddenly I was glad we didn't have front-row seats. I'd have had to scrape a puddle of Nash goo into a jar just to get him home.

Warm breath puffed against my neck an instant before the sound hit my ear. "Hey, Kaylee!"

I jumped, so badly startled I nearly fell into my chair. Tod stood on my right, and when the cowboy's swinging arm went *through* him, I knew the reaper was there for my viewing pleasure only.

"Don't do that!" I snapped beneath my breath. He probably couldn't hear me, but I wasn't going to raise my voice and risk the guy next to me thinking I was talking to myself. Or worse, to *him*.

"Grab Nash and come on!" From the front pocket of his baggy, faded jeans, Tod pulled two plastic-coated, official-looking cards attached to lanyards. His mischievous grin could do nothing to darken the cherubic features he'd inherited from his mother, and I had to remind myself that no matter how innocent he looked, Tod was trouble. Always.

"What's that?" I asked, and the cowboy frowned at me in question. I ignored him—so much for not looking crazy—and elbowed Nash. "Tod," I mouthed when he raised both brows at me.

Nash rolled his eyes and glanced past me, but I could tell from his roving stare that he couldn't see his brother. And that, as always, he was pissed that Tod had appeared to me, but not to him.

"Backstage passes." Tod reached through the cowboy to grab my hand, and if I hadn't jerked back from the reaper's grasp, I'd have gotten a very intimate feel of one of Eden's rudest fans.

I stood on my toes to reach Nash's ear. "He has backstage passes."

Nash's scowl made an irritated mask of his entire face, while onstage, Eden shed her jacket, now clad only in a bikini top and short skirt. "Where did he get them?"

"Do you really want to know?" Reapers weren't paid in money—at least, not the human kind—so he certainly hadn't bought the passes. Or the tickets.

"No," Nash grumbled. But he followed me, anyway.

Keeping up with Tod was a lost cause. He didn't have to edge past row after row of ecstatic fans, or stop and apologize when he stepped on one girl's foot or spilled her date's drink. He just walked right through seats and concertgoers alike, as if they didn't exist in his world.

They probably didn't.

Like all reapers, Tod's natural state of existence—if it could even be called natural—was somewhere between our world, where humans and the occasional *bean sidhe* reside in relative peace, and the Netherworld, where most things dark and dangerous dwell. He could exist completely in either one, if he chose, but he rarely did, because when he was corporeal, he typically forgot to avoid obstacles like chairs, tables, and doors. And people.

Of course, he could easily become visible to both me and Nash, but it was evidently much more fun to mess with his brother. I'd never met a set of siblings with less in common than Nash and Tod. They weren't even the same species; at least, not anymore.

The Hudson brothers were both born *bean sidhes*—that was the correct spelling, though most people knew us as banshees—from normal *bean sidhe* parents. As was I. But Tod had died two years earlier, when he was seventeen, and that's when things got weird, even for *bean sidhes*. Tod was recruited by the grim reapers.

As a reaper, Tod would live on in his own un-aging body. In exchange, he worked a twelve-hour shift every day, collecting souls from humans whose time had come to die. He didn't have to eat or sleep, so he got pretty bored for those other twelve hours of each day. And since Nash and I were among the few who knew about him, he typically took that boredom out on us.

Which was how we'd gotten kicked out of a mall, a skating rink, and a bowling alley, all in the past month. And as I bumped my way through the crowd after Tod, I had a feeling the concert would be next on the list.

One glance at the irritation glowing in Nash's cheeks told me he still couldn't see his brother, so I pulled him along as I tracked the headful of blond curls now several rows ahead of us, heading toward a side door beneath a red exit sign.

Eden's first song ended in a huge flash of purple light, reflected on the thousands of faces around me, then the lights went out.

I stopped, unwilling to move in the dark for fear that I'd trip over someone and land in an unidentified puddle. Or a lap.

Seconds later, the stage exploded with swirling, pulsing light, and Eden now swayed to the new beat in a different but equally skimpy costume. I glanced at her, then back at Tod, but caught only a fleeting glimpse of his curls disappearing through the closed side door.

Nash and I rushed after him, stepping on a series of toes and vaulting over a half-empty bottle of Coke someone had smuggled in. We were out of breath when we reached the door, so I glanced one last time at the stage, then shoved the door, grateful when it actually opened. Doors Tod walks through usually turn out to be locked.

Tod stood in the hall beyond, grinning, both backstage passes looped over one arm. "What'd you do, crawl all the way here?"

The door closed behind us, and I was surprised to realize I could barely hear the music, though it had been loud enough to drown out my thoughts in the auditorium. But I could still feel the thump of the bass, pulsing up through my feet from the floor.

Nash let go of my hand and glared at his brother. "Some of us are bound by the laws of physics."

"Not my problem." Tod waved the passes, then tossed one to each of us. "Snoozin', loozin', and all that crap."

I slipped the nylon lanyard over my neck and pulled my long brown hair over it. Now that I wore the pass, it would be seen by anyone who saw me; everything Tod holds is only as visible as he is at the time.

The reaper went fully corporeal then, his sneakers squeaking on the floor as he led us down a series of wide white hallways and through several doors, until we hit one that was locked. Tod shot us a mischievous grin, then walked through the door and pushed it open from the other side.

"Thanks." I brushed past him into the new hall, and the sudden upsurge of music warned that we were getting close to the stage. In spite of the questionable source of our backstage passes, my pulse jumped with excitement when we rounded the next corner and the building opened into a long, wide hall with a cavernous ceiling. Equipment was stacked against the walls—soundboards, speakers, instruments, and lights. People milled everywhere, carrying clothes, food, and clipboards. They spoke into two-way radios and headset microphones, and most wore badges similar to ours, though theirs read "Crew" in bold black letters.

Security guards in black tees and matching hats loitered, thick arms crossed over their chests. Background dancers raced across the open space in all stages of the next costume change, while a woman with a clipboard pointed and rushed them along.

No one noticed me and Nash, and I could tell Tod had gone non-corporeal again by the silence of his steps. We headed slowly toward the stage, where light pulsed and music thumped, much too loud for any of the backstage racket to be heard out front. I touched nothing, irrationally afraid that sneaking a cookie from the snack table would finally expose us as backstage-pass thieves.

In the wings of the stage, a small crowd had gathered to watch the show. Everyone wore badges similar to ours, and several people held equipment or props, most notably a small monkey, wearing a collar and a funny, brightly colored hat.

I laughed out loud, wondering what on earth America's reigning pop queen would do onstage with a monkey.

From our vantage point, we saw Eden in profile, now grinding in skintight white leather pants and a matching half top. The new song was gritty, with a crunchy guitar riff, and her dancing had changed to suit it; she popped each pose hard, and her hair swung out behind her. Guys in jeans and tight, dark shirts danced around and behind her, each taking her hand in turn, and lifting her on occasion.

Eden gave it her all, even several songs into the performance. The magazines and news stories hyped her hard work and dedication to her career, and the hours and hours a day she trained, rehearsed, and planned. And it showed. No one put on a show like Eden. She was the entertainment industry's golden girl, rolling in money and fame. Rumor had it she'd signed on for the lead in her first film, to begin shooting after the conclusion of her sold-out tour.

Everything Eden touched turned to gold.

We watched her, enthralled by each pose she struck, mesmerized by each note. We were under such a spell that at first no one noticed when something went wrong. During the guitar solo, Eden's arms fell to her side and she stopped dancing.

I thought it was another dramatic transition to the next song, so when her head fell forward, I assumed she was counting silently, ready to look up with those hypnotic, piercing black eyes and captivate her fans all over again.

But then the other dancers noticed, and several stopped moving. Then several more. And when the guitar solo ended, Eden still stood there, silent, a virtual vacuum sucking life from the background music.

Her chest heaved. Her shoulders shook. The microphone fell from her hand and crashed to the stage.

Feedback squealed across the auditorium, and the drummer stopped drumming. The guitarists—both lead and bass—turned toward Eden and stopped playing when they saw her.

Eden collapsed, legs bent, long, dark hair spilling around her on the floor.

Someone screamed from behind me in the sudden hush, and I jumped, startled. A woman raced past me and onto the stage, followed by several large men. My hair blew back in the draft created by the sudden rush, but I barely noticed. My gaze was glued to Eden who lay unmoving on the floor.

People bent over her, and I recognized the woman as her mother, the most famous stage parent/manager in the country. Eden's mom was crying, trying to shake her daughter awake as a member of security tried to pull her away. "She's not breathing!" the mother shouted, and we all heard her clearly, because the crowd of thousands had gone silent with shock. "Somebody help her, she's not breathing!"

And suddenly neither was I.

My hand clenched Nash's, and my heart raced in dreadful anticipation of the keening that would rip its way from my throat as the pop star's soul left her body. A *bean sidhe*'s wail can shatter not just glass, but eardrums. The frequency resonates painfully in the human brain, so that the sound seems to rattle from both outside and within.

"Breathe, Kaylee," Nash whispered into my ear, wrapping both arms around me as his voice cocooned my heart, his Influence soothing, comforting. A male *bean sidhe*'s voice is like an audio-sedative, without the side effects of the chemical version. Nash could make the screaming stop, or at least lower its volume and intensity. "Just breathe through it." So I did. I watched the stage over his shoulder and breathed, waiting for Eden to die.

Waiting for the scream to build deep inside me.

But the scream didn't come.

Onstage, someone's foot hit Eden's microphone, and it rolled across the floor and into the pit. No one noticed, because Eden still wasn't breathing. But I wasn't wailing, either.

Slowly, I loosened my grip on Nash and felt relief settle through me as logic prevailed over my dread. Eden wasn't wearing a death shroud—a translucent black haze surrounding the soon-to-be-dead, visible only to female *bean sidhes*. "She's fine." I smiled in spite of the horrified expressions surrounding me. "She's gonna be fine." Because if she were going to die, I'd already be screaming.

I'm a female *bean sidhe*. That's what we do.

"No, she isn't," Tod said softly, and we turned to find him still staring at the stage. The reaper pointed, and I followed his finger until my gaze found Eden again, surrounded by her mother, bodyguards, and odd members of the crew, one of whom was now giving her mouth-to-mouth. And as I watched, a foggy, ethereal substance began to rise slowly from the star's body like a snake from its charmer's basket.

Rather than floating toward the ceiling, as a soul should, Eden's seemed *heavy,* like it might sink to the ground around her instead. It was thick, yet colorless. And undulating through it were ribbons of darkness, swirling as if stirred by an unfelt breeze.

My breath caught in my throat, but I let it go almost immediately, because though I had no idea what that substance was, I knew without a doubt what it *wasn't*.

Eden had no soul.

"What is that?" I whispered frantically, tugging Nash's hand. "It's not a soul. And if she's dead, how come I'm not screaming?"

"What is what?" Nash hissed, and I realized he couldn't see Eden's not-soul. Male *bean sidhes* can only see elements of the Netherworld—including freed souls—when a female *bean sidhe* wails. Apparently the same held true for whatever ethereal sludge was oozing from Eden's body.

Nash glanced around to make sure no one was listening to us, but there was really no need. Eden was the center of attention.

Tod rolled his eyes and pulled one hand from the pocket of his baggy jeans. "Look over there." He pointed not toward the stage, but across it, where more people watched the spectacle from the opposite wing. "Do you see her?"

"I see lots of hers." People scrambled on the other side of the stage, most speaking into cell phones. A couple of vultures even snapped pictures of the fallen singer, and indignation burned deep in my chest.

But Tod continued to point, so I squinted into the dark wing. Whatever he wanted me to see probably wasn't native to the human world so it wouldn't be immediately obvious.

And that's when I found her.

The woman's tall, slim form created a darker spot in the already-thick shadows, a mere suggestion of a shape. Her eyes were the only part of her I could focus on, glowing like green embers in the gloom. "Who is she?" I glanced at Nash and he nodded, telling me he could see her too. Which likely meant she was *letting* us see her...

"That's Libby, from Special Projects." An odd, eager light shone in blue eyes Tod usually kept shadowed by brows drawn low. "When this week's list came down, she came with it, for this one job."

He was talking about the reapers' list, which contained the names and the exact place and time of death of everyone scheduled to die in the local area within a one-week span.

"You knew this was going to happen?" Even knowing he was a reaper, I couldn't believe how different Tod's reaction to death was from mine. Unlike most people, it wasn't my own death I feared—it was everyone else's. The sight of the deceased's soul would mark my own descent into madness. At least, that's what most people thought of my screaming fits. Humans had no idea that my "hysterical shrieking" actually suspended a person's soul as it leaves its body.

Sometimes I wished I still lived in human ignorance, but those days were over for me, for better or for worse.

"I couldn't turn down the chance to watch Libby work. She's a legend." Tod shrugged. "And seeing Addy was a bonus."

"Well, thanks so much for dragging us along!" Nash snapped.

"What is she?" I asked as another cluster of people rushed past us—two more bodyguards and a short, slight man whose face looked pinched with professional concern and curiosity. Probably a doctor. "And what's so special about this assignment?"

"Libby's a very special reaper." Tod's short, blond goatee glinted in the blue-tinted overhead lights as he spoke. "She was called in because that—" he pointed to the substance the female reaper now was steadily *inhaling* from Eden's body, over a twenty-foot span and dozens of heads "—isn't a soul. It's Demon's Breath."

Suddenly I was very glad no one else could hear Tod. I wished they couldn't hear me, either. "Demon, as in hellion?" I whispered, as low as I could speak and still be heard.

Tod nodded with his usual slow, grim smile. The very word *hellion* sent a jolt of terror through me, but Tod's eyes sparkled with excitement, as if he could actually get high on danger. I guess that's what you get when you mix boredom with the afterlife.

"She sold her soul...." Nash whispered, revulsion echoing within the sudden understanding in his voice.

I'd never met a hellion—they couldn't leave the Netherworld, fortunately—but I was intimately familiar with their appetite for human souls. Six weeks earlier, my aunt had tried to trade five poached teenage souls in exchange for her own eternal youth and beauty, but her plan went bad in the end, and she wound up paying in part with her own soul. But not before four girls died for her vanity.

Tod shrugged. "That's what it looks like to me."

Horror filled me. "Why would anyone do that?"

Nash looked like he shared my revulsion, but Tod only shrugged again, clearly unbothered by the most horrifying concept I'd ever encountered. "They usually ask for fame, fortune, and beauty."

All of which Eden had in spades.

"Okay, so she sold her soul to a hellion." That statement sound wrong in *sooo* many ways.... "Do I even want to know how Demon's Breath got into Eden's body in its place?"

"Probably not," Nash whispered, as heavy black curtains began to slide across the front of the stage, cutting off the shocked, horrified chatter from the auditorium.

But as usual, Tod was happy to give me a morbid peek into the Netherworld—complete with irreverent hand gestures. "When the hellion literally sucked out her soul, he replaced it with his own breath. That kept her alive until her time to die. Which is why Libby's here. Demon's Breath is a controlled substance in the Netherworld, and it has to be disposed of very carefully. Libby's trained to do that."

"A controlled substance?" I felt my brows dip in confusion. "Like plutonium?"

Tod chuckled, running his fingers across a panel of dead electronic equipment propped against the wall. "More like heroin."

I sighed and leaned into Nash, letting the warmth of his body comfort me. "The Netherworld is soooo weird."

"You have no idea." Tod's curls bounced when he turned to face Libby again, where the lady reaper had now inhaled most of the sluggish Demon's Breath. It swirled slowly into her mouth in a long, thick strand, like a ghostly trail of rotting spaghetti. "Come on, I want to talk to her." He took off toward the stage without waiting for our reply, and I lunged after him, hoping he was solid enough to touch.

He was—at least for me. Though I was sure Nash's hand would have gone right through the reaper.

"Wait." I hauled him back in spite of the weird look I got from some random stagehand in a black tee. "We can't just trot across the stage without being seen." Though, there were certainly times I wished I could go invisible. Like, during P.E. The girls' basketball coach was out to get me, I was sure of it.

"And I don't think I want to meet this super-reaper." Nash stuffed his hands in his front pockets. "The garden variety's weird enough."

Plus, most reapers hold no fondness for *bean sidhes*. The combined natural abilities of a male and female *bean sidhe*—the potential to return a soul to its body—are in direct opposition with a reaper's entire purpose in life. Or, the afterlife.

Tod was the rare exception to this mutual species aversion, by virtue of being both *bean sidhe* and reaper.

"Fine, but don't expect me to pass on any pearls of wisdom she coughs up…." Tod's gaze settled on me, and his full, perfect lips turned up into a wicked smile. He knew he had me; I was trying to learn everything I could about the Netherworld, to make up for living the first sixteen years of my life in total ignorance, thanks to my family's misguided attempt to keep me safe. And as creeped-out as I was by Eden's sudden, soulless death, I wouldn't pass up the opportunity to learn something neither Tod nor Nash could teach me.

"Nash, please?" I pulled his hand from his pocket and wound my fingers through his. I would go without him, but I'd rather have his company, and I was pretty sure I'd get it. He wouldn't leave me alone with Tod, because he didn't entirely trust his undead brother.

Neither did I.

I saw Nash's decision in the frown lines around his mouth before he nodded, so I stood on my toes to kiss him. Excitement tingled along the length of my spine and settled to burn lower when our lips touched, and when I pulled away, his hazel eyes churned with swirls of green and brown, a sure sign that a *bean sidhe* was feeling something strong. Not that humans could see it.

Nash nodded again to answer my unspoken question. "Yours are swirling, too."

I dared a grin in spite of the solemn circumstances, and Tod rolled his eyes at our display. Then he stomped off silently to meet this "special" reaper.

The fluttering in my stomach settled into a heavy anchor of dread as we followed Tod behind the stage, dodging shell-shocked technicians and stagehands on our way to the opposite wing. I needed all the information I could find about the Netherworld to keep myself from accidentally stumbling into something dangerous, but I didn't exactly look forward to meeting more reapers. Especially the creepy, intimidating woman swallowing the ominous life-source that had kept Eden up and singing for who knew how long.

"So what makes this reaper such a legend?" I whispered, walking between Nash and Tod, whose shoes still made no sound on the floor.

For a moment, Tod gaped at me like I'd just asked what made grass green. Then he seemed to remember my ignorance. "She's ancient. The oldest reaper still reaping. Maybe the oldest reaper ever. No one knows what name she was born with, but back in ancient Rome she took on the name of the goddess of death. Libitina."

I arched both brows at Tod. "So, you address the oldest, scariest grim reaper in history by a nickname?"

Tod shrugged, but I thought I saw him blush. Though, that could have been the red satin backdrop panels showing through his nearly translucent cheek. "I've never actually addressed her as anything. We haven't officially met."

"Great," I breathed, rolling my eyes. We were accompanying Tod-the-reaper-fanboy to meet his hero. It couldn't get any lamer without a *Star Trek* convention and an English-to-Klingon dictionary.

When we rounded the corner, my gaze found Libby just as she sucked the last bit of Demon's Breath from the air. The end of the strand whipped up to smack her cheek before sliding between her pursed lips, and the ancient reaper swiped the back of one black-leather-clad arm across her mouth, as if to wipe a smudge of sauce from her face.

I didn't want to know what kind of sauce Demon's Breath swam in.

"There she is," Tod said, and the eerie, awed quality of his voice drew my gaze to his face. He looked…shy.

My own intimidation faded in the face of the first obvious nerves I'd seen from the rookie reaper, and I couldn't resist a grin. "Okay, let's go." I took Tod's hand and had tugged him two steps in Libby's direction before his fingers suddenly faded out of existence around my own.

I stopped and glanced down, irritated to see that he had dialed both his appearance and his physical presence down to barely-there, to escape my grasp. "What's wrong?"

"Nothing a little dignity wouldn't fix," Tod snapped. "So could we please *not* mob the three-thousand-plus-year-old reaper like tweens at a boy-band concert?" He ran transparent hands over his equally transparent tee and marched toward Libby with his shoulders square, evidently satisfied that his composure was intact.

He grew a little more solid with each step, and I glanced around, afraid someone would notice him suddenly appearing in our midst. But when his shoes continued to make no sound, I realized he hadn't stepped into human sight. Not that it mattered. All eyes were glued to the stage, where the doctor still worked tirelessly—and fruitlessly—on Eden.

We followed Tod, and I knew by the sudden confidence in Nash's step that he could now see his brother. And that he was probably secretly hoping Tod would do or say something stupid in front of the foremost expert in his field.

We caught up with him as he stopped, and since they were the same height, Libby's bright green eyes stared straight into Tod's blue with enough intensity to make even me squirm. "Hi," Tod started, and I had to give him credit for not stuttering.

My own tongue was completely paralyzed.

Libitina was very old, very experienced, and clearly very powerful—all obvious in her bearing alone. She was also so impossibly beautiful that I was suddenly embarrassed by the makeup I'd probably sweated off during the concert and the long brown hair I could see frizzing on the edge of my vision, in spite of my efforts with a flatiron.

Libby wore a long, black leather trench coat, cinched at her tiny waist to show off slim hips. I would have said the coat was cliché for someone intimately involved with Death, except that as old as she was, she'd probably been wearing black leather much longer than it had been in vogue for hookers and superheroes alike.

Her hair was pulled back from her face in a severe ponytail that trailed tight, black curls halfway down her back. Her skin was dark and flawless, and so smooth I wanted to touch her cheek, just to assure myself she wasn't as perfect as she looked. She couldn't be.

Could she?

"Yes?" Libby said, her piercing gaze still trained on Tod. She hadn't acknowledged either me or Nash, and I was suddenly sure that, like most reapers, she hated *bean sidhes*. Maybe we shouldn't have tagged along after all.

Yet she hadn't become invisible to us….

"My name is Tod, and I work for the local branch office." He paused, and I was amused to realize Tod's cheeks were blazing— and this time that had nothing to do with the stage backdrop. "Can I ask you a couple of questions?"

Libby scowled, and a chill shot up my spine. "You are dissatisfied with my services?" She bit off the ends of her words in anger, distorting an accent I couldn't place, and we all three stepped back in unison, unwilling to stand in the face of her fury.

"No!" Tod held up both hands, and I was too busy choking on my own fear to be amused by his. "This has nothing to do with the local office. I'm off duty tonight. I'm just curious. About the process…"

Libby's thin, black brows arched, and I thought I saw amusement flicker behind her eyes. "Ask," she said finally, and suddenly I liked her—even if she didn't like *bean sidhes*—because she could easily have made Tod feel about an inch tall.

Tod stuffed his hands into his pockets and inhaled slowly. "What does it feel like? Demon's Breath. You hold it…inside. Right?"

Libby nodded briefly, then turned and walked away, headed toward a hallway identical to the one we'd followed to the stage.

We hesitated, glancing at one another in question. Then Tod shrugged and hurried after her. We actually had to jog to keep up as her boots moved silently but quickly over the floor.

"You breathe it in, deep into your lungs." Her rich accent spoke of dead languages, of cultures long ago lost to the ravages of time and fickle memory. Her voice was low and gruff. Aged. Powerful. It sent shivers through me, as if I were hearing something I shouldn't be able to. Something no one else had heard in centuries. "It fills you. It burns like frostbite, as if the Breath will consume your insides. Feed on them. But that is good. If the burning stops, you have held it too long. Demon's Breath will kill your soul."

The shivers grew until I noticed my hands trembling. I took Nash's in my left, and shoved the right into my pocket.

A couple of technicians passed us carrying equipment, and Tod waited until they were gone to pose his next question. "How long do you have?" He paced beside the female reaper now. Nash and I were content to trail behind, just close enough to hear.

"An hour." Her lips moved in profile against the white wall as she turned to half face him. "Any longer, and you risk much."

"What do you do with it?" I asked—I couldn't help it—and Libby froze in midstep. She pivoted slowly to look at me, and I saw *time* in her eyes. Years of life and death, and existence without end. The shivers in my hands became tremors echoing the length of my body.

I should not have drawn her attention.

"Who is this?" Libby faced Tod again.

"A friend. My brother's girlfriend." He nodded toward Nash, who stood tall beneath her hair-curling, nerve-crunching scrutiny. Then Libby whirled on one booted heel and marched on.

Cool relief sifted through me, and only then did I realize Tod hadn't given her either of our names. Nash had practically beaten that precaution into him; it was never wise to give your name to Death's emissaries. Though, if a reaper wanted to know your name, it was easy enough to find, especially in today's world. Which is why it was also unwise to catch a reaper's attention.

Sirens warbled outside the stadium then, and another gaggle of official-looking people rushed down the hall toward the stage, but Libby didn't seem to notice them. "There are places for proper disposal of Demon's Breath. In the Nether," she added, as if there were any question about that.

"If a reaper wanted to get into that—collecting Demon's Breath instead of souls—how might he get started?" Tod asked as we followed Libby around a sharp white corner, her feet silent on the slick linoleum.

"By surviving the next thousand years." Her accent grew sharper, her words thick with warning. "If you still live then, find me. I will show you. But do not try it alone. Fools suffer miserable deaths, boy."

"I won't," Tod assured her. "But it was awesome to watch."

Libby stopped, eyeing him with a strange expression caught on her features, as if she didn't quite know what she intended to say until the words came out. "You may watch again. I will return in five days."

"For more Demon's Breath?" I asked, and again her creepy green gaze slid my way, seeming to burn through my eyes and into my brain.

"Of course. The other fool will release hers on Thursday."

"What other fool?" Tod demanded through clenched teeth, and I glanced at him, surprised by his sharp tone. His brows were furrowed, his beautiful lips thinned by dread.

"Addison Page. The singer," Libby said, like it should have been obvious.

Tod actually stumbled backward, and Nash put a hand on his shoulder, but it went right through him. For a moment, I was afraid he'd fall through the featureless white wall. "Addy sold her soul?" Tod rubbed one hand across his own nearly transparent forehead. "Are you sure?"

Libby raised her brows, as if to ask if he were serious.

"When?"

"That is not my concern." The reaper slid her slim, dark hands into the pockets of her coat, watching Tod with disdain now, as if her hunch that he wasn't yet ready to collect Demon's Breath had just been confirmed. "Mine is to gather what I come for and dispose of it properly. Time marches on, boy, and so must I."

"Wait!" Tod grabbed her arm, and I wasn't sure who was more surprised—Libby or Nash. But Tod rushed on as if he hadn't noticed. "Addy's going to die?"

Libby nodded, then disappeared without so much as a wink to warn us. She was just suddenly gone, yet her voice remained for a moment longer, an echo of her very existence.

"She will release the Demon's Breath by taking her own life. And I shall be there to claim it."

"Addy sold her soul." Tod's voice sounded odd. Distant. I think he was in shock. Or maybe that was just an echo from the empty hallway.

If a voice isn't audible in the human range of hearing, can it echo?

"Um, yeah. Sounds like it," I said. The very thought sent chills through me, and I rubbed my arms through my sleeves, trying to get rid of the goose bumps.

"She's gonna kill herself." Tod's eyes were wide with panic and horror. I'd never seen him scared, and I didn't like how fear pressed his lips into a tense, thin line and wrinkled his forehead. "We have to stop her. Warn her, or something." Tod took off down the hall, and Nash and I ran after him. If we didn't keep up, he'd disappear through a wall or something, and we'd never find him. At least, not in time to finish arguing with him.

"Warn her of what? That she's going to kill herself?" Nash's shoes squeaked as we rounded a corner. "Don't you think she already knows that?"

"Maybe not." Tod stopped when the hallway ended in a T, glancing both ways in indecision. "Maybe whatever's supposed to drive her to suicide hasn't happened yet." He looked to the left again, then took off toward the right.

"Wait!" I lunged forward and grabbed his arm, relieved when my hand didn't pass right through him. "Do you even know where you're going?"

"No clue." He shrugged, looking more like his brother in that moment than ever before. "I know where her dressing room is, but I don't know how to get there from here, and I can't just pop in without losing you two."

I didn't want to know how he knew where her dressing room was, but considering how often he'd gone invisible to spy on me, the answer seemed obvious.

"Yeah, physics is a real bitch." Nash rolled his beautiful hazel eyes and leaned with one shoulder against the wall like he had nowhere better to be.

"You don't have to wait for us." As cool as it would have been to meet Addison Page, telling a rising star that she was going to end both her career and her life in less than a week was so not on my to-do list. "I think I'm going to sit this one out." I propped my hands on my hips and glanced at Nash to see if he was with me, but he and Tod wore identical, half amused, half reluctant expressions. "What?"

"I'm dead, Kaylee." Tod stopped in front of the first door we'd come to, his hand on the knob. "Addy came to my funeral. I can't show up in her dressing room two years after I was buried and tell her not to kill herself. That would just be rude."

I laughed at his idea of post-death etiquette, pretty sure that "rude" was a bit of an understatement. But I sobered quickly when his point sank in. "Wait, you want us to tell her?"

"If she sees me, she'll freak out and spend the last days of her life in the psych ward."

I bristled, irritated by the reminder of my own brief stay in the land of sedatives and straitjackets. "It's called the mental-health unit, thank you. And we are *not* going to go tell your famous ex-girlfriend to lighten up or she'll be joining you six feet under. *That* would be rude."

"She wouldn't believe us, anyway," Nash said, crossing his arms over his chest in a show of solidarity. "She'd probably call Security and have us arrested."

"So *make* her believe you." Tod gestured in exasperation. Like it'd be that easy. "I'll be there to help. She just won't be able to see me."

I glanced at Nash and was relieved to see my reluctance still reflected in his features. As much as I wanted to help—to hopefully save Addison Page's life—I did *not* want to be taken from her dressing room in handcuffs.

And my dad would be soooo pissed if he had to bail me out of jail.

But before I could even contemplate how bad that would be, something else sank in....

"Tod, wait a minute." He let go of the knob when I stepped between him and the door, but his oddly angelic frown said he wasn't happy about it. "How do we know this will even work? I mean, say she believes us and decides not to kill herself. Won't she just die of some other cause next week, at the same time she would have killed herself? If her name's really on the list, she's going to die one way or another, right? You can't stop Libby from coming for her, and frankly, I think you'd be an idiot to even try."

Nash and Tod had explained to me how the whole death business works right after I found out I was a *bean sidhe,* during the single most stressful week of my life. Evidently people come with expiration dates stamped on them at birth—much like food in the grocery store. It was the reapers' job to enforce that expiration date, then collect the dead person's soul and take it to be recycled.

As far as I knew, the only way to extend a person's life was to exchange his or her death date for someone else's, to keep life and death in balance. So if we saved Addison Page's life—which, as *bean sidhes,* Nash and I could technically do—someone else would have to die in her place, and that someone could be anyone. Me or Nash, or some random, nearby stranger.

As much as I wanted to help both Tod and Addison, I was not willing to pay that price, nor would I ask someone else to.

Tod blinked at me, and while his scowl remained in place, his sad eyes revealed the truth. "I know." He sighed, and his broad shoulders fell with the movement. "But I haven't actually seen the list yet, so I'm not going to worry about that right now. What I *am* going to do is try to talk her out of suicide. But I need help. Please, guys." His gaze trailed from me to Nash, then back.

Nash frowned and leaned against the wall beside the door again, striking the I-cannot-be-moved posture I recognized from several of our own past arguments. "Tod, you're the one who says it's dangerous for *bean sidhes* to mess in reaper business."

"And that knowing when they're going to die only makes a human's last days miserable," I added, perversely pleased by the chance to throw his own words back at him.

Tod shrugged. "I know, but this is different."

"Why?" Nash demanded, his gaze going hard as he glared at Tod. "Because this time it's an ex? One you've obviously never gotten over…"

Anger flashed across the reaper's face, mirroring his brother's, but beneath it lay a foundation of pain and vulnerability even he could not hide. "This is different because she sold her soul, Nash. You know what that means."

Nash's eyes closed for a moment, and he inhaled deeply. When he met Tod's gaze again, his held more sympathy than anger. "That was her choice."

"She didn't know what she was getting into! She couldn't have!" the reaper shouted, and I was floored by the depth of his anger and frustration. I'd never seen him put so much raw emotion on display.

"What was she getting into?" I glanced from brother to brother and crossed my own arms, waiting for an answer. I hate always being the clueless one.

Finally Nash sighed and turned his attention to me. "She sold her soul to a hellion, but he won't have full use of it until she dies. When she does, her soul is his for eternity. Forever. He can do whatever he wants with it, but since hellions feed on pain and chaos, he'll probably torture Addison's soul—and thus what remains of Addison—until the end of time. Or the end of the Netherworld. Whichever comes first."

My stomach churned around the dinner we'd grabbed before the concert, threatening to send the burger back up. "Is that what happened to the souls Aunt Val traded to Belphegore?" Nash nodded grimly, and horror drew my hands into cold, damp fists. "But that's not fair. Those girls did nothing wrong, and now their souls are going to be tortured for all of eternity?"

"That's why soul-poaching is illegal." Tod's voice was soft with sympathy and heavy with grief.

"Is selling your soul illegal, too?" A spark of hope zinged through me. Maybe Addison could get her soul back on a technicality!

But the reaper shook his head. "Souls can't be stolen from the living. They can only be given away or sold by the owner, or poached after death, once they're released from the body. There's a huge market for human souls in the Netherworld, and what Addy did was perfectly legal. But she had no idea what she was getting into. She couldn't have."

I didn't know what to say. I couldn't decide whether I was more horrified for those four innocent souls or for my aunt, who'd given up her own soul to save her daughter's. Or for Addison Page, who would soon suffer the same fate.

"We have to tell her." I looked into Nash's eyes and found the greens and browns once again swirling, this time with fear and reluctance, based on the expression framing the windows of his soul. "I couldn't live with myself if we didn't at least try."

"Kaylee, this is not our responsibility," he said, his protest fortified with a solid dose of ordinary common sense. "The hellion already has her soul. What are we supposed to do?"

I shrugged. "I don't know. Maybe we could help her break her demon contract, or something. Is that possible?"

Nash nodded reluctantly. "There are procedures built in, but Kaylee, it's way too dangerous…." But he knew he couldn't change my mind. Not this time. I could see it on his face.

"I can't walk away and leave her soul to be tortured if there's anything I can do to help. Can you?"

He didn't answer, and his heavy silence frightened me more than the thought of the hellion waiting for full possession of Addison's soul. Then he took my hand, and I exhaled deeply in relief. "Lead the way, reaper," he said. "And you better hurry. With Eden dead, Addy probably won't stick around for the finale." The previous shows had each closed with a duet from Addison's forthcoming album.

With Nash's warning in mind, we wound our way through the backstage area, Tod popping into locked rooms and side hallways occasionally to make sure we were on the right track. He also popped into Addison's dressing room twice, to make sure she was still there.

The closer we got, the more people we saw in the halls, and they were all talking about Eden's onstage collapse. She'd been rushed to the hospital moments after we left the stage, and though the EMTs had been giving her CPR and mouth-to-mouth when they left, no one seemed to think she would live.

Which we already knew for sure.

Thanks to the badges around our necks, no one tried to throw us out, or even ask where we were headed, so when we finally made it to Addison's dressing room, I couldn't help thinking the whole thing had been too easy.

I was right. There was a security guard posted outside her door. He had a newspaper rolled up in one fist and biceps the size of cannons.

"Now what?" I whispered, bending for a drink from the water fountain twenty feet from the closed door.

"Let me make sure she's still alone," Tod said, and I flinched over how loud he was speaking until I realized no one else could hear him. "Then I'll get rid of the guard."

Before we could ask how he planned to do that, the reaper disappeared.

Nash and I strolled arm in arm down the hall, trying not to look suspicious, and I grew more grateful by the second that he'd come with us—because I would have done it even without him. The security guard wore sunglasses, though it was night and we were inside, so I couldn't tell whether or not he was watching us, but I would have bet money that he was.

Out of nowhere, a hand touched my elbow, and Tod suddenly appeared at my side. I nearly jumped out of my skin, and the guard's head swiveled slowly in my direction.

"Don't do that!" I whispered angrily.

"Sorry," Tod said. But he didn't look very sorry. "Her mom's in there with her now, but she's about to leave to call the car."

He'd barely spoken the last word when the dressing room door opened, and an older, darker version of Addison Page emerged. She nodded to the guard, then clacked off down the hall past us, without a word or a glance in our direction.

"Okay..." This time Tod whispered, as if setting the tone for the Acme tiptoe routine we were about to pull. "You guys duck into the bathroom around the corner. I'll draw the guard away while you sneak into Addy's room, then I'll pop in with you. Get her attention fast, and don't let her scream."

But something told me that would be easier said than done.

"I'm gonna kill you if this goes bad," Nash hissed as we followed the reaper around the corner toward the public restroom.

"It's a little late for that," Tod snapped. Then he was gone again.

I opened the door to the ladies' room to make sure it was empty, then waved Nash inside and left the door slightly ajar. While he looked around in awe at the cleanliness and the fresh flowers, I peeked through the crack, waiting for some all-clear sign from Tod.

We'd only been in the bathroom a few seconds when rapid footsteps clomped toward us from the direction of Addison's dressing room. Tod appeared around the corner, fully corporeal now, a wild grin on his face, the security guard's newspaper tucked under one arm. The guard raced after him, but the poor man was obviously built for strength rather than speed, because Tod put more distance between them with every step.

"Get back here, you little punk!" the guard shouted, huge arms pumping uselessly at his sides.

Tod glanced at me as he passed the bathroom, and I could swear I saw him wink. Then he rounded the next corner, and the guard trailed after him.

As soon as they were gone, Nash and I jogged back to the dressing room, hearts pounding with exhilaration, afraid the guard would return at any moment. We stood in front of the door, hand in hand, and my pulse raced with nerves. Nash met my eyes, then nodded toward the doorknob.

"You do it," I whispered. "She doesn't know me, but she may remember you."

Nash rolled his eyes but reached toward the door. His hand hesitated over the knob for a second, then I saw determination—or was that resignation?—flash across his face. He twisted the knob and opened the door in one smooth motion, so brash I almost envied his nerve.

He stepped inside and pulled me in with him, then closed the door.

I braced myself, expecting to hear Addison scream for Security. Instead, I heard nothing and saw no sign of Addison Page.

But her room was *awesome*. A rack of flashy costumes stood against one wall, beside a full-length stand-alone mirror. Which was next to a vanity lit by several large, frosted bulbs. In one corner stood a small round table covered in an array of meats, cheeses, fruit, and bite-size desserts. And in the center of the room, a couch and two chairs were gathered around a flat-screen television hooked up to a PlayStation 3.

But no Addison Page.

Nash glanced at me with his brows raised in question, and I shrugged. Then jumped when the sound of running water drew my focus to an open door I hadn't noticed before. The dressing room had a private restroom. And Addison Page was in it.

"Is the car ready?" The singer stepped out of the restroom and crossed the floor toward her vanity, head tilted away from us as she pulled an earring from her left ear. Then she looked up and froze. For just a second, I thought she might actually scream. But then Nash spoke, and her features relaxed, just enough to hold true fear at bay.

"Hi, Addison," he said, and his Influence flowed over the room like a warm, comforting breeze, smoothing her ruffled feathers and taking the edge off my own nerves. Male *bean sidhes* rocked the whole audio-anesthesia thing, whereas the females of our species sported only an eardrum-bursting scream.

Not fair, right? But convenient at times.

A brief flicker of annoyance flashed across Addison's famous, pixieish features, replaced an instant later by a gracious, bright white smile. "Um, this isn't really a good time. I'm on my way to the hospital to check on Eden," she said, brushing back the blue streak in her pale hair while she grabbed a pen from the vanity. "But I guess I have time for a quick autograph."

She thought we were fans. And she didn't know Eden was dead. I wasn't sure which misunderstanding to correct first, so I started with the lesser of two evils.

"Oh, we're not fans." I shrugged, stuffing my hands into

my pockets. But then she frowned, and I realized how that had sounded. "I mean, we *are* fans. We love your music. But that's not why we're here."

Her frown deepened. Even with Nash's Influence, by my best guess, we had less than a minute before she would yell for the guard, who had surely returned to his post by now. "Then what do you want?" Addison narrowed beautiful, impossibly pale blue eyes, though her smile stayed friendly. Or at least cautious.

I glanced at Nash, hoping for some help, but he only shrugged and gestured for me to start talking. After all, I'd gotten him into this.

"We have to tell you something." I hesitated, glancing at the couch. "Could we maybe sit down?"

"Why?" She was openly suspicious now, and her hand snuck into her pocket, where a bulge betrayed her cell phone. "Who are you?"

"My name is Kaylee Cavanaugh, and this is Nash Hudson. I think you two used to know each other."

The lines in her brow deepened, and she propped one hand on her hip. "No, I… Wait. Hudson?" Understanding flickered behind her eyes.

Nash nodded.

"Tod's brother." Addison pulled her hand from her pocket and laid it across her chest, like she was crossing her heart. "I'm sorry I didn't recognize you. I haven't seen you since the funeral. How are you?"

"I'm fine." Nash gave her a small, sad smile. "But you're not."

Alarm flashed across her face and her hand slid into her pocket again, her thin, gold chain-link bracelet pushed up her arm with the motion. "What is this?"

Before I could answer, Tod appeared at my side, still winded from his race with the security guard. "What'd I miss?"

"Nothing," Nash said, having obviously heard, if not seen, him. "We haven't told her yet."

"Told who what?" Addison pulled the phone from her pocket and flipped it open, truly frightened now. "What's going on?"

"Say something," Tod urged, elbowing me. I glared at him, and Addison followed my gaze to…nothing. She couldn't see him, and she obviously couldn't hear him. "Start talking or she's going to call someone."

"I know!" I whispered, elbowing him back. There was no use pretending he wasn't there on her account. She already thought we were nuts. "Addison, please sit down. We have to tell you something, and it's going to sound very…strange."

"It already does. I think you should go." She edged toward the door, stretching one arm ahead of her, as if to point the way. "You're creeping me out."

"*Do* something!" Tod yelled this time, eyes wide and desperate.

Nash sighed heavily, and I knew what he was going to do a moment before the words left his mouth. But not soon enough to prevent them. "Okay, here's the deal. You're going to kill yourself in five days, and we're here to talk you out of it."

Addison blinked, and for a moment her fear gave way to confusion, then anger as her empty hand clenched the back of the sofa. "Get out. Now."

"What, you couldn't put a little Influence behind that one?" I snapped, glaring at Nash.

"Not if you want her to understand." His gaze shifted past me to Tod. "I told you she wouldn't listen."

"Who are you talking to?" Addison demanded, her voice rising in both pitch and volume.

"You're gonna have to show her," I told Tod, hyperconscious of the singer's near panic. "She won't listen to us, but she can't ignore *you*."

Tod glanced at Nash for a second opinion, but his brother only nodded, leaning with one hip against the arm of an overstuffed chair. "I don't see any other way."

Tod sighed, and I knew from the surprise on Addison's face that she'd heard him. A second later she jumped backward and her free hand went to her throat in shock. "No…"

She could see him.

4

"Addy, please don't freak out." Tod held his hands palms out, as if to calm her.

"There's another option?" Addison backed slowly toward her vanity, planting one wedge-heeled foot carefully behind the other with each step. "You're dead. I saw you in your coffin."

She had? I turned to Tod with one hand propped on my hip, surprised. "Wait, you were actually *in* the coffin?"

"Not for long," he mumbled. Then, "Not the point, Kay."

Oh, yeah. Soulless pop star contemplating suicide. *Focus, Kaylee.*

"Who are you?" Addison demanded. The backs of her thighs hit the vanity and she gripped the edge of it to steady herself. "How did you do that?"

It took me a second to realize she meant his sudden appearance out of nowhere. And maybe the whole coming-back-to-life thing.

"Addison, it's Tod. You know it's him," I said, desperately hoping that was true. That she was even listening to me, though her shocked, wide-eyed gaze was glued to her undead ex-boyfriend.

Her breathing slowed and her pale blue eyes narrowed. She

was studying him, probably trying to decide whether to freak out and shout for help, or to calm down and listen. I honestly don't know which I would have chosen in her position. But then she shook her head once, as if she were trying to toss off sleep, and denial shone bright in her eyes again.

"No. You're not him. You can't be. This is some kind of joke, or stunt. I'm being *Punk'd,* right? Ashton, if you're out there, this is *not funny!*" Her face flushed with anger, and tears formed in her eyes.

"You're gonna have to prove it," I whispered, glancing sideways at Tod.

He sighed, and I was impressed with how calm he stayed. "You know me, Addy. We went out for eight months in high school, back in Hurst, before you got the pilot. You were a freshman and I was a sophomore. Remember?"

Instead of answering, Addy crossed her arms over her chest and rolled her eyes. "Lots of people know that. I mentioned Tod in an interview once, and paparazzi followed me to his funeral. Nice try, but you're done. Get out before I yell for Security."

She talked about Tod to reporters? Wow. *They must have been really close....*

"Addy, you remember our first date? You didn't talk to the press about that, did you?"

She shook her head slowly, listening, though her arms remained crossed.

"We went to the West End for ice cream at Marble Slab, and we got a caricature done together by a guy with an easel set up on the sidewalk. I still have it. Then you got carsick on the way home and threw up on the side of the road. Do you remember? You didn't tell anyone else about that, did you?"

She shook her head again, her eyes wide. "Tod?" Addison's famous voice went squeaky, and broke on that one syllable. He nodded, and she hugged herself. "How...? That's impossible. I saw you, and you were dead. You were *dead!*"

"Yeah, well, it turns out that's not always as permanent as it sounds." Nash spoke calmly, softly, and the tension in my own body seemed to ease at his first words. "He was dead. But he's not anymore. Kind of."

Addison's shoulders relaxed as her gaze traveled from Tod to his still-living brother. "How? That doesn't make sense." Yet she wasn't as upset by that as she should have been. With any luck, Nash could strike a balance between too-terrified-to-listen and too-relaxed-to-understand.

"It doesn't make sense up here—" Nash tapped his temple "—but I think you know the truth inside. You've seen strange things, haven't you, Addy?" His voice lilted up with the question and he stepped forward, capturing her gaze. "You sold your soul, and you must have seen some pretty weird stuff in the process…."

Addison's shock broke through her mild daze for a moment, and she opened her mouth, but before she could ask how he knew about her soul, Nash continued. "But all of that was real, and so is this. So is Tod."

Her gaze slid to the reaper again, and now that Nash had calmed her fear and quieted that stubborn human denial, I could tell she really *saw* him. "How did you…get here?"

The reaper shrugged, and mild mischief turned up the corners of his lips. "I distracted the guard at the door, then doubled back."

Addison frowned, then a small smile began at her mouth and spread to include those famous, eerily pale eyes. "I see death hasn't killed your sense of humor."

Though, the great dirt nap hadn't exactly revived it, either….

She laughed over her own lame joke. "Wow. That's not a sentence I ever expected to say."

"So, are you okay with all this?" I asked, crossing my arms over my chest. "Done freaking out?"

She shrugged and propped both hands at her waist. "I can't

promise there won't be a relapse, but Tod's clearly here and alive. I can't really argue with the facts."

I liked her already.

"So, can we sit?" Tod gestured toward the plush seating arrangement.

"Yeah." Addy rounded one of the stiff-looking, green-upholstered armchairs and sank into it, waving a hand at the matching green-striped couch. "But my mom will be back in a few minutes, and she's not going to take this anywhere near as well as I am."

"No doubt," Tod mumbled. He sat in the chair opposite Addy's, while I took the couch. At Tod's signal, Nash locked the door to give us warning when her mother returned, then he joined me on the couch. "You remember my brother, right?"

"Of course. Nash. It's been a while." She crossed her legs and smiled, as if we hadn't come to discuss her immortal soul and impending suicide. Addison was much more poised than I would have been in her position, and I have to admit I was a little jealous of her composure. But then, maybe that was one of the advantages of being an actress.

That, and massive fame and fortune.

Her gaze slid my way, and she made actual eye contact. "And you're Kaylee, right?"

I nodded and gave her a genuine smile. People hardly ever remembered my name after only one introduction. I was pretty forgettable. At least, when I wasn't screaming.

Tod cleared his throat to get everyone's attention, and I turned to see him watching Addison intently from the chair opposite hers. One impeccably solid foot tapped the thick carpet. "Addy, you can't kill yourself," he said, and it took the rest of us a second to absorb his abrupt launch into a conversation no one else seemed prepared for.

Addison recovered first. "Hadn't planned to." She shrugged and smiled, then launched into a question of her own. "So, how are you alive now, when you were dead two years ago? Did your mom freak out, or what?" Unbridled curiosity illuminated her flawless features better than any stage lights could have.

"It's complicated." Tod tugged briefly on the blond fuzz at the end of his chin. "I'll tell you all about it later, but right now I just need to know you're not going to kill yourself." The gravity in his voice surprised me, and I'd never seen Tod look so frightened. So genuinely concerned for someone else. "Please," he said, and that last word wrung a bruising pang of sympathy from my heart, though I wasn't sure which of them I felt worse for: the soulless pop star with five days to live, or the reaper who would lose her again.

Addison's brows furrowed. "I said I won't. I love my life." She spread her arms to take in the entire room, as if to ask who *wouldn't* love her life.

Tod exhaled slowly, his features weighted by doubt and worry. He didn't believe her. How could he, considering Libby's inside information?

"Maybe she's not planning it yet." I shifted to lean against Nash's chest. His arm wound around me, his fingers spread across my ribs, and my pulse raced in response. "Maybe whatever drives her to it hasn't happened yet."

Tod nodded, and his gaze went distant. "Yeah." He turned back to Addison. "Is there anything wrong, Addy? You're probably under a lot of stress. Is your mother pushing you into this? Are you *on* something? There were rumors a couple of months ago...."

"No." Addison cut him off, her smile wilting like a cut flower. "Nothing's wrong, Tod. Nothing serious, anyway. There's pressure, but that's true no matter who you are or what you do."

Isn't that *the truth....*

"And am I *on* something...?" Her brows formed a hard line, and she clenched the arms of her chair, bracelet pressed into the upholstery. "I can't believe you'd even ask me that, with my mom still strung out on those damn pain pills."

Tod sighed and leaned forward with his elbows on his knees. I'd never seen him look so tense. So worried. "Is it bad again?"

Addy twisted her bracelet. "Nothing I can't handle."

"You sure?" Tod asked, obviously thinking the same thing I was. A strung-out parent could be a lot of stress. Especially for someone like Addison Page, for whom privacy was only a vague concept.

"As sure as I am that you're sitting there." Addy forced an awkward laugh at her own joke, and the reaper rolled his eyes. "Nothing's wrong, Tod. Other than Eden collapsing onstage. We're going to see her in a couple of minutes." She paused and glanced at the hands now twisted together in her lap. "You guys want to come? I don't think they'll let you in to see her, but I could use the company."

"Addison…" I began, but then hesitated. I'd never been the bearer of such bad news before, but someone had to tell her. "Eden died onstage."

Addison shook her head in echo of her earlier denial. "How do you know…?" She stopped as something occurred to her, and glanced at both of the guys. "Does this have anything to do with me…killing myself?"

I deferred to Tod, unsure about that one.

"We don't know," he said finally. "But, Addy, I need you to promise me…."

Suddenly the doorknob turned behind us, and was followed by a wooden *thunk* when someone walked into the door, obviously expecting it to open. "Addy?" a woman's nasal voice called. "What are you doing? Open the door."

Addison stood so quickly *my* head spun, rubbing her palms nervously on the sides of her jeans. "Just a minute, Mom," she called. "I'm…in the bathroom."

I stood and pulled Nash off of the couch, my pulse racing

now. No human mother—even one strung out on painkillers—would understand what we'd come to tell Addy. But Tod could go invisible, and Nash and I could pretend to be fans.

If Addison hadn't already panicked and lied…

She glanced at the door in dread, but before she could say anything else, Tod grabbed her hand. "Addy, promise me that no matter what happens, you won't kill yourself. *Promise* me."

"I…" Addison's gaze flicked from his face, lined in desperation, to the door, which her mother was now pounding on.

"Addison Renee Page, let me in right now! My nose is bleeding!"

"Are you okay in there?" her bodyguard called, and the knob twisted again.

Nash tugged me toward the wall, either to give the ex-couple more space or to put us out of the line of fire when the door gave way.

"*Promise* me!" Tod hissed, loud enough that I knew he'd gone inaudible to everyone outside the room. "You do *not* want to die without your soul. Trust me on this."

Addy's breaths came rapidly. Her jugular vein stood out in her neck, jiggling wildly in fear and confusion. Her voice was an uneven whisper. "How do you guys know about that?"

"The same way we know Eden's dead." Tod pulled her close, speaking almost directly into her ear, his voice low and gravelly with fear. "Addison, if you die while that hellion has your soul, he'll give you form in the Netherworld and will own you forever. *Forever,* Addy. He'll feed on your pain. He'll slice you open and let you bleed. He'll wear your intestines around his neck and peel your skin off inch by inch while you scream."

Tears formed in Addison's eyes, and her hands began to shake as she tried to push Tod away. But he wasn't done. "He'll twist your sanity with your own memories. He'll exploit your every fear, and every twinge of guilt you've ever felt. Then he'll heal you—inside and out—and start all over again."

Tod held her at arm's length so he could see her, and I jumped in, hissing softly as I tried to pull him away from her while Nash tried to hold me back. "Tod, stop it! You're scaring her!" And me.

But he meant to. He was scaring her to keep her alive. Though surely he knew such an effort was pointless. He'd taught me that you can't cheat death. Not without paying the price...

"Addison!" Ms. Page shouted from outside the door, and a fresh jolt of alarm shot up my spine and raced down my limbs. "Open up or I'll have Roger break down the door." But this time we barely heard her.

"You're serious?" Addison's terrified gaze was glued to Tod, her hands shaking worse than ever.

He nodded. "You have to get out of it, Addy. Get your soul back. There's an out-clause in your contract, right? That's hellion law. There has to be an out-clause."

Oh... He wasn't just trying to save her life, which was probably impossible, anyway. He was trying to save her soul.

Addison nodded, tears rolling down her face. "Eden did it, too," she sobbed softly. "Is she... Does he...*have* her now?"

Tod nodded and let her go, then wrapped his arms around her when she collapsed against him. "They didn't tell us that. About the torture." She sniffled against his shoulder. "They just said humans don't need their souls, and that if we sold ours, we could have everything. *Everything.*" She shook silently, then stepped back to look at him, eyes flashing with terror and indignation. Delirium, maybe. "He said we don't need souls!"

"You don't need them to keep you alive," Nash said softly. "Demon's Breath will do that just as well. But while a hellion has your soul, you can't move on. You'll be stuck there, a plaything for whoever owns you."

"You have to get it back, Addison," I ventured, hugging myself in horror. I hadn't known much about hellions, either. "You have to get your soul back, with this...out-clause." Whatever that was.

Addison eyed Tod fiercely, clutching at his arms. "Help me!" she begged softly. "I don't know what I'm doing. You have to help me. Please!" She glanced over his shoulder at me and Nash. "All of you, please!"

I had no idea what to say, but Tod nodded. "Of course we will."

Nash went stiff at my side, but before he could protest, more shouting came from the hallway.

"Okay, break it down!" the stage mother called, and Addison glanced around frantically, probably looking for somewhere to hide us.

"Wait, I'm coming!" she shouted. "Here," she whispered, pulling me toward the door by my arm. Nash followed, and she pressed us against the wall behind the door, so we'd be hidden when it opened. She tried to pull Tod into line with us, but he only smiled and shook his head.

"I can hide myself." He forced a smile, and Addy nodded, wiping tears from her face with her bare hands.

"Oh, yeah." She hesitated, then glanced at the door again. "Just a minute, Mom!" Then she turned to Tod and whispered, "I'm staying at the Adolphus, as Lisa Hawthorne. Call me tomorrow night and I'll sneak you guys up. Please?"

Tod nodded, but his smile was grimmer than I'd ever seen it. "I'll call you at eight."

"Thank you," she mouthed.

Tod winked at me and Nash, then blinked out of sight. Addy pressed one finger to her mouth in the world-wide signal for "shhhh," then unlocked the door and pulled it open.

"Mom! Are you okay? What happened?" Shoes brushed the carpet as she ushered her mother to the bathroom, but all I could see was the back of the door, an inch from my nose. Nash's hand curled around mine, and our pulses raced together.

"I didn't expect your door to be locked," her mother snapped as water ran, and I couldn't resist a grin. "Addy, you look like a tomato. Have you been crying?"

"I'm just worried about Eden. Hurry and get cleaned up so we can go." More footsteps brushed toward us, and Addy called out, "Roger, can you go get some wet rags or something?"

"Sure, Ms. Page," a deep voice said from outside the room. Heavy footsteps headed away, and Addy swung the door open, signaling the all clear.

I spared her one last, sympathetic smile, then Nash tugged me into the hall, still blessedly deserted.

We speed-walked through the maze of hallways, through the empty auditorium, and out to the half-empty parking lot, where Tod leaned against the closed passenger door of their mother's car.

Nash's hand went stiff in mine the moment he saw the reaper, and Tod had his hands up to ward off his brother's anger long before we got within hearing distance. "What was I supposed to do?" he asked, before either of us could get a word out.

"Not my problem!" Nash tried to shove Tod out of the way so he could unlock my door, but the reaper went non-corporeal at the last second, and Nash went right through him. His shoulder slammed into the car just above the window, and when he turned, anger blazed in his swirling eyes. "You could have done anything! *Except* tell her we'd get her soul back for her."

He pulled open the passenger side door and shoved it closed when I was settled in my seat and was still yelling when he opened his own door. "How are we supposed to do that? Wander around the Netherworld asking random hellions if they took possession of a human pop star's soul, and if so, would they please consider giving it back out of the kindness of their decayed hearts?"

Nash slid into his seat and slammed the door, leaving Tod alone in the dark parking lot with a handful of humans now watching us warily. He turned the key in the ignition, shifted into Drive, then took off across the asphalt, headed toward the exit with his parking receipt already in one fist.

As soon as we turned out of the lot, something caught my eye from the side-view mirror and I twisted in my seat to see Tod staring back at me, his usual scowl unusually fierce. "Don't do that!" I said, for at least the thousandth time since we'd met. "Normal people don't get in the car while it's still moving!"

Nash glared at him in the rearview mirror. "But as long as you're here, you need to understand something, and I'm only going to say this once—we are not tracking down Addison Page's soul. It's not our responsibility, and we wouldn't even know where to start. But most important, it's *too. Damn. Dangerous.*"

"Fine," Tod said through teeth clenched with either fear or anger. Or both.

"What?" Nash stopped for a red light and glanced in the mirror again, his brows low in confusion. He'd obviously expected an argument, as had I.

Tod shifted on the cloth seat, his corporeal clothes rustling with the movement. "I said fine. This is my problem, not yours. I'll do it myself."

"This isn't your problem, either," Nash insisted, and I turned in my seat again so I could see them both at once. "She sold her soul of her own free will for fame and fortune. The contract is legally binding, and it has a legally binding out-clause. Let her get it back herself." He stomped on the gas when the light changed, and the tires squealed beneath us as I grabbed the armrest.

"She didn't know what she was doing, Nash, and she still doesn't." Tod leaned forward, glaring into the rearview mirror. "She has no idea what rights she has in the Netherworld, and she can't even get there on her own. The out-clause is no good if you can't enforce it. You know that."

"Wait…" I loosened my seat belt and found a more comfortable sideways position as dread twisted my stomach into knots a scout couldn't untie. "She really can't do this on her own?"

Tod shook his head. "She doesn't stand a chance."

I sighed and sank back into my seat.

Nash glanced away from the road long enough to read my expression, shadows shifting over his face as we drove under a series of streetlights. "No, Kaylee. We can't. We could get killed."

"I know." I closed my eyes and let my head fall against the headrest. "I *know.*"

"No!" he repeated, his knuckles white on the steering wheel, jaw clenched in either fear or anger. Probably both.

"Nash, we have to. I have to, anyway." I stared at his profile, desperate for the words to make him understand. "I couldn't save the souls Aunt Val sold. Heidi, and Alyson, and Meredith, and Julie are going to be tortured forever, because I couldn't save them." My throat felt thick, and my voice cracked as tears burned my eyes.

"Kaylee, that's not your fau—"

"I know, but, Nash, I *can* help Addison. I can stop the same thing from happening to her." I wasn't sure how, but Tod wouldn't have offered our help if there was nothing we could do. Right? "I have to do this."

Nash clutched the wheel even tighter, and he looked like he wanted to twist it into a pretzel. Then he exhaled, and his hands relaxed. He'd made his decision, and I held my breath, waiting for it. "Fine. If you're in, I'm in." His focus shifted to the rearview mirror, where he glared at Tod. "But I'm in this for Kaylee, not for you, and not for your idiot pop princess." The look he shot me then was part disappointment, part anger, part loyalty, and all Nash. His gaze scalded me from the inside out, and I squirmed in my seat as that heat settled low within me.

But when he turned back to the road, the flames sputtered beneath a wash of cold fear. Nash would get involved for me, but the truth was that I had no idea what I was doing.

What had I just gotten us into?

5

"Okay, Kaylee, focus...." Harmony Hudson, Nash's mother, leaned forward on the faded olive couch, licking her lips in concentration as she watched me. She wore jeans and another snug tee, her blond curls pulled into the usual ponytail, a few ringlets hanging loose around her face. Harmony was the hottest mom I'd ever personally met. She looked thirty years old, at the most, but I'd seen her blow out her birthday candles a month earlier.

All eighty-two of them.

"Close your eyes and think about the last time it happened," she continued, and I sucked in a lungful of the fudge-brownie-scented air. "The last time you knew someone was going to die."

And that's where I lost my motivation. I didn't want to think about the last time. It still gave me nightmares.

Pale brows dipped low over Harmony's bright blue eyes—exact copies of Tod's—and her dimple deepened when she frowned. "What's wrong?"

I stared at the scarred hardwood floor. "Last time was...with Sophie and Aunt Val."

"Oh..." Harmony's eyes took on a familiar glint of wisdom, which, at first glance, seemed at odds with her youthful appearance. She was there when the rogue reaper killed my cousin and

tried to take her soul. She saw my aunt give her life instead of
Sophie's—a last-minute act of courage and selflessness that had
gone a long way toward redeeming her in my eyes.

Until I'd learned that the other souls she'd sold to Belphegore
would be tortured for eternity along with my aunt's. Now I was
leaning decidedly toward the Aunt-Val-deserved-what-she-got
school of thought.

Harmony watched emotions flit across my face, but as usual,
she reserved her own judgment. That was why I liked her. Well,
that, and the fact that she always had fresh-baked goodies ready
to be devoured after our how-to-be-a-*bean-sidhe* lessons. "Okay,
then, pick a different time. Just think back to any death premonition. One that was less traumatic."

But the truth was that they were all traumatic. I'd only known
I was a *bean sidhe* for six weeks, and so far every premonition
I'd ever suffered through had thoroughly freaked me out. And
every wail was largely uncontrollable.

Thus the lessons.

"Okay…" I closed my eyes and leaned against the soft, faded
couch cushions, thinking back to the most memorable premonition—other than that last one.

Emma.

My best friend's death had been unbearably awful, made even
worse because I'd known it was coming. I'd seen Em wearing
the death shroud for at least two minutes before she collapsed
on the gym floor, surrounded by hundreds of other students and
parents, gathered to mourn a dead classmate.

But I chose Emma's death to focus on because hers had a
happy ending.

Okay, a bittersweet ending, but that was better than the
screaming, panicking, clawing-my-way-out-of-the-Netherfog
ending most of them had. I'd suspended Emma's soul above her
body with my wail to keep it from the reaper who'd killed her,
while Nash had directed it back into her body. Emma had lived.

But someone else had died instead. That was the price, and the decision we'd made. I'd felt guilty about it ever since, but I'd do it all over again if I had to, because I couldn't let Emma die before her time, no matter who took her place.

So two months later I sat on Nash's couch beside his mother, picturing my best friend's death.

Emma, in the gym, several steps ahead. Voices buzzing around us. Nash's arm around my waist. His fingers curled over my hip. Then the death shroud.

It smeared her blond hair with thin, runny black, like a child's watercolors. Streaks smudged her clothes and her arms, and the scream built inside me. It clawed at my throat, scraping my skin raw even as I clenched my jaws shut, denying it exit.

As in memory, so in life.

The scream rose again, and my throat felt full. Hot. Bruised from the inside out.

My eyes flew open in panic, and Harmony stared calmly back at me. She smiled, a tiny upturn of full lips both of her sons had inherited. "You've got it!" she whispered, eyes shining with pride. "Okay, now here comes the hard part."

It gets harder?

I couldn't ask my question because once a *bean sidhe*'s wail takes over, her throat can be used for nothing else until that scream has either burst loose or been swallowed. I couldn't swallow it—not without Nash's voice to calm me, to coax my birthright into submission—and I wasn't willing to let it loose. Never again, if I could help it.

This lesson was on harnessing my wail. Making it work for me, rather than the other way around. So I nodded, telling Harmony I was ready for the hard part.

"Good. I want you to keep a tight rein on it. Then let it out a little at a time—like a very slow leak—without actually opening your mouth. Only keep the volume down. You want to just barely hear it."

Because the whole point was for me to be able to see and hear the Netherworld through my wail, without humans noticing anything weird. Like me screaming loud enough to shatter their minds. But that was easier said than done, especially considering how much time I'd spent trying to hold back my wail. Evidently suppressing it completely and letting just a little leak through were two very different skill sets.

But I tried.

Keeping my lips sealed, I opened my throat a tiny bit, forcing my jaws to relax. That's where the whole thing went downhill. Instead of that little leak of sound Harmony had mentioned, the entire wail ruptured from my throat, shoving my mouth open wide.

My screech filled the room. The entire house. My whole body hummed with the keening, a violent chord of discordant sounds no human could have produced. My head throbbed, my brain seeming to bounce around within my skull.

I closed my eyes. I couldn't take it.

Cold, smooth fingers brushed my arm, and I opened my eyes again to find Harmony speaking to me. The room around her had become a blur of colors and textures, thanks to my inability to focus on it. Her pretty face was twisted into a constant wince of pain from the shards of steel my scream was no doubt driving into her brain. Male *bean sidhes* hear a female's wail as an eerie, beautiful soul song. They crave the sound, and are pulled toward it. Almost seduced by it.

Female *bean sidhes* hear it as it is. As humans hear it. As a titanic racket loud enough to deafen, and sharp enough to shatter not just glass, but your ever-loving sanity.

Harmony glanced at her living-room window, the glass trembling in its frame. Because we shared a gender and species— though I was fuzzy on exactly how the whole thing worked—I could hear her words through my own screaming, but they sounded like they came from within my own head.

Calm down. Take a breath. Close your mouth….

I snapped my jaws shut, muffling the sound, but not eradicating it. It buzzed in my mouth now, rattling my teeth, and still seeped out like a moan on steroids. But I could hear her normally now.

"Breathe deeply, Kaylee," Harmony soothed, rubbing my arms until goose bumps stood up beneath my sleeves. "Close your eyes and draw it back in. All but that last little bit."

I let my eyelids fall, though that small effort took a lot of courage, because closing my eyes meant blocking her out and embracing my own private darkness. Being alone with the ruthless keening. With the memory of Emma's death, before I'd known it would be temporary.

But I did it.

"Okay, now pull it back. Deep inside you. Picture swallowing your wail—forcing it down past your throat into your heart. You can set it free in there. Let it bounce around. Ricochet. The human heart is a fragile thing, all thin vessels and delicate pumps. But the *bean sidhe* heart is armored. It has to be, for us to survive."

I pictured my heart with iron plating. I forced my arms to relax, my hands to fall into my lap. I listened to my wail as it seeped from my throat, forcing myself to hear each inharmonic note individually. And slowly, painfully, I drew them back into myself. Forced them down into my center.

I felt the wail in my throat, in reverse. It was tangible, and the sensation was eerie. Downright creepy. It was like swallowing smoke, if smoke were sharp. Prickly, as if it were bound in thorns.

When I'd swallowed all but the thinnest, most insubstantial thread, I felt a smile spread slowly from the corners of my mouth to my cheeks, then into my eyes. I heard only a ribbon of sound, so faint it could have been my imagination. My shoulders slumped as an odd peace filtered through me, settling into each limb. I'd done it. I called up my wail when I needed it, and restricted it on my own terms.

I opened my eyes, already grinning at Harmony. But my grin froze, then shattered before my gaze had even focused.

Harmony smiled back at me, curls framing her face, her dimples piercing cheeks that should have been rosy with good health and good cheer. But now they were gray. As was everything else. A hazy, foglike filter had slipped over my vision while I was modifying my wail, like my eyes had been opened farther than should have been possible.

The Nether-fog. A veil between our world and the Netherworld.

A female *bean sidhe*'s wail allows her—and any other *bean sidhes* near enough to hear her—to see through the fog into both the human world and that other, somehow *deeper* one simultaneously. Or to travel from one to the other.

My head turned, my eyes wide with horror. I wanted to learn about the Netherworld, but had no interest in going there!

"Kaylee? It's okay, Kaylee. Do you see it?" Harmony's words were smooth and warm like Nash's, but bore none of the supernatural calm his could carry. Harmony and I shared a skill set, and while Nash's voice could soothe and comfort human and *bean sidhe* alike, ours summoned darkness, and heralded pain and death.

Nash and I were two sides of the same weird coin, and I didn't like wailing without him.

My heart galloped within my chest, skipping some beats and rushing others, unable to find a steady rhythm. My palms dampened with sweat, and I rubbed them on the threadbare couch cushions, both to dry them and to anchor myself to the only reality I understood. The only truth I wanted any part of.

"Kaylee, look at me!" Harmony stroked my hand as she leaned to the side to place herself in my field of vision. "This is supposed to happen. I'm right here with you, and everything is fine."

No-no-no-no-no! But I couldn't speak as long as that last thread of sound still trailed from me. I could only glance around in panic at the fog layering Nash's house like a coat of dust too fine to settle. It hung in the air over Harmony's battered coffee table and old TV, darkening my world, my vision, and my heart.

My pulse raced, and each breath came faster than the last. I knew the pattern. First came the gloom, then came the creatures. I'd seen them before. Beings with too many or too few limbs. With joints that bent the wrong way, or didn't bend at all. Some had tails. Some didn't have heads. But the worst were the ones with no eyes, because I knew they were watching me. I just didn't know *how....*

Yet no creatures appeared. Harmony and I were alone in her house in the human world, and somehow alone in the Netherworld.

With that realization came the calm I craved. My tension eased, and my wail faded, thoughts of Emma's death melting into my memory to be used again when they were needed. Or better yet, forgotten.

The haze cleared slowly, until Harmony came into focus. Her hair looked more golden than ever, her eyes much brighter than I remembered in contrast to the drab shades of gray that had covered her moments earlier. "You okay?" she asked, forehead pinched with worry.

"Yeah. Sorry." I rubbed both hands over my face, tucking my own limp brown strands behind my ears. "I knew it was coming, but it still scared the crap out of me. I don't think I'll ever get used to that."

"Yes you will." She smiled and stood, motioning for me to follow her into the kitchen. "It gets easier with practice."

That's what I was afraid of.

Harmony waved an arm at the round breakfast table, and I pulled out a ladder-back chair with clear finish chipping off the back and one missing rung while she headed for the oven. The timer blinking above the stove was counting back with thirty-eight seconds to go, and it never failed to amaze me how Harmony always knew when it was about to go off. That timer had never once interrupted one of our lessons, and none of her treats had ever come out over- or underdone.

Unlike the cookies I'd baked two nights earlier.

"There's soda in the fridge." She slid her hand into a thick glove-shaped pot holder and pulled the oven door open.

"How 'bout milk?" I like milk with my chocolate.

"Top shelf." She pulled a glass pan of brownies from the oven and slid it onto a wire cooling rack on the counter. I took a short glass from the cabinet over the sink and filled it with milk, then sat at the table again while she poured one for herself.

"So, explain to me why I needed to learn to do that?" I sipped from my glass, suddenly grateful for cold, white milk, and all things normal and this-worldly.

Harmony shot me a sympathetic smile as she slid the carton onto the top shelf of the fridge, then swung the door shut. "It's mostly to help you learn to control your wail. If you can manipulate it on your own terms, you should be able to avoid screaming your head off in front of a room full of humans."

Because humans tend to lock up girls who can't stop screaming. Trust me.

"But other than that, it's helpful to be able to peek into the Netherworld when you need to. Though, I wouldn't suggest trying it unless you have to. The less you're noticed by Netherworlders, the easier your life will be."

She'd get no argument from me on that one. But I was curious on one point....

"So...why were we alone?"

"While you were wailing?" Harmony crossed the linoleum toward me and pulled out the chair next to mine while I nodded.

"Well, first of all, we weren't really there. We were just peeking in. Like watching the bears at the zoo through that thick glass wall. You can see them and they can see you, but no one can cross the barrier."

"So the Netherworlders could see us?"

"If anyone had been there, yes." She sipped from her glass again.

"So how come no one was there?"

"Because this is a private residence. Those only exist on one plane or the other. Only large, public buildings with heavy traffic exist in both worlds."

"Like the school?" I was thinking of all the weird creatures I'd seen when I peeked into the Netherworld from the gym, the day Emma died. "Or the mall?" That one brought even worse memories…

"Yeah. Schools, offices, museums, stadiums… Anywhere there are lots of people most of the time."

I frowned and took another sip of my milk as a new worry occurred to me. "How would I actually go there?"

"You wouldn't." Harmony's blue eyes were suddenly dark and hard, as if the sky had clouded over. They didn't swirl, because she had more than eighty years' experience hiding her emotions, but I could tell she was worried. "Kaylee, you have no business in the Netherworld."

Let's hope you're right.

"I know." I smiled to set her at ease. "I just want to make sure I don't wind up there accidentally, practicing what I learned today."

She relaxed at my explanation, and the light flowed back into her eyes. "You won't. The difference between looking through the glass and stepping through it is all a matter of intent. You have to *want* to go there to be there."

"That's it?" I frowned as she stood and rummaged through

a drawer, clanging silverware together in search of something. "Have desire, will travel?" It couldn't be that easy. Or that scary.

"Well, that and the soul song."

Of course. I felt the tension in my body ease, and I took another short sip of my milk, saving the rest to wash down my brownie.

Harmony finally pulled a knife from the drawer, followed by a long, thin metal spatula. She ran the knife across the glass dish, cutting the brownies into large, even squares.

"Harmony?"

"Hmm?" She slid the spatula under the first square and lifted it carefully out of the pan and onto a small paper plate. She liked baking but hated doing dishes.

"How can someone live without a soul?"

"What?" Harmony froze with a brownie crumb halfway to her mouth, the spatula still in her other hand. "Why are you...? What's going on, Kaylee?" Her eyes narrowed, and I felt guilty for making her worry.

I decided to tell her the truth. Part of it, anyway. "Nash and I saw Eden's concert last night in Dallas, remember?"

"Of course." Fear drained from her features again, and she scooped an extra-large brownie onto the second plate, then carried them both to the table, without forks. The Hudsons ate their brownies the proper way—with their fingers. My aunt would have thrown a fit, but I was enjoying being converted.

"I saw that on the news this morning." She set one plate in front of me, then sank into her chair with the other, smaller square. Her eyes brightened as the next piece of the puzzle slid into place. "Are you saying Eden died without her soul?"

I nodded, then chewed, swallowed, and washed the first rich bite down with a sip of milk before answering. "It was weird. She dropped dead right there on the stage, but I thought she'd just passed out, because there was no premonition. No death shroud. No urge to wail. But Tod said she was dead, and sure enough, a few seconds later, this weird, dark stuff floated up from her body. Too dark and heavy-looking to be a soul."

"Demon's Breath, probably." Harmony took another bite, licking a crumb from her lip before she chewed.

"That's what Tod said." I twisted my half-full glass of milk on the table. "That Eden sold her soul to a hellion."

She shrugged and brushed a ringlet back from her forehead. "That's the only explanation I can think of. A soul can't be taken from a living being. It can be stolen after a person's death—" or murder, as with Aunt Val's victims "—or it can be given up willingly by its owner. But then something else has to take its place, to keep the body alive. Usually, that something else is Demon's Breath."

"But I thought a person's soul is what determines his life span. If Eden's was gone, how did the reapers know when she was supposed to die?"

Harmony held up one finger as she swallowed, and I bit another huge, unladylike bite from my brownie. She wiped her lips on a paper towel, already shaking her head. "A person's soul doesn't determine how long he or she lives. The list does."

"So…where does the list come from? Who decides when everyone has to die?"

Harmony raised one brow, like she was impressed. "Now you're asking the good questions. Unfortunately, I don't have an answer for that one. But maybe that's a good thing.…"

I frowned, twisting my used napkin into a thin paper rope. "What do you mean?"

"No one actually knows who makes out the list. No one I know, anyway." She sipped from her cup before continuing. "Maybe the Fates traded in their thread and scissors for a pen and paper. Maybe the list comes from some automated printer in a secure room none of us will ever see. Maybe it comes straight from God. But there has to be a reason we don't know the specifics, and frankly, I'm pretty blissful about that particular nugget of ignorance."

"Me, too." I wasn't exactly eager to see whoever plotted my lifeline; I'd kind of drawn the short straw on that one. Though, it was very likely I'd live longer than I would have as a regular human.

"All we really know is that upsetting the balance between life and death is not an option. Somebody has to die for every entry on the list. Fortunately, there's a little wiggle room for special circumstances." Harmony hesitated, then met my eyes before continuing. "Which is how your mom was able to trade her death date for yours."

I cleared my throat and swallowed my last bite, trying to swallow my guilt along with it. I was supposed to die when I was three, but my mother took my place. I hadn't known the truth about her death until I discovered my *bean sidhe* heritage and my family was finally forced to tell me everything. Despite their insistence that what happened to my mom was not my fault, the fact was that if it weren't for me, she'd still be alive.

Guilt was inevitable. Right?

"Considering the sacrifice your mom made for you, I find it hard to understand how Eden—or anyone else for that matter—could possibly see her own soul as acceptable currency. As payment for something else."

I shrugged and dropped my wadded-up napkin on my empty plate. "I don't think she understood what she was getting into. Humans don't know about any of this."

"They're supposed to know, before they sign the contract. Hellion law requires full disclosure. But who knows if the poor fool actually read her contract before signing. What a waste." Harmony shook her head in disappointment and pushed the rest of her brownie toward me. "So much potential, squandered. For what, do you know?"

I shook my head, staring at her plate. I'd lost my appetite.

My best guess would be that Eden sold her soul for fame and fortune, but I didn't know for sure. All I knew for certain was that she was probably regretting that decision now, and that if we couldn't get Addison's soul back in four days, she would suffer the same fate.

I would not let that happen.

6

"So, what's with the fake name at the hotel? She's avoiding the press?" I tried to distract myself as I typed "hellion" into the search bar at the top of my laptop screen, then tapped the enter key. Links filled the screen faster than I could read the entries, and my vision started to blur with exhaustion. I hadn't slept very well the night before, thanks to nightmares of dead girls being tortured in the Netherworld, and had poured the last of my energy into my *bean sidhe* lesson that afternoon.

"I guess." Nash leaned back on my bed and I watched him in the mirror, my heart tripping faster when he put his hands behind his head and cords of muscle stood out beneath his short sleeves. Sometimes it still felt weird to be going out with a jock, but Nash Hudson wasn't your average football player. His *bean sidhe* bloodline, dead father, not-so-dead reaper brother, and familiarity with a world that would land most humans in a straitjacket meant that on the inside, Nash didn't fit in at school any more than I did.

He just hid it better.

And there were definite advantages to having a boyfriend as…aesthetically gifted as Nash. The downside was that I had trouble concentrating on anything else while he was around.

Focus, Kaylee... I took a deep breath and forced my thoughts back on track. "Isn't the whole fake name thing a little clichéd?"

He shrugged without dropping his arms. "So long as it works."

On-screen, the page had finished loading, and I skimmed the results. The first was about some kind of turbo engine for Mustangs, and the second was a link to a comic book Wiki. The rest of the links ran along those same lines. *So much for internet research.*

"Tell me again why we're doing this?" Nash's normally hypnotic voice was pinched thin and sharp with reluctance. And maybe a little annoyance.

"Because Addison needs help and I believe in karma." I glanced in the mirror again to find Nash watching me in amusement now.

"I meant dinner."

"Oh." I pushed my chair away from the desk and almost tipped over when one of the back wheels caught on the ratty carpet. Standing, I tugged my tee into place, then sank cross-legged onto the bed facing Nash. "Because my dad's trying really hard to make this whole single-parent thing work, and Uncle Brendon's the only one he has to talk to."

After my mom died, my father sent me to live with my aunt and uncle, to help hide me from the reaper-with-a-vendetta who'd traded my mother's life for mine. But we both knew my resemblance to her was at least as strong a motivator for my dad's absence from my life. Every time he looked at me, he saw her, and his heart broke a little more.

But after what Aunt Val had done, he'd come back, assuming it would be easier to protect me himself, now that I was in on the big secret of my species. And I was pretty sure he felt guilty for being gone so long. So, my dad had given up a good job in Ireland for crappy factory work in Texas, and together we were trying not to screw up the whole father-daughter thing too badly. So what if that meant a tiny rental house, no extra money, and weekly dinners with my uncle and mean-girl cousin?

Nash's knees touched mine and he took my hands in his, letting them lie in the hollow between our legs. "I know, but Sophie's turning into a real pain."

He was right about that.

Sophie didn't understand what had happened the night her mother died. My cousin had awakened from what we'd told her was a simple loss of consciousness due to shock—but was actually her own temporary demise—to find her mother dead on the floor, and me holding a heavy cast-iron skillet like a baseball bat.

Though the coroner had said Aunt Val died of heart failure, Sophie remained convinced that I was somehow responsible for her mother's death. But I couldn't really blame her, considering how confusing and scary her life had recently become. My cousin had no idea that the rest of her family wasn't human, or that the world contained anything more dangerous than the ordinary criminals on the FBI's most-wanted list. But she knew there was something we weren't telling her, and she resented us all for that.

She knew better than to blame me openly, or to even throw a hostile word my way on family dinner nights, but at school it was open season on Kaylee. And Nash wasn't the only one who had noticed.

A metal clang rang out from the kitchen, and I laughed. I couldn't help it. My father wasn't much of a cook, but he was really trying.

"What's for dinner?" Nash's thumb stroked the back of my hand, sending shivers of anticipation through me.

"Lasagna and bagged salad."

"Sounds good." The browns and greens in his eyes swirled lazily, wickedly. "And I already know what I want for dessert…."

He leaned forward and his lips met mine, softly at first. Then eagerly.

I tilted my head for a better angle and kissed him back, loving the feel of his lips on mine, his hand at the back of my neck. My fingers found his chest, trailing lightly over his shirt to feel the firmness beneath.

My heart raced, adrenaline pulsing through me in a steady, charged rhythm, leaving my limbs heavy, my body eager. My mouth opened beneath Nash's, and he moaned. The sound of his need skimmed lightly over my skin like a shadow given form, warming me as it slid down my neck, over my collarbones, and between my breasts to burn deep inside me.

He pulled me onto his lap and I crossed my ankles at his back, holding us tightly together while his lips moved over my neck. I could feel what he wanted through both layers of denim separating us, and my head swam with the knowledge that he was excited by *me*.

Nash Hudson could have had just about any girl he wanted—and he'd already had more than a few—but he was with me.

It's because you're a bean sidhe, some traitorous voice spoke up from deep inside me as I tangled my fingers in a handful of his thick brown hair. *You're a novelty. New prey to chase. But once he's truly caught you, the game will be over, and he'll move on to the next hunt.*

And I'd have no one to help me control my wail.

No. Nash wouldn't do that. He wouldn't help me help Addison if he was just trying to get my pants off. I wasn't that much of a catch, and there were easier ways to get laid, especially for him. And he hadn't even really pushed the issue.

Not that much, anyway.

Nash pulled my head down until our mouths met again, and I wrapped my arms around his neck and shoved my doubts aside. His hands found my hip, squeezing as our kiss intensified. Deepened. His fingers traveled up gradually as his lips slid down my

chin and over my neck, singeing a path toward my shoulder. My
head fell back, my mouth open, each breath slipping in and out
silently as I concentrated on the pleasure of his skin on mine.

He pushed aside the neckline of my T-shirt, and his lips closed
over the point of my shoulder, sucking gently. Nibbling just a
little. My hand tightened around his biceps. Not stopping him.
Not urging him. Just…waiting.

I inhaled softly as his other hand slid up my side, under my
shirt. He kissed my shoulder again, his lips hot against my flesh,
and his thumb brushed the underside of my right breast. My
breath hitched, my heart pounding as infant flames of longing
licked lower, deeper.

My skin felt flushed, my body pulsing with sudden awareness,
impulsive craving….

"Don't stop on my account."

I jumped, and Nash leaned away from me so fast my head
spun, my skin suddenly cold in his absence. "*Damn* it, Tod!" he
snapped as I straightened my shirt, my cheeks flaming.

Avoiding the reaper's eyes, I climbed off Nash and pushed
my bedroom door the rest of the way closed; my dad probably
wouldn't hear Tod, but he could definitely hear the other half of
the conversation. I glared at my uninvited guest. "If you don't
learn to knock like regular people, I swear I'll…tell your boss
you're abusing your reaper skills to pursue a life of voyeurism
and debauchery."

Tod shot us a wry grin. "He already knows."

I huffed and sank onto the bed with Nash, relaxing into him
as his arm went around my waist. "What's up? And make it fast.
My dad's home." And as grateful as he was to Tod for helping
save Sophie, my father wasn't very comfortable with the idea of
me hanging out with a reaper, or—as he called them—one of
death's minions.

And honestly, sometimes neither was I.

Tod rolled his eyes and glanced at the door, then his gaze slid back to me. "I just talked to Addy and she's arranged for some privacy tonight at eight-thirty, for an hour at the most. In her room at the Adolphus."

Eight-thirty? That only left an hour and a half for dinner and the drive into Dallas. We'd never make it.

"Uncle Brendon's going to be here with Sophie any minute, and I can't skip out early."

"Four days, Kaylee." The reaper's usual scowl deepened. "Addy only has four days."

I shrugged. "You're welcome to explain what we're doing to my entire family…."

Tod flinched, and that one movement told me just how much he respected the combined threat of my father and uncle standing together. *Bean sidhes* might not have any obvious offensive abilities, but together, my dad and uncle had almost three hundred years of experience. And they weren't exactly small men.

"Fine. Just get there as soon as you can."

"Do you have a plan, or are you just throwing us all into the deep end?" Nash's finger traced lazy figure eights on my lower back, and I wanted to lean into his touch. Or better yet, pick up where we'd left off.

Tod sank wearily into my desk chair, arms crossed over the back. "Well, obviously we need to know which hellion she sold her soul to."

"Yeah, good luck with that." I pointed at the computer screen behind him, and the reaper twisted in his seat to look. When he met my gaze again, a cocky smile had turned up one side of his mouth, and his blue eyes glinted in shadowed mirth.

"You thought you could figure that out online? Somehow I don't think hellions are much into social networking."

"You got a better plan?" Nash pulled me closer, and my heart beat a little faster in response to his.

"Yeah. I thought we'd ask her."

"You can do that on your own," Nash snapped.

Tod shook his head. "I need Kaylee. Addy likes her."

"And Addy always gets what she wants?"

I could practically hear the scowl in Nash's voice, and I twisted to look at him in amusement. "Like you're one to talk!"

His brows rose, and his steamy gaze traveled south of my face. "I don't have everything I want. Yet." I flushed, and turned back to Tod in time to see his eyes roll. "Well, you guys aren't going without me." Nash stretched one leg out on my rumpled comforter. "But do you honestly think she'll know this hellion's name?"

Tod shrugged again. "I think it's worth a shot—"

Before he could finish, my door creaked open and my dad appeared in the gap. His gaze hardened when it landed on me and Nash, now reclined together on the bed, and I knew that if he had less control over his emotions, my father's irises would be churning furiously.

"Kaylee, I know I'm new at this, but I'm not *that* new. This door stays open when you two are alone in here."

I glanced at Tod, who smirked at me from my own desk chair. "We're not—" And that's when I realized my father couldn't see the reaper, and that I probably shouldn't remedy that. I'd rather my father think Nash and I were breaking the normal human rules than the weird *bean sidhe* ones. "Doing anything," I finished lamely.

"We were just talking, Mr. Cavanaugh." Nash didn't even glance at his brother, who was now making obscene gestures and rolling his eyes madly.

Unconvinced, my dad nodded curtly, then disappeared into the hall, just as the doorbell rang. "Kaylee, can you get that? I'm burning the bread."

"Eat fast." Tod leaned back to cross both arms over his chest as I stood. Then he was gone before I could reply. At least, I thought he was gone, but it was hard to tell with Tod.

Nash followed me to the door, behind which my cousin's

voice rang out loud and clear. "...don't see why we can't do this at our house. There's barely room to turn around in their kitchen, and Uncle Aiden's place smells funny."

"It does not smell funny, and we hosted last week." Uncle Brendon sounded exhausted, but much more patient with his only daughter than I would have been. Especially considering how much he'd suffered from his wife's loss, in spite of what she'd cost us all. But Sophie seemed oblivious to her father's pain. "It's their turn."

I shot Nash a resigned smile, then pulled the door open, bracing myself for Sophie's acidic presence. "Hey, guys, come on in."

My cousin brushed past us into the house as if she hadn't heard my greeting, mumbling beneath her breath about how she'd rather spend a Sunday night. She left us to choke on a cloud of her perfume, overwhelming in our small, dark entry.

"I'm sorry about that." Uncle Brendon pushed the front door shut as he stepped inside. "She's...still suffering."

And making sure her misery has plenty of company.

Half an hour later, all five of us sat around the square card table in our eat-in kitchen, me straddling the corner between Nash and Sophie. There wasn't enough room to actually put the food on the table, so if anyone wanted seconds, he'd have to get up and refill his plate from the dishes on the counter. But that didn't seem to be much of a worry, considering that the rim of Sophie's plate was ringed with small bits of marinara-stained waxed paper, which my dad had forgotten to remove from the slices of cheese he'd layered into the lasagna.

If it hadn't embarrassed my father to no end, it would have been almost funny to watch her face twist with fresh horror each time she pulled a limp bit of paper from her food. Not that it mattered. She didn't eat enough to keep a squirrel alive, anyway, and had lost several pounds in the weeks since her mother's death.

There wasn't much conversation over dinner, but every now

and then, my uncle would look across the table at his brother and chuckle as he pulled a piece of cheese paper from his pasta and folded it into his napkin, breaking the tension for another few moments. For which I was profoundly grateful.

Nash and I excused ourselves immediately after dinner, nodding at my father's reminder to be home by ten-thirty, and I drove, because Nash's mom had their car. I'd rarely driven in downtown Dallas and had never been to Addison's hotel, so I counted us lucky to get there in one piece.

The lobby of the Adolphus was full of dark, ornate furniture and fancy chandeliers, and I felt underdressed clomping through the lobby in jeans and sneakers. Fortunately, before I could work up the nerve to ask the snooty clerk behind an oversize desk which room "Lisa Hawthorne" was in, Tod appeared from around a corner, wearing respectably clean and intact jeans and an unwrinkled button-up shirt open over his usual dark tee. He jerked his head toward a cluster of elevators on one end of the lobby, and we followed him gratefully into the first one to open.

"She's pretty nervous, so go easy on her," Tod said, eyeing Nash as soon as the mirrored doors closed and the elevator slid into motion.

"She's not the only one." I ran one shaky hand over my ponytail, wondering if I should have worn my hair down. Or wiped my feet before walking through the lobby. But the overpriced hotel wasn't really the cause of my nerves.

I'd peeked into the Netherworld that afternoon, and wasn't anxious to do it again anytime soon. But as badly as the prospect of actually walking into that shadow-world scared me, my horror was much greater at the thought of condemning Addison Page to an eternity there. Even if she had signed away her own soul.

Tod was right. She didn't know what she was getting into. She couldn't have.

The elevator binged in warning and slowed to a smooth stop,

then the doors slid open almost silently. Tod got off first, and Nash and I followed him down a thickly carpeted hallway past at least a dozen doors before he stopped in front of the very last one, nearest the emergency staircase.

"Hang on a minute," he said, then popped out of sight before we could protest, leaving me and Nash standing in the hall like idiots, hoping no one came out to ask if we'd lost our key. Or to call Security.

Who me? Paranoid?

Absolutely.

Several seconds later, the door opened from the inside, and for the second time in as many days, we walked into the private rooms of Addison Page, rock star. I had a fleeting moment of panicked certainty that once again, she wasn't expecting us. That Tod had made the whole meeting up. But Addison stood in the middle of the sitting room, watching us through red-rimmed eyes, and she didn't look surprised to see us. Thank goodness.

"Thanks for coming," she said as we made our way to a collection of couches gathered around yet another flat-screen television. "I know you guys probably think I don't deserve your help, and the truth is that I'm not sure I do."

Neither was I, but the fact that she had her own doubts made me want to help her for her own sake, beyond my need to make up for not being able to save the girls my aunt had damned to eternal torture.

"Yes you do." Tod guided her to a boldly patterned armchair with one hand on her lower back. She didn't pull away from him, and I was impressed all over again by her composure. I wouldn't have been so calm if I had an undead ex-boyfriend.

Or the staggering lack of a soul.

Nash sank onto the cream-colored couch and pulled me down with him, his lips firmly sealed against the dissenting opinion I read clearly on his face. He wasn't convinced that we had any business there. Or that Addison had any right to ask for our help.

Tod sat in the other chair, leaning forward with his elbows on his knees. His gaze hadn't left Addy since we'd walked into the room, and I had a feeling it wouldn't anytime soon.

Addison wrung her hands together, twisting her fingers until I was sure one of them would break. "So…what's next? How can I help?"

"We need to know who—" Tod began, but Nash cut him off boldly.

"Addy, before we get started, you need to understand how dangerous this is. Not just for you, but for us." His voice was as hard and unrelenting as I'd ever heard it, and he squeezed my hand as he spoke. "We're putting our own lives in danger for you, and honestly, the only reason I'm here is for Kaylee. Because I don't want her to get hurt."

My heart jumped into my throat, and a smile formed on my face in spite of the solemn circumstances.

"I understand…." Addison said, but Nash interrupted again.

"I don't think you do. I don't think you *can*. We're *bean sidhes*." We both watched her face very carefully for a reaction, but got none. "Do you know anything about *bean sidhes?*"

"A little," she admitted, glancing briefly at the reaper. "Tod told me…some stuff." Her cheeks flushed, and I wondered what else Tod had told her.

"Good." Nash looked relieved to finally hear something he approved of. "Did he tell you that the Netherworld is a very dangerous place for *bean sidhes?* That we have no defenses against the things that live there? That we can't even pop out like he can, if something goes wrong?"

She nodded again, shyly. Guiltily. And I could see that Addison Page wasn't accustomed to asking for help. She looked… humiliated. As if the admission of her own powerlessness might break her.

And that alone told me she was stronger than she thought she was. Stronger than Tod thought she was.

Good. She'd have to be.

"Okay, then, the first thing we want to know…" He glanced at me for confirmation, and I nodded in spite of the suspicious glint shining in Tod's eyes. Nash and I had already discussed this. "Is how you got yourself into this mess. Why the hell would you sell your soul? I know I'm looking at your life from the outside, but I gotta say that from where we stand, it looks like you've got everything you could ever want."

Addison smiled wistfully, regretfully, as Tod glared at us. "I do now," she said, her famous, melodic voice so soft I could barely hear it. "But when they came to me with this deal, I had nothing but dreams and desperation. I know that sounds melodramatic, but it's the truth. They said they could make or break me, and they were right."

"Who?" I asked, speaking for the first time since we'd entered her room.

"Dekker Media."

A chill swept the length of my body, leaving me cold from the inside out.

Dekker Media was an entertainment *titan.* They had theme parks, production studios, television channels, and more large-scale marketing clout than any other company in the world. Dekker Media had its sticky fingers in every pie imaginable. Kids grew up watching their movies, listening to their CDs, playing with their toys, wearing their officially licensed shoes and clothes, and sleeping between sheets plastered with the faces of their squeaky-clean, family-friendly stars.

The company was pervasive. Ubiquitous. Obnoxious.

They signed most of their stars straight out of junior high, churning out one teenage cash cow after another.

"Wait, I don't understand," Nash said, having obviously regained his head before I had. "You sold your soul to Dekker Media?" He frowned at me briefly, then let his gaze slide toward his brother. "I thought she sold it to a hellion."

"She did." Tod's jaw bulged in barely repressed anger. "But the deal went through John Dekker himself."

Wow. I was stunned into silence for the second time in as many minutes.

John Dekker was the CEO and public face of Dekker Media, grandson of the legendary company founder, and more recognized by tweens around the world than the U.S. president.

"Okay, can you start from the beginning?" I leaned back on the couch, my head swimming from information overload.

Addison nodded, and once she got started, the words flowed quickly, and I had to listen carefully to keep up.

"It was two years ago, just after I turned sixteen. *The Private Life of Megan Ford* had just finished its first season and was up for renewal. John Dekker found me on the set on the first day of filming the second season and took me to his office. Alone. He said that the ratings were only okay so far, and that whether or not the show continued was up to me. It was my choice. But that if I wanted it badly enough, Megan Ford could be a huge hit. Make me famous. Make me *rich*."

"You sold your soul for fame and fortune?" Nash asked, contempt so thick in his voice I almost looked down to see if some had dripped on the carpet.

Addison flinched, but Tod spoke up, his own anger rivaling Nash's. "It wasn't like that. Don't you remember her family? Her dad was long gone and her mom was unemployed. Always strung out on one pill or another. They were living on Addy's income, and Dekker told her that if she didn't sign on the dotted line, that would all dry up. That he'd make sure she never worked again. He said her mother would go to jail for prescription drug fraud and neglect, and Addy and her little sister, Regan, would be split up in foster care."

Addison's hands shook in her lap, but she added nothing to Tod's speech. Nor did she deny any of it.

"He scared the shit out of her, Nash."

"Did you tell anyone?" I asked gently, trying not to upset her any more than she already was. "Your mom?" But I knew as soon as I said it that her mother would have been no help. "A friend?"

Addison nodded miserably. "I told Eden." She sniffled, obviously holding back sobs. "She'd done a guest spot on the show, and we'd become friends. She said I was lucky. That they only offered that deal to the best of us. The ones with real star potential. She said she'd signed two years ago and hadn't regretted it for a minute. And her first CD had just gone platinum. *Platinum!*" she repeated, glancing at Tod in desperation, begging him with her eyes to believe her. To understand her decision. "I could sign on to be a star, or I could put the entire crew out of work and let my family starve. I did it for them…."

I saw the struggle on Nash's face. He understood her choice. But he didn't want to.

However, I'd already moved on to the bigger picture.

They only offered that deal to the best of us. Addison's words haunted me, and their implication sent fresh chills down my spine to pool in my limbs as my teeth began to chatter.

They'd done it before. A lot. Dekker Media was making deals with demons—and letting its teenage stars pay the price.

7

"Wait, Dekker Media is blackmailing kids into selling their souls?" Nash looked as horrified as I felt.

"Honestly, I doubt we all had to be blackmailed." Addison leaned back in the hotel chair and ran her palms nervously over designer jeans–clad thighs.

Nash glanced across the coffee table from her to Tod. "But how does that benefit the company?"

"Greed, plain and simple. Right?" I looked to Addy for confirmation.

She shrugged and swallowed thickly, like her dinner was trying to come back up. "That's my guess. I mean, if we're rich and famous, so are the suits and pencil pushers, right?"

Nash frowned. "So what if their stars leave the corporation? Go mainstream, like Eden did?"

Addison crossed her arms over her chest, probably to keep her hands from fidgeting. "Eden went mainstream on-screen two years ago, but only after six years and three contracts with Dekker, during which she brought in cash faster than any other child star in history. But she's still on their record label, and so am I."

The singer inhaled deeply, as if her next words would be

difficult to say. "When you sign with Dekker, even if you're not selling your soul, you're selling out. They get most of us before we hit puberty, and you become whatever they want you to be. They design your look, cast you in their shows, and put you in at least one made-for-TV movie a year. The movies themselves don't make much, but the merchandising brings in some serious cash." She sighed and began ticking points off on her fingers. "They pick the songs you'll record, schedule your appearances, and book your tours. They'll even choose your haircut unless your agent is a real shark. But most of the agents are in John Dekker's pocket, too, because they want clients who have guaranteed careers."

So. Creepy. Dekker Media was starting to sound scarier than the Netherworld.

"Okay, maybe I'm misunderstanding, but we're talking about *the* Dekker Media, right? The child-friendly, shiny-happy sit-coms? With the cartoon squirrel and the squeaky-clean animated fairy tales? *That* Dekker Media is actually reaping the souls of its stars in exchange for commercial success?"

Addison's lip curled into a bitter smile. "Ironic, isn't it?"

I didn't know how to answer. Until they grew up and went mainstream, Dekker's stars didn't even bare their midriffs. Yet they were all soulless shells of humanity. Irony didn't even begin to cover it.

And I'd thought the whole *bean sidhe* wail thing was weird….

Tod shot a smile of support at Addison, and Nash rubbed his face with both hands. Acid churned in my stomach, threatening to devour me from the inside out, and the very air tasted bitter, heavy with the aftertaste of such sour words. But I had to ask…

"Addison, how long has this been going on? This soul trafficking?"

She shrugged and pulled a strand of white-blond hair over her shoulder, twisting the end of it as she spoke. "I don't know, but rumor has it a couple of their stars from the fifties sold out, back when they were still broadcasting in black and white. Who was the girl who did all those bonfire slasher movies after she left Dekker?"

"*Campfire Stalker* movies," Tod corrected.

"Yeah, those. That girl sold her soul. And she's getting old now...." Addison's voice trailed off, but the horror on her face was easy to read.

"Guys, this is much bigger than we thought." I crossed my arms over my chest, glancing from one somber, shocked face to the next. "Too big." The thought of tracking down one hellion with a secondhand soul was scary enough. But I had no idea how to go up against the Netherworld *and* Dekker Media over an arrangement they'd evidently had going for more than half a century.

All we could really do was take Addison to the Netherworld so she could enforce the out-clause.

"So, what's the deal with this out-clause? What happens if you ask for your soul back?"

"They take everything." Tod stood and waved one arm to indicate the hotel suite, and Addison's entire career, then crossed the room toward a small refrigerator against one wall. "Everything she's worked for will just be...gone."

"If she wasn't prepared for that, she shouldn't have sold her soul," Nash snapped, his irises a churning sea of brown and green. But I knew he wasn't so much mad at Addy as he was worried about us. In his opinion, risking two mostly innocent lives and one afterlife for a single compromised soul made little sense.

I was starting to agree with him. I wanted to help Addy, but not if she wasn't willing to help herself. What were fame and fortune compared to an eternity of torture? "That's kind of how the whole contract thing works, Addison. You fulfill it, or you have to pay back everything they've given you. But isn't your eternal soul worth it?"

She blinked at me, and her tears finally overflowed. "It's not about the money, or even the fame. There are days I'd like to trade my face in for one no one's ever seen." Addison swiped tears from her cheeks with both hands, smearing expertly applied eyeliner in the process, and I pushed a box of tissues across the table toward her.

"So, what is it about?"

She took a deep breath. "If I demand my soul back, they'll take back everything I ever got as a result of signing that contract—and everything anyone else ever got from it through me. They'll ruin me, but the fallout will hit my agent, my lawyer, my publicist, and everyone who ever worked for me. It'll devastate my whole family." She sniffled, but now there was a sharp edge of anger in her voice. "My mom. Regan. My dad, and whatever twenty-year-old he's shacked up with this week. And I'm not just talking about money. We've been poor, and we can be poor again. I'm talking debt, disgrace, and public humiliation, a thousand times worse than any of them would have suffered if I'd turned down the original offer."

Nash's eyes narrowed as Tod kicked the fridge shut and returned with four cans of diet Coke, evidently all Addy kept on hand. "They can't do that. Can they?"

Addison laughed bitterly, and accepted the can Tod handed her. "You remember Whitney Lance? Lindy Cohen? Between the two of them, they have three divorces, seven arrests, five stints in rehab, and two children taken away by the courts. And it gets much worse. Others have had nude photo scandals, public breakdowns, and weeks spent in the psychiatric ward. Carolina Burke served two years for tax evasion, and Denison Clark was arrested for drunk driving two months before his twenty-first birthday. Then again for statutory rape six months later."

"Yeah, but they all actually did those things, right?" Nash popped open his can, looking less sympathetic by the moment.

"Please tell me you don't have an arrest record or a love child hidden away somewhere."

"Of course not." Addy's eyes flashed in anger, and I was glad to see it. If she couldn't stand up to us, how could she possibly have enough nerve to demand her soul back from a hellion?

"Well, if you haven't given them any rope, how are they supposed to hang you?"

"I'm not perfect, Nash!" Addison used the arms of her chair to shove herself to her feet and stood staring down at him. "Don't tell me you've never had a drink. Or that you're a virgin."

Nash's face hardened, but he remained silent.

"My contract keeps me bubble wrapped, but if I get my soul back, not only will they strip the padding, they'll start throwing knives at me. They'll twist every decision I make and hurl it back at me. Every drink I take will be a public binge. Every relationship I get into will be a disaster played out in full color on newsstands all over the world. Exes will sell stories and pictures to magazines." She was pacing now, words falling from her lips almost faster than I could understand them. "The paparazzi will get shots of my mom all strung out. Hell, she'll probably go to prison for buying narcotics online, or something like that. My dad's DUIs will catch up with him, and without me to bail him out when he gets in over his head, his creditors will eat him alive. And I don't even want to know what'll happen to Regan. She just scored a role in a new tween drama. Her career will be over before it begins."

Addison fell into the chair again and practically melted into the upholstery. "They'll drive me crazy, and that will only fuel the media frenzy."

I leaned back, trying to absorb it all. Trying to imagine my own life under the microscope, my every indiscretion on display. "Okay, yes, it sounds bad. But your parents dug their own holes, and you can't hold yourself responsible when they fall in."

I popped open my own can and took a sip, still thinking. "Are poverty and embarrassment really worse than eternal torture?"

Addy shook her head halfheartedly. "No, and I know I probably deserve whatever I get. But Regan doesn't, and neither does anyone else I wind up hurting." She met my gaze, her pale blue eyes swimming in tears again. "Remember last year, when Thad Evans flipped his car? He killed two people and messed up his own face for good when he went through the windshield. Then he lost nearly everything he owned in lawsuits from the dead kids' parents, and the rest of it to crooked accountants and lawyers. And what about—"

"Whoa, wait a minute." I rubbed my temples with both hands, fighting off a headache from information overload as everything she'd told us finally began to sink in. "Are you saying that all the Dekker stars with wholesome images and squeaky-clean backgrounds are actually soulless human husks, and Hollywood's bad boys and girls are really the good guys, because they got their souls back?"

She stared down into her can. "I wouldn't exactly call them good guys for taking the out-clause."

"What does that mean?" Nash pulled a throw pillow from behind his back, then dropped it on the floor beside the couch.

Addison glanced at Tod instead of answering. The reaper sighed and leaned forward with his elbows on his knees, and his focus shifted from Nash to me, then back to Nash. "There's a little complication with the out-clause."

My stomach churned. Something told me his definition of a "little complication" and mine wouldn't have much in common.

"Addy doesn't actually have a copy of her contract…."

"I was barely sixteen," Addison interrupted, her cheeks flaming in embarrassment. "It never occurred to me to ask for a copy to keep."

Nash scowled at her, hazel eyes swirling rapidly with mounting anger. "Or to actually read the damned thing before you signed it, I'm guessing."

"Wait, isn't sixteen too young to sign a contract without your mom's permission?" I asked, hoping I'd just discovered a brilliant legal loophole.

Tod's blue-eyed gaze seemed to darken. "The Netherworld considers humans adult once they hit puberty."

I frowned. "That's messed up."

He shrugged. "It's the Netherworld. And she had no idea she was entitled to a copy of her contract, and hellions aren't known for explaining your rights up front." He deliberately shifted his focus to me. "Anyway, I asked around a little bit today…"

The sick look on his face told me I didn't want to know who he'd spoken to, or what he'd had to do for the information.

"… and if Addy's contract reads like all the rest of them do— and I'm sure it does—her out-clause requires an exchange."

"What?" I blinked, hoping I'd heard him wrong, or was misunderstanding something. "An exchange like my mom made? A life for a life?" The horror crawling through me had no equal. I rubbed my arms, trying to keep goose bumps at bay, but they rose, anyway.

"A soul for a soul," Tod corrected, staring at the floor for a second before meeting my gaze again. "But basically, yes. Addy can only get her soul back by trading it for another one."

"Wait…" Nash rubbed his forehead, like that might help the new information sink in. "Souls can't be stolen. They can only be taken when someone dies, or given up freely by their owner."

I searched Addison's face, struggling with my own mounting nausea. "So, all those people you mentioned? They all had to kill someone to get their souls back?"

"Or recruit someone," Tod said, twisting the tab on his can, as if unbothered by the new development.

"And you call that a *little* complication?"

Tod shrugged and glanced at Nash as if he wanted a second

opinion. "I know we're short on time, and I'd suggest steering clear of murder just to keep things simple, but I'm sure Addy knows someone looking for a quick career boost—"

"No!" she and I shouted in unison, shooting twin looks of horror at the reaper. "I can't take the out-clause, Tod," Addison continued. "Even if I were willing to throw my family to the wolves, I can't put someone else in my position."

"Would you rather die without your soul?" He looked irritated with her for the first time that I'd seen. Was he really ready to damn someone else to the Netherworld to save Addison?

Yes. I could see that in his eyes, in how they lit up every time she spoke. In the way his gaze never left her for long. He'd literally do anything for her, and that knowledge scared me almost as badly as the thought of traveling to the Netherworld.

"No," she answered finally, spinning her can slowly on the coffee table. "That's why I need your help. I need to get my soul back without using the out-clause."

"Damn it!" Nash slammed his empty can down on the coffee table, his irises flashing with a confusion of angry colors.

"She's right," I said softly. Then I pinned Tod with my gaze. "I won't help you lead another lamb to the slaughter. If we do this, we do it without the exchange."

Tod scowled, and again his willingness to take the easy route chilled me. But then he glanced at the raw desperation on Addison's face and nodded.

"Nash?" I took his hand and folded my fingers around his. "I understand if you want to back out."

He exhaled heavily. "Like I can let you do this alone. I'm in."

My relief was a bitter mercy. I didn't want to do this any more than he did. But I wanted to do it without him even less.

"So...how do we start?" Addison glanced from me to Nash, then to Tod. "What can I do?"

I took a deep breath, then gulped from my can. "First, we

need to know who this hellion is. It is a he, right?" I asked, as it occurred to me that I'd been thinking of the hellion as male.

"Yes, it's a…um…guy demon." She flushed and shook her head. "But I don't know his name. I didn't even know for sure that they had names."

"But you did actually meet him, right?" Frustration flavored my words, and we could all hear it.

"She did." Tod answered for her, clenching his hands into tense fists in his lap. "The transfer process is…hands-on."

Wow. So many things that *could mean…*

"Good. Tell us everything you remember." I rubbed my damp palms on my jeans, half dreading whatever we were about to hear. But if I was *half* dreading it, Addison was all the way there. She glanced at Tod, reluctance obvious in the lips she'd pressed together and the panic swimming in her eyes.

"It's okay." He leaned forward to rub her bare arm. "We need to know what you know." But Addison's hands began to shake, in spite of his reassurance.

I elbowed Nash and glanced at Addy. He rolled his eyes, then nodded curtly. "Just tell us what you remember." In spite of his reluctance to coddle her, his voice radiated safety and comfort, flowing over us all like a warm, familiar blanket. "Close your eyes, if you need to. Pretend we're not here." After a moment, Addy nodded and leaned back in her chair, her eyes closed. "Start from when you signed the contract," Nash soothed. "Where were you?"

"In John Dekker's office. He had the curtains closed and the air cranked. I was freezing."

"Okay, good…" Nash said, and I glanced at my watch. Addison's hour of privacy would be up in about twenty minutes and I was not up for another high-pressure getaway. "So you signed the contract. Then what happened?"

Do you sign a demon contract with ink, or with blood? I couldn't help but wonder.

"Dekker took the contract into another room. When he came back, he had a woman with him. She was tall and pretty, but she looked at me weird. Like she was hungry and I was dinner."

I shifted uncomfortably on the couch until Nash took my hand again, squeezing gently. The feel of his skin against mine did almost as much as his voice to calm me. "What did the woman do?" he asked.

Addy cleared her throat and continued, eyes still pinched closed. "She held my hands and I started to feel dizzy. I closed my eyes and when I opened them—" she opened her eyes to look at us then, as if acting out her memory "—Dekker's office was gone."

Both brothers met my gaze, confirming my suspicion. Dekker had a rogue reaper in his pocket.

"Where were you?" I asked. I couldn't help it. I'd peeked into the Netherworld several times, but had never actually been there.

"I don't know." Her eyes went distant as she sank back into her own memory. "We were standing on a white marble floor in a room so big I couldn't see the walls, but I could tell from the echo that there *were* walls. And there was this weird gray haze over everything for a minute or so. Then that cleared all at once, like it was never there. But I know I saw it…."

Nash glanced at Tod, and something unspoken seemed to pass between them. I elbowed Nash, hoping for an explanation, but he only held up one finger, asking me to wait. I nodded reluctantly, then sipped silently from my can as he continued. "What happened next, once the haze cleared?"

"Nothing, at first." Addy's eyes regained focus, and her gaze held mine for a moment before sliding to Tod. "Then I heard footsteps on the marble, and saw someone walking toward us from behind the woman."

"That was the hellion?" Tod asked, his words clipped in anger. Or was that fear? "What did he look like? Tell us everything you can think of."

Addy closed her eyes again in concentration. "He looked pretty normal. Like any businessman. He wore a plain black suit and had brown hair. He didn't look very scary, so I started to relax. But then I saw his eyes. They had no color. At all." Her eyes opened then, glazed with fear so fresh I could almost taste it. "They were just solid black balls stuck in his head, with no pupils or irises. It was...weird. I couldn't tell if they were moving, and didn't know whether or not he was looking at me."

Tod and Nash looked at each other again, then back at Addy. "What did he do?"

"He kissed me." Addison's voice broke on the last word, and she began to tremble all over. When Tod stood and crossed between her chair and the couch, her eyes caught his movement and were drawn back into focus.

"Are you okay?" I asked as Tod slid the closet door into the wall and pulled a blanket from the bottom shelf.

"Yeah." She smiled in thanks when Tod draped the blanket over her lap and tucked it around her sides. "I just don't want to think about what I did. About what I let him do."

I nodded sympathetically, and Nash cleared his throat. "Okay, so he kissed you...?"

"Yeah, only it wasn't really a kiss." Addison leaned forward to sip from her can, then set it on the table and pulled the blanker tighter around herself. "His mouth opened, and he...sucked on me."

"He sucked on you?" I repeated, confused by her phrasing. "Isn't that kind of what a kiss is?" *Unless* I've *been doing it all wrong...*

Her teeth began to chatter, and it took obvious effort for her to speak clearly. "He sucked on me like I was a human Popsicle, and it felt like I'd swallowed a hurricane. Like he'd stirred something up, and I could feel it whipping around inside me. Then it just went...through my lips and into him."

Wow. Hellions suck. Literally.

"When it was over, I was cold on the inside. I was shaking so badly I could hardly stand. I felt so empty I thought my body would collapse in on itself, like I was a vacuum that couldn't be filled. I knew then that I'd made a mistake. But it was too late."

Addy leaned forward to pick up her can again, but it shook violently in her hands and sloshed soda over the sides. She set it down in disgust and pressed her hands together between her knees, trying in vain to stop shivering. "The man—the hellion—just stepped back and licked his lips, like I tasted good. He smiled at me, and I felt dirty. Like I could scrub for hours and never get rid of his filth." Her hands rubbed at her jeans again, pressing so hard her fingers went white. "Then he leaned down and kissed me again, only this time he exhaled into my mouth, and his breath felt thick and heavy."

She paused and closed her eyes, rubbing her face roughly as if to wipe the memory from her mind. But it wouldn't go. I knew that from experience. The worst memories stick with us, while the nice ones always seem to slip through our fingers.

"I'd thought I was cold before, but that was nothing compared to being filled with his breath. Filled with *him*. The demon took part of me and left part of himself in its place. I could feel him rolling through me. Exploring me from the inside, so cold he burned every part of me he touched. The first few times I exhaled, my breath was white, like in the middle of winter. My teeth chattered for two days afterward. But the worst was the chill." She shuddered and clutched the blanket tighter. "That awful, hollow cold, swallowing me from the inside out…"

"When did that go away?" I asked, my voice so soft and horrified I barely heard it.

Addison looked at me and smiled softly, her expression empty, and all the creepier for that fact. Then she reached up with one hand and pulled her left eyelid up. With her free hand, she pinched the front of her eye, and something fell out onto her palm.

"When did the chill fade?" She blinked then, and when she looked at me, I saw that without her contact lens, her left eye was solid white, with no pupil and no iris. "It never did."

8

"Whoa." Nash leaned closer for a better view, as my heart leaped into my throat. And if I weren't busy being horrified by Addison's featureless eye, I might have been surprised by his fearless curiosity. "The demon did that to your eye?"

Addison nodded. "Both of them." She held out her hand so we could see the small, curved, plastic disk cradled in her palm. It was too big to be a regular contact lens, and she must have seen my confusion. "Demon technology. Dekker provides them, to make us look normal."

My pulse still racing uneasily, I leaned over for a better look and noticed that the lens was detailed with the specifics of a human eye. Addison's eerie pale blue iris was right there in her palm, surrounding a pinpoint black pupil.

"The pupils even dilate and constrict, depending on the amount of light in the room." She smiled bitterly and blinked with a creepy, mismatched set of eyes. "Don'tcha just *love* foreign technology?"

I had no answer for that, and hoped she was being ironic. I wasn't particularly fond of technology that allowed elements of the Netherworld to hide in our world. But I did have questions.

"Why did he do that? Wouldn't it be in the hellion's best interest to avoid making you stand out?"

"He had no choice." Tod scowled. "It's a side effect of the process. You know how they say the eyes are the windows to the soul?" he asked, and I swallowed thickly before nodding. I didn't like where this was headed. "Evidently they mean that literally. Once the soul is gone, there's nothing to see through the windows."

Nash whistled softly. "That has to be the weirdest thing I've ever seen." And that meant a lot coming from a *bean sidhe*.

"You want me to put the contact back in, don't you?" Addison cocked her head and gave him a small, eerie smile.

"That'd be great, thanks." Nash nodded decisively.

Addy stood and crossed into the attached bathroom. She was back in under a minute, and her eye looked normal. Only it also still looked weird, probably because I now knew what the contacts hid.

"So, when she gets her soul back, her eyes will go back to normal?" Nash aimed his question at his brother, rather than Addison, and I realized he was avoiding looking at her. Her eyes freaked me out, too, but I couldn't help being amused that Nash was more comfortable dealing with a grim reaper—a living dead boy who killed people and harvested human souls—than with an otherwise normal human girl who'd lost hers.

"They should."

"Okay, wait a minute. I've seen several dead people—" not a statement I could have imagined saying a few months earlier "—and none of them looked like that, even after the reaper took their souls."

Tod nodded, Addy's hand held between both of his. "When your heart and brain stop working, your eyes stop working. They reflect the state the soul was in when the person died. It's kind of like when a clock battery runs down. The hour and minute hands don't disappear, but they don't keep ticking, either. They freeze on the last minute they measured."

"Okay, that makes sense." In a really weird way. But I didn't plan to dwell on it. I was ready to give Addison her privacy and go work on her problem somewhere her empty soul-windows didn't stare at me from behind their eerie human facades. But first we needed the information we'd actually come for. "Addison, did you notice anything about the hellion that might help us identify him? A crooked nose or a dimpled chin? Bad teeth?"

But even as I asked, I realized her answer probably wouldn't help, even if she had noticed something. I didn't know much about hellions, but I did know they could assume more than one form, so any description she gave us might not fit the hellion a moment after she'd met him.

She shook her head slowly. "No. Other than the eyes, he looked normal. Brown hair. Average height. Normal clothes. And I didn't see any birthmarks or anything."

"And you sure you didn't hear the hellion's name?" Nash asked.

"If I had, I don't think I could have forgotten it."

"What about your contract?" I asked, struck by a sudden bolt of brilliance. "He signed, too, didn't he? Did you see what he wrote?"

She shook her head miserably. "They must have done that after I left. The spot for his name was still blank when I signed."

My hand tightened around Nash's; my frustration was getting harder to control. "Okay, then, think carefully. Did he say anything to you? Or to the woman who took you to him?" No need to tell her the woman was a reaper. I wasn't sure how much she knew about Tod, or the Netherworld in general.

"Um…" Addy closed her eyes in concentration, but opened them after only a few seconds. "No. He never spoke. I never even heard his voice."

"What about the woman?" Nash's foot bounced on the carpet, and his knee bumped the coffee table over and over. He was obviously as eager to go as I was. "Did she say anything to either of you?"

"No." Addy didn't hesitate that time. "No one spoke while we were in...that place." Her nose wrinkled in disgust, or maybe in fear.

"What about when you got back?" I laid my hand on Nash's knee to make it stop bouncing. "Did she say anything when you got back to Dekker's office?"

"Yes!" Addy's weird, fake eyes widened, and I noticed absently that the pupils *did* dilate with varying levels of light. That would have been cool, if it weren't so strange. "When we got back, Dekker was still there. On her way out of the room, the woman kind of trailed her hand up his arm and over his shoulder, smiling at him like he was edible. She said, 'Your avarice is secure for another year.' Then she just walked out the door."

Avarice... I could practically hear the gears in Tod's head grinding, as he searched his memory, but if he came up with anything, I couldn't tell.

"Does that mean anything to you?" Addison studied the reaper's face in obvious hope. "Avarice means greed, right?"

"Yeah," I said when Tod didn't answer. I ran my thumb over Nash's knuckles, where his fingers were still wrapped in mine.

"So, does that tell you who the hellion is?"

"No." Though, I hated to admit it. "But with a little research it might." I stood, signaling to the guys that I was ready to go. Immediately. "Tod, can you try to get a copy of Addy's contract? Surely Dekker has it in a file somewhere." That seemed to me to be the easiest way to identify the hellion, considering that Tod could pop into and out of places at will.

He nodded, but his face betrayed little hope.

"Good." I turned back to Addy and scrounged up an encouraging smile. "We'll let you know what we find out."

★ ★ ★

I shoved the front door open and pocketed my keys, glancing into first the living room, then the kitchen to make sure Nash and I were alone. My dad worked an extra half shift most Mondays, so he shouldn't be home until after nine, which would give me and Nash several hours alone together.

But I couldn't get used to having the house to myself—Aunt Val had almost always been home—so I shouted for him just in case, as Nash closed the door behind me. "Dad?"

No response, but I dropped my backpack in his recliner, then checked his bedroom to be sure. He'd kill me if he found out I was messing in reaper business. Again. Not to mention the hellions.

My dad's room was empty, and by the time I got back to the kitchen, Nash had shed his jacket and pulled two cans of soda from the fridge. I shrugged out of my coat and tossed it over the back of an armchair, barely glancing at the ripped upholstery.

It would have cost too much for my dad to bring his furniture over from Ireland, so we'd been slowly furnishing our new-to-us home as we could afford to. Fortunately the rental house was tiny, so we didn't need much. And Uncle Brendon had insisted I keep everything I'd used at his house, so my bedroom looked much the same here, except for the plain white walls and little available floor space.

I didn't care about any of that. All that mattered was that Sophie wasn't around to stick her nose in my business. Except on Sunday nights. And even then, she usually ignored me completely.

"You hungry?" I opened an overhead cabinet and pulled out a flat, folded bag of popcorn.

"Starving," Nash said, so I stuck it in the microwave and set the timer. While the microwave hummed, I popped open my can and stood with my back against the countertop, watching the view as Nash rooted through the fridge. Evidently two and a half minutes was too long to wait for a snack.

But then, with the state football play-offs coming up, Coach Rundell had been working him extra hard for the past couple of weeks. No wonder Nash was always hungry.

"So, any ideas?" I asked as the first pop echoed from the microwave. Between conflicting schedules at school, his football practice, and my shift at the Cinemark, we'd barely had a chance to talk all day.

Nash stood with a jar of salsa in one hand, and I tossed him a half-empty bag of corn chips from the countertop. "Not even one." He rounded the peninsula and sank into a chair at the folding card table currently furnishing our eat-in kitchen. "Find anything online?"

"Role-playing games and band lyrics," I said, pulling open the grimy door when the microwave buzzed. Obviously, the Netherworld had yet to extend its influence to the internet. Which was probably fortunate, now that I thought about it.

I dumped the popcorn into the largest bowl in the cabinet and shook a small bottle of nacho-cheese-flavored seasoning over it, then grabbed my soda on the way to the table. "So...what do you know about hellions?"

"Nothing more than what Addy told us last night." Nash dipped a corn chip into the wide-mouthed jar, and it came out loaded with chunky hot salsa.

"After seeing her eyes, I never want to lay mine on a hellion. Ever." I crunched on several pieces of popcorn. "But it doesn't look like we'll have much of a choice."

"I could kill Tod for getting us into this."

"It's a little late for that." I wrinkled my nose in distaste when he dipped a piece of popcorn into the salsa jar, then tossed it into his mouth.

"Weird." Nash cocked his head to one side, chewing as he considered the odd combination. "But good-weird."

"You want something to put that in?" I stood to grab a bowl before he could answer. "When's Tod supposed to be here?"

He glanced at his watch. "He's taking his break in about fifteen minutes. But knowing my brother, he's already here somewhere, spying on us."

I set the bowl on the table and poured salsa into it. "He needs a life of his own. A girlfriend. Addison seems pretty interested in him…." I ventured, leaning over his shoulder to dip a popcorn kernel into the sauce. I hesitated, then finally closed my eyes and stuck it in my mouth.

Eww! You'd think nacho seasoning and salsa would go well together, but they don't. At least, not on popcorn.

Nash laughed at me while I washed the taste from my mouth with a gulp from my can. "The last thing Tod needs is a soulless human husk of a girlfriend. Especially a famous one. He's legally deceased, and she's followed around all day by photographers. I can see the headline—*Addison Page dates dead boy!*"

"Okay, so it's not an obvious paring." I shrugged and grabbed another handful of regular popcorn. "But it's not like you and I are exactly simple." Not with his mom teaching me *bean sidhe* stuff, and my dad watching his every move. Though, there was the little matter of our mutual species….

"I like a challenge." Nash stood, his irises swirling lazily. Hungrily.

"Oh, yeah?" I smiled up at him and retreated slowly until my hip hit the countertop, my insides smoking from the heat of his gaze.

"Yeah…" Nash stepped close enough that I could feel the warmth of his chest through both of our shirts. But he didn't touch me. His head dipped toward my neck, and I inhaled sharply when his breath brushed my collarbone.

I tilted my head back. My heart slammed against my ribs, and I held my breath, waiting to feel his lips on me. They would be soft, and hot. I knew it. I wanted it. But it didn't happen.

His head rose gradually, his breath traveling up my neck unbearably slowly. My pulse raced faster with each hot, damp puff against my skin. "Nash…" My arms rose, and my fingers hovered millimeters from his shirt when his warm hands wrapped around my wrists. Holding me. Stopping me.

"Mmm?" His breath brushed my ear then, and shivers shot up my spine, lingering in pleasant places all over my body.

"Let me touch you." It came out as a moan, and part of me was mortified by the need in my voice. But he liked it. I could tell, and that made it okay.

"Not yet," he murmured, his words indistinct, a groan granted the bare minimum of consonants. The sound buffeted my earlobe. Scalding me.

"Now," I whispered. I couldn't breathe. Not until I could touch him. Or he touched me. "Now. Please, Nash."

"Are you sure?" His words surged over me like a wave of heat, pulsing with barely controlled desire. Power. Compulsion. Considering his particular talents, he could probably have talked me into anything he wanted me to do, and that knowledge scared me and thrilled me at the same time. But he wouldn't do it. He wanted me to want him on my own.

Oh, and I did. I wanted him so badly every part of me ached, some places worse than others.

Nash pulled back enough so that I could see the brown of his eyes, churning in a sea of green. And still his breath brushed my chin, sending a wave of sensation over me, so delicate I froze to keep from shattering it.

Then I nodded. I was *totally* sure.

Nash let go of my wrists, and one hand slid over my skin to the back of my neck, cradling my skull. He tilted my head to one side and his lips met mine, just as hot and soft as I'd known they'd be.

I opened my mouth for him, drawing him in farther. Deeper. As much as I could take, and still I wanted more. My hands skimmed his chest, traveling boldly over each plane, each ridge, and soon that wasn't enough, either, so I tugged his shirt up, eager for the feel of his flesh beneath my fingers.

Nash's free hand found my waist, squeezing. His fingers slid beneath the waistband of my jeans, gripping my hip, scalding me with each touch. I moaned into his mouth when his fingers tightened, and he kissed me harder, teasing me.

My hands wrapped around his waist, traveling up the broad expanse of his back, smooth and hard, and…

"Give it a rest, already," Tod snapped from somewhere behind his brother. "It already smells like sex in here, and you're both still dressed. You have no idea how messed up that is."

Nash stiffened and pulled away from me. Then his forehead fell against my shoulder, and he growled in warning at his brother, as my hands slid down his back and out of his shirt. Nash breathed heavily against my neck as he pulled his fingers slowly from my waistband. He wanted more. Was ready for more.

I could feel his readiness against my hip.

I couldn't make my heart stop pounding. Couldn't control my ragged breathing. Couldn't cool my burning cheeks.

Nash finally stepped away from me, and he was still breathing heavily, too. He shoved his hands into his pockets and collapsed into his chair.

"You're lucky no one else walked in on you," Tod continued, snatching a chip from the bag, completely oblivious to our discomfort, as usual. "If I were her dad, you'd be hobbling home with your balls in hand tonight, little brother."

"Shut up, Tod!" I snapped, tugging my jeans into place below my navel, both delighted and mortified to realize I could still feel the warmth of Nash's bare hand on my hip. "Or you're not going to be in any shape to help Addison!"

"Speaking of which…" Tod dipped his chip into the salsa, then crunched as he spoke. "I'd appreciate it if you two could keep your sticky fingers out of my personal life…."

"What life?" Nash mumbled angrily. "Just sit down so we can get this over with. Kaylee's dad will be home by nine, and we'd like at least a couple of hours alone before then."

Tod smirked. "You think she's ready for any more time alone with you?"

"Not your business, Tod. I'll decide what I'm ready for." I dropped into the chair across from him. "Your business is finding the hellion who has Addy's soul, and figuring out how to get it back from him. Did you find her contract?"

Tod scowled in defeat. "No. It took me three hours of digging and snooping this morning just to find out that all copies of demon paperwork are kept in the Netherworld."

"So, she never really had a shot at enacting her out-clause." I shoved the bowl of salsa across the table, suddenly too angry to snack. "How did the others do it?"

"They probably actually read their contracts," Nash snapped.

"Or else they went through Dekker again. I'm guessing he doesn't care if they renege, so long as they provide a replacement soul." Tod rocked back and forth on the uneven legs of his folding chair.

"Lovely," I spat, closing my eyes briefly in disgust. "Any idea how to ID the hellion on our own?"

"No." The reaper sighed in frustration and grabbed a handful of popcorn. "I've never actually met a hellion, and so far as I know, there's no demon directory to refer to. Not that we have a name to look up."

"But hellions have specialties, right?" Nash asked. "Like, there's a demon of pain, and a demon of lust…"

"…and a demon of joy, and a demon of hope, and even a demon of love," Tod finished, gesturing with a corn chip. "There's a hellion for every emotion and weakness known to man. More than one. There are hundreds of hellions in the Netherworld. Maybe thousands. Knowing what Addy's demon specializes in won't be much help without something more specific."

"But it's a starting place, right?" I twisted my can on the table. "It's more than we knew yesterday."

Tod nodded slowly. "For what little good it does us."

"Wait…" My thoughts had stalled on something he'd said, like a thorn caught on a loose thread. "How can there be a hellion of love? Or of hope? I thought hellions fed on pain and suffering. And chaos. How can they possibly feed on emotions that make people happy?"

Nash smiled at me, but it was a sweet, pitying smile, like he was humoring me. As if I were too naive for words. But it was Tod who answered, as usual more than willing to enlighten me on the darker side of life.

"A hellion can wring pain and chaos from any emotion, Kaylee. If you want love, he gives you unrequited love. Pangs of it so torturous you go insane and die. If you ask for hope, he makes it vain hope, hope so fruitless that after grasping at it, clutching it, you eventually go insane and die. And if you beg for faith, you get blind faith. Faith you cling to, and build upon, until the day you discover that it's unfounded, and you—"

"I get it," I interrupted, a chip halfway to my mouth. "You go insane and die. Hellions are the sum of all things cruel and evil. Thanks for clarifying."

Nash chuckled, and I couldn't hold back a grin.

"You two are cracked," Tod snapped.

My smile widened. "Says the undead man in love with the soulless pop star."

Tod scowled, and I thought I saw his cheeks flush. Which struck me as kind of weird for a man who'd died two years ago. "I'm not in love with her."

"So you pulled us into a potentially deadly scheme to save the soul of some girl you don't even care about?"

His scowl deepened, and Tod scooted his folding chair across the faded linoleum. "Fine. You don't want to help? I'll do it myself." He stood. "So what if I get killed in the process? Permanently, this time."

I rolled my eyes. "Sit down, reaper, we're going to help." I just couldn't resist getting back at him for constantly invading our privacy. "But we're suffering from a conspicuous lack of ideas, here. We need someone who knows more about hellions. Or at least about the Netherworld in general."

"Hello? *Reaper* here." Exasperated, Tod laid one hand flat on the tabletop. "I know about the Netherworld."

"Not enough, apparently." Nash tossed another piece of popcorn into his mouth, ignoring Tod's annoyed under-his-breath muttering. "We need to talk to someone who's been around longer." He eyed me solemnly. "Kaylee, we need to talk to your dad."

"No." I shook my head firmly. "No way. If I even mention the word *hellion* he'll lock me in my room and swallow the key."

"He's the oldest non-human I know, and you don't have to tell him what we're doing." Nash shrugged, as if my decision should have been a no-brainer. "Just tell him you're curious. Or come up with something that won't make him worry. Besides, he promised not to keep any more secrets from you."

"Yeah, but he never promised to give me the inside scoop on demons." I looked him straight in the eye to convey my final word on the subject. "If I ask my dad about hellions, this whole thing is over." Then I smiled as an alternate solution came to mind. "Why don't you ask your mom?"

Nash frowned, and Tod's expression echoed the sentiment. "Because not only would she freak out, she'd call your dad so they could freak out in stereo."

"So we're back where we started." My shoulders slumped, and I dipped a chip into the bowl of salsa. "We need someone old enough to have lots of experience in the Netherworld, but who won't care what we're up to."

Tod sat up straight in his chair, as if the lightbulb over his head had just blinked to life. "Libby. We need to talk to Libby."

9

"How much trouble are you going to be in if we get caught?"
Nash asked, concern lining the edges of his perfect, practically
edible mouth. A tall, skinny guy in a letter jacket rushed past
us in the hallway, carrying a huge black tuba case. He narrowly
missed smashing my shoulder with it, and when Nash tugged
me out of the way, the tubaist ran into the lockers instead with
a horrible metal-crunching crash.

"You mean if we get caught here…" In the human world.
"Or there?" I whispered, unwilling to say "the Netherworld" in
public. Especially at school, with the tuba player still regaining
his balance a few feet away.

"Either one." Nash veered away from the dark green lockers
and I followed him, ducking into an alcove near the first-floor
restrooms.

"Well, I doubt Coach Rundell will even notice I'm not
there." I had American History last period, and with the football play-offs coming up, the coach had been too busy studying
his playbook to come up with actual lesson plans, so we'd been
watching installments of a documentary about the Civil War
for the past week and a half. "But if he does, and they call my

dad…" I'd have to be home before dusk for the remainder of my adolescence.

My father was trying really hard to be a good dad, and he wasn't doing too bad a job, considering he'd been absent for the past thirteen years of my life. But he was going overboard on a few vital issues. Like quality family time—thus, our Sunday-night dinners—and his need to know where I was at all times.

That was appropriate the last time we'd shared a home—back when I was three. But at sixteen, I needed a little more freedom, and a lot less nosiness.

"And if we get caught *there*…" I shrugged. "All bets are off."

Nash swallowed thickly. "With any luck, we won't have to actually cross over. Yet." But we both heard the uncertainty in his pause. "Where does your dad think you're going?"

"Downtown with me," Emma said. Startled, I spun to find my best friend leaning against a bright purple chess club flyer taped to the wall behind us. "After work, we're grabbing pizza and going birthday shopping for my mom." Emma winked one deep chocolate-colored eye at me and smiled to show even, white teeth. She was pretty enough to be spectacularly popular, but smart enough not to give a damn, and I loved her for it.

I'd convinced a lovesick coworker at the Cinemark to switch my Tuesday shift for his Friday shift just by mentioning that he'd spend all four hours alone with Emma in the ticket booth. As soon as I said her name, he'd offered to trade entire schedules.

"I said I'd have her home by ten-thirty, so don't be late," Emma teased Nash.

He grinned and pulled me closer, and I wanted to melt into him. "No problem." But I couldn't help mentally crossing my fingers. Tod had done some digging and found out that Libby would be pulling in another dose of Demon's Breath that night in Abilene. But Abilene was a six-hour round-trip. Counting rest stops, dinner, and however long it took to actually convince her to help us, it was bound to be a long night.

"So, where are you really going?" Em tucked a strand of long, straight blond hair behind one ear and eyed us both with a knowing grin. "Or do I even want to know?"

"Probably not. It's not what you think." I sighed, wishing it was what she thought. Wishing *hard*.

Her grin melted into a look of concern to match Nash's, and she tugged her backpack higher on her shoulder. "*Bean sidhe* business?" she whispered, glancing around dramatically for potential eavesdroppers.

"Yeah." We'd had to fill Emma in on some basic Netherworld stuff when Nash and I had reinstated her soul, thus saving her life. And accidentally ending another, a fact which haunted me constantly. But Emma didn't know about Tod, or that reapers even existed, and I wasn't going to tell her anything that could bring her to the attention of any dangerous Netherworld elements. I hadn't saved her just to let her go again. Ever.

Which is why I felt guilty asking her to cover for me. Unfortunately, I had no other options, since Nash would be with me. *I really needed to find more friends....*

"You're not missing French, are you?" Panic peeked around the edges of Emma's expression, and I laughed.

"No, just history." Emma's memory for foreign vocabulary was as fragile as mine for dates and numbers. I helped her out in French, and she returned the favor the next hour, in history. It was a good system, and we weren't really cheating. We were just...helping.

I'd probably never need to know when the War of 1812 ended, anyway. Right?

"Then come on, we're gonna be late."

Grinning, Nash leaned forward and kissed me, but Emma dragged me back by one arm before I got much more than a taste of him. Nash winked and took off in the opposite direction. I watched him for several seconds, until Emma hissed my name, and I followed her, still looking over my shoulder.

When I finally turned, I gasped to find myself less than four inches from Sophie's overglossed sneer. "You almost flattened me," she snapped, icy green eyes glittering with anger that went deeper than resentment of my intrusion into her social circle.

"Sorry," I mumbled, thrown off by the unexpected confrontation. It was easier to stay mad at her before, when her general bitchiness was superficial in nature. But now that pain and grief peeked out at me from behind the armor of her arrogance, I found it much more difficult to do anything but pity her.

Even if she did blame me for her mother's death.

When my pride wouldn't allow me to step out of her path—well, pride and Emma's tight grip on my arm, refusing to let me back down—Sophie sidestepped me with a look so pompous it might have seared the soul of someone with a lesser spirit. But I could only return her look with pity, which fueled her anger even more.

"Your cousin is *such* a freak," Sophie's best friend, Laura Bell, said at her side.

Sophie rolled her eyes at me as she turned to march off down the hall. "You have no idea...."

"Just ignore them," Emma insisted, as I followed her around the corner and through the first door on the left, just as the bell rang. "Laura's jealous of you and Nash." Because she'd had him first, a fact she reminded me of at every possible opportunity. "And Sophie's always been a bitch."

I slid into my fifth-row seat as Madame Brown—who'd probably never even been to France—cleared her throat at the front of the class. "She lost her mom, Em."

"So did you!" Emma hissed, flipping open her textbook in search of the homework she kept folded between the pages. When she'd actually done it. "And you don't practice 'bitchy' like it's a lost art."

Before I could remind her that I'd had thirteen years to get over my mother's death, Madame Brown eyed Emma from the front of the class, a black dry-erase marker poised and ready in one hand. "Mademoiselle Marshall?" she said, thin black brows arched dramatically. *"Avez-vous quelque chose pour dire?"*

"Uh…" Emma's cheeks went scarlet, and she flipped frantically through more pages in her book, muttering under her breath. *"Dire…dire…"*

"Something to say," I whispered, without moving my lips. I was getting really good at that. "'Do you have something to say?'"

"Oh. *Non, Madame,"* she said finally, loud enough for the entire class to hear.

"Bon." Madame Brown turned back to the white board.

Emma slumped in her chair in relief, smiling at me in thanks. "How do you say, 'I hate this class' in French?"

"Should we wait for him?" I tapped my fingers on the steering wheel, and glanced at the clock on my cell phone for the thousandth time in the last five minutes. "Maybe he got stuck at work." As a rookie reaper, Tod worked from noon to midnight every day at a local hospital, ending the lives of the patients on his list, then taking their souls to be recycled. It was a creepy line of work, in my opinion, but creepy seemed to suit Tod.

"Nah, he traded shifts with one of the other death-dealers. Tod will show up whenever and wherever he wants." Nash bent at the waist to see me through the open passenger side door of my car, and behind him, digital numbers scrolled upward across the front of the gas meter as the price rose with each fraction of a gallon he pumped. "Calm down. It'll be fine."

I forced a smile and clutched my hands together in my lap. But the moment my hands stilled, my foot began tapping uncontrollably on the floorboard. I'd never skipped a class before, and knowing my luck, getting caught seemed inevitable. But so long as we didn't get caught until after we'd returned Addison's soul, I was willing to face the consequences.

Nash tore his receipt from the paper slot on the pump and slid it into his back pocket, then dropped into the passenger seat and pulled the door shut. "Let's go!"

I'd only had my license for about six months and had never driven farther than Fort Worth. Fortunately, once we got out of the Metroplex, Abilene was a straight shot along I-20, and with Nash navigating, the most complicated part of the road trip was deciding where to stop for dinner.

At least, until Tod popped into my backseat with no warning, as I was bending for a sip of my watered-down soda. His bright blue eyes suddenly staring back at me in my rearview mirror startled me so badly I stuck the straw up my nose instead of into my mouth. "Ow!" I clutched my nose and dropped my cup in my lap, but Nash grabbed it before it could spill. His free hand went to the wheel, in case I dropped that, too.

Fortunately, one good swerve put us back between the lines on the highway, even as my heart thumped painfully after a near miss with the guardrail.

"Damn it, Tod!" Nash shouted into my ear, and I flinched even though I'd known it was coming. Those were the three words he yelled the most.

When I'd recovered from the shock—to both my nose and my heart—I glared at Tod in the rearview mirror. "What took you so long?"

"I was with Addy." He stared out the rear passenger's side window, but even at that angle, I could see tension in the tight line of his square jaw. "She's a wreck, and I hate to leave her alone with her handlers. Damned parasites are worse than Netherworld leeches, sucking her dry one radio ad or guest spot at a time. I'll catch up with her after we talk to Libby."

"What's she doing in Abilene?"

"Collecting Demon's Breath from some eighty-year-old oil tycoon." Tod didn't look at me until I cleared my throat for his attention, as I flicked on my blinker and changed lanes to make room for a cop stopped behind a station wagon on the side of the road.

"Where exactly is this oil tycoon supposed to die?" I envisioned a sickroom in a huge old house decorated with doilies and dust-covered photographs of laughing grandchildren. Where there would be nowhere for us to hide, if we could even get in.

Maybe we should have let Tod go alone....

"He's in a nursing home. I know the reaper on duty tonight, and he's planning to take an extra-long coffee break. I think Libby kind of freaks him out."

I had the feeling we should have been freaked out by her, too, and the fact that we weren't was starting to scare me a little.

An hour later, I followed Nash's directions into the parking lot of the Southern Oaks nursing home, just as the sun sank below the roof of the low, orange-brick building. We were running late, so we jogged across the asphalt, the early November air stinging our lungs, and through the double front doors, where we paused to catch our breath to keep from making the staff suspicious.

Except for Tod. He'd blinked straight from the car into the nursing home as soon as we got to Abilene, so he could watch Libby work again. And to keep her from leaving before we caught up with her. He could have come alone, but Tod seemed to think Libby liked me—she'd actually acknowledged my presence in the concert hall—and would be more likely to answer our questions if they came from me.

I was skeptical, but willing to give it a shot to help Addison.

We'd just passed the front office, nodding politely at the nurse on duty, when Tod appeared behind us. The nurse didn't even blink at his sudden appearance—she obviously couldn't see him.

"Henry White." Tod waved us forward with one hand. "Room 124. Hurry, it's almost time."

But even knowing I wouldn't have to wail, I was less than eager to watch some poor old man die. I'd seen quite enough of death in what little of my life I'd lived so far. Unfortunately, even with me dragging my feet, we got there just in time for the show.

Libby stood in one dark corner, dressed in another variation of black-on-black leather, looking psychotic-scary in deep blue and gold eye shadow. Sweat stood out on her forehead, an obvious sign of the effort it took to suck in the dark substance leaking slowly, thickly from the wrinkled man lying limp on the bed.

Henry White was alone in his room, except for us and the monitor near his head, leaking a steady, high-pitched tone, which speared my brain almost as sharply as my own wail would have. I rubbed my temples, both surprised and sad that White's only deathbed visitors were two *bean sidhes* and two reapers, one of which had come to kill him. Where were his kids? Grandchildren? Or even the poor man's accountant, or money-grubbing lawyer? Surely he'd meant enough to someone to warrant a little company when death came a-knockin'.

Even as that last thought passed through my head, footsteps rushed down the hall. A heavyset nurse appeared in the doorway, wearing bright purple scrubs. She glanced my way and smiled sympathetically as she brushed past me to press a button on the monitor. "Are you family?" she asked, as the annoying beep ended and welcome silence descended.

"No." I glanced from her to Henry White's still form, then to the corner, where Libby was slurping up the last of the Demon's Breath like some kind of putrid, ethereal sludge.

"We're...visitors," Nash finished, threading his fingers through mine when my hand began to tremble. Tod watched Libby in fascination, practically drooling as she wiped her mouth with one delicate, black-gloved finger. But I was so creeped out, chill bumps had burst to life all over my body.

If she burped up black smoke, I was out of there, no matter what she could tell us.

Clutching Nash's hand, I backed toward the wall. I kept

hoping the shock would wear off. That death would eventually become routine for me. But it hadn't, and on second thought, I decided that was probably a very good thing. If death ever ceased to bother me, it would be because I'd seen entirely too much of it.

The nurse continued taking Henry White's pulse, though it was obvious by that point that he was already gone. "Well, then, you'll have to go," she said, without looking up from her work.

I was happy to oblige. "Why didn't she give him CPR?" I asked Nash on the way out of the room. We all knew she couldn't bring him back, but she didn't even try.

"Honey, he signed a DNR years ago," she said, watching me with more of that weird, detached sympathy behind her eyes. She probably would have made a good reaper.

I glanced back at her from the hall. "DNR?"

"Do not resuscitate. He signed a form asking not to be brought back when his heart gave out. He was ready to go."

Her words sent fresh chills down my spine. I had no doubt that if Henry White had known what his afterlife would consist of, he'd never have signed that paper. Or his demon contract.

Tod and Libby trailed us into the hall, though no one else could see or hear them. "Are you following me?" she asked Tod.

"Um, yeah. Kind of," Tod said, and I turned to find him grinning up at Libby. "I'm, um, seriously interested in doing this. Collecting Demon's Breath instead of souls. When I found out you were going to be here, I couldn't resist coming to ask you a few more questions."

"This job is not for children." Libby's eyes flashed fiercely. Her grim smile looked more like a snarl. "You have five minutes."

Tod exhaled in relief, and the reapers followed us into the frigid parking lot, while Nash and I pretended to be alone, a skill I was getting pretty good at. Behind the nursing home, Libby sat on the hood of my car and lit a cigarette, watching

Tod expectantly, and I wondered if passersby would be able to see the smoke she exhaled.

"Is that..." Tod's words puffed from his mouth on a white cloud. "Does that help you hold the Demon's breath?"

"This?" She held the cigarette up, flicking ash onto the asphalt. Tod nodded, and she shook her head slowly. "It just tastes good."

Tod flushed beneath the light overhead. As uncomfortable as I was hanging out with a reaper who'd been old when the New World was discovered, it was almost worth it to see Tod too embarrassed for words.

Almost.

"Three minutes," Libby prodded, without even a glance at her watch. "When I have finished with this—" she held up the cigarette again "—I will be finished with you."

"Right." Tod glanced at first me, then Nash, but we only stared back at him. This was his show; the reaper had yet to acknowledge either of us existed. "Um...does all Demon's Breath taste the same, or does it vary from hellion to hellion? You know, like 31 flavors?"

Libby's eyes narrowed as she watched him, and I was sure she'd ask a question of her own, and our little road trip would end in disaster. But after a moment's hesitation—just long enough to blow smoke into his face—she answered. "It all tastes the same. Foul. It would probably kill you, so do not consider trying it."

"I won't." But Tod didn't look anywhere near as put off by the idea as I thought he should be. "So...you can't tell what hellion this particular breath...came from?"

"No." She inhaled from her cigarette and crossed her opposite arm over her chest. "Nor do I care."

Tod exhaled in frustration and glanced at us again, but I could only shrug. I had no idea where to go from there. "When they give you your list, does it say what hellion owns the target's soul?"

"No." Libby dropped her half-smoked cigarette and ground it beneath her boot, and I was sure she'd simply disappear without another word. Instead, she turned to face us. All three of us. And I literally squirmed beneath her gaze. "Why are you following me, asking about hellions? Demon's Breath is nothing for children to play with."

I wanted to insist that we weren't children, but I kept my mouth shut because arguing with Libby probably wasn't the best way to get information out of her. And because compared to her, even poor old Mr. Henry was a child.

"I'm just curious…." Tod began. But his mouth snapped shut at one angry glance from the older reaper, who could clearly smell his lie. "We… We're trying to help a friend."

"Who?" Libby pushed off of my car and crossed both arms this time, glaring down at us.

Nash and Tod exchanged glances but remained silent, so I answered. Silence obviously wasn't getting us anywhere. But the truth might.

"We're trying to help Addison Page get her soul back."

"That cannot be done," Libby said, without missing a beat. Any surprise she may have felt was instantly swallowed by her perpetual scowl. "And you will die trying. But she can reclaim it herself. Her contract has an out-clause. They all do."

"We know." I sighed and let my shoulders slump, hoping she couldn't tell from my posture that I was about to tell a half truth—I was afraid she wouldn't help us if she knew what we were really planning. "But she doesn't know the hellion's name. She can't enact the out-clause if she can't find him, and she only knows he's a hellion of avarice."

"I do not have direct contact with hellions." Libby scowled. "Stupid humans." She closed her eyes briefly before meeting mine again. "She does not have a copy of her contract?"

"No, and we couldn't come up with a copy, either."

"Those bastards never play fair," Libby muttered. "But there is nothing you can do about it. Go home." She turned then, as if to walk away, but I knew it wasn't over. If she were truly done with us, she would simply have disappeared.

"Please." I started after her and she whirled around, long leather coat flaring out behind her. Libby's surprised, angry gaze found me immediately, and I made myself speak, in spite of the nerves tightening my throat. "Anything you could tell us might help."

"I do not know who has her soul, and I will not ask for you. That is beyond what is safe, even for me."

"Fine. I understand. But…" I closed my eyes, thinking quickly. "What else can you tell us about your job? Where do you take the Demon's Breath after you collect it?"

One corner of her mouth twitched, like she was holding back a smile, and I was suddenly sure she was proud of me. As if I were on the right track, and she secretly wanted me to follow it.

"There are disposal centers in the Nether. The closest is near Dallas. In the large stadium."

"Texas Stadium? The old one, right?" I asked, still thinking, and she nodded. "Would anyone there help us?"

Libby's mouth quirked again. "No. Definitely not."

But then, she hadn't planned to help us, either. "Thank you." I exhaled slowly, sure we were headed in the right direction. "Thank you so much."

"Child," she called, as I turned toward my car, key already in hand. When I glanced up at her, something unfamiliar passed over her face. Concern? Or maybe amusement? Figures that I'd amuse a reaper. "Demon's Breath is very powerful, and it attracts both the desperate and the dangerous. Watch out for fiends."

I nodded, trying not to reveal fear in my posture. But as I

started my engine, Nash buckling himself into the seat next to me, I couldn't stop my hands from shaking.

I had no idea what a fiend was, but something told me I would soon find out.

≪ 10 ≫

"I can't believe you did that!" Nash said, and I glanced away from the dark highway long enough to see him grinning from ear to ear in the passenger seat, his irises swirling in the deep shadows. He looked…excited.

"Did what?" A car passed us going the opposite direction, and when it was gone, I flicked my brights back on.

"He can't believe you asked a several-thousand-year-old reaper for help getting a human's soul back," Tod answered from the backseat. He had both arms crossed over his usual dark T-shirt, but I knew by the tilt of his fuzzy chin and the shine in his eyes in the rearview mirror that he was pleased. Maybe even a little impressed.

I shrugged and stifled a giddy smile as I turned back to the road. *It* was *a bit of a rush.* "I figured it couldn't hurt to ask…"

"But it could have." Nash aimed the heater vents toward the center of the car and closed the broken one, which wouldn't twist. "You keep forgetting that most reapers don't like *bean sidhes.* And vice versa."

"Maybe I keep forgetting that because the first *bean sidhe* and reaper I met are brothers. Neither of whom seems to hate me."

Still half grinning, Nash twisted to look at Tod. "Maybe we should have introduced her to Levi first."

"There's still time," Tod said, and that time he actually smiled. A little.

Levi was Tod's boss, the oldest and most experienced reaper in Texas. Except for Libby, who worked all over the southern U.S., whenever and wherever she was needed. But evidently Levi was enough of a threat to keep several hundred other reapers in line.

"So, what's the plan?" I turned down the heat now that my goose bumps were gone. "I have to be home by ten-thirty, so we can't look for this disposal station tonight. So...tomorrow after school?"

Nash nodded and flipped another vent closed, but Tod's frown deepened in the rearview mirror. "Are you seriously saying your curfew is more important than Addison's soul?"

"You're in no position to complain." Nash twisted in his seat to face us both, gripping the back of my seat. "Kaylee and I don't owe either you or Addy a damn thing, and if you don't lay off, we'll both just walk."

Only they both knew I'd never do that. I'd said I was in, and I meant it. But...

"If I get home late, I get grounded, and I won't be much help to Addy while I'm stuck in my room." I eyed Tod in the mirror and flicked off my brights as another car approached in the opposite lane. "She's not supposed to die until Thursday, so we still have all day tomorrow, at least, right?"

Instead of answering, Tod scowled, and his curls shone brightly in the glare from the passing car's headlights. "Can't you sneak out after your dad goes to bed?"

I nodded and flicked my brights back on. "Probably. But if I get caught, we're right back where we started, only getting caught sneaking out is much worse than being late for curfew in the first place. I could be late because of traffic, car trouble, or the built-in delay of hanging out with Emma. But sneaking out implies that I'm up to something my dad won't like." Which was true, but not in the way my father would be thinking. "And then he'll start checking up on me all the time. He's new at this, and way overzealous."

Nash and Tod had it easy. They were both legal—Nash had turned eighteen in late August—and thus mostly free from curfews and other unreasonable parental restrictions. Especially Tod, who was not only of age, but technically dead.

It's hard to ground someone who doesn't even officially exist. And can walk through walls.

"Whatever." He ran one hand through his mop of curls. "Can't you skip school tomorrow?"

"Love to," I said, and Tod's eyes brightened. Until I continued. "But I can't. I skipped last period today for this little road trip, and if I miss again, the school will call my dad."

"High school's a pain in the ass," Tod snapped, and I almost laughed out loud at the absurdity of such an understatement. "I'll be glad when you turn eighteen."

That time I did laugh. "Me, too."

"That makes three of us." The heat in Nash's eyes said his agreement had nothing to do with helping either Tod or Addison, and everything to do with uninterrupted privacy. At least where my father was concerned.

Something told me getting rid of Tod would be a little more difficult.

My phone rang as I took a long, gradual curve in the highway, and Nash helped me hold the wheel while I dug my cell from my pocket. I didn't recognize the number, which meant my father probably hadn't figured anything out yet.

I flipped my phone open and held it to my ear with my right hand, while I steered with my left. "Hello?"

"Kaylee?" It was Addison, and she sounded stuffy, like she had a cold. Or like she'd been crying.

"Addy, what's wrong?" I asked, and Tod's image in the rearview mirror lurched when he leaned forward. His arm brushed the back of my shoulder as he hovered near my phone to listen in.

"Tod doesn't have a phone, so he gave me your number," Addison began, sniffling into my ear. "I hope that's okay." She sniffed again, and I wanted to tell her to blow her nose.

"It's fine. What's wrong?" I asked again, as Tod's breath warmed the back of my neck, stirring my ponytail. How weird that he was alive enough to breathe hot air, but not to carry a cell phone. Maybe it was hard to get an account in a dead man's name….

"It's Regan." Addison sobbed haltingly while I twisted the wheel to the left to keep us on the road when it curved. Suddenly it felt like I was trying to do a dozen things at once. And failing.

"What's wrong with Regan?" Tod asked over my shoulder, and she must have heard him.

"John Dekker offered her the contract, and she said yes!" Her voice rose in disbelief on the last word, and it echoed like a siren going off in my head. For a moment I wondered how certain we were of Addison's humanity. "He's on his way here now. He always brings the contract personally—he doesn't trust anyone else with it."

My heart beat so hard my chest felt bruised. John Dekker was coming to Texas, and he was bringing a soul-sucking demon with him.

The road swam before me as my horror and confusion crested in a startling wave of disorientation. Nash grabbed the wheel again, though I hadn't let go of it, and I took a deep breath, forcing my thoughts apart. Each to its own distinct corner of my mind. That was the only way I could concentrate on one at a time.

I tightened my grip on the wheel, eased up on the gas, and focused on the road, nodding absently to tell Nash I was fine. Until a semi blasted past on our right, nearly blowing us off the highway.

Maybe I should pull over....

"Wait, your sister sold her soul?" I said, hitting the speakerphone button as I glanced over my shoulder to make sure there was nothing in the other lane. But the entire highway was blocked by Tod's face, crinkled with fear—an odd expression to find on a reaper.

"Move!" I mouthed, handing the phone to Nash, and Tod immediately dropped back into the rear passenger seat. I swerved too quickly into the right lane—blessedly empty—then onto the shoulder of the road.

"She hasn't actually signed the contract yet," Addison continued, oblivious to my driving woes. "But she will as soon as Dekker gets here. You guys have to help me. Please. She won't listen to me, but she can't argue with you. She knows Tod's dead. You all have to come tell her what you told me. What will happen to her when she dies."

"Why won't she listen to you?" I shoved the gearshift into Park, and Nash stabbed a button on the dash to turn on the hazard lights.

"She thinks I'm trying to hold her back." Addy sobbed again and springs creaked as she sat on something. It sounded like a bed, rather than a chair. "She said she was tired of 'singing in my shadow.'"

Nash spoke loudly, to make sure she could hear. "Addy, where's your mom?"

Addison sniffled again, sounding much younger than eighteen. I guess true terror does that. "She went out, and she's not answering her phone." She didn't elaborate, but I recognized the embarrassed, disgusted tone in her voice. Her mom was strung out again, and gone when she was needed most.

"Does she know what your sister's about to do?" Nash continued.

Addison sobbed miserably. "Yeah, but she doesn't understand. I tried to tell her Regan was selling her soul, but she thought I was speaking in metaphors." She sniffled again. "I doubt she'd care, anyway. She'd just see dollar signs."

I already hated Mrs. Page, though I'd never met her.

Tod leaned forward with his arms folded across the back of Nash's seat this time. "Where's Regan now?"

"We're both at home," Addy said. "My mom's house in Hurst. Do you remember how to get here?"

Tod nodded, then realized she couldn't hear him. "Yeah." But then he faltered, obviously at a loss for how we could help.

But I had an idea—a stroke of genius, really—that sent adrenaline racing through my veins fast enough to leave me lightheaded. "After she signs the contract, Dekker has to take her to the Netherworld like they did with you, right?" My small car rocked violently as another huge truck blasted past us on the highway, without bothering to move into the far lane.

Addison cleared her throat, and more springs groaned. "Yeah, but we can't let that happen. We have to stop her from signing."

"I know." I held up one finger to tell Nash and Tod to wait—that I really was going somewhere with this. "But my point is that in order to take her to the Netherworld, Dekker has to bring along that reaper, right? The lady who took you to the hellion?"

"Yeah, I guess…"

"And, Tod…" I twisted in the driver's seat to face him, though the steering wheel bruised my side. "Using your soul-wrangling abilities for anything other than reaping from the approved list is illegal for a reaper, right? Including taking humans to the Netherworld to facilitate the removal of their souls?" He nodded, and I continued. "Would you call that a firing offense?"

"Definitely." His eyes lit up, as my point became clear.

"And would your boss be interested in the chance to fire such a reaper?"

His brows arched. "It would make his decade."

"That's what I thought." I faced forward again to spare my ribs, just as the first drops of rain went splat on the windshield.

"And without his pet reaper, Dekker has no way to get Regan to the Netherworld. Right?" My excitement grew as Tod and Nash both nodded eagerly. We had a chance to save Regan from making a huge mistake *and* bring justice to the rogue reaper involved. Plus, if I could peek into the Netherworld, I could at least get a good look at the hellion we needed to identify. "So, what do you think? Will it work?"

Nash grinned from ear to ear and made a gruff happy noise deep in his throat. "I think it might."

"So, wait, you have a plan?" Addy squeaked over the line.

"Yeah, I think we do." I twisted my key in the ignition, and the car rumbled to life, more like an ailing house cat than a purring tiger, but so long as my poor car moved, I wasn't going to complain.

"What should I do?"

I rebuckled my seat belt and flicked the switch to start my windshield wipers. "Stall them until we get there." The passenger side wiper stuttered across the glass once, then died without so much as a whimper. Fortunately, I didn't need to see through that side. "Say whatever you have to say. But don't let her sign that contract, and do *not* let the reaper take Regan to the Netherworld."

"Okay, I'll try." But she sounded less than confident.

"Try hard, Addy." I punched the button to make the hazard lights stop blinking and glanced over my left shoulder before pulling into traffic again. "You only have one sister, right? And she only has one soul."

"Yeah, okay." She sniffled again, but this time determination echoed in her voice like a vow sworn in a cavern. "I'll keep her here if I have to chain her to the kitchen cabinets."

"I hope you're kidding, but in case you're not, that won't work. Neither your cabinets nor your chain exist in the Netherworld, because they're in a private residence." *Huh. Look at that.* I'd actually learned something in how-to-be-a-*bean-sidhe* lessons…

"Yes, but the concept has some real potential," Tod muttered from behind me, and I glanced in the mirror to see him grinning lasciviously.

"I'll come up with something," Addison said. She obviously hadn't heard the reaper's last comment.

"Good. We'll be there as soon as we can." I nodded at Nash, and he closed my phone, but held on to it, so I wouldn't have to dig for it if it rang again. Then I stomped on the gas, and nearly had a heart attack when my poor little car hydroplaned a good ten feet before finding traction again.

"I'd rather be late-but-whole than punctual-but-dead," Nash suggested, teasing me much more calmly than I could have managed if he'd nearly killed me.

"I'm gonna find Levi and meet you guys there," Tod said, and I frowned when I realized the fear shining in his eyes probably had as much to do with my driving and the possibility of his own second death than with being late to Regan's soul harvest.

Was that some kind of residual human fear, or could a car crash actually hurt a reaper, if he didn't blink out in time? And for the first time, I wondered exactly how dead Tod was....

"Wait!" I shouted, and Nash reached for the wheel again when I stretched my neck to catch his brother's gaze in the rearview mirror. Tod arched one brow at me. I'd caught him right before he would have disappeared. "Reapers don't have death dates, because they're already dead, right?" I asked, and Tod nodded. "So...do you guys still have souls?"

He scowled. "Do my eyes look empty to you?"

I breathed a little easier, knowing the dead boy in my backseat wasn't soulless—even if his conscience wasn't exactly bright and shiny. "So, what happens to a reaper's soul once it's confiscated?" I asked, watching his face for any unspoken reaction. Because a fired reaper was a dead reaper. Permanently dead.

"It's recycled, just like a human's," Tod said, and I could see the gears grinding behind his eyes, as he tried to follow my thought process. His brother's expression was eerily similar, only without that edge of suspicion. Nash might not have known exactly what I was up to, but he trusted me completely.

I wasn't sure whether that made him sweet or naive.

"So…who collects it?" I asked, not surprised to see my brow crinkle in the mirror. "Can just any reaper kill a fellow reaper and take her soul?"

Tod shrugged, and suddenly looked completely invested in the conversation—a relative rarity for him. "In theory, yes. But that would be a really good way to piss off your coworkers. So we usually leave that to managers and Dark reapers, like Libby."

The rain had started to slow, so I dared a little more pressure on the gas pedal. "Does it work the same way it does with humans?"

"As far as I know. Though, reaper souls are much rarer than human souls, so I've never actually seen it done."

"What are you getting at, Kaylee?" Nash asked, as I put my blinker on to pass an old pickup in the right lane.

"I was just curious," I said, not yet willing to mention the kernel of an idea sprouting slowly in my head. "Do you know how to get to Addison's mom's house?" I asked Nash, and when he nodded, I eyed Tod in the mirror. "Go find Levi. We'll meet you there as soon as we can."

He nodded, then disappeared.

I drove as fast as I could without risking an accident or police intervention, and when we got to Hurst, Nash gave me directions to her neighborhood. Which is where we got lost. The roads in Addison's subdivision wound around in interconnected circles and cul-de-sacs, several of which seemed to share variations of the same name. And all the houses looked the same, especially in the dark.

My ten-thirty curfew came and went while we wandered the neighborhood, trying to call Addy the whole time, but she never answered her phone. Finally, Nash suggested I let him drive while I took a peek into the Netherworld to see if I could give him a general direction from there. Reluctantly—very reluctantly—I agreed.

In the passenger seat of my own car, as a late-night mist still sprayed my windshield, I called up the memory of Emma's death, forcing myself to relive it one more time. I told myself I was doing a good thing. Trying to save the soul of a thirteen-year-old girl who had no idea what she was getting herself into, rather than simply exploring my own abilities.

It didn't help.

Summoning my own wail was still one of the most difficult things I'd ever had to do, probably because I didn't really want to remember how Emma had looked when she'd died. How her face had gone blank, her eyes staring up at the gym ceiling as if she could see straight through it and into the heavens. *Though, she actually saw nothing at all....*

That did it. The wail began deep in my chest, fighting to break free from my throat, but I held it back. Swallowed most of it, as Harmony had taught me. What came out was a soft, high-pitched keening, which buzzed in my ears and seemed to resonate in my fillings. And finally a thin gray haze formed over everything, in spite of the fact that there was very little light to filter through it. To reflect off of it.

Since I was just peeking into the Netherworld, rather than going there, my vision seemed to split as one reality layered itself over the other. It was a bit like watching a 3-D movie without the proper cardboard glasses. The images didn't quite line up.

And the Netherworld—rather than being lit by what paltry moonlight shone in the human plane—was illuminated by a ubiquitous white glow from above, similar to the way the lights of a city in the distance reflect off low-lying clouds in the dark. This light was indistinct and somehow cold, and seemed to blur the world before me, rather than to truly lighten it.

However that was par for the course, at least as far as I could tell. I'd never been able to see very far in the Netherworld, which gave me the impression that if I took one step too many, I'd fall into some huge, gaping pit, or step off the edge of the world. That thought, and the cool, hazy light, made me want to step very carefully. Or to close my eyes and shake my head until the Netherworld disappeared altogether.

But I resisted the urge to deny the Netherworld, though every survival instinct I had groaned within me. I'd never find Regan and Addy in time if I didn't look in both worlds.

"What do you see?" Nash asked. Because he could hear my keening, he would have been able to see into the Netherworld with me, if he'd wanted. But someone had to drive.

I couldn't answer him—not while I was holding back my wail. So I shrugged, and squinted into the distance, turning slowly in my seat. At first there was nothing but the usual gray fog, paler toward the sky, and the eerie impression of movement just outside my field of vision.

As Harmony had explained, human private residences didn't exist in the Netherworld, so when I peeked into it, Addy's neighborhood was suddenly overlaid with a second, similar series of gravel streets and walkways, which ended in nothing. And some darkly intuitive part of my mind insisted that the gravel was really crushed bone. Though, from what sort of creature I couldn't begin to imagine....

I wondered what I'd see if I were actually in the Netherworld. What would the homes look like? Could I go in one? Would I want to?

"Well?" The urgency in Nash's voice reminded me of the ticking clock. I squinted into the fog again and this time made out a series of darker-than-normal shapes in the ever-present gray spliced into our world. Shapes that weren't moving. Or at least, weren't moving *away*.

I pointed to my right, and was surprised when my hand smashed into the glass of my own window. Though I still sat bodily in the human world, my senses were so intensely focused on that other world that I'd become oblivious to my physical surroundings. The car didn't exist in the Netherworld, where I seemed to float over the road alone, in an invisible chair.

Weird.

Nash turned the wheel in the direction I'd pointed, and vertigo washed over me as I moved along with a vehicle I could only see and feel on one plane. In one reality.

Double weird. Evidently I get carsick in the Nether-reality.

As we drew closer, the shapes became a little more distinct. Two tall forms, and one small. Small, like a little girl. A young teenager, maybe.

Crap. Regan had already crossed over.

A little more of my wail slipped out, and I was surprised all over again when the echo of my voice bounced around in the car, rather than rolling out to points unknown. Nash followed my finger, and I had to slap a hand over my mouth to keep from vomiting when the car tilted up suddenly, and he slammed my gearshift into Park. We were in a sharply sloping driveway, only feet from those three dark figures now.

The driver's side door opened, and cold air swirled around me. A moment later, my door opened, and Nash helped me out of the car by one arm. Icy mist settled on me, rendering me instantly damp and cold, and distantly I wished I'd worn a jacket.

Nash's lips brushed my ear. "Let it go…" His words slid over me like warm satin gliding over my skin. I felt myself relax, even as the largest of those gray figures turned to walk away. "We're here now, so just let it go."

I let the wail fade, and the grayness melted from my vision, leaving me with a scratchy throat and haunting images lingering behind my eyes. And a crystal-clear view of a large brick house with a stone facade around a bright red front door, illuminated by a series of floodlights.

Parked on the street in front of the house was a plain black limousine—if a limo can ever be considered plain—with the engine still running, the driver half asleep behind the wheel. That would have been a remarkable sight on my street, but in Addy's neighborhood, it was probably commonplace.

Nash dashed toward the house, and I sprinted after him, without taking time to truly reorient myself in the human world. I tripped over the front step, but he caught me with one hand, already twisting the knob with the other.

It opened easily. Dekker and the reaper obviously weren't expecting company. Fortunately, Addison was.

We rushed through the tiled foyer into a large, plush living room, where John Dekker held Addison Page by her upper arm, his other hand gripping an expanding file folder closed with a built-in rubber band.

Was that Regan's contract? Excitement surged through me like an electrical charge. Could the hellion's name really be so close?

An instant later, two female figures appeared in the center of the floor, holding hands.

The taller form I assumed to be the rogue reaper. The other was Regan Page. I recognized her from the ads for her new tween drama. Except that on TV, she had crystalline blue eyes only a couple of shades darker than her sister's.

Now her eyes were solid white orbs, shot through with tiny red veins, as if the whites had absorbed her pupils and irises.

Despair crashed through me, heavy and almost too thick to breathe through. My hand tightened around Nash's. We were too late. She'd sold her soul, and the brief, dark-'n'-blurry glimpse I'd gotten of the hellion who took it wasn't enough to let me identify him, much less find him.

I'd failed—again—and another girl had lost her soul.

"Regan…" Addison moaned, staring into her sister's featureless eyes, slowly shaking her head. Her own eerie, fake-blue eyes filled with tears and her hands began to tremble.

"You made the right choice," Dekker told Regan, flashing that famous, million-dollar smile. The caps that launched a thousand amusement park rides. His grandfather would have been proud. "You'll be rich and famous for the rest of your life."

Sudden anger flamed behind the icy blue rings of Addy's contact lenses, blazing through her weaker emotions like kindling. She ripped her arm from Dekker's grasp and pulled Regan away from the reaper. "Is the hellion still there?" she demanded, her focus shifting between me and Nash as she held her sister's thin arm with a granite grip. "If we destroy her contract, will that kill the deal?"

"No!" Regan tried to twist away, and Dekker followed Addison's gaze to me and Nash, standing at the edge of the room like freshmen at the prom.

"Who are they?" he asked calmly, clearly speaking to his female colleague, though he looked at us.

The reaper sneered but looked like she really wanted to hiss. *"Bean sidhes,"* she spat.

"Friends," Addison said. "I...invited them."

Dekker dismissed us at a glance and turned back to Addy, flipping open his folder so we could all see that it was empty. Because, as Tod had discovered, demon paperwork was kept in the Netherworld. "It doesn't work like that, Addison." Dekker shot her a smug, patient smile. "Hellion contracts are indestructible by human means. Like fireproof, Kevlar paperwork. And if Regan invokes her out-clause before she has a pedestal to fall from, her willpower and decorum will corrode until she wouldn't recognize a good decision if it ran her over on the street. You'll likely be an aunt in a couple of years, and I'm sure the brat's father will be a convict, or a dealer, or something equally prestigious.

"Regan's flaws will be exploited and magnified, and because her sister's famous, her every stumble will be front-page news." He paused, and his eager brown eyes seemed to spark with a little extra oomph. "Oh, and any tendencies toward addiction—something she might have inherited, for example?" His raised eyebrows said Dekker was more than familiar with Ms. Page's fondness for prescription drugs. "Well, let's just say they'll be awfully hard for a new, disgraced teen mother to resist...."

Regan stared at Dekker in growing horror, and rage flushed Addy's cheeks. "It doesn't matter," she insisted, while her sister's head whipped back and forth in denial. "She's not taking the out-clause."

"Why not?" Regan demanded, but Addy turned to me without answering her.

"Is the demon still there? I want to talk to him."

"He's gone," I said, remembering the largest of the three dark figures I'd seen in the Netherworld. The one who'd walked away as I let my wail fade.

"Take us," Addy demanded softly. "We'll find him."

"No." Nash shook his head firmly. "You can't go there, and neither can Kaylee. It's not safe."

"Neither is this!" Addison shoved her sister forward, and Nash flinched as his gaze found Regan's newly empty eyes.

"What's happening?" Regan shouted, tears filling her eyes. "Who're they?" She waved one arm at me and Nash, then her bewildered gaze slid back to Dekker. "Why is he threatening to wreck my life?"

Dekker crossed his arms over his chest, the empty folder flat against his side. "I'm not threatening you. I'm simply stating facts. You've signed a contract, and you'll be expected to stand by your word."

"She had no idea what she was signing," Addy said. "You didn't tell her the truth."

"I never lied," Dekker insisted calmly.

"What are you guys talking about?" Regan demanded, more bewildered than truly scared.

"We're talking about *this!*" Addison whirled her sister around until she faced a mirror hanging on the wall above a beige couch. "Look!"

Regan looked, and her eyes went anime-wide. But though her cheeks flushed bright red, no color returned to her eyes. That beautiful blue was gone, along with her soul.

"What…?" Regan started to step closer to the mirror for a better look, then changed her mind and stepped back instead, shaking her head slowly in denial. Then she whirled on John Dekker and his reaper with a rage and confusion almost equal to her sister's. "What's wrong with my eyes? How can I see if I don't have eyes? You didn't say anything about this."

"It was in the fine print." The reaper crossed her arms over a gaunt, black-clad chest, contempt glittering in her normal gray eyes. "You are old enough to read, aren't you?"

Dekker laid one hand on her forearm, and the reaper seemed to fold into herself, as if he'd just jabbed her off button. "There's nothing wrong with your eyes." His voice was calm and smooth, but it had nothing on Nash. "It's a side effect of the process. And we have an easy fix for this, don't we, Addison?"

Dekker glanced at the older Page sister, but she only glared at him, jaw clenched in vicious anger as he handed two small white boxes to her sister. "These are your prescription, I believe, and a virtual match to your own eye color. I'll have new boxes hand-delivered every six months. These should last until then, but please be careful with them." He winked his own nondescript brown eyes. "They aren't exactly cheap."

Regan's empty eyes filled with tears again, and I couldn't remember ever being scared of a crying eighth-grader before. But I was scared then. The incongruity of her very human tears with those distinctly *in*human eyes gave me chills in places I didn't even know I could get cold. "Will they stay like this?" She turned hesitantly toward the mirror again, then away before she could possibly have really seen herself. "Why do they look so…empty?"

"Because they're empty," Tod said, and we all spun around at the sound of his voice. Tod stood near the kitchen doorway, next to a small redheaded boy who barely came up to the reaper's shoulders. "The eyes are the windows to the soul, and without your soul, there's nothing for them to reflect."

Dekker's pet reaper went stiff on the edge of the room. Was Tod really that scary?

"Do you have another brother?" I whispered, standing on my toes to reach Nash's ear. "And did your dad have red hair?"

"That's Levi," he whispered back, and the little boy nodded politely at me, shrugging with his hands in the pockets of a baggy pair of khakis.

"Levi-the-reaper?" I asked, a little embarrassed when my voice went high with surprise. After all the truly weird stuff I'd seen since discovering I was a *bean sidhe,* a freckle-faced little-boy reaper shouldn't have fazed me in the least. But it did. "Tod's boss, Levi-the-reaper?"

"The one and only." Levi shot me a disarmingly sweet smile. One his eyes didn't match. Then he turned a ferocious glare on the rogue reaper. "Bana."

She froze with that one word—her own name, spoken in a child's high, soft voice—and her fingers twitched nervously at her sides. She looked like she wanted to run, but couldn't.

"I wasn't sure who to expect, but I must admit your name never occurred to me." Levi strolled forward like a kid in the park, and I had the absurd thought that he should have been carrying a baseball bat on his shoulder, or a skateboard under one arm. He stopped several feet from Bana and her boss, and gave John Dekker only a fleeting glance, as if he didn't recognize one of the most famous faces in the world.

Which struck me as especially ironic, considering the reaper's apparent age.

"Who is this?" Dekker asked, but before Bana could answer—and I seriously doubt she would have—the boy pulled his freckled right hand from his pocket.

"Levi Van Zant. Senior reaper in this district. I've come to relieve Bana of her duties. And her soul."

Bana's arms went stiff in anticipation, and I realized she was trying to blink out of Addy's house, and out of Levi's reach. My breath caught in my throat. We were going to lose her. But did it even matter? We were too late to stop her from ferrying Regan to the Netherworld.

But despite her obvious effort to disappear, she remained fully corporeal.

And before I could release my breath—before Bana could even suck one in—Levi's small hand shot out and wrapped around her wrist. His fingers barely met on the back of her arm, but any doubt I had about the strength of his grip was put to rest with one look at her face, twisted in agony, as if his very touch burned.

"Bana, look at me."

She tried to refuse. Her free hand clawed uselessly at the wall behind her, scratching the Sheetrock, resistance etched into the terrified, angry lines of her jaw and forehead. But she couldn't resist. Nor could she blink out. Somehow, Levi was blocking her abilities. Guaranteeing her cooperation.

Would Tod ever have that power?

"Look at me, Bana."

Her eyes flew open, and a cry leaked from her mouth. She looked straight into Levi's green eyes, which seemed to…shine. To glow with a bright, cold light.

We watched, every one of us fascinated. Including Dekker, but especially Regan Page, who was getting her first terrifying glimpse of the world she'd just entered. The world she'd sold herself to.

Bana's shoulders slumped and her eyelids fluttered, as if they'd close. Levi's grip on her arm tightened visibly. Dekker stepped back and the reaper went suddenly stiff. Her eyes opened again, but began to dull immediately. To simply…go dark.

And that's when the panic hit. My heart pounded, bruising the inside of my chest. Sweat formed between Nash's hand and mine. The cry rose in my throat, clawing me from the inside out, demanding an exit. An audience. Bana's soul song wanted to be heard.

I clenched my jaw against the wail, my mind whirring with questions.

A soul song for a reaper? It made sense—she did have a soul— yet somehow I'd never expected to actually wail for a reaper. Did that mean that Nash and I could save her if we wanted to? But why would we want to? And if we did, would someone else be taken in her place? Did doomed reaper souls require an exchange?

Surely not. Tod had said reaper souls were much rarer than human souls, so if we were to save Bana, would another reaper have to die? Because one human soul wouldn't be enough, would it?

The kernel of an idea I'd had earlier exploded in my head so violently it felt like my skull would split wide open. Because it wasn't just an idea. It was an *idea*. The kind of idea that could change lives.

Or save souls.

My hand clutched Nash's, and he tore his gaze from Bana to look at me in surprise, at almost the exact moment the scream leaked from my sealed lips. Just a sliver of sound at first, sharp and painful, but controlled. For the moment.

"Bana?" he whispered, hazel eyes wide, forehead crinkled.

I nodded and let another slice of sound slide from me.

Tod noticed then, and shot a questioning glance at Nash, who could only shrug. "You can make it stop, Kaylee," he said finally, his lips brushing my ear, his peaceful Influence brushing my heart. "I've seen you do it. Bring it back. Hold it in."

But I twisted away from him, shaking my head adamantly. I didn't want to hold it in. I wanted to let it go. Let my shriek pierce every skull in the room and rattle the windows. And let it capture Bana's filthy soul.

The rogue reaper was about to pay for her part in Dekker's soul-trafficking ring, and I was going to personally wring the recompense from her.

Addy and Regan watched me now, rather than Bana and Levi, and their stares made me nervous. Broke my concentration.

I closed my eyes briefly, then opened them along with my mouth. Sharp spikes of sound burst from me, washing over the room like a wave of glass shards. Addy, Regan, and Dekker flinched as one, as their brains were pierced by the evidence of my intent. Their hands flew to their ears. Their eyes squeezed shut. Their noses wrinkled in displeasure bordering on pain.

Levi shuddered, but his concentration never faltered. Bana was in too much pain from the brutal removal of her soul to even notice what I was doing. But Nash and Tod each wore odd smiles, their faces almost slack in pleasure. They heard my wail as a beautiful, eerie song, a melody without equivalent in the human world. A gift from the female *bean sidhe*, which only the males of our species could experience.

Even the undead males, apparently.

The panic ebbed inside me, riding the sliver of sound out of my core and into the room. With that pressure released, I was able to focus on my part in the plan I was forming. And to somehow communicate Tod's part to him.

An instant later, the last ember of light died in Bana's eyes, and her soul rose from her body. It looked exactly like a human soul—pale and formless. I'm not sure what I was expecting, but that wasn't it. Shouldn't a reaper's soul be different, somehow? And if it wasn't, would my plan even work?

Only one way to find out…

I sang for her soul. Called to it, suspending it in the air like a thick fog as Levi let go of the dead reaper's arm. He stepped back, and she collapsed on Addy's plush living-room carpet, a tangle of bent arms and awkwardly twisted legs.

Dekker jumped away from his dead employee so fast he tripped over his own feet and would have gone down if not for the chair he grabbed for balance. If I hadn't been screaming loud enough to rouse the dead, I'd have laughed. I wouldn't have thought someone who dealt so closely with reapers and hellions would be spooked by a little death.

But despite my fleeting amusement, my plan was not funny. It was born of desperation and inspiration, and it would never work if Tod didn't get on board. Fast.

Unable to take my eyes from Bana's soul, I felt around on my left, reaching blindly for Tod's arm. I found it, and pulled him forward just as Nash bent to whisper into my ear. That was the only way I could hear him over my own wail, and I probably wouldn't have heard a human voice. "What are you doing? She's dead. Let her go. I'm *not* bringing her back."

I shook my head vehemently, frustrated by my inability to communicate. When Tod's head came into my field of vision, I shoved him toward Bana, pointing at her hovering soul with my free hand then at Tod. Specifically, at his mouth. I needed him to suck up her soul, like Libby had sucked up the Demon's Breath.

To hold it, just for a little while.

And finally, he seemed to get it. "You want me to take her soul?" he asked, and I nodded, relief washing through me so quickly the edges of my vision went black.

I grabbed Nash for balance and concentrated on maintaining my song.

"Why?" Tod asked, shrugging when Levi shot him a questioning glance.

But I couldn't explain until he took the soul so I could stop screeching. I made more frantic gestures with my arms, and he finally nodded in concession. Then he opened his mouth and sucked in Bana's soul. In seconds, it was gone.

I closed my mouth and the room went silent, but for the awful ringing in my ears, which I knew from experience wouldn't fade completely for a couple of hours.

Tod wiped nonexistent soul crumbs from his mouth, and I shuddered.

"That was...surreal," I said, my voice as scratchy as an old record player. I stumbled, weak from exertion, and Nash caught me. He half carried me to the couch along the far wall, which was when I realized John Dekker was gone. He'd slipped from the room while everyone else watched me scream, and the front door still stood open.

Outside, tires squealed on the street and headlights faded from the front window. The limo we'd seen out front was gone. As was Regan's soul.

I whirled on the Page sisters, my eyes wide. "Did you catch the hellion's name?"

Addy shook her head slowly, angrily. "They never said it." Her features darkened with tortured disappointment and she glanced at her sister. "Do you know his name?"

Regan shook her head silently, offering no excuses.

"Great. So, what was all that?" Addison asked me, wrapping one arm around her sister's shoulders. Regan only stared, too shocked to form a coherent question.

I knew exactly how she felt.

"Could they see any of that?" I asked, rubbing my throat.

Nash shook his head. "Tod, explain what you can. Kaylee's losing her voice. I'm gonna get her something to drink." With that, he kicked the front door closed and headed into Addy's kitchen, face flushed in barely controlled anger.

Addy didn't seem to notice.

"Bana was a grim reaper," Tod began, guiding both stunned sisters to the empty couch opposite the one I sat on. "Like me and Levi." He nodded toward the boy still standing in the corner, small hands once again hidden in his pockets, evidently content to watch and listen for the moment. "Only she was... bad. So Levi fired her."

"You mean he killed her," Addison said, obviously struggling not to stare at the corpse on her carpet.

"Well, technically she was already dead." Tod shrugged. "So he really just finished the job. And Kaylee was singing her soul song."

"That wasn't singing." Regan's nose wrinkled like she smelled something awful. "That was a vocal *slaughter.*"

If my throat didn't feel like I'd just swallowed barbed wire, I would have laughed. I totally agreed.

"It wasn't a song like you think of music." Nash emerged from the kitchen with a glass of ice water. "It was a call to Bana's soul. Kaylee suspended it long enough for Tod to...take it."

"Speaking of which…" Tod sat on the other couch, as close as he could get to Addison, their legs touching from thigh to knee while Levi watched with an odd expression I couldn't interpret. "Why did I take her soul? Does this have anything to do with all your reaper questions in the car?"

"In fact, it does," I said, after one long sip of the water. My throat still hurt, but my voice had decent volume, considering what I'd just put it through. "We're going to barter with Bana's soul."

Nash's brows arched like he was impressed, and the sudden light in Tod's eyes said he understood at least part of what I was getting at. "You said a reaper's soul is rarer than a human's." I shifted my focus from Tod to his boss. "Am I correct in assuming that makes it more valuable?"

Levi nodded, and now his smile showed a line of small white teeth. They were all there, fortunately. If any had been missing, he would have been too creepy to look at.

"As valuable as, say, two human souls?" I glanced at the Page sisters, then back at Levi, whose brows arched in surprise.

"She's smart, this one," he said. "Of course, I can't officially condone what you're thinking, so I'll take my leave now…."

"But I'm on the right path?" I asked as he knelt next to the dead reaper.

"I'm afraid I don't know what you're talking about." Levi winked at me, still grinning. Then he picked up Bana in both arms as if she weighed nothing, though she had more than a foot on him, and they both disappeared.

"What is going on?" Regan finally demanded, impotent fists clenched at her sides.

I smiled gently, trying to set her at ease, though those eerie, empty eyes creeped me out. "We're going to trade Bana's soul to the hellion. For both of yours."

≪ 12 ≫

"Shh," I whispered to Nash as I closed the front door softly, wondering what the chances were that my father had fallen asleep early and hadn't noticed I was late. The living room was dark, and in the kitchen, only the over-the-sink light was on, so it was looking pretty good so far....

"Kaylee, get in here. Now."

Or not.

Nash squeezed my hand and followed me into the living room, where my father's silhouette leaned forward in the lumpy armchair, outlined by what little light penetrated the curtains from the street lamp outside. I stood in the middle of the floor, staring at the dark spot where his eyes would be, Nash's chest pressed against my back. "Why are you sitting in the dark?"

A shadow-arm reached up and to the left. The floor lamp clicked and light flooded the room. My dad still wore the flannel shirt he'd worked in, and his eyes were red from exhaustion. "Why are you an hour and a half late?"

Technically, it was only an hour and twenty-four minutes, but he looked even less eager to be corrected than I was to discuss my whereabouts.

"It's not even midnight." I tugged Nash forward and he

took that as his signal to intervene, though that wasn't what I'd intended.

"Sorry, Mr. Cavanaugh. We didn't realize it was so la—"

"Go home, Nash." A muscle jumped along the line of my father's jaw. "Your mom's waiting for you, too."

Nash's eyebrows rose, and he frowned. "I'll talk to you tomorrow, Kaylee," he said, already turning toward the front door with my hand still clasped in his, our arms stretched between us.

"That remains to be seen," my dad snapped.

I grinned, hoping to lighten the mood. "You gonna ground me from school?"

He was un-amused. "Good night, Nash."

"I have to drive him." I probably should have taken him home first, but I was hoping my dad would be asleep and we could discuss our next move, in light of that evening's failure. I dug my keys from my pocket and turned to follow Nash, but he shook his head with one look at my dad.

"I'll walk. It's only a few blocks." As the door closed behind him, I suddenly wished we didn't live so close together.

"Where were you?" my dad asked as I sank onto the couch on his left. "And before you start, I know you didn't work tonight, and you clearly weren't with Emma."

Great. "It's not whatever you're thinking." I could virtually guarantee that. But I couldn't tell him where I'd really been, because he'd like that even less than the thought that I was out drinking, smoking, or sleeping with Nash.

"Then where were you?" He crossed both arms over his chest, and I thought I saw his irises swirl just a little, though that might have been the flicker of a passing headlight on his eyes.

"Out driving." *Mostly.*

When he leaned forward to peer into my eyes, I realized his irises really were swirling. Weird. He usually had better control over his emotions…

"Is Nash going to be a problem?" My dad's voice was deep and rough. Worried.

I fiddled with a frayed spot of denim over my knee. "Why would he be?"

He closed his eyes briefly, and when they opened, his face held a new resolve and the colors in his irises had stopped moving. He'd regained control over…something. Something I didn't understand and he didn't seem ready to explain. "Kaylee, I know you like him, and I know he's…not a bad kid. And we all know he was there for you when I wasn't, and I'm sorrier about that than I could ever explain. But I don't want you to…"

He hesitated and rubbed his forehead, then started over. "It isn't a good idea for you to get too involved with him. You're so young, and… Damn, I wish your mother was here to explain this…."

Sudden understanding flooded me and blood rushed to my cheeks. "Dad, is this about sex?"

That time he blushed, and I almost felt sorry for him. Full-time parenthood was new for him, and we were still feeling our way around in some areas. Like curfews, and apparently that mortifying after-school-special talk.

"It's not just about sex…."

"Okay, please stop." I held up both hands, palms out, and rolled my eyes. "This is just weird—"

"Kaylee…"

"—and it's really none of your business—" I gestured with one arm.

He stood, frowning down at me. "This most certainly is my business—"

"—and I don't need you stepping in to tell me what I can and can't do!" I stood to put us on equal ground.

"That's my job." His mouth quirked up in an ironic smile, but I refused to see the humor.

"Well, you're not very good at it!"

His smile collapsed, and his eyes swirled slowly. Sadly.

I felt guilty immediately. He was trying so hard. "I didn't mean it like that."

"I know." He exhaled heavily. "But you're still grounded. For coming home late—not for hurting my feelings."

Great. I closed my eyes, trying to think quickly. I knew how to deal with my aunt and uncle, but with my dad, I was in mostly unexplored territory. "Okay, but this is really kind of a disastrous time for me to be grounded." I crossed my arms over my chest. "Can't we work something else out? I'll do the dishes all week. And the laundry." Of course, I already did most of the clothes, anyway, because he kind of sucked at sorting.

"Did Bren and Val really go for that?" Anger edged his voice now. I was nearing some kind of boundary, and I really had no desire to cross it. My dad was actually pretty laid-back for the most part, and I didn't want to trigger whatever auto-lockdown mechanism most parents have hardwired into their brains. Even recently returned itinerant parents.

"No." They'd rarely actually grounded me; Sophie was usually the one in trouble. Though, I couldn't remember them actually grounding her, either, come to think of it…. "But I have something important to do this week."

"What?"

My entire body felt heavy with guilt. "I can't tell you."

"Like you can't tell me where you were tonight?"

"Kind of." I exhaled heavily and met his gaze. "Dad, I need you to trust me. This is really important."

He held out one hand, palm up. "Give me your phone."

My hand snuck into my pocket, curling protectively around my cell. "Seriously?" He couldn't mean that.

"Yes. One week, no phone."

"No!" Spikes of righteous anger shot up my spine, tingling all the way into my fingers. I was trying to help someone! If he'd been around long enough to get to know me, he'd know that, even without the details. "It's not safe to run around without a phone!" Especially for someone so deep in hellion business she'd have to look up to wave to the devil.

"Well, that won't be a problem, because you're not going anywhere. Give me your keys. You can take the bus to school tomorrow."

"This is ridiculous!" I shouted, reluctantly digging my phone from one pocket, my keys from the other. "And completely unwarranted. It's not like I was out drinking and sleeping around."

My dad rubbed his forehead and sank back into the armchair, looking as weary as I'd ever seen him. "Kaylee, I don't know what you were doing, because you won't tell me!"

"Fine." I slapped my phone into his waiting palm. "But my reasons for not telling you everything now are just as important as your reasons for not telling me anything over the past thirteen years. And it's completely messed up that you expect me to trust you when you're not willing to return the favor."

My jab found its mark and my father flinched again. "I'm tired, Kaylee, and I don't have the energy for this." He set my phone on an end table and rubbed his face with both hands. "Give me your keys and go to bed. Please."

And what was I supposed to say to Addy and Regan? *Sorry, I can't save your immortal souls, because I'm* grounded?

I dropped my keys on the kitchen counter, then plodded down the hall to my room, sorting through possible ways around this new complication. How were we supposed to find the hellion without a car? Walk all over the Metroplex?

With my bedroom door open, I sank cross-legged onto my bed and listened as my father locked up, then plodded down the hall to his own room. Fifteen minutes later, his snores echoed in the hall and a bolt of irritation lanced me. Our first real fight hadn't interrupted his sleep in the least.

Still irritated, I crossed the hall to use the bathroom and brush my teeth, then changed into a halter top and baggy pajama pants before collapsing onto my bed again. I had chemistry homework to do, and I was too mad to sleep, but I'd left my books in my car and couldn't get to them without my keys.

"You okay?" Tod asked from the wing chair by my headboard, and I almost jumped off the bed in surprise. "Sorry." He grabbed my arm to steady me.

I was tempted to yell at him, but resisted because for once his intrusion might actually come in handy. And because I didn't want to wake my dad up. "How much of that did you hear?" I waved one arm in the direction of the living room to indicate my fight with my dad.

"Just the last bit. Nash asked me to check on you." He waggled both eyebrows and donned a mischievous grin. "Don't worry, I turned around when you changed."

I couldn't help a laugh. Tod might flirt with me to bug Nash, but he obviously really cared about Addy, beyond whatever crush they'd shared in school. "I'm glad to hear you've retained at least a little moral fortitude since your unfortunate demise."

"I reserve it for special occasions. And people I like."

I threw my pillow at him.

"So is this all because you're late?"

"That, and because I wouldn't tell him where I'd been. I'm grounded for a week."

Tod frowned. "But you're still coming after school tomorrow, right?"

I cocked my head at him, eyes narrowed in mock confusion. "What part of 'grounded' don't you understand?"

"The part where it gets in the way of my plans." But I knew from the serious cast of his scowl that it wasn't really his plans he was worried about. It was Addy's soul.

Since we hadn't gotten there in time to stop Regan from selling out or even to identify the hellion who bought her soul, we were back to plan A: hoping someone at the Demon's Breath disposal facility would be willing to help us. But we had to get there first, which would be difficult without a car.

At least now we had something to bargain with, once we found the hellion. Fortunately, Tod could hold Bana's soul much longer than a reaper could hold on to a lungful of Demon's Breath. Not that I was exactly eager to enact that particular part of the plan...

"Look, it's your fault I'm grounded," I whisper-hissed at Tod. "None of this would have happened if you hadn't dragged me into this in the first place. What do you want me to do?"

"Sneak out." He shrugged, as if that should have been a no-brainer. But that was easy for him to say. He was dead. What else could they do to him, take away his birthday? "If you get caught, I'll make it up to you. I swear. Please, Kaylee. We can't do this without you."

"Yes you can!" I switched to a whisper again, in case my father woke up and heard the single most incriminating words I'd ever spoken. "You have Bana's soul. You can make the deal on your own."

His face fell, and he stared at the pillow in his lap for a moment before meeting my gaze again, frustration flaring like flames behind his eyes. "No I can't. I'm still a rookie reaper, Kaylee. I can only carry a limited amount of cargo to the Netherworld at a time, and I've already got Bana's soul to deal with. Even if I can take Addy, too, I need you to bring Regan. And Nash. I have a feeling we're going to need him."

I felt my eyes go wide, and my reflection in the mirror looked as terrified as I felt. "Can I do that?"

"Can't you?" Confusion flitted across his features. "Isn't that what my mom's supposed to be teaching you?"

"I don't know! She hasn't shown me a syllabus. Can she ferry people?"

"Yeah." He nodded firmly. "And you have to get her to teach you how. We can't do this without you, Kaylee."

I sighed, and the bleak weight of responsibility settled almost physically over me. I had no choice. But my dad was going to kill me when he found out, and the collateral damage would likely include both Nash and Tod. And Harmony, when he discovered her unwitting assistance. But hopefully that wouldn't be until after we'd returned Addy's and Regan's souls to their rightful bodies.

"Fine. But you owe me. Starting now."

"Absolutely." Relief half relaxed his features, and the reaper leaned forward in my chair. "Whatever you want."

"Can you get my phone out of my dad's room without waking him up?"

"No problem." He was gone before I could warn him to be careful.

Several seconds later, as I sat frozen on my bed, irrationally afraid to move in case the squealing springs woke my father, Tod popped back into my room, cradling my slim red phone in one palm.

He shot me a crooked grin, blue eyes sparkling with mischief. "Did you know your dad sleeps in boxers?"

"Ew. Thanks for the visual." I grabbed my phone and scrolled through the menu to check my missed calls. Five from my dad and four from Emma. We must have hit a dead zone on the highway, and I hadn't checked my messages.

I selected the last voice mail Emma had left and held the phone to my ear, one hand on my hip as I glanced at Tod. "I need my books from my car, then I'll need you to put this back wherever my dad left it."

Tod gave me a mock bow. "Anything else? Can I fan you with a big palm leaf? Feed you grapes while you write your homework in my blood?"

"Shh!" I hissed, waving him off as Emma's voice spoke to me from my phone. "You said you owed me!"

He frowned and popped out of my room in time for me to

hear most of the missed message. "...tried to cover for you, but he called the theater first, and they told him you weren't working. You better call him and do some damage control, Kaylee. I'll see you tomorrow...."

The phone beeped in my ear as her message ended. She'd tried to warn me.

Tod popped back into my room holding my chemistry text and a notebook as I pressed a button to call Emma back. She answered on the third ring, and I gestured for him to set my stuff on my desk.

"Kay? It's twelve-thirty in the morning," Emma mumbled. It sounded like she had her face buried in the phone. "What's wrong?"

"Sorry, Em, but it's kind of an emergency. Can Nash and I get a ride to school tomorrow?"

"'Course." She sounded a little more alert, and springs squealed as she sat up in bed. "What happened to your car?"

"My dad took my keys and my phone for a week."

"Ouch. I'll be there at seven-thirty." Which meant seven-forty-five, in Emma-land. We'd be late to school, but that was better than riding the bus with the freshmen.

"Thanks. You're awesome."

"I know," she slurred, already half asleep again. "Bye." The phone clicked in my ear and Emma was gone. I spared a moment to hope she remembered us in the morning. Then I sank onto my bed, suddenly very sleepy, now that the immediate problem was resolved.

"Tell Nash to be here at seven-thirty if he wants a ride." I'd driven him to school most mornings since we started going out. I glanced at the textbook on my desk, briefly considering my homework. But I was too tired to mess with that. I'd do it at lunch. "So what's the plan for tomorrow?"

"We go downtown and find the disposal facility, then start

asking questions until we hear what we need to know," Tod said, slouching in my chair again.

"Simple. I like it." I sat on my pillow and slid my legs beneath my covers. "When?"

"After school?"

"Nope. My dad'll call, and if I'm not here to answer, he'll...I don't know. Call the cops or something."

Tod scowled, an odd look on his cherubic features. "You're not looking at the big picture, Kaylee. Addy's soul is at stake. I've traded two hospital shifts in a row and will probably have to do it again tomorrow. The least you can do is drop off your dad's radar for a couple of hours after school."

"Okay, first of all, we're not out of time just yet. Tomorrow's Wednesday, and Addy's not supposed to die until Thursday. And we can't do this until I learn how to turn myself into a Netherworld ferry." Which meant I'd have to convince my father to let me go for my how-to-be-a-*bean-sidhe* lesson after school, in spite of the grounding.

Then I'd have to talk Harmony into teaching me what I needed to know, without telling her why I needed to know it.

"Besides, we need a car. You can blink into Dallas whenever you want, but Nash and I can't. And I'm not taking the bus in the middle of the night."

"Middle of the night?" He leaned forward in my chair, brows dipped low in concern. "Isn't that cutting it kind of close?"

"We don't really have any choice, Tod." I scooted down on the bed until the covers gathered at my waist. "The only time my dad won't check up on me is when he's asleep, which means we can't leave until tomorrow night. That gives you almost a day to explain everything to Addy and Regan, and to find us a car." Because his mom worked the night shift at the hospital and would need hers. "Do *not* steal one. The last thing we need is to get arrested on the way to the Netherworld."

I could already see the headline: Mentally Fragile Teen Arrested in Stolen Car; Says She Was Looking for a Demon.

Sophie wouldn't have to work hard to convince everyone I was nuts after that.

"That's not enough time, Kaylee." Tod looked as grim as I'd ever seen him.

"It'll have to be." I wasn't sure how best to comfort a reaper. "By Thursday morning, Addy will be in full possession of her soul."

It wasn't much of a promise, but since I couldn't guarantee her life, her soul was all I could offer him.

"Now, could you please put my phone back where you found it? And turn the light off on your way out." With that, I lay back and pulled the covers over my shoulder. I needed sleep.

Tomorrow promised to be the weirdest Wednesday in history.

≪ 13 ≫

"I really should just leave you here. You deserve to ride the bus, for keeping so many secrets." Emma slammed her locker closed as the last bell rang, but her bright brown eyes gave her away. She wasn't really mad. She was fishing for hints about the super-secret *bean sidhe* mission she imagined we were on.

I settled my backpack higher on my shoulder and tugged my snug tee down over the waistband of my jeans. "Trust me, you're not missing anything." If she knew the truth, her curiosity would no doubt give way to terror. Which was why I couldn't tell her.

But Emma would give us another ride, anyway, to make up for making us all nearly half an hour late to first period. I should have known she wouldn't remember a middle-of-the-night, sleep-foggy promise. She'd actually made it all the way to the school parking lot five minutes ahead of the tardy bell before remembering me and Nash. I would have texted her, but my dad left for work with my phone, and I didn't have her number memorized. Nor did Nash have it programmed.

We all three got unexcused tardies, which made a matched set with my unexcused absence from history the day before. Add to that the half-finished chemistry homework I'd spilled nacho-cheese sauce on during lunch, and I was starting to think

I couldn't handle both school and *bean sidhe* business. Not to mention work.

"Hey, Emma," a male voice called from down the hall. We looked up to see Doug Fuller strutting with a huddle of football players in matching school jackets, Nash among them. "You got plans tonight?"

The cluster closed around us in a tall wall of broad green-and-white-clad shoulders, blocking most of the hall from view and effectively trapping us, though Emma didn't seem to notice the sudden suffocating lack of personal space. I stepped back and my bag hit the lockers. There was nowhere else to go unless I was willing to break through the offensive line and expose my confinement issues. Which would be like waving a red flag in front of a whole herd of bulls.

Nash must have seen the swirl of panic in my eyes, because he was suddenly at my side. I let my backpack slide to the floor, and he wrapped both arms around me from behind. His breath brushed my ear in a private, whispered greeting, and I relaxed into him as if the other ass-letes weren't even there.

They'd accepted me into their company easily enough—though I'd only hovered on the fringes before, thanks to Emma's various adventures in dating—because Nash and I were practically attached at the hip.

Or at the crotch, as the other guys no doubt assumed. After all, why else would he hang out with Emma's curveless, penniless best friend, even if I did have a not-hideous face?

A very good question…

Nash had no more money than I did. Maybe even less. But he was wealthy in another currency: athleticism. He'd helped lead the football team to the regional play-offs—they were the heavy favorites for Friday night's game—and would do it again when baseball season arrived in the spring. That prowess, along with a face and body—not to mention a voice—few girls could say no to, kept him firmly anchored in the bright, shining kingdom of

Social Acceptance, a world surely stranger and more frightening than anything I could stumble across in the Netherworld.

Emma had a free pass into that world, issued solely upon the basis of her flawless face and generous curves. She flitted among the chosen ones at will, lingering whenever a strong chin or bulging arm caught her eye. But it never lasted long. She bored easily—especially of guys with wandering hands—and would soon come back bearing tales of bumbling inadequacy unenhanced by enthusiasm.

Outside of school, it was easy to forget that Nash belonged to that world, too, and that he had a lot in common with his friends, minus the bumbling inadequacy part. But I'd rather walk the Netherworld alone, with my soul safety-pinned to my sleeve, than spend a few hours alone with any one of his teammates. Somehow, that seemed safer.

"Yeah, I have plans." Emma stood on her toes and pressed herself into Doug's chest so that her breasts flattened against his letter jacket, her nose inches from his chin. His hand slithered around her waist to spread at the base of her spine, fingers inching lower. "I have very interesting plans...."

His friends snickered and Emma stretched higher, letting her lips brush his jaw near his ear as his hand slid lower, gripping the upper curve of her backside. "Too bad they don't include you."

With that, she dropped onto her heels again and smiled up at him, one hand propped on the dramatic flair of her hip.

I laughed. I couldn't help it. Emma's game was a bit like taunting an angry gorilla through a flimsy window screen, but what can I say? She was fun to watch.

"You'll change your mind." Doug grinned and winked, walking backward away from us to keep Emma in his sight. He was a much better sport than I'd given him credit for.

"Not likely." Emma turned to her locker and threaded the padlock through the holes in the latch, then snapped it shut as Nash waved off several summonses from his friends, so he could hang out with me. And his mother. "Come on, pedestrians, where am I dropping you? Your place or his?"

"His," I answered so quickly Emma's brows shot up in amusement.

"Trouble at home?" She shrugged her backpack onto one shoulder as I grabbed mine from the floor, and we followed her down the hall in the opposite direction of the offensive line.

"No more than usual, but I have a lesson this afternoon." I left it vague because she knew what I was talking about.

Nash climbed into the back of Emma's metallic blue Sunfire and I took shotgun. Her car was far from new—it was a hand-me-down from one of her older sisters—yet it made mine look like an antique in comparison. However, the major advantage to Emma's vehicle over mine was that she was actually in possession of her keys.

I buckled as she pulled out of the lot onto a side street, barely glancing in her rearview mirror before changing lanes right in front of the first stoplight. "Give me a hint." Em glanced sideways at me, when she really should have had her eyes on the road. "Just a little one. Is someone else going to die? Is it another cheerleader?"

I laughed at her lighthearted inquisition.

"Maybe you should tell her," Tod's voice said out of nowhere, and I jumped so hard the seat belt cut into my neck.

"Stop doing that!" Nash shouted, and I turned to see Tod on the bench seat next to him, one finger pressed to his lips in an exaggerated "shh" signal, while his other hand pointed at Emma.

"Sorry!" she snapped, assuming Nash was talking to her. She swerved into the right-hand lane without bothering to flick on her turn signal, and the driver of the car behind us honked, gesturing angrily. "It's not like I'm actually wishing for more dead cheerleaders. I'm just saying, if *someone* has to go…"

Tod snorted. "I like her!"

Nash elbowed him in the side, and Emma raised both brows at

him in the rearview mirror. She'd seen the gesture, but couldn't see the reaper now holding his ribs, nor did she hear his *oof* of pain. "Sorry." Nash finally met her gaze. "I wasn't talking to you."

Her mouth opened, but I cut off a question I was sure we wouldn't be able to answer. "Em, go." I pointed out the windshield, where the cars in front of us had already driven through the intersection when the light turned green. The man behind us honked again, and Emma stomped on the gas. We lurched forward, and she forgot about Nash's odd behavior. At least for the moment.

"Does this have anything to do with Eden dropping dead onstage?"

I couldn't think of an answer fast enough, and Em's lighthearted smile died when she realized she'd actually hit the bull's-eye.

"Kaylee..." Tod said from the backseat.

"What's wrong?" I twisted so I could see all three of the other occupants.

"I just didn't see the light change." Emma slammed on the brake when the school bus in front of us slowed to a rumbling stop, the pop-out stop sign swinging away from its side.

Of course, I wasn't talking to her. I was talking to the uninvited, invisible reaper in her backseat.

"I can't get Addy and Regan alone long enough to explain the plan to them. They're constantly surrounded by this whole entourage. Assistants, and publicists, and Security, and their mother, who, by the way—" he turned to Nash "—hasn't changed one bit, except for a whole web of new wrinkles. She still has her nose in everything Addy does."

"Is there a point to this?" I looked from one brother to the other.

"A point to what?" Emma glanced in the rearview mirror

again to see what she was missing. "What is wrong with you guys today?"

"Sorry, Em." I turned to face her more directly. "It's—"

"*Bean sidhe* business. I know. And I'm getting pretty damn sick of the whole thing." She smacked the steering wheel with the heel of one palm, then swerved into a right-hand turn without even touching the brake.

I grabbed the door grip, but she only stomped on the gas again before the wheel even straightened out. "I lied to your dad last night, and I got stuck in the ticket booth with Glen 'the human sprinkler' Frank for *four hours* yesterday. And I've driven you around today like your own personal chauffeur. The least you could do is explain why you two are acting so weird."

Sighing, I glanced at Nash, then pointedly at Tod, raising my brows in question. *Should we tell her?*

He shrugged, leaving the decision up to me. She was my best friend.

I shifted to face Emma, exhaling slowly. "I don't want you mixed up in all this. It's dangerous."

She rolled her eyes, and when she turned to look at me, she accidently turned the wheel, too, and the front right tire scraped the curb. Emma didn't seem to notice. "I'm not asking to go with you on some kind of scary field trip. I just hate being in the dark all the time."

I knew exactly how she felt, but before I could say anything, Tod shrugged at me, blue eyes shining in mischief. "Sounds like she wants to help. Ask if we can borrow her car. Preferably before she drives it into the side of a building…"

"No!" Nash and I snapped in unison. Then, before Emma could get even angrier, I glared at Tod. "Show her."

"You sure?" He frowned, no doubt thinking of my standing order for him to stay as far from Emma as possible, and never to let her see him. I didn't want death getting a crush on my best friend.

"Yeah, I'm sure."

"Wha—" Emma started. Then she squealed, and her eyes went huge as she stared into the rearview mirror in total shock. I grabbed the wheel when her hands fell away from it, trying to keep us on the right side of the road while her foot got heavier and heavier on the gas.

"*Told* you this was a bad idea," Tod said from the backseat, as Nash growled wordlessly at him in frustration.

"Em!" I yelled. "Hit the brake!" We were racing toward a four-way stop, where a group of tweens waited to cross the road on bicycles.

"Who...? How...?" She blinked, then actually twisted to look into the backseat, and the car lurched forward even faster when she braced herself against the gas pedal instead of the floorboard.

"Emma, stop!" I shouted, and she whirled around and stomped on the brake, bringing us to a screeching halt two feet from the crosswalk.

"Okay, we probably shouldn't have done that while she was actually driving." Nash studied her profile in concern.

"You call that driving?" Tod crossed his arms casually over his chest as if we hadn't nearly flattened three kids and totaled Emma's car.

The tweens rode their bikes across the street, glaring at us through the windshield. The last one flipped us off, then tossed long, purple-striped hair over his shoulder and rode off, standing on his pedals.

In the driver's seat, Emma sat frozen, staring wide-eyed into the rearview mirror. Her chest rose and fell heavily with each breath, and her hands shook on the wheel.

"Want me to drive?" I offered, laying one hand on her arm.

She shook her head without taking her gaze from Tod. "I want you to tell me what the hell just happened. Who is he, and how did he get in my car?"

"Okay, but we can't sit here forever." Another car had stopped behind us at the four-way, already honking. "Pull into the lot up there and we'll explain." *Part of it, anyway.*

Emma forced her attention from the rearview mirror with obvious effort. "This is part of your *bean sidhe* business? Who *is* that?" She glanced quickly at Tod again, as she drove slowly through the intersection.

Nash braced his arm on the back of my seat, steeling himself for something he obviously didn't want to say. "Emma, this is my brother. Tod." Calm flowed with his words, and I could tell the moment it hit Emma, because her shoulders relaxed, and her grip on the wheel loosened just a bit.

"You have a… Wait." She turned the car smoothly into a small lot in front of a park full of preschoolers and their parents, then pulled into the first empty spot, facing the road. Emma cut the engine and twisted onto her knees to peer over the back of her seat. "You have a brother?" she said to Nash, after a quick glance at me for confirmation. No one from Eastlake High knew about Nash's dead brother, because he and Harmony had moved—and changed schools—after the funeral two years earlier. "And he can…what? Teleport into strange cars? Is that a *bean sidhe* ability?"

"No…" I started, trying to decide how much to tell her. But then the reaper took that decision right out of my hands, in classic Tod-style.

"Okay, we're kind of on a tight schedule here, so let's get this over with…."

"Tod—" Nash snapped, but his brother held up one hand and rushed on before either of us could stop him.

"I'm a *bean sidhe*, just like Nash and Kaylee. Except that I'm dead. Teleportation—never really heard it called that—isn't a *bean sidhe* ability. It's a reaper ability. I'm a grim reaper. I can appear wherever I want, whenever I want, and I can choose who sees and hears me." He hesitated, and I wondered if my face could possibly be as red as Nash's. Or my eyes as wide as Emma's.

"You're Nash's brother. And a *grim reaper?*" She blinked again, and I readied myself for hysterics, or fear, or laughter. But knowing Emma, I should have known better. "So you, what? Kill people? Did you kill me that day in the gym?" She clenched the headrest, her expression an odd mix of anger, awe, and confusion. But there was no disbelief. She'd seen and heard enough of the bizarre following her own temporary death that Tod's admission obviously didn't come as that much of a surprise.

Or maybe Nash's Influence was still affecting her a little.

"No." Tod shook his head firmly, but the corners of his mouth turned up in amusement. "I had nothing to do with that. I do kill people, then I reap their souls and take them to be recycled. But only people who are on my list."

"So, you're not…dangerous?"

His pouty grin deepened into something almost predatory, like the Tod I'd first met two months earlier. "Oh, I'm dangerous…."

"Tod…" I warned, as Nash punched his brother in the arm, hard enough to actually hurt.

"Just not to you," the reaper finished, shrugging at Emma. "I see you all the time, but you've never seen me, because Kaylee said if I got too close to you, I'd suffer eternity without my balls."

"Jeez, Tod!" I shouted, my anger threatening to boil over and scald us all.

The reaper leaned closer to Emma and spoke in a stage whisper. "She's not as scary as she thinks she is, but I respect her intent."

Em looked like she didn't know whether to laugh or cry, and I rolled my eyes at Tod. "Do you have to be so difficult?"

He shrugged and leaned back in his seat. "You wanted me to show her, so I showed her. Now ask her if we can borrow her car so I can get back to my part in the plan."

"Borrowing a car *was* your part of the plan, and we are not taking Emma's." Even if she was willing to lend it to us, I wasn't willing to ask. I wanted as little contact between her and the Netherworld as possible.

And I was already regretting asking Tod to show himself.

"Wait, why do you need my car?" Emma glanced from Tod to Nash, then to me.

"Kaylee's dad took her keys," the reaper said.

"We don't need your car." I glared at Tod. "Though, we really appreciate you taking us to Nash's house. Assuming you're not completely freaked out by all this."

"Oh, I'm totally freaked." Emma smiled slowly, and I wondered how deep her shock went. "But I asked, right? Besides, this isn't much weirder than you and Nash bringing people back to life. Not really." As if she were trying to convince herself. "And it's much better than listening to you talk to people who aren't there. Or yell at me." She raised one brow at me. "You were yelling at him, not me, right?"

"Yes." I returned her hesitant smile easily. "We yell at Tod a lot."

"I can see why. So…" She glanced at all three of us again. "You need to borrow my car?"

"Yes," Tod said, just as Nash and I said, "No."

"Look." Tod turned a dark look my way. "Everyone I know is dead, and has no use for a car. Except Mom, and she needs hers to get to work tonight. So either you let me take one, let me get your keys back from your dad, or we borrow Emma's car. Those are the options."

"What about Addy?" I demanded, before Emma could break in and volunteer her car. And that's exactly what she would have done. I recognized the gleam of curiosity in her eyes, and I knew that if we used her car, she'd insist on coming with us. And that could not happen. "You can't tell me Addy doesn't have a car."

"She doesn't." Tod scowled, and I got the distinct impression he was a little irritated with his pop princess. "She never got her license, because there's always someone else around to take her wherever she wants to go. Which poses a whole new problem. If we can't get some time alone with her, whether or not we can find a car won't matter."

"Who's Addy?" Emma asked.

"No one." I glared at Tod to keep him from contradicting me. "Just some girl Tod has a crush on."

"It's not a crush," he spat, as if the word burned his tongue. "I'm trying to save her life."

"Not really her *life*," I corrected, when Emma's brow wrinkled in worry. She knew that each life had a price, and I couldn't let her think we were willing to kill some likely innocent bystander to save Tod's girlfriend. "We're trying to save her soul."

"What's wrong with her soul?" Emma asked Tod, having obviously come to the conclusion that he was her best source of information.

The reaper shrugged. "Nothing. She's just not actually in possession of it. At the moment."

"Whoooa…" Emma sank back into her seat slowly, her expression bleak, and I realized that somehow she understood the gravity of what she'd just heard, though she wasn't privy to the whole story. And if I had my way, she wouldn't be. "I get off at eight. My car's yours after that."

"Emma, no." I shook my head, one hand gripping the side of my headrest, but she only shook hers back at me. "Thanks, but…"

"You need the car. Take the car. Don't let some poor girl lose her soul because you were too stubborn to drive a loaner."

I sighed and closed my eyes briefly before giving in with a short nod, despite my better judgment. "Thanks, Em."

"You're welcome." Her smile grew, and her eyes glinted with mischief eerily similar to what I usually saw in Tod's. "And you're buying your own gas. Unless you let me tag along…"

"No." I smiled, to soften the blow. "It's too dangerous. And if you argue, I won't take your car."

"Yeah, I figured. Okay, let's go. I have to be at the Cinemark by four." Emma straightened in her seat and started the car again. "Though, how I'm supposed to serve popcorn for four hours after this, I have no idea...."

14

"Hey, come on in." Harmony Hudson held the front door propped open for us before we'd even made it out of the car. "What's wrong with Emma?"

Nash glanced back at her as he crossed the dead grass, and I followed his gaze to find Emma looking a little dazed as she locked her car, as if what she'd learned had finally truly sunk in. The reaper had disappeared entirely.

"She just met Tod." I stepped into Nash's dark, warm living room and dropped my bag on the floor by the couch.

"Aah…" Harmony smiled knowingly as Emma stepped onto the porch. "You're going to need some processed sugar. Come on in and have a cookie."

Emma didn't even try to resist. She'd had enough of Harmony's treats to know better than to turn down the offer, even though she was already running late for work, thanks to our short detour.

Harmony closed the front door and followed us into the kitchen, where we gathered around the island and a plate of still-warm chocolate cookies, glittering under the fluorescent lights with a sprinkling of granulated sugar.

"I swear, Harmony, if you don't stop baking, I won't be able to fit in my own car. Assuming I ever get it back." I let my backpack slide to the floor while I bit into the cookie, surprised to discover a sweetened-peanut-butter center. "I'm sorry my dad bugged you last night," I said around another mouthful. "He totally overreacted."

"You know, it wouldn't hurt you to check in with him every now and then, to keep him from worrying." Nash's mom reached across the island to smack her son's shoulder. "You, too. You have a cell phone for a reason."

Nash shrugged and avoided answering by shoving an entire cookie into his mouth. But I felt obligated to answer.

"He's my dad. He's going to worry no matter what I do." And part of me was grateful that he was concerned over something legitimate, rather than something stupid, like the lead content of my shampoo bottle. But the other part of me couldn't quite escape the irony. For the past thirteen years, he hadn't even known when my curfew was, and now he'd gone all father-of-the-year.

Before Addy'd called, we were on track to get home before anyone expected us. If I'd known what was going to happen, I'd have called my dad, even if only to make up a reason I'd be late. But after Addy's call, things had moved so fast I'd honestly forgotten I had a cell, much less a curfew.

"Mmm," Emma groaned around her first bite, and I swear her eyes nearly rolled back into her head. "Can I take one for the road?"

Harmony beamed and immediately began rooting through one of the island drawers. "I'll pack several for you."

Emma left five minutes later, armed with a paper bag of pea-nut-butter-surprise cookies and a private promise to meet us in Nash's driveway at midnight. His mom would already be at work, and surely my dad would be asleep by then. Assuming I didn't wake him sneaking out of the house.

With Emma gone, Harmony sent Nash to his room with a

plateful of cookies and a strong suggestion that he take advantage
of the privacy to do some homework.

When his Xbox whirred to life a minute later, we shared an
eye roll. Nash would leave his homework until the last possible
moment, and likely only half finish it. And he'd still manage
straight Bs. If he'd ever actually applied himself, he could probably have been valedictorian.

Harmony poured soda over ice in two glasses, then gestured
with a nod of her head for me to grab a couple of cookies on our
way into the living room. "Your dad knows you're here, right?"
She sipped from her glass as she walked backward through the
swinging door, to hold it open for me.

"Yeah. These lessons were his idea. He says arming myself
with information is the best way to avoid trouble. Or something
like that." A fact I'd reminded him of when he threatened to
make me come straight home from school.

With any luck, he wouldn't guess that the knowledge I was
about to arm myself with could get me into more trouble than
he could possibly imagine.

Hopefully it would be enough to get us all out of trouble, too.

I had a vague plan for how to get Harmony to teach me what
we needed to know, and to make her think it was her idea.
Reverse psychology. It only works on preschoolers and adults.

"We could just skip today's lesson and gorge on junk food
instead." I sank onto the couch and set the napkin-wrapped
bundle of cookies on the coffee table. "We don't have to tell my
dad."

The shades of blue in Harmony's irises churned languidly, and
her frown looked impossibly cute for an eighty-two-year-old
woman. But then again, she was holding up remarkably well
for an octogenarian. "Kaylee, you need to learn about your *bean
sidhe* heritage and your abilities. I'd hate for you to stumble into
something by accident later, like you did with Belphegore."

"Oh, I won't. Not now that I know what I am. And it's not

like I'm ever going to use any of this, right?" I shrugged, but inside I flinched from her hurt look. "I mean, I already know how to hold back my wail, and that's all I really need, right?" I hated feigning disinterest in what she had to show me, when I was really very curious. And I hated it even worse that I sounded ungrateful for her help. But Addy's and Regan's souls depended on making Harmony want to teach me something my father wouldn't approve of. Something she'd normally never show me.

"You never know, Kaylee." She drank from her glass again, probably to hide her disappointment, which had virtually erased the deep dimples from her cheeks. "Emergencies happen, and you might need to know how to go to the Netherworld someday, instead of just peeking into it."

I frowned, showcasing my hesitance as I chewed my last bite of cookie. "Isn't that dangerous?"

She shrugged and pushed up the sleeves of her snug lilac sweater. "Unsupervised, yes. But the risk would be pretty minimal if we cross over from here."

"Because human houses don't exist in the Netherworld?" I was thinking of what she'd told me on Sunday.

"That's true, but Netherworlders do have homes of their own, and if you cross over without knowing where you'll come out, you could wind up somewhere you don't want to be."

I was betting that was a pretty big understatement.

"Can't we just peek in and see what's here on the Netherworld plane?"

"Kind of." Harmony sat straighter; she was perking up now that I was openly curious. "When you peek into the Netherworld from here, or vice versa, you're seeing the two realities layered, one over the other. That can be really confusing if you aren't used to mentally sorting out what you're seeing. You could easily overlook something important. Or dangerous."

"So, how do you know it's safe to cross over from your

house?" I asked, then let my brows rise in eagerness. "You've done it, haven't you? Where would we wind up?"

Harmony set her glass on the end table, then met my gaze frankly. "Yes, I've done it. I had to cross over when we first moved here, to make sure it was safe in case of an emergency. I still do it periodically, to make sure nothing's changed."

"What could change?"

She shrugged. "The landscape there evolves, just like ours does, based on the needs of the populace."

"So, is it safe?"

She smiled, obviously enjoying my interest. "Yes, it's safe. Comparatively speaking, anyway. This spot in the Nether-world—" she spread her arms to take in her entire house "—is... unoccupied. But, Kaylee, things are different there. It's like a warped reflection of our world. Everything is skewed, like the world kind of *shifted* after everything was built."

I knew exactly what she meant, though I'd never actually been to the Netherworld, because I'd seen the things that lived there. They were skewed, too. Disproportionate, like images stretched or squished in carnival mirrors. I could only imagine what their surroundings must look like.

And I only *wanted* to imagine. But my imagination wouldn't get the Page sisters back their souls. Or get me out of my house if my father didn't go to bed at a decent hour...

"Have you ever crossed over from my house?" My heart thumped painfully as I said the words. She'd see through my question. She'd know what I was up to. She'd tell my dad, and it would all be over. Addy would die soulless, and Regan would follow her sister, whenever her time came.

But Harmony only cocked her head to one side, frowning at me as the unpleasant possibilities occurred to her. "Only once. Why?"

I thought quickly, and went with a half truth. "It creeps me out to think that someone else—some weird Netherworld family—could be living in an alternate version of my house. What if I have one of those emergencies and have to cross over? I'd rather know what I was getting into before I actually get there. To make sure it's safe." I quoted her own words back to her, and Harmony's bright blue eyes darkened for a moment, before clearing like the sky after a summer storm.

I admired her control. Her perseverance. Harmony had picked herself up and pieced her life together twice, after the deaths of both her husband and her oldest son, and she still found enough of herself to share with people who needed her. To protect both me and Nash, and by extension, Emma, Addy, and Regan.

"You don't have to worry about that." She handed me the cookie she had yet to taste, as if a little sugar really could make everything all better. "The Netherworld is much more sparsely populated than our world," she continued as I bit into the cookie. "So it's not like every house here represents a house there. If you crossed over from home, you'd find overgrown fields, with buildings in the distance, in the direction of our downtown district. Very similar to what you'd see if you crossed over from here."

Good. I kept chewing to disguise my exhalation of relief.

"But, Kaylee, that doesn't mean you should try it." She was solemn now, blue eyes glittering with urgent warning. "The Netherworld is dangerous, especially for *bean sidhes,* and you should never go there unless you literally have no other choice."

I could only nod. "But if I needed to? If I had that emergency?" I paused and met her eyes, letting mine shine with equal parts eagerness and careful dread. As if I wanted the knowledge but hoped never to have to use it. Which was totally true; my fear was real enough to pass scrutiny. "You said it works just like peeking, right?"

"Yeah." She held her glass in both hands and leaned back against the arm of the couch, looking easily a quarter of her actual age with one foot tucked beneath her slim leg. "The difference is in the intent. If you call your wail on purpose, like you learned to do on Monday, but with the intent of going to the Netherworld, rather than just peeking in, you'll cross over." She set her glass down again and sat straighter, as if to underline the importance of whatever she was about to say. "It's frighteningly simple, Kaylee. The most important thing to learn is how *not* to go, when you just want to peek, because once you've crossed over that first time, your body remembers how. And sometimes it seems like *it* wants to be there, even if you don't."

Okay, that's *scary.* I shivered with a sudden surge of fear that left chills the length of my arms.

"Which is why we're not going to try it." Harmony leaned back again, and her usual pleasant smile was in place. "I think theoretical knowledge is enough for now."

I found myself nodding, even though I really needed the actual experience. "Once you're there, do you get back the same way? By wailing with the intent to go home?"

Harmony nodded. "But, Kaylee, this knowledge is for emergencies only. I can't emphasize that enough." I nodded, but she continued. "Do not go sightseeing in the Netherworld. You practically shine with youth and vitality, and that will attract… people. Netherworlders."

Aaaand, it gets even creepier….

"Don't worry." I exhaled and smiled to set her at ease. "I don't go around looking for danger." Yet somehow, it always seems to find me….

"I know."

She drank the rest of her soda and we sat in silence for nearly a minute, listening to the canned fight sounds from Nash's room. Then, though I was more on edge than I wanted to admit by what I'd already learned, I played my last card, desperate for that remaining piece of information.

"Since you checked to make sure it was safe to cross over from here, my dad probably did the same thing, right? Crossed over from our house to make sure it's safe?"

Harmony grinned like I'd just asked her to explain the difference between boys and girls. "Not exactly," she said, still smiling. "Your dad can't cross over on his own." Which I'd already known, thanks to Tod. "So I took him. Humans and male *bean sidhes* can't cross over without a female *bean sidhe's* wail."

"Oh," I let my eyes widen in surprise and concern. "What if we have an emergency and we both need to cross over? How can I do that? Take him with me?"

I didn't think she'd answer. I truly didn't. And she probably wouldn't have, if not for the obvious guilt she felt over having scared the crap out of me with the knowledge that I might someday have to abandon my father in a burning building because he can't cross over.

"You just have to be holding on to him when you cross over, and he'll come with you. That's the same way it works with whatever you're holding or wearing. Which is what keeps you from showing up naked in the Netherworld." Harmony grinned at her own joke, and I forced a laugh to let her know I wasn't totally freaked out.

"You two about done?" Nash asked, and I looked up to find him watching us from their short, dark hallway. He glanced pointedly at his watch, then at me. "It's nearly four-thirty. What time are you supposed to be home?"

"My dad'll probably call to check on me soon. You know, to make sure I'm not having any fun or acting like a teenager." I stood and picked up my backpack, and Harmony stood, too. She got the message.

"Go easy on your father. He's pretty new at this."

"I know." But that was his fault. He'd had the past thirteen years to reestablish his role in my life after my mother died, and so far, late was proving to be only marginally better than never. "Walk me home?" I asked Nash, already headed for the door.

"Love to."

"Thanks for the cookies, Harmony. And the lesson," I added, still trying to make up for acting like I didn't care about her efforts to help me.

"No problem." She headed toward the kitchen with both empty glasses. "And, Nash, please don't linger. I doubt hanging out with you is on Kaylee's list of approved activities at the moment."

That was an understatement, considering that whatever my dad thought I'd been doing, he knew I'd been doing it with Nash.

Nash rolled his eyes at his mom and held the screen door open as I stuffed both arms into my jacket sleeves, then took the backpack he held for me. "Bye, Mom…"

We didn't hear her reply, because the door closed behind us, and we were already walking hand in hand, in spite of the cold numbing my fingers. We walked in comfortable silence, and I opened my own front door with a key ring conspicuously missing my car key. Nash came inside, in spite of his mother's warning.

"Want a snack?" I shrugged out of my jacket and backpack and let them fall onto the couch, and when I looked up, Nash was there, so close I caught my breath.

"I want you." His eyes smoldered, and his lips came apart a tiny bit. Just enough to make me want to fill that gap with my own. To taste his lower lip, and leave a trail of kisses over the stubble on his jaw and down his neck.

"Mmm," I murmured as his lips found the hollow below my ear, and vaguely I realized that was the same sound Emma had made when she bit into her first cookie.

Nash was just as delicious, in a completely unsatisfying way. Unsatisfying, because no matter how much time we spent together, no matter how closely I pressed myself against him, I always wanted more.

But what if more was too much for me, and just enough for him? That fear lingered, that secret certainty that if I slept with Nash—if I gave us both what we wanted—he would move on in pursuit of the next challenge. It had happened before, over and over again. The list of his past conquests was long and distinguished, at least by Eastlake standards.

I couldn't put my paranoia to bed. In fact, it grew with every groan he let slip, because they told me how badly he wanted me. But what if wanting me was like waiting for popcorn to pop, or coffee to brew? They both smelled so good, but the taste could never live up to such delectable scents. And neither made a very satisfying meal.

What if I was the sexual equivalent of popcorn? Suitable for light snacking only?

Nash's lips met mine, and I pushed those fears away. I opened for him, sucking his tongue into my mouth, tasting it. He leaned into me, and we would have fallen onto the cushions if he hadn't braced his hand against the back of the couch. He shoved my backpack and jacket to the floor, then lowered me gently, slowly. With infuriating patience.

Even drowning in my own doubts, I had no patience.

He settled over me, hips pressing into me, chest heavy on mine, holding himself up on one elbow. His knee slid between mine and I gasped, sucking air from him. Heat rose from the pit of my stomach, tingling all the way up. He tasted so good. Felt so good. And I understood him in a way no human girl ever could.

Surely he knew that…

Nash's lips trailed down my neck, setting off a series of tingly explosions, adrenaline pumping through my heart. My hand clenched the tail of his shirt, then I pushed it up, trailing my fingers over his stomach.

And in that moment, I became a fan of football, for the simple fact that it had literally shaped him. I couldn't resist running my hands around to his back as it twisted and bunched beneath my fingers. He was strength personified, and simply touching him made me stronger. Harder. More capable of everything ahead of us.

If I had Nash, I could do it. I could do anything.

The phone rang, and Nash groaned into my ear, his breath a puff of warm frustration fueling my own. "Your dad?"

"Probably."

He collapsed on me, pinning me to the couch momentarily as the phone rang again, and I didn't want to move. Didn't want him to get up. He had to, of course, but he did it slooowly, sliding off me one delicious inch at a time until he sat on the floor beside the couch, one hand flat over my stomach.

I arched one arm over my head and grabbed the phone, moving as little of my body as possible. "Hello?"

"I take it you're at home?" my father said as metal clanged in the background.

"I answered the phone, didn't I?" I closed my eyes in regret; my answer had come out harsher than I'd intended, my voice sharpened by irritation at having been interrupted.

My dad sighed, and I heard hurt in his exhalation. "Is Nash there?"

"He walked me home."

He sighed again and raised his voice. "Nash, go home."

Nash scowled. "I was…just going."

"Say hi to your mom," my father said. Then there was only silence and the clang of more metal over the line, and I realized he was waiting for Nash to leave. Right then.

"Um, I will." Nash stood and leaned down to kiss my cheek, the most he would do with my father there, even if only in spirit. And in voice. "See you later, Kaylee," he said, then closed the door on his way out.

"Happy?" I snapped into the phone. I wasn't sorry that time.

"No, Kaylee. I'm not happy. I'll be home by seven-thirty with dinner. What do you want from the Chinese place?"

I bit my lip to keep from saying something I'd regret later. Likely much later. "Shrimp fried rice. Want me to call it in?"

"That would be great. Thanks." He hung up, and I stared at the empty living room, wishing I knew of some way I could get along with my father *and* save Addy's soul. But so far, the two seemed to be mutually exclusive. Fortunately, it would all be over in a matter of hours, and my life would go back to normal.

Assuming I survived the night.

≪ 15 ≫

My dad walked in the front door at seven twenty-four, carrying a white paper bag and smelling of metal and sweat. He looked awful. Exhausted. I felt bad for him. And really guilty.

After my mother died and I'd been handed over to my aunt and uncle, my father had gone to Ireland to run the pub his parents owned. He'd made a decent living, but most of his extra money went to pay for my incidentals and to fund my college account. So when he came back to the States, he'd brought nothing but a suitcase and enough cash to put down a deposit on a rental house and buy a second used car—I still had the one he'd bought me for my sixteenth birthday.

Now he worked in a factory all day, taking overtime where he could get it, because he thought he should at least try to make as much money as his brother did.

I didn't care about the money. A little money only made people want more of it. And I liked our used furniture, because if I spilled on it, no one got mad, which meant I could snack in the living room, in front of the television. But my father insisted we eat dinner together every night. Our crappy kitchen card table was the magic wand he kept waving to turn us into a real family. But on some nights, all that magic seemed to do was irritate and frustrate us both.

And still he tried....

"I got some fried wontons." He set the greasy bag on the card table and draped his jacket over the back of a folding metal chair.

"Thanks." He knew they were my favorite. He knew all my favorite takeout, because he rarely had time to cook, and I didn't care if I never ate another bite of homemade health food after living with Aunt Val for thirteen years.

We ate in near silence, except for the occasional intrusion upon my thoughts when he asked if I'd done my homework— yes—and how Nash and Harmony were doing—fine. He never asked about Tod, which was just as well, because if he had, he'd know from my answer that I'd been hanging out with the reaper, too. And that would just make him even angrier, and more worried.

"How long is it going to be like this?" my dad asked as I pushed back my chair and tossed my paper plate into the plastic trash bin. "How long are you going to be mad?"

"I'm not mad." I trudged into the living room and shoved my trig and history books into my backpack, the corresponding homework assignments folded in half inside them. "I just..." *Have things I can't tell you. Things you could probably help me with. But you won't. So talking does us no good.* "I have stuff on my mind. It has nothing to do with you."

I wanted to explain that things would get better. He would stop trying so hard—start realizing I was sixteen, not six—and eventually he'd understand that Nash was keeping me out of trouble, not getting me into it. When that happened, we could both relax. Maybe he could even tell me about my mother without tearing up and making some excuse to stop talking.

But not yet. None of that could happen while I was still helping Addy and Regan behind his back. Because he knew something was wrong, and he couldn't move beyond that until it was resolved, and I couldn't look him in the eye until I was done lying.

Soon, though. It would be soon.

My dad fell asleep in his recliner shortly after eleven, and he sat there snoring for several minutes before I thought to turn off the television. I could only stare at him from the couch, boiling with frustration.

He was supposed to fall asleep in his bed, not in the living room!

I could wake him up and tell him to go to bed. That would still leave more than half an hour for him to go back to sleep before I had to leave for Nash's. But the last time I'd done that, he'd decided he wasn't ready for bed yet, and he'd stayed up to watch some stupid action movie until after midnight.

I could leave him where he was and hope he didn't check on me when he went to bed. But then I'd run the risk of waking him when I opened the front door. Because the window in my room was painted shut, and the screen on the back door squealed like a pissed-off harpy.

That only left my backup plan, which I'd really hoped to avoid.

My dad's bedroom door stood open, and I saw my cell phone on his nightstand, all alone and sad-looking. He'd never know if I took it, and I'd have a safety net in case something went horribly wrong while I was out.

I took my phone—I was too big of a wimp to walk into something so dangerous without a safety net—then stared at myself in the mirror over my dresser, wondering if I had the courage to do what needed to be done. I tucked a strand of straight brown hair behind my ear and wondered if my irises were swirling. I couldn't see them myself, but if Nash were there, would he see the shades of blue twisting with the fear that pulsed through my veins, leaving icicles in its wake, threatening to shatter with my next movement. Could I walk into the Netherworld like I belonged there? Could I demand an audience with a hellion and offer him a trade?

Even if I could, would I survive such an audience? And if I did, what was I opening myself up to? It seemed like an extraordinarily bad idea to bring myself to a demon's attention. Pretty much the opposite of my dad's lay-low-to-survive philosophy.

At least I wouldn't be alone. I'd have Nash and Tod. Assuming I survived sneaking out of my own house.

What should I take?

Something that would actually function in the Netherworld. Traveling light seemed wise, but did I really want to step into another reality carrying nothing but a useless phone and some pocket lint? I slid my pitifully incomplete key ring into my pocket. Cash would do me no good in the Netherworld—Nash said they spent other, unthinkable currency—but it might come in handy before we crossed over.

A small stone box on my dresser held everything of tangible value I owned: my mother's engagement ring and the forty-eight dollars left over from my last paycheck. I stuffed the bills into my front pocket. Usually a small lump of cash felt reassuring; it represented emergency gas money, or bus fare home, should I need it. But this time I still felt woefully unprepared to face the world with so little going for me.

What I really needed was a weapon. Unfortunately, the most dangerous thing in the entire house was my dad's butcher knife, and something told me that wouldn't be much use against anything I ran into in the Netherworld.

I pulled my hair into a ponytail and shrugged into my jacket, then pronounced myself ready to go. At least, as ready as I was going to be.

My heart beat fiercely, and suddenly my throat felt too thick to breathe through. My father would wake up if I tried to unbolt and unchain the front door, but there was no telling what *else* I'd wake up if I crossed into the Netherworld. Harmony said there'd just be an empty field, but what if she was wrong? What if things had changed since she'd last crossed over?

I shook off fear, forcing my spine straight and my head up. The best way to enter the lion's den is one step at a time.

With that, I dove into my remembrance of death. It was like tumbling headfirst into a pool of grief and horror, and at first, it seemed I would sink. I would drown in sorrow. Then I forced my heartache into focus, scrambling desperately for a handle on my own emotion. *Sophie. Emma.* And finally my mother—what little I could remember of her. The memories of their soul songs bubbled up inside me. Darkness enveloped me, and sound leaked from my throat.

I pressed my lips together to keep it from bursting forth in a silence-shattering wail of grief and misery. If my father heard me keening—or singing, from his perspective—it was all over. So I swallowed the sound, like Harmony had taught me. Forced it down and into my heart, where the echo resonated within me, hammering at my fragile self-control, clawing at my insides.

It was easier this time, just like she'd promised. Or rather, like she'd warned. I could see the Netherworld haze blooming before me, a gray filter laid over my room, covering my bed, my dresser, and my desk in various shades of gloom. Now I only had to add intent to my wail.

Whatever that meant…

I intend to cross over, I thought, closing my eyes. When I opened them, my room was still gray, and still just as *there* as it had been a moment before.

It would be so much easier if there were a secret password, or handshake. *Netherworld, open sesame!*

Yeah, that didn't work, either.

I closed my eyes again, careful to keep the wail deep in my throat—all but one slim curl of sound that wound its way up and into the room, like a thin ribbon of Netherworld energy being pulled through me and into the human plane. If I could just follow it, like a bread-crumb trail, I was sure it would lead me where I needed to go.

Where I was already going…

The background hum of the refrigerator faded and cool air brushed my face. I opened my eyes and gasped so suddenly I choked on my own keening. I coughed, and the thin stream of sound ended in a wet gurgle.

My room was gone. As was the whole house. The walls, the doors, the furniture. All gone. My father, too.

I stood in the middle of a large field of some kind of grass I didn't recognize. It grew tall enough that the thin seed clusters on top brushed my elbows, and I knew without taking a single step that it would be a pain to walk through.

I ran my fingers over the grains, surprised by the rough, whispering sound they made against my skin. The stalks were stiff and brittle, and oddly cold to the touch, as if they were nourished by a chill wind rather than by the sun. And they weren't green or even fall-brown like the November-hued grass was in my world. The entire field was an earthy olive color, with shades of deep umber near the base of the stalks.

Curious, I bent one seed cluster and nearly jumped out of my own skin when it broke with an audible *snap* and shattered between my fingers. It didn't crumble. It splintered into hundreds of tiny, cold plant shards. The slivers tinkled like tiny bells as they fell, brushing the other stalks on the way down.

One sharp grass shard got caught with its point through the weave of my jeans. When I tried to brush it off, I accidently pushed the splinter deeper, flinching when the tiny point jabbed my skin. I used my fingernails like tweezers to pull it out carefully, and was surprised to see a little dot of blood staining my jeans.

Stupid sharp grass had cut me! *This gives all new meaning to the phrase "blades of grass…."*

I looked up slowly, then turned to see as much as I could of the grass surrounding me without breaking any more stalks. I was in the middle of the field, at least a hundred feet from the nearest edge, which was in front of me. I couldn't walk through the grass without getting shredded in the process.

Crap! When Harmony said the Netherworld was dangerous, I'd thought she'd meant the residents!

I glanced around at my foreign surroundings, hoping for inspiration from the scenery. What I could see of the Netherworld was beautiful, in a dark, eerie way. The night sky was a deep, bruised purple streaked with ailing shades of blue and green, as if the earth had beaten its canopy into submission.

The slim crescent of a moon was dark red, like the harvest moon after a slaughter, and its sharp points seemed to pierce the sky, rather than to grace it. It was beautiful-scary, but absolutely no help in getting me out of the field. I could *not* make it across one hundred feet of fragile glass spires without getting all sliced up.

But maybe I wouldn't need to….

I only had to stay in the Netherworld long enough to get out of my house, to keep from waking my dad.

Would it have killed Harmony to mention that the plant life in the Netherworld was painful?

Okay, Kaylee, focus…. How far was it from my room to the side yard outside my window?

Before I'd crossed over, I was standing in front of my mirror. I closed my eyes and visualized turning, then crossing my narrow room toward the far wall.

Ten steps, give or take. If I could make it eight feet to my right, I'd wind up just outside my bedroom window. Assuming I didn't misjudge and cross over inside the brick wall…

Better go nine feet, to be safe.

I took a deep breath and lifted my arms to keep them from brushing the grass stalks and getting chewed up. Then I slid my right foot to the side, one step.

Four glasslike stalks shattered as my foot went through them. They collapsed to rain sharp chunks of Netherworld vegetation on my leg, and those chunks shattered even further. But the damage to my body was minimal, because I didn't try to brush the shards off.

On my left, something growled softly, and a slithering sound approached from near the ground. Ten feet away, several stalks shook without breaking.

My pulse raced, and I began to sweat in spite of the cold. A stray strand from my ponytail fell over my eyes, and I brushed it back, on alert for more movement or noise from the ground around me. But there was none, at least for the moment.

I moved quickly after that, shuffling sideways through the grass, pausing after each step to let the vegetation settle and to make sure I hadn't been cut very badly. More dry rustling met my ears, and was followed by a quick, nausea-inducing burst of panic. But I saw no more movement.

Plants crunched beneath my shoes, and I soon learned to angle my right foot so that the stalks fell away from me, rather than on me. The slithering noises continued, like a dark echo from some panicked part of my brain, and I moved in the opposite direction, praying that whatever was making those sounds wouldn't pounce. Or bite. Or whatever.

Ten steps later, I was sure I'd gone far enough. I closed my eyes and stuck my fingers in my ears to block out sights and sounds of the Netherworld, unconcerned with how stupid I must look.

I wanted to look stupid in my own yard.

The wail came even easier this time, and rather than worrying about that, I reveled in it, grateful that I didn't have to fight for concentration with that slither-creature sliding toward me. Intent wasn't hard to come by that time, either. I seriously wanted to go home. Just in time to sneak out.

I kept my eyes open, and was amazed to see the Netherworld

simply fade around me, going first gray, then insubstantial. The sharp stalks blurred, then finally disappeared, and I found myself standing in short, dead grass, a mere six inches or so from the brick wall of the house and my bedroom window.

Oops, cut that one kind of close. Though, I'd gone two extra steps, just to be sure. Were distances skewed in the Netherworld?

My brain danced around the possible implications of that thought, but then I shook it off. I had to get to Nash's.

I spared a moment to pluck the obvious shards of Netherworld grass from my jeans, vaguely frightened that they hadn't simply faded from existence with the rest of the Nether. Then I zipped up my jacket and took off toward Nash's house at a jog, hoping the remaining slivers would shake free with the movement.

Any other night, I would have been nervous to be out alone, but after several minutes in the Netherworld, edging my way through a field of deadly grass to get away from something slithering through the stalks after me, nighttime in the human-world seemed downright welcoming.

I was breathing hard by the time I got to Nash's house, where he, Tod, and Emma were piling into her car. "Leaving without me?" I panted, leaning with my hands on my knees to catch my breath.

"Kaylee, jeez, you scared me!" Emma cried, loud enough that if any of the neighbors had been awake, they'd have heard her.

"We weren't leaving without you." Nash greeted me with a tame kiss on the tip of my nose, a greeting that spoke of relief, rather than heat. "We were coming to find you."

I wrapped my arm around his waist, pressing into him to share his warmth. "I'm only a couple of minutes…" My voice trailed off as I glanced at my watch. It was twelve thirty-five. I'd left my room around eleven fifty-five, and it had taken me no more than ten minutes to jog from my house to Nash's. And I'd spent less than five minutes in the Netherworld. I was sure of it.

Which meant I was missing twenty-five minutes….

Fear washed over me like a cold ocean wave, and both Hudson boys saw it on my face.

"How did you get out of your house, Kaylee?" Tod asked, his voice deep with suspicion, and when all heads turned his way, I knew Emma could both see and hear him.

I squeezed Nash and stared at my feet. "My dad fell asleep in the living room. I didn't have any other choice."

"So you crossed over?" Nash's voice was lower and more dangerous than I'd ever heard it, and his words held no hint of calm. He held me at arms' length, both hands on my shoulders. "Don't ever do that again. Do you understand?"

I shrugged out of his grip, my temper flaring to a hot, sharp edge. "It'll be pretty hard to get Addy's soul back without crossing over," I snapped.

"Crossing over?" Emma's brows sank in confusion. "To where?"

"I mean alone," Nash clarified, ignoring her question. "You can't go there alone, Kaylee. You have no idea what...stuff is out there."

"What stuff is where?" Emma demanded, propping both hands on her hips.

"Well, I know a little better now." Turning from Nash, I slid into the passenger seat, then I caught Emma's eye and tossed my head toward the driver's side, urging her silently to get in.

The guys followed our lead reluctantly.

"What happened?" Nash demanded softly, as he clicked his seat belt home in the backseat. "Did you see something?"

I twisted around and smiled to relax him. I didn't like the bossy side of him, but knew it stemmed from concern for me. "Just a field full of weird grass with something slithering through it."

"Lizards," Tod said, and I knew based on Emma's reaction— or lack thereof—that he hadn't let her hear him that time. Which meant we weren't talking about ordinary lizards.

I glanced at Nash with my brows raised in question, but he only shook his head. We'd talk about it later, after we'd dropped Emma at her house. Or rather, after she'd dropped herself off.

Em was still irritated by our refusal to explain what was going on, but she hugged me when she got out of the car and told me to be careful doing…whatever we were doing.

I hugged her back and thanked her sincerely. Then I hugged her again, hoping it wouldn't be the last time I'd see her. I really didn't want to die in the Netherworld. Or anywhere else, for that matter. Not yet, anyway.

I slid into the driver's seat and Nash climbed over the center console to sit next to me. Then I twisted to look out the rear windshield as I backed slowly out of Emma's driveway, while she let herself into her house. "So, time moves slower in the Netherworld? That would have been nice to know."

"If we'd known you were going, we would have told you," Tod said matter-of-factly. "Along with the fact that most species of Netherworld lizards are poisonous to humans."

"And to *bean sidhes,*" Nash clarified, in case I didn't get it.

"Yeah, thanks. And the plant life isn't exactly amber waves of grain."

Tod grinned, and I knew that he, at least, had forgiven me. "It won't be like that closer to the city. The Netherworld is like a reflection of our world, anchored at certain, highly populated spots. Like public buildings. But the farther you go from those meccas, the less the Netherworld resembles our own. Including plant and animal life. And space and time."

So I really *had* gone farther in the Netherworld than I had on the human plane.

"Space and time?" I took the next corner too fast, distracted by the new information.

"Yeah." Tod shifted onto the center of the back bench seat so I could see him better in the mirror. "The human world is the constant, and time in the Netherworld will never go faster than it does here. And you'll never move farther here than you would have there. But time will move slower in the parts of the Netherworld that are least firmly anchored to the human plane, and it's very easy to think you've traveled far enough, yet when you cross back over, you haven't gone as far here as you thought you had."

Which was exactly what had happened to me.

"So, how are we supposed to get around in the Netherworld, if we never know where or when we'll be when we cross back over?" I shot a worried glance at Nash.

"Very carefully," he said, his voice grim and dark again. But this time he let a thread of calm snake through it to wrap around me, and I settled into that calm, inhaling it just for the taste of Nash. "Because most mistakes made in the Netherworld can't be fixed."

We took I-30 to Highway 12, in Irving, where the Dallas Cow-
boys were finishing their last season in the old stadium. I drove
and Nash navigated. Fortunately, he'd been to Texas Stadium a
bunch of times, and except for one missed exit—I hate it when
highway signs aren't marked well in advance—we had no problems getting there. Though, I was a little creeped out by the
late-night, nearly deserted feel of the area.

We parked in a lot south of the stadium, and the sound of
my car door closing echoed across the expanse of bare concrete.
The air outside was warmer and more humid than in the car, but
goose bumps popped up all over my arms, as if my skin knew
better than my head that I ought to be afraid.

The dark chill of anticipation could probably be attributed
to my imagination. Or to the fear that I would cross over from
the human plane into another field of glass spears, or something
even worse.

"You ready?" Tod asked from the other side of Emma's car,
one hand on the roof between us. Nash stood next to him,
watching me carefully, as if I might melt into a puddle of fear
and raw nerves any minute. Or maybe burst into tears.

Did he really think I was that fragile?

No, I was not ready. But neither was I going to delay our mission. Addy's time was running out.

"This is a public place with a very large concentration of human life force most of the time, so this section of the Netherworld should be pretty well anchored to ours," Tod began, stuffing his hands into his jacket pockets. "Which means that, for the most part, you can trust that time and space are running along pretty normal lines."

"But there hasn't been a game here in a couple of weeks, right?" I glanced from one brother to the other. "Shouldn't that lack of human activity cause the anchor to slip a little?"

Nash rounded the hood of the car to take my hand, and his brother shrugged. "It might slip a bit during the off-season, but there's been so much human energy built up here over the years that two weeks isn't enough to make much of a difference." The reaper ran one hand through his blond curls and joined us at the front of the car. "There might be a slight time and space discrepancy because it's the middle of the night and no one's around right now, but it'll be very small. Definitely much less than what you felt at home."

"What about the grass? Are we going to be shredded by vegetation when we cross over?"

Nash rubbed my upper arms through my jacket as I shivered. "I doubt it. There's too much activity here for razor wheat to get a foothold on the land. It takes a while for that shit to establish strong roots, which it can't do with Netherworlders stomping through it all the time. Right?" He glanced at Tod for confirmation, and the reaper nodded. Then Nash lifted my chin until my gaze met his. "And by the way, if you ever have to do that again—which I would not recommend—wear waders. Waist high, at least. Mom says that's the only way to get out of razor wheat without getting sliced to bits."

I nodded and bit my lip to keep from telling him about the whole sideways-step procedure, because that would make it sound like I'd mastered the razor wheat and intended to maintain my skill. Which I did not.

Unless I had to.

Still, waders sounded like a good idea....

"So, if the Netherworld parallel to my house is a field of razor wheat, that means no one's been there in a while, right?"

"It means there hasn't been enough activity there to keep it from growing or to stomp it down," Nash said as Tod headed across the lot toward the stadium, with us trailing him. "That's probably why your dad picked that section of the neighborhood."

His guess felt right. I could easily see my father trying to protect me by isolating us from centers of Netherworld activity.

A pang of guilt rang through me at that thought, for the way I'd yelled at him. Yes, he was being a real pain, but only because I wouldn't tell him what I was doing. It wasn't his fault. When this whole mess was over and I was done lying, I'd make him a pan of brownies.

Chocolate says "I'm sorry" so much better than words.

"The fact that there probably won't be razor wheat doesn't mean the plant life will be safe." Nash sounded grim and almost angry as he stepped over a concrete wheel stop. He didn't want to cross over, and honestly, neither did I. "Don't touch anything, just in case."

"So, all the plants are dangerous?"

Tod cleared his throat and pivoted to walk backward, facing us as he spoke, walking right through steel barricades and light posts. "The sun in the Netherworld doesn't shine as purely as it does here. It's kind of...filtered. Anemic. So the plants have adapted. They supplement their diet with blood, from wherever they can find it. Mostly rodents, and lizards, and other scuttlers. But they'll try for your blood, too, if you flaunt it."

Lovely... A dark chill washed over me, and I rubbed my arms for warmth. I hated the Netherworld already, and I'd spent only minutes there. "It sounds like *Little Shop of Horrors.*"

Tod gave a harsh huff and turned smoothly to face forward. "That was only one plant."

I stepped onto the raised sidewalk in front of the stadium, walking confidently to hide the fear pumping through my veins, chilling me from the inside out. "So, don't touch anything and stay away from the plant life."

"Right." Tod nodded, apparently satisfied. "Let's go. It's not getting any earlier, on either plane."

Keening was even easier that time than the time before, and to my surprise—and concern—I was able to do it without consciously remembering anyone's death. Instead I forced myself to endure the nightmare unfolding in my mind, like a bloom dripping blood.

Nash's death.

It wasn't a premonition. I knew that at the first touch of the terror-soaked, thorny vine creeping up the base of my skull. I wasn't predicting Nash's death. I was imagining it in horrifying, soul-wrenching detail. My biggest anti-wish. It played out behind my closed eyes, drawing from me a wail so strong the first thin tendrils of sound scorched my throat like I'd choked on living flames.

I wanted to spit those flames back up. Needed to purge them from my body for my own sanity. But I made myself swallow them, all but a ribbon of sound vibrating from my vocal chords, bypassing my sealed lips. My insides smoldered, ethereal smoke making the back of my throat itch.

I opened my eyes, and the world had gone gray.

The stadium was still there, rising in front of me like a domed, steel-and-concrete mushroom. But now an otherworldly fog shrouded the exposed beams and the underside of the massive stands.

Nash stared at me, his eyes churning colorlessly in fear for me. Fear for us all.

Tod watched us both carefully, and I read doubt in every line on his face. He wasn't sure I could cross over. Or at least that I could take Nash with me.

The reaper's skepticism fueled my determination, pushing me past the pain in my throat and the awful bloated feeling in my core, as if my insides would soon rupture from holding back my own wail. I thought of the Netherworld, and my intense need to be there. To find the hellion who'd sucked the Page sisters' souls. To get those souls back.

At first nothing happened. Then, just when frustration threatened to rip the full cry from throat, I realized the problem. I was still thinking about the razor wheat, and my desire never to step into it again. And those thoughts interfered with my intent to actually cross over.

Growling a bit, in sharp, dissonant harmony with my keening, I forced thoughts of the glasslike stalks from my mind and concentrated on Nash's assurance that it couldn't grow in such a populated area.

Suddenly the stadium began to fade into that featureless haze, and for one long moment I saw nothing but gray. Felt nothing but gray. I'd had my eyes closed the first time I'd crossed over, so I'd missed this claustrophobic emptiness, as if the world had swallowed me whole and wrapped me in fog.

My hands flailed in front of me, reaching desperately, blindly for Nash, before it was too late to take him with me. I did not want to have to cross over again.

His hands closed over mine with a familiar, soothing warmth. My finger brushed the pencil callous on the middle finger of his right hand, and the long, raised scar on his left palm, where he'd sliced it open working on his bike when he was twelve. I squeezed his hands, and an instant later the world whooshed back into focus around me.

Only it wasn't our world. It was the Netherworld. Again.

My previous crossover had prepared me for this trip no more

than a trip to the farm would prepare an alien visitor for an evening in New York City.

My biggest surprise was that the Netherworld had sidewalks— a sign of civilization and advanced order I had not expected. I'd known the stadium would exist on both levels. As a center of high-volume human activity, it was one of the anchors pinning the human plane to the Netherworld like a dress pattern over a bolt of cloth. Where the pin pierced both, the layers remained flat and even, and time and space were relatively constant. But between the pins, the bottom layer—the Netherworld—could bunch, and shift, and wrinkle. And that's where things were likely to get the weirdest.

Not that they were exactly normal even at one of the anchors....

"How did the Netherworld get sidewalks?" I whispered, letting go of Nash's hands to wipe nervous sweat on the front of my jeans. My pulse pounded in my ears so fast I was actually a little dizzy. "And parking lots? Is there some kind of creepy concrete company around here?" I didn't even want to know what the Netherworld mafia might bury in building foundations....

"No." Tod sounded amused again, in his own bleak way. "All of this is drawn through from our world, along with enormous amounts of human energy. The stronger the anchor, the more closely the Netherworld mirrors our world."

"So, the Netherworld equivalents of places like L.A. and New York must look—"

"Just about the same," Nash finished for me, smiling in spite of the circumstances. "Except for the people walking down the sidewalks."

I propped both hands on my hips, below the hem of my jacket, and took a long look around. "The stadium doesn't look much different—" though, the few vehicles sprinkled around the lot and the area surrounding the huge complex on the human plane were gone "—so where's the disposal facility?"

"Um…" Tod gestured toward the stadium. "I think that's it." He shrugged. "It's not like they actually play football here, right?"

I studied the stadium more carefully, looking for some sign of activity. Surely if this place was a repository for dangerous substances, there would be Security, or warning signs, or something. "Where is everyone? What about those fiends? Shouldn't they be around here somewhere?" Not that I was eager to find them. Unless, of course, finding them helped us avoid them.

"I don't—" Tod started.

But then Nash grabbed my arm, whispering fiercely. "Did you see that?"

I followed his gaze to the main entrance and the thick bank of shadows cast over it by the strange red crescent moon. On its own, such a feeble moon shouldn't have been able to produce much light, but again I noticed that the Netherworld night sky was not as dark as the one I'd grown up beneath, and the odd purple expanse cast a weak glow of its own.

Still, the shadows were virtually impenetrable, and at first I could see nothing in their depths.

Then something moved. The long, dark expanse seemed to writhe. To *wriggle,* as if the shadows cloaked some huge nest full of bodies crawling all over one another, vying for what little light reflected from the oddly colored sky.

"What is that?" I'd wandered several steps closer before I even realized I'd moved. Nash came with me, but Tod put a hand on my shoulder to hold me back.

"I think those are the fiends."

Great. "Okay, maybe there's a back door." 'Cause we were not fighting our way through a mass of wriggling fiends. Whatever those were. "Let's walk around," I suggested. And since neither of the guys had a better idea, we walked.

I couldn't get over how normal things looked—so long as I stared at the ground. The parking lot was virtually identical to the one in front of our own Texas Stadium, potholes and all. There were faded, chipped lines of yellow and white paint on the asphalt, and even several dark streaks of burned rubber, which had crossed over with the entire lot.

The closer we got to the building, however, the more the small differences began to jump out at me. The first was the flags. On the human plane, the stadium was ringed with a series of blue-and-white flags showing a football player in his helmet, and the Texas Lone Star. But in the Netherworld, those flags were stained, streaked banners of gray, torn by some other-worldly wind. Several had been reduced to ribbons of colorless cloth, virtually shredded by time and neglect.

The murals, too, were gray and largely featureless, showing just a hint of a humanlike outline. Several of them seemed to have extra limbs. And I could swear one had two heads.

"This is weeeeird," I sang beneath my breath, curling my fingers around Nash's when his warm hand found mine. "Let's just find a way in and ask the first person we see. Maybe Libby will be here…."

"She won't help." Tod veered slightly to the right, away from the main entrance, where those writhing figures were slowly coming into focus. "She's already told us everything she can, and I doubt any other reaper will do more. We'll have to ask someone else."

"What *are* those?" I asked, again squinting into the shadows beneath the awning. I could discern individual bodies now, and was surprised to realize that they were not serpentine in the least, in spite of the mental image their writhing had called up in my head.

They had heads—one apiece, fortunately—and the proper number of arms and legs. But that's where the similarity to my species ended. These creatures were small—though I couldn't judge how small from such a distance—and naked. Their skin was darker than mine and lighter than Libby's, but I couldn't tell how much of their coloring was due to the thick shadows they crawled through.

Oh, and they had tails. Long, thin hairless tails that coiled and uncoiled around legs and other appendages with such fluidity that they couldn't possibly have contained rigid bones.

And their tails weren't the only hairless parts. These little creatures were completely bald, and some part of me wondered if they wallowed all over one another just to stay warm. Some sort of group defense against the cold?

"Those are the fiends," Tod said softly, and for the first time, I realized he was acting weird. Speaking softly. Walking with us, rather than blinking to the other side of the stadium to scan for other entrances. Did his reaper abilities not function in the Netherworld?

"They can't be fiends," I said, deciding to hold my question for later. "They're too small." They didn't even come up to my waist, and the way Libby described fiends, I was expecting huge, burly monsters, pounding on the doors of the facility, literally fiending for another hit of Demon's Breath.

"Size isn't everything," Tod said, and my jaws clenched in irritation over his wise-man tone. "Those are the fiends. Look how they're crawling all over one another to get to the door. Not that that'll help. It's probably bolted from the inside."

Oh. They weren't trying to stay warm. They were trying to break in. I kicked a loose chip of concrete, thinking. "If it's bolted from the inside, how do the reapers get in?"

"They probably cross over from inside the stadium." An easy feat for a reaper, who could blink himself right onto the football field on the human plane, even after hours.

"So how are we going to get in?"

"Don't know yet." Tod frowned, still watching the fiends.

"Can't you just blink yourself inside from here?"

He shook his head slowly and feigned interest in a crack in the sidewalk.

Nash huffed, sounding almost smug. "Most reaper skills don't work here," he said, confirming my earlier hunch.

Tod sighed and met my gaze, his forehead lined deeply in frustration. "I could have done it from the human plane, but I doubt whoever works in there would be eager to help one rookie reaper who pops in without permission, bearing no Demon's Breath."

"So you're just like us down here?" I couldn't tear my gaze from the small bodies climbing all over one another in a bid for the door. As I watched, one creature's tail encircled another's neck and wrenched him forcefully from the top of the pile, only to drop him several feet from the ground. The displaced fiend bumped and rolled down the mountain of squirming bodies until he hit the concrete, where he scraped the side of his face and came up bleeding.

Wow. It was like watching a panicked crowd fight its way out of a burning building, only they were trying to get in.

And that's when I noticed that several fiends stood at the edge of the crowd, watching their spastic brethren jostle for position. Other than the occasional manic, full-body twitch, they looked pretty normal. For little naked guys with tails.

"Maybe we should ask one of them," I whispered, pointing out the fiends on the fringe. "They look like they come here pretty often."

"Kaylee, you can't just walk up to a fiend and start a conversation," Nash whispered, pulling me close with one arm around my waist. But this time, the motion felt less like it was intended to comfort me than to protect me. To draw me away from the minimonsters.

"Why not?" I frowned and glanced again at the pile of fiends trying to scale the exposed beams and smooth, glass doors. Okay, yes, they looked pretty fierce. But they were also pint-size. If one attacked, surely we could just…step on him.

"Because they're poisonous," Tod answered, coming to an abrupt stop. "And they bite."

"They eat people?" I took several slow, careful steps backward, squinting harder at the fiends. They weren't big enough to eat more than my hand in a single sitting.

Maybe they share....

Though, judging from the competitive nature of their desperate climb, I highly doubted it.

"No, they don't eat people. Not humans or *bean sidhes,* anyway. There aren't many of us around here. But they bite anything that gets in their way, and their saliva is toxic to creatures native to the human world."

"Lovely." I took another step backward, but it was too late. We'd caught their attention. Or rather, I had.

The fiend in the middle crossed the lot toward me, almost bouncing with each step, and two more came on his heels, twitching noticeably every few seconds.

"Snacks?" the second fiend asked, his voice high-pitched and eager, like a child high on sugar. And when he opened his mouth, I glimpsed double rows of sharply pointed, metallic-looking, needlelike teeth, both top and bottom.

They glinted like blood in the red moonlight.

The fiends grew closer, fingers twitching eagerly. Saliva gathered in the corners of their thin gray lips.

My heart lurched into my throat, and to my own humiliation, I yelped and grabbed Nash's arm. I tried to take another step back, but my foot caught on something, and I would have gone down on my face if not for my grip on Nash's jacket sleeve.

One glance down revealed the problem, and pumped more scalding fear through my bloodstream, fast enough to make my head swim. A thin, bright weed grew from a crack in the concrete, red as Japanese maple leaves in the fall. The damn thing had wound around my right ankle, clinging to my jeans with thorns as sharp as the teeth of a tiny saw.

I jerked on my foot, my gaze glued to the fiends still approaching slowly, but that only pulled the vine tight. The thorns pierced denim and speared my flesh in a dozen tiny points of pain. "Ow!" I cried, then immediately slapped my hand over my mouth. The last thing I needed was to draw more attention our way.

Nash glanced down, and in a flash he'd dropped to one knee, a pocketknife drawn and ready. He couldn't fit it between the vine and my leg without cutting me, so he simply sliced the weed out of the ground, and pulled me back before the surviving, grasping tendrils could grip me again.

The severed weed dripped several drops of dark red on the concrete. Or maybe that was my blood. A sick feeling wound around my stomach, tightening like the vine around my leg.

What am I doing *here?* My ankle burned where the thorns had pricked me, my pulse raced in my ears, so loud I could hardly hear the scrambling of the fiends against the glass anymore.

Was there time to cross back into the human world before the approaching fiends pounced? Because I was suddenly certain that's what they were planning.

"They smell yummy," the third said, followed by a peal of high, maniacal laughter. "Do they kiss hellions?" His teeth clanged like hollow metal when he closed his mouth, and my pulse lurched again. "Do they breathe Demon's Breath?"

"No," the first one said, as Nash, Tod, and I slowly backed farther from the small monsters now clearly stalking us. I wasn't sure if they could hurt Tod, but he obviously wasn't taking any chances. "They are clean."

"Pity…" the second high-pitched voice sang. Then the two fiends in back turned on their small, bare heels and twitch-bounced back to the group scaling the walls of the stadium.

My pulse slowed just a bit, with the threat decreased by two-thirds. But the first fiend still eyed us. Eyed *me*. He sniffed, tiny, flat nostrils flaring. "Foreign." His left arm twitched violently, as if it were trying to fight free from the rest of his body. Then his right foot jiggled, like he was trying to wake it up. Only, I was sure he hadn't done it on purpose. He was in desperate need of a hit, and his body wouldn't work properly until he got it.

"You don't belong here, humans." He stepped forward as one corner of his mouth began to jump. The fiend eyed me boldly, assessing me, and I realized that though he was clearly in the grip of some sort of withdrawal, he was still thinking and speaking somewhat coherently. At least, more so than his friends. "Stay, and something bigger will surely eat you…."

"We're not—" I started, but Nash squeezed my hand ruthlessly, stopping me from denying our humanity. "We're looking for a hellion," I said instead, and Nash groaned audibly. Evidently that wasn't a good conversation-starter in the Netherworld.

Who knew?

But the fiend surprised me. "As are we all," he said wistfully, and I felt my brows arch almost off of my head. Yet that made sense. They were desperate for a hit of Demon's Breath. Of course they were looking for a demon.

"Um, I mean we're looking for a *particular* hellion." This time, Tod squeezed my other hand, but I ignored him. If the fiend wanted to bite us, he could already have done it several times over. "Do you know a hellion of avarice?"

The fiend's flashing yellow eyes gleamed brighter, and they may have moistened just a bit, as if with a fond memory. "Ah, avarice…" he breathed, squeaky voice piercing right to the center of my brain. "My favorite flavor."

Excitement traced my veins, chasing out those last, healthy jolts of fear. He knew the hellion of avarice. Or at least, he knew *a* hellion of avarice.

I dared one step forward, fighting the urge to squat and look him in the eye, and Nash held tightly to my hand so I couldn't go any farther. "Can you tell us where to find this hellion?"

"I can." The creature nodded his bulbous, bald head, and in

the reddish moonlight, I got a good look at the dark veins snaking over the top of it, bulging like a serious weight lifter's. "But there is a price."

I frowned. "I don't have much money. Not quite fifty—"

"Kaylee..." Nash refused to relinquish my hand when I tried to dig in my pocket.

"I have no use for your worthless paper currency," the fiend spat, gray lips turning down around razor-sharp teeth. "I will tell you where to find your hellion—for a portion of his breath. Payable in advance..."

"What?" Anger burned in my cheeks. The fiend's nostrils flared again, as if my ire scented the air, and for all I know, it did.

"Let's go...." Tod tugged on my other arm.

"No!" I turned back to the fiend, trying to get my voice under control. My anger clearly pleased him, and that wouldn't help my case. "If we knew where to get a dose of his breath, we wouldn't have to ask you where to find him!"

But the fiend only blinked up at me, tiny hands twitching, clearly unconcerned with how I came up with the payment. Did logic have no place in the Netherworld? How was I supposed to...

I stood straight as a sudden possibility occurred to me. "Is an hour soon enough?" My lips curled up into what felt like a sly smile.

The fiend nodded slowly. Eagerly. "I will wait here. One hour. My time," he said, as if in afterthought.

"Deal." My smile widened.

Nash and Tod frowned at me, but instead of explaining, I dismissed the creepy little monster and rushed across the lot with both guys on my heels, my focus on the ground ahead, on the lookout for anything that could poison, grab, or eat me.

Because the guys were right: If I wasn't careful, I had no doubt this monstrous wonderland would swallow Alice whole...

‹ 17 ›

"Where are we going?" Nash asked from the driver's seat as I propped my right foot on the dashboard, glad to be back on my own side of the looking glass, even if only temporarily.

"I don't know yet. Here." I twisted to toss my phone over the backseat to Tod. Unfortunately, he was no longer fully with us—non-corporeal due to stress, maybe?—and the phone dropped through his body to land on the seat, like it had fallen through a hologram. His rear and my phone now occupied the same space at the same time.

Wasn't an event like that supposed to make the world explode, or something?

The reaper glanced down in surprise, then reached through himself to grab my phone from the seat—which had to be one of the weirdest things I'd ever seen. Even weirder than killer plants and little bald fiends with tails and needle-teeth.

Tod's body solidified, and he stared at me blankly. "What's this for?"

"Well, most people use it as a form of communication, but it would probably work as a projectile, in a pinch."

Tod frowned. "Funny. Who am I supposed to call?"

"Addy. Find out where she is. I have an idea." While he

dialed, I turned my attention to the thorny coil of vine still wrapped tightly around my ankle. Nash had cut it close to the ground to get me loose, but there was still enough of the weed left to encircle my leg twice, long, thin thorns piercing both the denim and my skin. At two-inch intervals, thin four-leaf clusters dangled, dark green at the centers, bleeding to red on the serrated edges.

"Be careful with that," Nash warned, glancing from the road to my ankle, then back. "I think that's crimson creeper, and if it is, the thorns are poisonous."

Of course they were. Was anything in the Netherworld nontoxic?

"It's a little late for that. The stupid thorns went all the way through my jeans." I pinched the end of the creeper vine between my thumb and forefinger, completely horrified when thin red liquid dribbled from the severed tip, and gingerly pulled it away from my leg. Fortunately, now that the weird red vine was dead, it uncoiled easily. But each time a thorn pulled free from my skin, a fresh jolt of blazing pain shot through my ankle, as if I were being struck by tiny bolts of lightning. By the time I dropped the plant on the floorboard—the vine had to be eight inches long—a hot ache had settled into my ankle joint, throbbing with each beat of my heart.

I bit my bottom lip as I carefully rolled up the cuff of my jeans. Then I gasped in shock. My ankle was already swollen. Each of the dozen or so tiny holes was raised and puckered, and the wounds were almost as red as the vine itself.

"Shit!" Nash whistled through his teeth. "Definitely crimson creeper. My mom will know what to do for that, but if we tell her, she'll call your dad." Nash's eyes found mine, and I wondered if I looked as conflicted as he did. "Do you think you can wait a couple of hours, or do we need to go now?"

To the hospital, of course. Where Harmony worked as a third-shift RN on the orthopedic ward, where the patients were least likely to die.

I pressed my foot against the dashboard experimentally. The pain was constant, and did not increase with pressure, which meant I could probably walk on it. "I can wait." I closed my eyes briefly and exhaled, mourning the last of my hope that my dad might never discover what we were up to. Now that I was injured, full disclosure was unavoidable—hopefully after we'd reclaimed Addy's and Regan's souls.

When this was all over, I'd probably be spending a lot of time alone in my room.

"Hello, Addy?" Tod said from the backseat, and I loosened the chest strap of my seat belt so I could twist around to watch him, studying his face for any clue about Addison's half of their conversation. "Did I wake you up?"

She laughed bitterly over the line, but I couldn't make out her actual words.

"Yeah, I probably couldn't, either." Tod plucked a frayed thread from the thin layer of denim over his right knee. "Listen, where are you? I think we need to drop by for a minute...." He glanced at me to confirm, and I nodded while Addison said something else I couldn't understand. "Good. Can you arrange for a few minutes of privacy?" Another pause. "We'll be there in ten minutes."

"Twenty," I corrected him. "We have to make a stop first."

Tod relayed the correction to Addison, then said goodbye, hung up, and tossed my phone back to me. "She's at her mom's house. It's the only place she can avoid most of her entourage."

"Good." I slid my phone into my pocket and glanced out the windshield to read the passing highway signs. "Nash, we need an all-night Walmart, or grocery store. Or maybe a drugstore."

He nodded and slid smoothly into the right-hand lane, barely pausing to flick on Emma's blinker. "There's a twenty-four-hour Walgreens a couple of miles from Addy's house. Will that work?"

"With any luck. Do you think I should get something for this, while we're there?" I raised my cuff to show him my ankle, and Tod sucked in a sharp breath from the backseat, then leaned forward, gripping my headrest.

"Damn, Kaylee, is that from the weed?"

"Yeah." I poked gently at one of the swollen puncture marks, then hissed when a fresh jolt of pain shot through my tender flesh and into the core of the joint. A small bead of clear fluid oozed from the hole, and I dabbed at it with a tissue from the box on Emma's center console. "Nash thinks it's crimson creeper."

"He's right. Thank goodness it was a little one. Of course, if it was fully grown, you never would have stepped on it."

"Fully grown? How big do they get?"

Tod raised both brows, surprised by my cluelessness. Though, he shouldn't have been, considering that a couple of months ago I didn't even know my own species. "Fifty feet or better. And a puncture from one that size will kill you in a couple of hours, if it doesn't break your spine first. They're like giant pythons with roots."

"And thorns," I added bitterly.

Tod looked like he wanted to say something else, but whatever he was thinking was lost when Nash spoke up.

"You're gonna need something for that ankle." Nash glanced at it again, until I pulled my cuff down and set my foot on the floor. "But I have no idea whether or not human-world medicine will work on Netherworld toxin." He paused and flicked the right blinker on again, when he spied our exit. "So what else do we need at Walgreens?"

"Balloons." I smiled at Nash's perplexed expression, enjoying understanding more than he did for once.

Tod stuck his head between the front seats, looking just as confused as his brother. "We're taking Addy balloons? Should we stop for a cake and a present, too?"

My smile widened. "The balloons aren't for Addison. They're for the fiend. Addy's just going to…blow one up for us."

For a moment, Tod's eyes narrowed even further. Then his expression smoothed as comprehension settled in, and one half of his mouth quirked up.

"Clever…" Nash nodded at me in obvious respect. "I like it."

"Let's just hope it works."

At Walgreens, Tod found a bag of multicolored latex party balloons while Nash and I hunted down a tube of antibiotic cream. When we met at the cash register, the reaper also snagged three bars of chocolate. I paid—I knew my "paper currency" would come in handy!—then we rushed to Addison's house, beyond grateful for the light, middle-of-the-night traffic, because we had to be back at the stadium in half an hour.

We parked next to a shiny Lexus in Addison's driveway, and she must have heard the engine, because she pulled the front door open as we climbed the steps, then ushered us into the empty living room.

Addy closed the door behind us and stood in the entry with her hands deep in the pockets of a pair of snug, faded jeans. She was still fully dressed. She hadn't even tried to go to sleep. Not that I could blame her.

"Where's your mom?" Tod asked from the middle of the room. No one sat.

"She's passed out in her room." Addy's ironic smile said that for once, she was grateful for her mother's "issues."

"What about Regan?" I rubbed my left shoe against my right ankle, barely resisting the urge to bend over and scratch because that would have exposed my Netherworldly injury and led to questions we didn't have time to answer. And because I was pretty sure scratching would make more clear liquid run from my puncture wounds, rather than easing the fierce, burning itch that had settled in.

"She's sleeping off a couple of Mom's painkillers." Addison

glanced at me, then down at her unpainted toenails. "I *had* to give them to her. She was freaking out, and I just wanted her go to sleep and shut up. I tried to warn her, but she didn't listen. She never listens…."

My heart ached for Addy, and her splintered relationship with her sister. They reminded me of me and Sophie, and that thought left a bitter taste in my mouth, as if I'd swallowed one of Addy's mother's pills.

"It's fine." Tod clearly didn't care what happened to Regan. He had eyes—and concern—only for Addison. "We're a step away from finding the hellion, but first we need you to blow up one of these."

"Maybe two or three of them," I interjected, tossing Tod the bag of party balloons. "I'm not sure what dose the fiend is looking for, or what the concentration is…inside her. So it might take more than one."

Tod ripped open the bag while Addison glanced from one of us to the other like we'd lost our minds.

"It's in your breath," I explained, while Tod pulled a cherry-red balloon from the bag and stretched it to make it easier to inflate. "The Demon's Breath. It rests in your core. And in your lungs, and I think that every time you exhale, you breathe a little bit of it into the air."

I'd gotten the idea from the fiends, who'd wanted to know if we exhaled Demon's Breath. We didn't, of course. But Addy might.

I wasn't sure how it worked. If she lost a little bit of the force keeping her alive with each exhale, or if the Demon's Breath replaced itself as each little bit was lost. But I was virtually certain—based on the fiends' odd dialogue—that Addy carried within herself the very currency we needed.

She took the balloon from Tod and stared at it for a second as if it might grow teeth and bite her. Then Addy put the latex to her mouth as we watched from a loosely formed semicircle on the beige carpet.

"Wait." I shrugged, my arms still crossed over my chest. "It seemed to me when Eden died that Demon's Breath is heavier than air, so it's probably at the bottom of your lungs. You'll have to empty them to exhale what we really need. So blow out as much as you can on each breath, okay?"

Addison nodded hesitantly, then put the red balloon to her lips again as Tod pulled a yellow one from the bag. She began to blow, and the balloon grew slowly, becoming more translucent with each millimeter it gained in circumference. She blew without inhaling, forcing more air from her lungs than I'd have thought possible, until her face was nearly as flushed as the balloon.

Singers must have very good lungs.

When she could exhale no more, the balloon was half-filled. She pinched it closed between her thumb and forefinger, and I took it from her to tie off the opening. When I let it go, the balloon sank quickly, as if it were tethered to some small weight.

Tod handed her the yellow balloon and she repeated the process without a word or a glance at any of us. When the second balloon had joined the red one on the floor, I couldn't help but smile as I stared at them, the room silent but for Addy's forceful exhaling into a third, purple, one.

The balloons on the floor looked festive, in a cheesy, child's-birthday-party kind of way. They seemed to mock their own dangerous content. But then, maybe that was appropriate, considering the origins of that content: a world where the residents would gladly eat us alive. If the plant life didn't get us first.

When Addy had finished the third balloon, Nash decided we had enough. Not because we were sure we actually *did* have enough, but because we were running out of time. Why hadn't I asked for two hours?

Not that it mattered. Addy's life-clock was ticking toward

its last tock even without the fiend's deadline. According to the digital numbers on her DVD player, it was just after one o'clock on Thursday morning. Addy would die sometime in the next twenty-three hours—probably sooner, rather than later—and every moment we wasted brought that unknown time closer.

"We'll come back for you as soon as we can," Tod said as I gathered the filled balloons. "Get Regan up and moving." If she'd already been conscious, we could have just taken both Page sisters with us. "We'll call when we're on the way, but I can't promise much notice."

Because we had no idea where this hellion was going to be, or how long it would take to get there. And to find him.

"I'll try." Addy frowned, glancing toward the kitchen. "She won't touch coffee, but I think we have some Jolt in the fridge."

"Good. I'll call you when we know more," Tod promised, and left a kiss on her cheek on his way out the door.

Addison watched us from the front porch as we backed down the dark driveway, her arms crossed over the front of a thin, long-sleeved T-shirt, apparently oblivious to the middle-of-the-night November cold. My guess was that it was nothing compared to the chill inside her.

Nash drove again, and I spent the first part of the ride to the stadium applying antibiotic cream to my ankle, and the second part desperately wishing I hadn't. I'd barely wiped the thick white cream from my fingers when the puncture wounds began to bubble and hiss softly, as if I'd poured on hydrogen peroxide instead. The annoying ache/burn I'd been trying to ignore for the past forty minutes roared into a full-blown bonfire in my ankle.

I wiped off all the cream I could with more of Emma's tissues, wishing she had something wet so I could get all of it. The little bit that remained in the holes in my flesh bubbled softly, leaking tiny drops of white-tinged liquid now. By the time we pulled into the stadium parking lot, thin, red, weblike lines had begun to snake out from the double ring of punctures in all directions. The webbing extended less than an inch so far, but I had no doubt it would keep spreading.

Nash glanced at my ankle twice, his frown deepening each time, and I seriously considered his offer to take me to the hospital. To end the pain creeping up my leg and get our confession over with. But that would effectively end our night, leaving Addy to die without her soul. Damning her to an eternity of torture. And I couldn't do that. Not knowing what had happened to the souls my aunt had bargained with. How could I let Addy suffer the same fate?

Besides, there would be time to treat my injury after we'd reclaimed the Page souls, right? Because according to Tod, no matter how bad my ankle got, I wouldn't die until my name showed up on some reaper's list, and if that happened, no amount of Netherworldly cream or pills could save me. I refused to think about the fact that Tod's list couldn't predict the loss of my leg or foot. So I pressed on, in spite of the pain.

We negotiated the parking lot on the human plane—brightly colored balloons tucked under both of my arms and one of Nash's—to avoid stepping on any more crimson creeper, and we didn't stop to cross over until I judged that we were approximately where we'd stood when we'd bargained with the fiend. Then we moved several feet to the left, to avoid that stupid vine. I was pretty sure my estimate of the distance was good enough, because as far as I could tell, we hadn't lost any time crossing over earlier. The anchor at the stadium was very strong.

Tod crossed over first, to make sure all was clear, and that the fiend was waiting for us, because I wasn't going to make the effort if the little monster had ditched us, or if it wasn't safe to be in the Netherworld at that particular place and time. Only once he'd returned with the all clear did I summon my wail—with less effort than ever now—and haul Nash into the Netherworld with me.

The fiend stood very close to where we'd left him, running the tip of his tail through one small, loosely clenched fist over and over. His gaze jumped from place to place. His twitches had grown stronger, and he clearly could not stand still. And suddenly it occurred to me with an indescribable jolt of horror that I'd become a Netherworld drug dealer.

After several deep breaths, I decided I could live with that, so long as the ends justified the means. I hadn't gotten the little monster hooked on Demon's Breath in the first place, and I was only enabling him for one hit. Right?

The fiend's eyes widened at one glimpse of the balloons we carried, and I noticed for the first time that his bright yellow eyes were drastically dilated and shiny.

"Give!" he panted, reaching up with both short, stubby hands for the red balloon, the first to capture his attention. I wondered briefly if he were color-blind, and I was relieved to notice that he had no fingernails. At least I wouldn't have to worry about him clawing me in a rush for his fix.

"Information first," I insisted, holding both balloons over my head by the knots sealing them.

"No!" His arms began to tremble, even as his tail twitched furiously. He was hurting badly, and if he didn't get what he needed soon, someone was going to get hurt. Unfortunately, I didn't have needlelike metallic teeth with which to defend myself.

But my spine was starting to feel quite a bit like steel.

"Tell us where to find the hellion of avarice, or we'll pop the balloons one at a time. Too high up for you to inhale." I nodded at Nash, and he produced his folding knife from one pocket, flipping it open with the press of one button.

"No!" the fiend screeched, jumping for the balloon in vain.

Nash jerked back in surprise, and the point of his knife pierced the balloon he held. The latex exploded, showering him with bits of purple rubber. He coughed and waved a hand in front of his face, casually clearing away the very substance our little informant craved. *Needed…*

The fiend dropped to his knees, picking up one scrap of latex at a time, sniffing them desperately. But after several seconds, he looked up at us in bitter, pained defeat.

I held up the red balloon. "Tell us, or we'll pop this one, too," I threatened softly, hoping not to attract the attention of the fiends still madly trying to scale the stadium walls. Many of them now lay unconscious on the sidewalk, either from denial of their chemical fix, or from being stomped on by their stronger brethren.

The fiend squealed in fury, and his hands squeezed into tiny fists, his tail whipping behind him angrily, stirring dust from the surface of the parking lot. "Fine. Human monsters. No mercy…" he mumbled, and I almost laughed. His entire species seemed ready to bring about its own end for one more hit of a substance they had no business snorting. Or sniffing. Or whatever. Yet *we* had no mercy?

"Talk." I held the red balloon closer to Nash's knife, as he posed with it threateningly.

The small creature drew himself up straight and squared his shoulders, drawing what little dignity he still possessed around himself like a cape. "Hellions loiter where they feed. You want Avari, a hellion of avarice. He will be where greed best festers."

"Which is where?" I inched the red balloon closer to Nash's knife point.

The fiend shrugged, but the motion was not smooth enough to disguise the tremor now shaking his entire body. "Downtown. The greatest bastion of greed I know." The fiend gasped, as if he couldn't suck in a deep-enough breath. At least, not one that wasn't polluted with his poison of choice. "Humans call it Prime Life."

"The insurance company?" Nash cleared his throat gingerly,

as if it hurt. Prime Life was the largest insurance firm in the country, and it was headquartered in Dallas.

Hmm, I thought, a moment before the fiend nodded silently. *That kind of makes sense.*

"Bastion of greed…" the fiend repeated. "Probably there now…" He extended both small arms, like a child begging to be picked up. Only this child wanted a party balloon filled with addictive Nether-toxins.

I handed it over, though my stomach churned in response to a less-honorable action than any I'd ever taken. After a second thought, I gave him the yellow balloon, too. We had no use for it, and he clearly needed it. The thought of which made my stomach pitch even harder.

But we'd gotten what we'd come for, and I crossed back into the human world satisfied, if not exactly pleased with myself.

The ends would eventually justify the means, right? So how come I felt like *I'd* just sold *my* soul…?

"You okay?" Nash asked, when he noticed me limping back to the car.

"Fine." Though, I wasn't at all sure of that. My ankle burned fiercely, and was so swollen it seemed to jiggle with each step. But I was afraid to look at it, so I glanced at my watch instead.

It was 2:15 a.m. on the day Abby was fated to die. Unfortunately, we hadn't thought to ask Libby for a specific time, and Levi had been closely guarding the reapers' list ever since Tod stole a peek at it six weeks ago, so I already felt like we were working in the dark. Regardless, there wouldn't be time to seek medical attention until Addy and Regan had their souls back and evil had met its match. Until then, I would pretend my ankle was made of steel, like some kind of bionic joint, and that I could feel no pain. I was superhuman. I could do anything.

But I'd take some Tylenol, just in case. Lots of Tylenol.

Nash slid behind the wheel of Emma's car again, because I didn't feel like driving. I felt like sleeping, but sleep, like everything else appealing, wasn't an option at the moment.

Nash twisted the key in the ignition and glanced in the rearview mirror at his brother. "We'll pick up Addy and Regan." He turned the wheel to the left as far as it would go, to cut a tight circle in the deserted parking lot. "You go on to Prime Life and see if you can find Avari. Here, take this." Nash arced one arm backward over his shoulder to Tod, his cell phone clenched loosely in his fist.

"That won't work in the Netherworld," I said. And even if it did, I bet he'd rack up one hell of a roaming charge.

Tod scrolled through his brother's contact list. Or maybe his playlist. "Yeah, but once I find Avari, I can cross back over and call you."

Oh, yeah.

Tod pocketed the phone and leaned forward to stick his head between the seats. "Thanks, guys. I really owe you for this."

I'm sure my grin looked more like a grimace. "And for this…" I propped my foot on the dash again and pulled up my jeans cuff to reveal my ankle. At which point my grimace contorted into an expression of disgust and fear, and my words trailed into shocked silence.

My ankle was twice its normal size. The flesh beneath the double ring of punctures was inflamed and covered in those weird, red webbed veins, which now crept beneath my sock and halfway to my knee. Fluid sloshed beneath the skin over my ankle, hanging lower at the back, just above my shoe, where gravity tugged hardest.

Nash's sudden intake of breath hissed throughout the car, and I looked up to see him watching me, rather than the road. "Kaylee, we have to get that looked at."

"Ya think?" I tried to smile, but my sense of humor had deserted me. "Eyes on the road!"

He jumped, then turned the wheel back on course, but kept sneaking glances at my ankle while I tried to decide whether or not to poke it. "That antibiotic cream made it worse," I said. "Will a human doctor even know what to do for this?"

"I doubt it." Nash divided his attention between my ankle and the lightly populated highway. "But Mom will."

I glanced at Tod, eager for a second opinion. "What do you think? Can this wait?"

The reaper swallowed thickly and studied my ankle for a moment. Then he met my gaze, his blue eyes shadowed in the backseat. "I think so."

"You sure?" I asked. Because he didn't sound very sure.

"Yeah." Tod nodded firmly. "You'll be fine. We're not looking to drag this out, anyway."

"Okay. Good." I sank back into my seat, feeling a little better now that we'd decided on a course of action. "As soon as we're done at Prime Life, we'll call your mom and have her meet us at your house," I said to Nash, then twisted to look at Tod. "I'll call Addy and tell her we're on the way. You go find this hellion. Avari. But try not to let him see you. And if he does, don't tell him we're bringing Addy and Regan. Somehow I doubt he'll be eager to give their souls back, even if he thinks he'll be getting two more in exchange."

For once, Tod nodded without arguing. Then he gave me an unexpected kiss on the cheek and disappeared with Nash's phone before I could recover from the surprise.

"I take it that's a thank-you," I mumbled, rubbing the spot on my cheek where the reaper's lips had touched me. They were warmer than I'd expected from a dead man.

Nash huffed, but he didn't really look mad. His brother's kiss spoke more of gratitude than anything else.

While he watched out for our exit, squinting beneath streetlights at regular intervals, I pulled my phone from my pocket. But before I could scroll through the call history for Addy's number, a small message at the bottom of the display popped up to tell me I'd missed five calls.

Crap. My dad had discovered my empty bed.

Please *tell me he didn't call the police!*

Three messages were from him, as expected. The first two had come in less than an hour after I'd left the house, while we were in the Netherworld bargaining with the fiend the first time. They were virtually identical—my father's angry voice demanding to know where I was, and what the *hell* I was doing. My dad didn't cuss much. Only when he was really, really mad. Or scared.

The third call was from Emma, warning me that my father had called her house at one o'clock in the morning. Which woke her mother up and led to all kinds of questions Emma'd had to dance around.

Oops. I made a mental note to bake a pan of brownies for Emma, too, to try to make up for the trouble I was getting her into.

Fortunately, her mother hadn't noticed the missing car, and it hadn't occurred to my father—yet, anyway—to ask if I'd borrowed it.

The fourth call was from Harmony, who was worried, and even sounded a little angry. She said my dad was "beside himself" and about two seconds from driving the streets in search of me. Then she wanted to know if I'd seen Nash, who wasn't answering his phone, either. Which meant he would have messages, too.

That was her way of warning us that she knew we were in this together—whatever *this* was—and that we'd better have a good explanation when we finally turned ourselves in.

I liked Harmony, and I was afraid that once she found out what we were doing, she'd shorten the long leash Nash had enjoyed since way before I'd met him. And that would be my fault, too.

The fifth call was from my dad again, saying he was going to drive around town looking for me, and if he hadn't heard from me by three, he'd go to the police.

Wonderful.

A quick glance at the clock on my phone display said it was two fifty-four in the morning. "I gotta call my dad," I said, glancing at Nash in dread. He nodded grimly, having obviously heard at least part of the messages.

As my dad's phone rang in my ear, I tugged my pants leg down and set my foot on the floor, gasping when even that slight movement made the accumulated fluid slosh.

"Kaylee?" my dad barked into my ear. "Is that you?"

"Yeah, it's me. I'm fine," I added before he could ask. And that was true, relatively speaking. I hadn't been mugged, or kidnapped, or turned out on the streets. "Look, I don't have much time to talk, but the bottom line is that I'm sorry I snuck out, but I *had* to. I have to finish something important, then I'll be home. A couple of hours, at most."

"Is Nash with you?"

I sighed, and let my head fall back against the headrest, watching as the highway lights passed over us in a steady, hypnotic rhythm. "This isn't his fault," I insisted. "I asked him to help. I'll explain everything when I get home."

"Kaylee—"

"I gotta go, Dad. I just wanted to tell you I'm okay. And please don't go to the police. They won't understand." With that, I slid my phone closed and pressed the button to ignore the incoming call when it began to ring an instant later. Instead of answering, I called Addison. She answered on the first ring and assured me that Regan was up, if not exactly perky.

I told her to funnel another Jolt down her sister's throat and get her dressed. We'd be there in ten minutes.

Again, Addy met us at the door, but this time Regan sat on the couch in designer jeans and a couple of snug, layered, long-sleeved tees. She stared across the room with those weird, solid-white eyes until our arrival caught her attention and she smiled blankly at me, her lips barely curling up enough to qualify as an actual expression.

"She's gonna have to put her contacts in," I said, forcing myself to look somewhere other than Regan's eyes. Anywhere else. "She can't go out like that."

Addison crossed the room toward her sister, a brown leather jacket folded over one arm. "I don't think I can get them in her eyes, and she's not up to it yet. Can't she just wear sunglasses?"

"It's the middle of the night." I picked up one of Regan's listless arms and slid it through the jacket sleeve her sister held.

"We're not trying to make a fashion statement, Kaylee." Addy stuffed her sister's remaining hand through its sleeve. "We're just trying to avoid notice."

"Will we have to worry about paparazzi at three in the morning?" I asked as Addison knelt to slide a pair of glittery canvas shoes on her sister's bare feet. Not exactly winter attire, but it would work in a pinch. As would the sunglasses.

"Not in your car," the pop princess said, and I didn't bother to tell her it wasn't my car. She would have been much more embarrassed to appear in mine than in Emma's. "Not unless someone tipped them off. And if that's the case, we have bigger things to worry about." She rose and pulled her sister up by both hands.

Regan just stood there.

"How much did you give her?" Nash stepped closer to the youngest Page with his arms out, as if to catch her. Because she looked pretty wobbly.

"You mean Jolt or pills?"

"Pills."

"Two. But I think part of this is shock."

Nash exhaled deeply, frowning. "Grab another Jolt for the road." He wrapped one arm around Regan's shoulders and led her toward the door. Addy ducked into the kitchen while I snatched a pair of oversize, super-dark sunglasses from the bar between the living room and kitchen, sliding them in place over Regan's ears right before Nash pushed her gently over the threshold and onto the porch.

Addy sat by her sister in the back, and I slid into the passenger seat, buckling my seat belt as Nash started the engine. I resisted the urge to take another look at my ankle because I didn't want Addy or Regan to see it.

I didn't really want to see it, either.

"Regan, can you hear me?" Nash asked, as we took the on-ramp back onto the highway.

"Yeah…" Regan said, frowning slightly.

"Here, drink this." Addison popped the top on the drink can and held it to her sister's lips.

"No…" Regan pushed sluggishly at the can, and Addy pulled it back to keep from spilling.

"We need you coherent, Regan," I said, wishing I had Nash's Influence rather than my own much harsher abilities. "Don't you want to get your soul back?"

Regan shrugged, and I couldn't even tell if she was looking at me from behind those huge sunglasses.

"Keep making her drink." I settled into my seat, concentrating on the pain in my leg to keep from falling asleep.

My eyes were just starting to close when my phone buzzed in my pocket. My dad had called me twice more on the way to Addy's house, but I checked the display just in case. It was Tod, calling on Nash's phone.

"Hello?" I jabbed Nash's arm as I answered, then mouthed his brother's name.

"Kaylee? I found him. If you guys get here before he leaves, this might just work." Tod sucked in a tense, worried breath. "But, Kay, this place isn't like the stadium. It's…busy. You'll have to cross over in the parking lot, then bring everyone in through the side door, because the building's still closed in the human world. And be careful. Don't touch anything—"

"Like I haven't learned my lesson on that one…" I interrupted.

"And don't let Addy and Regan touch anything, either. Or talk to anyone."

"We'll be careful." I was as eager as the next person to walk out of this alive. "Make sure he doesn't leave. We're about fifteen minutes away." Fortunately, we were too early for morning rush-hour traffic, and most of our fellow highway drivers were truckers on overnight routes.

"I don't think he will. Everyone's here to absorb the bleed-through of human life force, and they're not going to leave before the workday starts. That's when the energy here will go through the roof." Another pause. "But hurry, just in case."

"We're going as fast as we can." Without getting splattered all over the highway.

By the time Nash pulled into a spot on the bottom floor of the Prime Life parking garage, Regan was starting to come around, either because the pills were wearing off, or because the Jolt was kicking in. Or maybe the importance of our mission was finally starting to sink in.

Her hand trembled as Nash helped her out of the car, and she rose unsteadily, almost knocking her sunglasses from her face when she tried to wipe her eyes. I stood, intending to help him with her, but the moment my right foot hit the ground, the echoes of my previous pain were swallowed in a wave of fresh agony so fierce I almost fell on my face right there in the parking lot.

Addison caught me. "What's wrong, Kaylee? Are you okay?" she asked, as I regained my balance and stepped carefully away from her.

"Yeah." I eased weight onto my injured leg, wincing as flames of pain flashed as far north as my hip. "I hurt my ankle earlier, and it's getting worse." I glanced up, smiling at Nash to assure him that I was okay.

"Let's get this done so we can take care of your leg," he said, one arm still around Regan, and I could only nod in agreement.

Moving slowly because of my limp and Regan's chemically induced stupor, Nash led us to the locked glass doors, where we both turned to face Addison and Regan. "I'm going to cross us all over," I explained, "kind of like Bana did for you both, by holding your hand. When we get there, it won't be like last time. Tod says Prime Life is…populated this time of day in the Netherworld, so there are a couple of ground rules you need to follow, at all costs."

Both sisters nodded, Addison's fake-blue eyes wide with both fear and determination. I couldn't see Regan's eyes through her glasses—not that it would have mattered if I could—but I knew from the thin line her lips were pressed into that she was listening and taking me seriously.

Thank goodness.

I accidently put too much weight onto my bad leg and hissed in pain, so Nash continued while I breathed through it. "Don't touch anything," he began. "Don't make eye contact with anyone. Don't even look at anyone but us."

"And make sure you don't step on anything," I added, smiling wryly when my pain seemed to scare Regan. "Ready?" I asked. Both sisters nodded, taking the hands I held out. Nash held on to my arm, but I was afraid that if he wasn't actually touching my flesh, he couldn't come along for the ride, so I shoved up both my shirt and jacket sleeve, and he held on to my bare wrist.

Crossing over was a little harder this time, which left me oddly relieved, in light of Harmony's warning that it would eventually become too easy. This time, the pain in my leg was so distracting, it was hard to convince myself I actually wanted to return to the source of my injury. But after a few frustrating minutes, my need for closure transcended pain, and my intent to cross over became real.

I opened my eyes when Regan gasped, not surprised to find her staring in openmouthed wonder through the glass doors at my back. The Netherworld version of Prime Life was already open for business, and based on the number of beings I could now hear milling around inside, I had to wonder if they ever closed.

"What is this place?" Regan whispered, stepping closer to the door. She pulled her sunglasses off as if they impeded her vision, and I was almost as glad to see her finally returning to true consciousness as I was unnerved all over again by the sight of those eerie white eyes. They fit in much better here than they did in our world.

Nash must have been thinking the same thing. He glanced from Regan, holding her sunglasses, to Addy, wearing her contacts, to me and my normal, boring blue eyes. "Um, Addy, I think you'll be safer here without your contacts," he said. "And Regan, give Kaylee your glasses."

"Why?" she asked as Addison dug a plain white contact case from the pocket of her jeans, shooting Nash a questioning look almost identical to her sister's.

"Because most of the things in there—" I pointed over my shoulder; I hadn't yet worked up the nerve to actually *look* at the lion's den we'd be walking through "—have no reason to bother you if they know you have no soul. But my eyes will give me away in an instant."

Neither of them argued, and I almost felt guilty for not mentioning that some of them might try to eat us, whether or not we had souls. But not guilty enough for full disclosure, which might send them screaming into the Nether-night.

Regan handed me her glasses, which I slipped on immediately, then she held her sister's case while Addy took out her contacts. Nash seemed willing to go in with his eyes unguarded, and I had to trust that he'd crossed over more than I had, therefore knew what he was doing. And finally, when we were all ready to go inside, I made myself turn and look.

The shock of what I saw was almost as powerful as the pain shooting up my bad leg with every movement.

Though I'd never been in our world's version of Prime Life,

I was willing to bet my next paycheck that the world-anchor had pulled it through in its entirety. Furniture, marble floors, stone fountain, and all. But the creatures occupying that space had little in common with their real-world counterparts.

We should not be here, I thought as Nash pushed open the door. He held it for us as I led Addy and Regan inside. Though, once again, Regan needed a little push to get her going. Not that I could blame her.

When the door closed behind us, I concentrated on putting one foot in front of the other on the slick, marbled floor. *Step-ow! Step-ow!* Over and over again, breathing through the pain and doggedly avoiding eye contact with any of the creatures in the room. At least, any of them who actually had eyes.

Regan's breathing sped up until she was practically panting, and out of the corner of my eye, I saw her hand shaking. I wrapped my hand around hers and squeezed to tell her she was fine. Everything was okay. Then I made myself look up, though not at anything in particular, when I realized that walking with my eyes down practically advertized my status as prey.

And I would not be prey.

Near the fountain in the center of the room, two headless human-ish forms stood with their backs to us. One was male and one female, and she was bent to let her hand dangle in the flow of water that looked thick and smelled foul. When and if they turned, we'd find their facial features imbedded in their chests, as if they'd swallowed their own heads, and the lost parts were trying to break free from the inside. I knew that because I'd glimpsed this species briefly the day Emma died.

But what I hadn't known—since peeking renders everything in shades of gray—was that their skin tone would be a smooth, delicate pink, as if they'd never lost the soft flush of the birthing process. If creatures like that were even birthed in the first place.

"Just keep walking," Nash whispered, and I glanced quickly at his profile to find his jaw tense, his hands in his pockets. "Tod's waiting for us by the elevators. We're almost there."

I followed his line of sight. Tod was indeed waiting for us by a bank of very normal-looking elevators, his arms crossed over his chest. His expression was strong, closed-off, and arrogant, as if to say he might not belong there, but neither was he afraid.

But we were not almost there. We'd gone less than a quarter of the way—just far enough to attract attention.

As we crossed the room, oddly lilted, strangely pitched snippets of conversation began to fade into silence as one creature after another noticed our presence. Then, as we passed an arrangement of formal, burgundy-colored couches, that conversation started back up, as if I'd just yawned to pop my ears and could suddenly hear again. This time I caught actual words here and there.

"Overworlders…"

"…taste their fear…"

"…used-up husks…"

"…plump, soft flesh…"

"…beacons of energy…"

"…swimming in pain…"

"…strong, young hearts…"

Chills traveled up my arms and down my spine. I became aware of a steady movement toward us, as the creatures slowly converged, slinking, slithering, lurching, and gliding in our direction from every corner of the room. I caught glimpses of extra arms, coiling tails, and flashing eyes in all manner of *wrong* colors. Whispered hisses followed us. Outstretched appendages welcomed us.

Something brushed a strand of hair from my shoulder, then trailed lightly down my back. I swallowed a shudder of revulsion and forced myself to face forward. To keep walking.

"This one smells like warm rot…." a female voice whispered into my ear, though as near as I could tell, the speaker was all the

way across the lobby, beside the reception desk. Skeletal hands
peeked from beneath long, wide sleeves, but she stood on nothing that I could see. No feet. No paws. No flippers. She simply
hung on the air, sunken eyes glowing a dark, eerie blue.

As we moved forward, the crowd parted reluctantly, some
beings moving so slowly we had to wait for them to vacate our
path. Oddly textured hems brushed my jeans. Scalding fingers
tugged on mine. And something cold and airy, like a breeze
somehow made solid, wound around my ankles, forming an
almost physical resistance to my forward motion and introducing
a new, prickly cold pain to the agony still throbbing in my leg.

When we finally reached Tod and the bank of elevators—
I'd come to view them as salvation itself—my sigh of relief was
audible. Without a word, he pressed a button on the wall, and a
set of doors slid open. We stepped inside, and Addy jabbed the
"close door" button repeatedly with one trembling finger.

When the door closed, she turned on us, tears welling in her
oddly blank eyes. "What the *hell* was that?"

"Hell's about right," I mumbled, and she whirled on me,
fierce anger overwhelming her fear for the first time.

I was glad to see it. Leaking fear in the Netherworld was like
leaking blood in a shark tank.

"You could have warned us!"

"What did you think you were getting into when you sold
your soul?" Nash demanded, and I glanced at him in surprise.
Contempt shone in his eyes. "These creatures live off the human
life force that bleeds through from our world to theirs. Some
of them eat souls. Some of them eat flesh. Some of them just
like new toys. Either way, walking through that lobby was like
dangling a bloody steak in front of a tiger, and Kaylee and I did
that for you two, even though she's in horrible pain and huge
trouble with her father. And neither of us have a thing to gain
from this. So if you have any further complaints, you can lodge
them right up your own ass, *pop star,* because nobody here gives

a damn who you are or how much you're worth. Without us, you're meat, pure and simple. Got it?"

Addison blinked her big, empty eyes. Then she nodded, still trembling, and I couldn't resist a smile.

But then the elevator binged and the doors slid open, and my heart jumped so far up my throat I could have spit it on the floor.

Tod stepped out first and we followed quickly, pleased to find the hallway deserted. And carpeted, which meant our shoes were silent. The reaper led us to a door near the end of the hall, where he stopped and turned to whisper. "He's in there. I peeked right before you got here." He hesitated, and forced a tense smile at Addy and Regan. "You guys ready?"

Addy nodded hesitantly and squeezed Regan's hand until she nodded, too.

"Good. Let's do this." Tod put one hand on the knob. My heart raced so fast I felt dizzy. He twisted the knob, and my pulse pumped scalding ribbons of adrenaline through my veins. He pushed the door open, and I had to swallow back vomit.

Behind a desk in the middle of a normal-looking office sat a normal-looking man in a suit, tie, and pair of sunglasses. He showed no surprise at our arrival. *This* was the hellion of greed?

"Avari?" Tod said, and the man nodded slowly, silently. "We're here to bargain for the souls of Addison and Regan Page."

And as the impossibility of what we were about to attempt truly sank in, I focused on one thought to keep myself calm: *Weirdest. Wednesday. Ever.*

19

Avari rose, placing both palms flat on the glossy work surface of a desk that stood empty in the Netherworld, but was probably cluttered with some worker-drone's papers, pens, and coffee mug in our world. "Come inside," he said, his words as smooth and dark as good fudge, but nowhere near as sweet.

His voice sent shivers through me, leaving tiny icicle shards to chill the blood in my veins.

Tod stepped inside and we followed him reluctantly. I brought up the rear, fighting to control the wince of pain my features wanted to form, and to deny the groan lodged in my throat. I would not expose myself as the weakest member of the herd.

With the casual wave of one hand, Avari closed the door behind us, from across the room. "Addison. Regan." The hellion nodded formally, rounding his desk to stand in front of it. "I assume you've come to invoke your respective out-clauses?"

"No." Addy spoke firmly and clearly, in spite of the trembling hands she clasped at her back. "We won't damn someone else to eternity with you. We're here to make a different sort of trade."

Avari sat with one hip on the corner of his desk, tugging the sleeves of an immaculate, coal-gray suit jacket into place. If not for the sunglasses—and the ability to close doors without touching them—he could have been any ordinary cog in the life-insurance machine. "What makes you think I'm open to such an exchange?" Power radiated from him in waves of bitter cold, drawing goose bumps from my skin, even beneath my jacket.

"You're a hellion of avarice," I began, but when the demon's head turned my way, the words froze in my throat, and I had to cough to force them up. "Why wouldn't you want more for less?"

Avari's brows rose above his sunglasses, and my heart thumped painfully from the knowledge that both his attention and his gaze were focused on me. Being scrutinized by a hellion was definitely not part of the plan.

Nash stepped protectively closer to me, his hand brushing mine, but Avari took no notice.

"You reek, *bean sidhe*." The hellion's words wove through me on a gust of frigid air, coiling around my chest until I could hardly feel my heartbeat through the simultaneous numbing cold and stabbing, icy pressure. "The rot spreads inside you quickly. I smell it. I feel it, though you disguise your pain with uncommon strength and fortitude. Both qualities I find quite appetizing in a soul."

He rose from his desk and took a single stride toward me. I answered it with a backward step, swallowing a cry as my bad foot hit the floor. Needlelike pain shot down my foot and up my leg, this time enveloping my entire pelvis, as well.

I was getting worse. Fast.

The hellion's long, straight nose twitched as he inhaled, and a terrifying flash of hunger flickered across his otherwise empty expression. "I can eat your pain. I can spare your life."

Panic shot through me and I squelched it all, except the tremor in my hands. "When my death comes, you can't stop it, and I won't even try. If I'm supposed to die from crimson creeper venom, so be it." Not that I was exactly eager to go, but I would *not* die without my soul. Not even for the promise of a quick, painless death.

"And if you were not meant to die of such poison?" Avari's brows lifted once more as he stepped forward, and again I limped backward, my vision going gray with the sudden, harsh movement. "I see your lifeline spread before me like a length of road, and the miles should tick away your fleeting, insignificant life for some time to come. Yet the stench of death clings to you. It flows through your veins like a river through its channel, and the toxin will reach your heart within minutes."

He paused, and I thought I glimpsed a dark flash of pleasure, even through the opaque tint of his lenses. "If you stay in the Nether much longer, you will die here."

Fresh fear skittered up my spine to lodge in my throat, and my gaze flitted from Nash's horrified expression to the smug hellion. Then I asked the question he clearly wanted to hear, in spite of some strong instinct urging me to retreat into silence. I had to know. "But you said my lifeline goes on." I stopped to breathe through another agonizing wave of pain. "How can I die here?"

"The date stamped on your feeble body means nothing in the Netherworld. If you suffer a mortal injury or contract a deadly infection here, you will die among us. As one of us. But you have a few minutes yet. Enough time to barter for your friends. Or to escape to your own world."

Was he telling the truth?

Horror drew my hands into fists so tight my fingernails cut into my flesh. If I fled the Netherworld to save myself, there would be no one left to suspend Addy's and Regan's souls once the hellion released them, so Nash could guide them back into the proper bodies. But if I stayed to help them, I would die.

Unless I sold my soul to Avari.

"Which will it be, little *bean sidhe?*" The hellion's faux-sympathetic smile sent a spike of terror through my heart. "Your life, or your friends'? Or your soul?"

"Tod?" I turned on him, silently demanding the truth, keeping the hellion safely in my peripheral vision.

The reaper's tortured, conflicted expression greeted me. "Kaylee, he's just trying to buy your soul."

I knew that, of course. But I also knew Tod would say anything to save Addison's soul. He would also *not* say anything with that same goal in mind. "Tell me the truth, Tod. Can I die here?"

The reaper sighed but nodded. "Your expiration date means nothing here. You know, 'Offer not valid in the Netherworld, the Bermuda Triangle, and various undiscovered warp zones across the globe....'"

I closed my eyes briefly and exhaled. "Awesome, Tod. Thanks for that." Anger flamed through me, thawing some of the chill Avari's voice had left in my veins. But it could do nothing to ease the agony clawing its way up my right leg and into my torso. "Thanks for warning me *before* we crossed over."

And suddenly I realized. I remembered. "You knew!" He'd almost said something in the car. He'd started to tell me my ankle couldn't wait. But then he didn't.

On the edge of my vision, Nash's hands curled into fists at his sides, and his eyes churned furiously in fear and rage.

"I'm sorry, Kay," Tod began as Addy and Regan stared at me in horror. "I'm so sorry...."

I turned my back on him, ignoring his silent plea for forgiveness. "If I die, it will be with my soul in my possession," I said to the hellion, summoning every ounce of that fortitude he'd mentioned. "It will never be yours." I paused, as cold, treacherous anger flowed swiftly over the demon's face. "Got that, Tod?"

"I got it," he whispered from behind me. He would take my soul if I died, to keep it from the demon. It was the least he owed me. That, and a few tears spilled over my grave...

"So be it, *bean sidhe*." Avari's voice was as still and deadly as an Arctic winter. He turned that toxic hunger on Addison. "What do you offer?"

Addy nodded at Tod, who'd recovered most of his composure. "Your colleague Bana is no longer with us," the reaper said. "Not in body, anyway."

The hellion's expression did not change, but I suffered in silence for several tense moments before he spoke again. "You have Bana's soul?"

"Yes." Tod let a slow smile stretch across his face. "She was more than one hundred years old. Her soul has more accumulated energy than both Addison's and Regan's combined, and I can personally attest to the quality of that energy." He patted his stomach, like he'd just eaten a particularly satisfying burger.

Again, Avari betrayed no thought or emotion, and frustration spiked with my pulse. I couldn't tell if he was even interested in our bait, much less how close we were to a deal.

The entire right side of my body throbbed during Avari's silence, pain cresting and falling with each beat of my heart. Small, sharp tongues of anguish licked at the base of my spine, replacing the numbing cold with a searing heat. I could almost feel the creeper venom flowing through me, taking over my body one cell at a time, one limb after another.

"No." Finally the hellion spoke, and I concentrated on his words to distract me from the pain that hunched my back and singed my nerve endings. "Human souls are pure, and particularly innocent are the souls of children." His gaze seemed to focus on Regan then, though I couldn't be sure with his eyes hidden. "If you want your souls back, you will offer a fair exchange. That is the agreement you signed."

Regan moaned, and Addy squeezed her sister's hand. "Please," the pop star begged, stepping in front of Regan to block her from the demon's sight, and vice versa. But the moment the word left her mouth, both Nash and Tod went stiff, and it didn't take me long to catch on. Addison had just shown the hellion another weak link in our chain, and exactly how to exploit it.

The demon smiled, and the temperature in the room plummeted. My goose bumps grew fatter, and my nose started to run, like I'd caught a cold. I began to shiver, and each small movement sent fresh waves of pain throughout my body, one after the other, cresting in my injured ankle.

"You want to save your sister?" Avari's voice pierced me like a massive icicle through the chest, and I couldn't hold back a gasp. I wasn't the only one; Regan looked like her blood had just frozen in her veins.

Addison hesitated, and Nash tried unsuccessfully to catch her eye without speaking. "Yes," Addy said finally, her pretty face twisted with fear and desperation.

The hellion's smile widened almost imperceptibly, and some small motion caught my eye from his desk. I glanced down to see a thin, blue-tinted film of frost forming on the glass desktop, crawling across the surface in tiny, flat ice-vines. The frost branched steadily in all directions, a network of captured snowflakes. It was beautiful.

It was also one of the scariest things I'd ever seen.

"I will trade one unspoiled human soul for this reaper's accumulated energy." Avari's soft words rolled over me like thunder as ice continued to spread toward the edge of the desk. "Show me Bana's soul."

"You first," I gasped, clutching my abdomen as the toxin spreading within me set my stomach on fire. Soon the poison's flames would meet the ice Avari's words had driven through my chest, and I knew better than to hope the two would simply cancel each other out. "Give us the soul first," I repeated, ignoring the shocked faces staring at me. "Or there's no deal."

A growl rumbled from the demon's throat to shake the entire room, and a sudden gush of frigid power sent more frost surging over the edge of the desk and onto the floor. Avari ripped the sunglasses from his face and they froze in his hand, tiny icicles hanging from the earpieces and the left lens. His fist closed, and the frozen plastic shattered, clinking to the floor like glass.

His eyes, now exposed, were spheres of solid black, just like Addison had said. But what her words had failed to convey was the utter *darkness* encompassed in those obsidian orbs. Looking into Avari's eyes was like looking into the depths of oblivion. Into the distillation of nothingness.

He was the very absence of all things light and good, and staring into his eyes called forth my own worst fear: that if I were to look into my own heart and soul, I would find nothing more. That I would be just as empty. That my own void would mirror his.

But I wouldn't let it. If I had to die, at least I could die helping a friend.

"You dare make demands of me?" the hellion roared, shattering a heavy stalactite of ice that had grown from the ceiling. It crashed to the floor, and both Page sisters jumped.

I only smiled. I was a little light-headed, and more than a little out of my mind with pain and with the very thought of my rapidly approaching demise. "I *totally* dare. You don't scare me." I barely noticed the sick look on Nash's face, growing worse with every word I spoke. He aimed eyebrow acrobatics my way, trying to shut me up, but I ignored him. What did I have to lose? "I'm going to die, anyway," I continued. "And if you don't release one soul now, Tod will take off with Bana's, as well as mine, and you'll have gained nothing from this little gathering."

How well did *that* concept sit with the demon of greed?

Avari growled again, and more spears of ice dropped from the ceiling to shatter at our feet. But then his growl died, and the floor went still beneath me, a temporary mercy for my tortured right leg. And when the sound faded, the hellion's lips turned up in the single most terrifying smile I'd ever seen.

"Fine. Have your soul, for what good it will do you…." He exhaled deeply, without sucking in a preparatory breath, and what I at first mistook for warm air puffing into the cold room soon revealed itself as a soul. A human soul.

We'd done it!

I glanced at Nash and Tod in relief and in pure joy, ignoring the pain that now wound its way over my ribs toward my right shoulder.

"Kaylee!" Nash whispered fiercely, desperately, and I followed his gaze to the soul now floating steadily toward the icicle-studded ceiling.

Oops. I'd forgotten the most important part. Since Regan wasn't actually dying, I'd had no urge to wail for her, and her soul was getting away. So I used what I'd learned from Harmony to call my wail up on demand, suspending the soul with the thin sliver of sound that leaked from my tightly sealed lips.

The soul bobbed just below the ceiling, surrounding one of the stalactites of ice. Sweat broke out on Nash's forehead, in spite of the freezing temperature, as he concentrated on guiding the soul into Regan's body while everyone else watched. Tod stared at his brother in relief, while Addy and Regan looked on in amazement—evidently in the Netherworld humans can see souls.

But Avari looked…amused?

Was I missing something?

I focused on my wail, on holding most of it back, to distract myself from the pain that now pierced my right shoulder and was inching its way down my arm. Nash brought the soul steadily closer to Regan, and in a sudden moment of comprehension, Addison pushed her sister toward the bobbing soul, to make Nash's work easier.

My heart beat harder in anticipation. The rush of adrenaline through my veins tried to overwhelm the pain in my bones. Any second, Regan and her soul would be reunited. We could claim success on the part of at least one Page sister.

We couldn't help Addy—she'd made her own choice—but we'd done what we could.

Nash's sudden wide-eyed, horrified expression was the first sign that something had gone wrong. "It doesn't fit!" he breathed, and I wasn't sure whether I'd actually heard him or read his lips. "It's not hers!"

Suddenly the hellion's unprecedented agreeableness and his amused expression made sense, and we all seemed to draw the same conclusion at once: Avari had tricked us.

He'd released Addison's soul instead of Regan's.

20

"No!" Addison shouted, her voice strong and shrill, powered by a singer's trained lungs. Which I could have used in that moment, as my muffled keening thinned. But her protest meant nothing to Avari.

"This is my offer," he said, softer than before, yet still his words sent cold, ethereal fingers over my flesh, making my goose-pimpled skin crawl. "The choice is yours."

"Nooo." Addison moaned that time. "No. Take me. You said you'd take my soul."

Avari shook his head slowly, a cruel teacher scolding a naive student. "You misinterpreted my words. That happens more than you might think."

As my wail wavered, my mind raced while I tried to remember everything the hellion had said. Had he actually said he'd trade Regan's soul for Bana's? Or just *a* soul? I couldn't remember....

"Choose." Avari clucked his tongue at Addison. "Your friends cannot hold your soul forever. Not with this one near death." The demon's gaze met mine, and suddenly his cruel truth sank in. I was dying. The poison had spread to my right hand, and now flowed over my left side on its way to my heart. I couldn't hold Addy's soul for long.

My gaze pleaded with her as I struggled to keep the sound steady in my throat.

Addison's eyes watered and she glanced from me to Regan, who stood frozen in terror, clenching her sister's hand so hard it had turned purple. Then her gaze swung my way, and she focused on something over my shoulder. And I thought I saw some glimmer of hope in her grotesquely blank eyes.

Was that possible? Had she thought of something?

Addy turned to Tod and mouthed something I couldn't interpret.

I was next, and what she said silently to me was "One more minute. Please." I closed my eyes briefly, then opened them and nodded. I would hold on, for just a little longer.

Addison smiled her thanks, then she nodded decisively, again looking over my shoulder.

An instant later, Addy collapsed. Her legs simply folded under her and her head smacked the frosted marble floor. Not that it mattered. She was dead before she hit the ground.

"No!" Regan shouted, tears pouring down her cheeks. She lurched toward her sister, but Tod held her back, wrapping his arms around her shoulders to keep her still.

Surprise dried up the trickle of sound flowing from my throat, and Addy's soul bobbed, until I keened again a second later. Then things got even weirder.

A figure stepped forward from behind me and to my right, her mouth open, already sucking in a long, thick stream of Demon's Breath from Addy's still form.

Libby. My heart ached as I realized Addison had seen her over my shoulder. She'd nodded to Libby, not to me.

Then Tod spoke, Regan now sobbing on his shoulder, and I began to put the pieces together. "The deal has changed, Avari. If you want Bana's soul, you take Addison's with it and return her sister's. Or else, we'll leave with both of the souls in our possession, and you'll keep only the one you have now."

Damn. Shock wound through me, blending with the pain now arcing across every nerve ending in my body. Somehow, Addison had known who Libby was and why she'd come. Had Tod told her, or did understanding simply come in the last moments of her life?

Either way, with a single nod of her head, Addison had asked Libby to end her life, to force the hellion into trading her soul for Regan's. Because Addison's was ready to reap now, and Regan's wouldn't truly be his until she died, likely decades later.

Avari's face paled with rage, and the void in his eyes seemed to churn, though I could detect no motion when I looked directly into those dark spheres.

"Five seconds, or you're out of luck," Tod said as Nash continued to sweat, and my voice warbled. "We're in a bit of a rush." He gestured to me, and I realized he planned to get me home before I died. He was trying to save me, since he couldn't save Addison.

All I could do was sing. And watch Libby claim the Demon's Breath. And wait.

"Five... Four..." Tod taunted as Regan heaved with silent sobs and Avari bellowed in rage. The floor grew slick with ice beneath my feet, and my breath puffed visibly into the frigid air.

Then, just when I thought it was over—thought Addison's death had been for nothing—the hellion spat one short, powerful exhalation into the room, and Regan's soul bobbed near the ceiling.

At Nash's signal, I let go of Addison's soul and sang for her sister's. Libby swallowed the last of the Demon's Breath and popped out of existence without so much as a glance at the rest of us. Avari slurped up Addy's soul in a fraction of the time it took Nash to guide Regan's home. And only then did Tod release Bana's soul into the room.

While Avari devoured it, Nash rushed toward me across the slick floor, tugging a shocked Regan by one hand. I had a moment to notice that her eyes were again beautiful, and blue, and normal. Then they converged on me, sliding so quickly they almost bowled me over.

"Now!" Nash whispered desperately, tugging me into an agonizing squat so that I touched both him, Regan, and Addison's limp arm. "Take us back now!"

That time, intent to cross was no problem, and I was already keening. Avari's roar of fury faded swiftly from my ears. An instant later I collapsed to the floor of a generic office full of cubicles and cheap industrial carpet. Addy lay at my side, and Nash and Regan stared down at me, a mixture of grief and relief coursing over their features.

A moment later, Tod popped into existence next to his brother.

"Are you okay?" Nash knelt at my side, but by then I could only shake my head. I'd lost my voice completely, and was in so much pain it hurt to draw a breath. "Call Mom," Nash ordered, sliding one hand behind my back, the other beneath my knees. He carried me out of the office and into the hall while Regan followed, crying and scrolling through the entries in Nash's phone for a name she wouldn't even recognize, because Tod carried her sister's body.

Each second we waited for the elevator was pure agony. I hurt all over, and worse wherever he touched me. But I was grateful for that touch.

"You'll be fine," Nash whispered. "Your expiration date is in full effect here, so you won't die. But you're going to hurt like hell until we get this fixed."

I'd guessed as much.

I'd just decided that Prime Life shut down their elevators after hours when the mirrored doors slid open with a soft ding. Downstairs, we crossed the eerily empty lobby and Nash set

me on a burgundy couch while he kicked open the locked glass
doors leading to the parking garage. It took him three tries, but
I was still impressed.

Harmony answered her phone as Nash buckled me into the
front seat, and Regan gave the phone to Tod as he closed the
trunk, where he'd gently laid Addison. He explained the basics,
demanding his mother meet us at my house with the necessary
supplies. She said she'd be there in ten minutes.

It took us twenty, and once he'd dropped me and Nash off,
Tod took the Page sisters home, where Regan would "find" her
sister's body on the floor of her own room. Then he returned
Emma's car.

My front door flew open before Nash and I even got to the
porch, and my father took me from him without a word. His
anger had momentarily been eclipsed by fear I hadn't seen since
that long-ago day I barely remembered.

The day my mother had died to save me.

"Not again," he muttered, laying me on the couch. I moaned,
and tears overflowed his eyes.

"She'll be fine." Harmony pushed him aside gently. I hadn't
even known she was there, but suddenly she was at my side, her
fingers cold on my arm, a filled syringe ready in her other hand.
"Tod said it's crimson creeper."

"Where the hell did she find crim—" His eyes widened in
horror, and some of that anger returned. "Kaylee, what did you
do?"

"She can explain it later, Aiden," Harmony said firmly. The
needle slid into my arm, and though it was blissfully cold, the
medicine that invaded my body scalded like one of the original
pinpricks from the creeper. "For now, let her sleep. She'll need
another dose of this in four hours." She held a second syringe
up for my father to see, and he nodded. "If the red webbing isn't
gone four hours after that, call me."

But she'd be back to check on me before then. Nash would see to that.

"Come on, Nash," Harmony said, and the hard edge in her voice said he wouldn't get off easy, either.

"No…" I moaned, surprised when my voice actually produced the cracked, tortured sound. I grabbed his wrist with the last of my strength.

Harmony frowned at me, then at my father. "Can he stay, Aiden? She wants him to stay."

My father hedged, and I begged him with my eyes. I needed them both. I'd never hurt so badly in my life, but Nash's voice could help. I knew it could. "Fine," he said finally. "But you have to go to sleep, young lady."

We'd argue about the "young lady" part later. But I agreed with the rest of his statement.

The last thing I saw before sleep—blissful, pain-free sleep—claimed me were their faces, side by side, watching me with identical expressions of concern.

21

"Thanks for coming." Regan smoothed her black dress over her flat stomach. Her perfect blue eyes were red from crying, but her expression was pure strength and poise. Her mother stood beside the coffin, staring past all the headstones in a chemically induced oblivion. She was coping with Addy's death the only way she knew how—with pills, and alcohol, and seclusion. She hadn't left her house in nearly a week, and had only come out this time for the funeral. Because Regan made her.

"We wouldn't have missed it," Nash said, and I nodded. He spoke for us both.

Regan had made all the arrangements, choosing her sister's favorite flowers, music, and poetry, as well as the coffin and the plot. It was a lot of responsibility for a thirteen-year-old already devastated by her sister's death—her sacrifice—and it broke my heart that she'd had to rise to such a tragic occasion.

But she would be fine. The determined line of her jaw and straight length of her spine said that clearly. Whatever else happened, Regan Page would be just fine.

Addy had seen to that.

Regan glanced briefly at her mother, then at the crowd of

paparazzi gathered behind a long barricade before returning her attention to me. "How are you feeling?"

"I'm fine now. Really," I added, when doubt flickered behind her mercifully real eyes.

The red webbing had faded from my skin by the time the sun went down the day Addy died, but it took three more days before the last of the pain abated. And the puncture marks around my ankle left scars—a double ring of bright red dots. I'd missed school for the rest of that week, but Harmony had only let Nash miss Thursday, and only because we'd been up all of Wednesday night.

And since I was well enough for the funeral, I would be returning to school on Monday.

Addy's service was private, but Regan got us in. Tod cried through the whole thing, but I think I was the only one who could see him. Addy's death nearly killed him. Again. Levi had given him a couple of weeks off, and was personally covering his hospital shifts. And we hadn't seen Tod once between that night and the funeral.

I think he was having a lot of trouble with the knowledge that Addison's soul was now the property of a hellion of greed, and that the rest of her existence would be spent in agonizing pain, of every possible variety.

I wasn't dealing with that very well, either. I'd really wanted to save her. And I would have plenty of time to think about my failure, because I was grounded for a solid month. My father was unmoved by our altruistic intentions. He considered nothing else on the face of the planet—or in either world—worth risking my life.

After he said that, I found it pretty hard to complain about being grounded, even though I would only see Nash at school and at *bean sidhe* lessons.

The only positive thing to come out of the whole mess—other than returning Regan's soul—was the fact that we were never fingered for the "break in" at Prime Life. Thank goodness. That one would have been impossible to explain to the cops. It was no picnic to explain to my dad, either.

"So, what are you going to do?" I leaned into Nash's chest for both comfort and warmth.

Regan shrugged and tucked a strand of blond hair behind her ear. "Take care of my mom, I guess. And stay far away from John Dekker."

I nodded. Regan had done us all proud. In honor of Addison's sacrifice, she'd already broken her contract with Dekker Media and was pursuing other acting opportunities. Rumor had it the Teen Network—Dekker's biggest competition—wanted her to do a pilot for them, but she wouldn't even accept their calls until she'd laid Addison to rest.

The fact that the wolves were already nipping at her heels made me wonder if anyone in the entertainment industry remained in possession of a soul.

As for Dekker Media, as far as I knew, they couldn't continue to provide souls for Avari without someone to ferry teenage stars to the Netherworld for them. So, for the moment at least, the adolescent population of Hollywood was secure. Though I still got a sick feeling every time I thought of all the soulless victims still waiting to suffer throughout the afterlife at Avari's hands.

But there was nothing I could do about that.

My dad said I couldn't save them all, and on my good days, I have to admit that he was right. Eventually, people have to learn to make their own choices, and to deal with the consequences.

Including me.

"I think that's your dad over there," Regan said, and I twisted to follow her gaze. Sure enough, my father—more handsome than ever in his dark suit—stood in front of his freshly washed car, waiting patiently for me.

"Yeah, I better go." I stepped away from Nash as Regan opened her arms to hug me.

"Thank you, Kaylee," she whispered into my ear, as she squeezed me so tight I could barely breathe. "Thank you so much." She sniffed, and her next words sounded thick, as if she were holding back more tears. "I won't forget what you did for me. What you helped Addy do."

I hugged her back, because I didn't know what to say.

No problem? But it was a problem. I'd nearly died.

Anyone else would have done the same? But that wasn't true, either.

I'd helped Addy and Regan because I couldn't *not* help them. Because in most cases, I believe that people deserve a second chance. And because I couldn't have lived with myself if I'd stood by and let them both die soulless, when I could have helped.

Finally, Regan stepped back and looked into my eyes, her own still brimming with tears. "I want you to know that I understand what Addy gave up for me. And I'm going to do my best to deserve it."

"I know you will." With that, I squeezed her hand, then turned toward Tod, who stared at the coffin from beneath the skeletal branches of a broad oak. I needed to talk to him before I left, because I wasn't sure when I'd see him next.

Or if Nash could see him at that moment. But then his hand stiffened on my arm when he saw where I was leading him, and I knew he could see his brother. "Kaylee, do we have to do this now? He's really hurting."

"So is Regan," I pointed out, and my free hand slid into the pocket of my formal black coat, bought just for Addy's funeral. "I have to know if he did this."

"Does it really matter?" Nash asked, and I looked up at him to find his eyes swirling slowly, though I couldn't quite identify the emotion. "What's done is done, and justice isn't always pretty. And, anyway, do you really want to know?"

"Yes. I need to hear it." Because part of me couldn't believe he'd actually done it.

Nash frowned, but tagged along. When we stopped beneath Tod's tree, Nash's body shielding us from the stragglers still loitering around the coffin, I pulled from my pocket a news clipping folded in half. "Do you know anything about this?"

Tod took the clipping and unfolded it. He couldn't have read more than the headline before handing it back to me, his face carefully blank, though rage churned violently in the cerulean depths of his eyes. The fact that I could see it surely meant he harbored it deep inside his soul. And that thought scared me.

"Kaylee, don't ask questions you don't want answered," the reaper said, his voice harder and more humorless than I'd ever heard it.

"You killed him," I accused, glancing at the headline for at least the fiftieth time.

BILLIONAIRE CEO MISSING; SISTER FEARS THE WORST

"No. Death is too good for John Dekker," Tod said without a hint of remorse. His ruthless expression gave me chills.

"Where is he?" Nash asked, when he realized his brother wasn't going to elaborate.

"I dropped him off in Avari's office."

My heart jumped into my throat, and suddenly I could hear my own pulse. "You stranded him in the Netherworld?"

The reaper shrugged. "A live plaything is rare on that side. They won't kill him."

"They'll do worse," I spat.

Tod cocked one eyebrow at me. "Does he deserve any less?"

I had to think about that. John Dekker had been responsible for dozens of teenagers losing their souls, and he'd worked to keep Addy and Regan from reclaiming theirs. Did he deserve any less than eternal torture?

Probably not. But that wasn't my call to make. The very thought of wielding so much power terrified me.

Though, it didn't seem to have bothered Tod.

"I can't believe you did that...."

"And yet you haven't asked me to bring him back." He ran one hand through his hair. "I think you have no trouble believing it. I think you wish you'd done it yourself."

"No." I shook my head, bothered by the spark of anger raging unchecked inside him. Was this why my father didn't want me hanging out with a reaper? Because, as he'd always insisted, Tod *was* dangerous?

I shook that thought off. It was too much to think about with Addy not yet in the ground, and my failure on her behalf haunting me. I took Nash's hand again and shoved the clipping deep into my pocket. "I have to go," I said, already turning toward my dad's car.

"Kaylee, just say it," Tod called after me, and I was glad no one else could hear him. Not even Nash, this time. I could tell from the relief on his face—he was happy to be walking away from his brother. "Say the word, and I'll bring him back. I'll rescue him from never-ending torture. It's your call...."

Hot, bitter tears filled my eyes, as horror filled my heart. It wasn't my call. He couldn't put a decision like that on me. It wasn't right.

Yet as I headed toward my father with my boyfriend at my side, my lips remained sealed, and I was more terrified than I could express by the thought of what my silence probably said about me, deep down inside.

My dad started his engine, and Nash kissed me gently before I sank into the front passenger seat. Then I tucked my skirt beneath me and he closed the car door. I put John Dekker and Tod out of my mind. Forced them to the back of my brain to make room for Nash.

I would only think about Nash. I trusted Nash. I loved him. I understood him, like I would never understand his brother.

Nash waved at me in the side-view mirror as our car pulled forward slowly, my father carefully avoiding stray members of the press. I leaned with my head against the cold window, watching as his image grew smaller and smaller in the mirror. Trying not to think about how long it would be before we could be alone together again.

Three weeks, five days, and four hours until my grounding ends.

Three weeks, five days, four hours, and fifty-four seconds. Fifty-three seconds… Fifty-two seconds…

But who's counting?

★ ★ ★ ★ ★

Acknowledgments

Thanks, as always, to my husband, and to my critique partner, Rinda Elliott, for being my first sounding boards. Thanks to Alex Elliott, the first reader from my target audience. Thanks to my editor, Mary-Theresa Hussey, and to the entire editorial and production teams, for believing in this book. And a huge thank you to my agent, Miriam Kriss, for holding my hand and keeping me sane.

From *New York Times* Bestselling Author

JULIE KAGAWA

Book 1

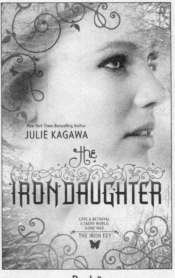

Book 2

"The characters of the series are really what have driven this book from fantasy to fantastical."
—*New York Journal of Books*

"The tension between Ash and Puck is non-stop, but it's Ash's unfailing loyalty to Meghan that just melts the heart."
—*TeensReadToo.com*, 5-star rating

www.TheIronFey.com

HTIRONFEY3BKTR1R2

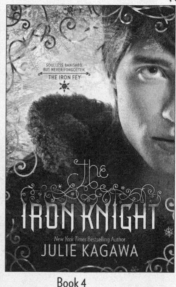
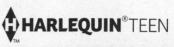

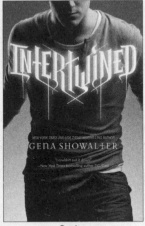
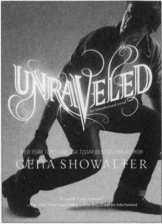
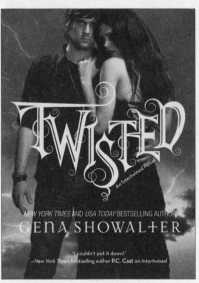